INKED ATHENA

LITVINOV BRATVA
BOOK 2

NICOLE FOX

INKED ATHENA

LITVINOV BRATVA BOOK 2

Running from him once was hard.

Doing it again will be impossible.

Especially once he finds out I'm pregnant with his child.

When he learns the truth, Samuil whisks me away to his Scottish castle.

He says it's to keep me safe.

But the bars on the windows say they're there to keep me contained.

I want to hate him for locking me away.

But when his touch melts my resolve and his kisses promise protection,

I start to wonder if his prison might be the only place I'm truly free.

Because the way he looks at me now—like I'm carrying his whole world inside me—

Makes me want to believe in forever.

Problem is, forever might be shorter than we think.

Dark forces are closing in on all sides,

Led by his ex-wife and his own brother, who want to destroy everything Sam's built.

I say, Let them come.

That day on the beach, Rufus knocked a stranger into my arms.

Now, I'm carrying his heir.

I'm commanding his castle.

And I'm about to show his enemies

Why even the gentlest creatures have teeth.

***Inked Athena** is Book 2 of the Litvinov Bratva duet. The story begins in Book 1, **Inked Adonis**.*

1

NOVA

Samuil.

A shadow against shadows in this moonlit room, but I'd know him anywhere. My Samuil. The man who showed me what safety felt like, right before he took it away.

My heart thunders against my ribs as I grip the chair at my side, steadying myself. The windows of Hope's family cabin frame the angry pewter sky beyond, a perfect backdrop for the man who's waiting for me with death in his hands.

Every desperate, yearning pulse pushes me to run to him.

He's strong and sure and powerful. He'll protect you. He would never, ever let anything hurt you.

It doesn't take much to prove that wrong.

One small step forward is all it takes for reality to shatter the desperate fantasy that he's here to save me. Pain shoots through my ravaged leg, and I stumble. In the same moment, his fingers curl around the handle of the gun in his lap.

The sight steals my breath. Not because I'm afraid of the weapon—God knows I've had enough of those pointed at me lately—but because it's Samuil holding it. The same hands that cradled my face like I was precious. The same fingers that traced poetry on my skin in the dark.

He rises from the armchair in one fluid movement, all coiled power and lethal grace. His silver eyes lock onto mine, arctic cold in the shadows. Those eyes used to warm when they found me. Used to crinkle at the corners when I made him laugh.

Now, they're empty.

Or maybe they're full of conviction about what needs to be done with a traitor.

My pulse races as his eyebrows draw together, studying me like I'm a stranger. Like the past months meant nothing.

I should explain. Should tell him why I was at the Andropov building. Should make him understand that everything I did was to protect him, to protect us.

But the words stay trapped in my throat, held hostage by the certainty that he won't believe me. That he'll pull the trigger before I can make him understand.

When he takes a step toward me, my body makes the choice my mind can't. I stumble backward, my injured leg threatening to buckle. The crutch I've been leaning on clatters to the floor, the sound explosive in the silence.

His hand shoots out—to steady me or grab me, I'll never know. Because I'm already moving, already running. The cabin door bangs against the wall as I burst through it into the gathering storm.

The wind knifes through my thin layers, carrying the bite of approaching rain. Tears blur my vision—from the cold or from leaving him, I'm not sure. There's no time to figure it out. No time for anything but survival.

Heavy clouds swallow the last traces of sun as I force my battered body forward. The pain in my leg is a constant scream, but I've gotten good at ignoring screams. Growing up in my father's house taught me that much.

"Nova!"

His voice booms through the trees, echoing from every direction. My heart twists—even now, even running from him, my body yearns to go to him when he calls. But I can't trust that instinct anymore. Can't trust anything but the need to survive.

I weave between the tree trunks, each step a gamble between speed and stealth. The forest floor is treacherous with fallen leaves and hidden roots, slick from yesterday's rain. One wrong step could end this.

But stopping isn't an option.

The trees press closer, branches reaching for me like grasping fingers. I dodge and pivot, making my path as unpredictable as possible. The rational part of my brain knows I'm leaving an obvious trail—broken twigs, disturbed leaves, probably blood from where my stitches have torn. But rationality took a vacation the moment I saw that gun in his hands.

A branch snaps somewhere behind me. Close. Too close.

"Nova!" His voice is different now. Rougher. More desperate.

My lungs are on fire. Each breath feels like inhaling glass. But I push harder, veering left where the undergrowth is thickest. If I can't outrun him, maybe I can outlast him. Find somewhere to hide until—

Until what? Until he gives up? Until help arrives? Until I wake up from this nightmare?

The duffel bag I left behind haunts me. Everything I need to escape is in that bag—money, documents, the burner phone Hope gave me. I might as well have gift-wrapped my own trap.

Another crack of branches. Closer still.

I risk a glance over my shoulder and my foot catches on something—a root, a rock, it doesn't matter. I stumble, overcorrect, and crash into a tree trunk. The impact drives the air from my lungs.

For a moment, I can't move. Can't breathe. Can only press my forehead against the rough bark and try to remember how my body works.

That's when I hear it. The steady crunch of leaves under deliberate footsteps.

He's done running.

He's hunting now.

Fear floods my system with fresh adrenaline. I push off from the tree, ignoring how my vision swims. The dense growth to my left looks like salvation—thick enough to hide in, dark enough to disappear.

My bad leg drags as I force my way through the undergrowth. Branches snag my clothes, scratch my face, but

I keep going. The ground beneath my feet feels different. Softer. Less stable.

"I know you're there, *zaychik.*" His voice is closer now, almost gentle. Like he's trying to coax a frightened animal. "Stop running."

The word slices through me. He taught me what it meant, late one night beneath a canopy of white bedsheets, his breath mingling with mine, skin on skin, heart on heart, closer than any two people have a right to be.

Zaychik. Rabbit. His little rabbit.

But rabbits get hunted. Rabbits get caught.

I push deeper into the thicket, where the branches are so tight they form a natural fortress. Just a few more steps. Just a little further. Just—

The ground disappears.

For one suspended moment, I'm weightless. My stomach lurches as the world tilts. My hands grasp at empty air, at trailing vines that snap under my fingers.

Then gravity remembers me.

The fall is both endless and instant. My body pinwheels through space, through darkness. Branches whip past me. My shoulder slams into something solid. Pain explodes through my already battered body.

I think I scream. I must scream, because I hear Samuil shout my name. Not in anger this time.

In terror.

The sound follows me down into the ravine, chasing me all

the way to the bottom where the darkness swallows everything whole.

My last thought before unconsciousness claims me is that maybe this is better. Maybe this way, he won't have to live with pulling the trigger.

The black takes me before I can find out if I'm right.

2

SAMUIL

A FEW HOURS EARLIER

I crouch in the shadows, eyeing the cabin nestled in the dense Wisconsin woods. It looks harmless enough—all worn wood and moss-covered stone, like something ripped from a children's storybook. There should be smoke curling from the chimney, the scent of fresh bread drifting through open windows.

Instead, there's only silence and decay.

I move through the overgrown grass, avoiding the gravel path that would betray my presence. The late afternoon sun catches on the algae-slicked windows, nature slowly reclaiming what man abandoned.

At the back corner of the cabin, I find my entry point—a window partially hidden by decrepit shutters.

One sharp strike shatters the glass.

I pause, listening for any reaction, but there's only the whisper of wind through the leaves. Methodically, I clear the frame of remaining shards before hauling myself through.

The wooden shutters groan as I pull them closed behind me, concealing the evidence of my break-in.

The bedroom I've entered reeks of mothballs and rotting wood. My eyes adjust slowly to the gloom as I move through the space, checking corners, analyzing sight lines.

The main room beyond is modest. Kitchen, dining area, living space all flowing together. A loft stretches overhead, but the thick layer of dust coating everything tells me no one's been here in months.

No one except Hope Levy, who rented a car in Chicago this morning and drove north. And where Hope goes, Nova will follow.

My Nova, who's been missing for days. Who appeared in that video looking broken and bloody, conspiring with my enemies.

My hands clench as the footage replays in my mind for the thousandth time. I've memorized every frame, every bruise on her face, every pained step she took.

None of it makes a bit of fucking sense.

When I left her, she was whole. Safe. Protected.

Someone touched her. Someone dared to harm what's mine.

I lower myself into an armchair facing the door, laying my gun across my lap. The rage I've been containing since I found her bloodied sweatshirt in that abandoned garage threatens to explode. I want to tear apart everyone responsible with my bare hands.

But first, I need answers.

I need *her*.

Time passes in the growing darkness. I don't move. I barely breathe. I've learned patience in my years leading the Bratva. I'll wait here forever if that's what it takes to see her again, to understand why she ran.

The crunch of gravel under careful footsteps breaks the silence. Wood creaks on the porch. A key slides into the lock.

And there she is.

She's backlit in gold, almost blinding to look at. I'm sure I've conjured her with my obsessive thoughts alone. It's sheer will that has put her in front of me.

Then she pushes the door closed and limps into the living room.

She stumbles into a chair and the couch as she clumsily makes her way through the cabin, and I soak in the sight of her. Even broken and filthy and exhausted, *she's here.*

As I watch her move, an ice-cold rage I've been shoving down since I walked into the dilapidated car dealership and found her sweatshirt crumpled on the dirty floor rises in me.

Someone hurt her. Touched her. Someone fucking dared.

My hand fists on the arm of the chair, desperate to tear out the throat of every single person responsible.

The only damper to the rage is the guilt.

Because I should've been there.

No one would've gotten close enough to touch her if I'd been with her, if I hadn't left things the way I did.

I'm shifting between the twin emotions, growing angrier and angrier with myself and this world, when she turns towards me and gasps.

Her golden-brown eyes are saucers in the dark, locked on me. The bruises along her jaw stand out purple and angry against her pale skin—so much worse than they looked in the video. She's dirty and shaking and tired and weak.

A longing I've never felt before unfurls in my chest. I want to gather her in my arms and piece her back together. I want to solve this puzzle together.

Still, my jaw is clenched as I manage to say, "I've been waiting for you."

Nova teeters unsteadily, shifting towards me like she wants to close the gap between us as much as I do.

But she falters. She falls sideways into the couch.

I grab the gun to get it out of my way, to have both hands free to catch her, to hold her face and lower her to the couch so she can rest. She looks so tired.

But she springs backwards.

Her gaze flicks from me to the weapon, and I know what she's thinking. I see it written there plainly half a second before she turns and flees through the door.

Fuck.

"Nova!"

I curse again, toss the gun in the chair, and tear after her, but she's fast. Faster than she has any right to be in her condition, and I know she must be hurting herself. It'll only get worse if I chase her, but as she disappears into the trees, I don't have a choice.

Some dark part of me thinks I'll always be chasing after this woman.

The sky is gloomier than it was even a few minutes ago. Heavy rain clouds have rolled in, blotting out the sun. Still, I can follow her path through the trees. There are sliding tracks in the mud and broken branches where she's weaving and dodging the trees—and me.

Because she thinks I'm going to shoot her. That I'm here to kill her.

I'm not sure what's worse: knowing she's hurting herself more with every step or knowing that what she's running from is *me*.

"Nova!" I call again. "Stop!"

I need to catch her, make sure she's okay, and then kill the people responsible. We don't have time for this.

I follow her path until, finally, in the distance, I see her. She's clinging to a tree with both arms, panting to catch her breath.

As I close the distance, her eyes snap to mine. Our gazes lock for a moment, and I think she'll stop. She'll see the truth in my eyes that I want to hold her and help her and figure out what the fuck is going on.

Instead, she stumbles away from the tree and into the dense foliage hiding a steep ravine.

There isn't even time to issue a warning before she pushes through the leaves and falls away.

"NOVA!"

I throw myself into a sprint, barely slowing as I reach the edge of the ravine. I angle my body to the side and ski down the steep bank, using my foot to slow my fall.

Stones and branches and gnarled roots rip open my skin, but I don't care about any of it. All I can focus on is Nova, lying in a crumpled heap at the bottom of the gully.

"No, no, no," I snarl. "Please, please, please…"

I never beg. Never pray. God and I haven't been on speaking terms since I was five years old. But I'll fall to my knees right now and build a thousand churches if it means she's alive.

I skid to a stop and crawl the rest of the way over to her. "Nova."

She doesn't move except for the shallow rise and fall of her chest.

Carefully, I pick her up and cradle her against my body. She smells like damp and dirt, and fuck me, this isn't how it was supposed to be.

I prop her more securely against my chest, and she lets out a faint, exhausted moan.

I want to tell her it's going to be okay.

I want to tell her that she's safe now.

I want to tell her that I'm going to take care of her.

Instead, I hold her close and carry her back to the cabin.

A weak moan escapes her lips as I adjust my grip. "I've got you," I murmur in Russian, the language of my heart. "You're safe now."

The trek back is slow and careful. I pick my path methodically, protecting her from every jolt and bounce. Her skin is cold against mine, clothes filthy from the forest floor.

I need to get her warm, check her injuries, find out what happened.

But first, I need to make sure she doesn't try to run again when she wakes. Because she *will* wake up. She has to.

I've only just found her.

I refuse to lose her again.

3

NOVA

This must be it. The ground. Death. Whatever lies on the other side of the pain and fear.

Except I'm not moving.

And when I reach out my fingers, I find that the afterlife is soft and plush against my fingertips.

That doesn't make sense. None of this does. I can still hear the bone-crunching thud of impact, the way the air rushed out of my lungs. And beneath it all, a deep voice saying my name again and again…

I blink my eyes open slowly, my vision watery until I can make out the inky-black sky overhead. And the skylight framing it.

I fist my hands in blankets on either side of me as I take in the wooden beams above me, the rough timber ceiling.

"You're awake."

His voice is baritone and familiar, but nothing is safe anymore. I can't trust anything or anyone.

My body tenses before my brain can stop it. Pain immediately sears through my arm. My leg. My head. I cry out, stars swimming in my eyes, still trying to twist away from the weight I feel on the edge of my bed.

"Nova, stop." His voice is firm, but the hand he curls around mine is gentle. He gives my fingers a tender squeeze.

I don't see any restraints, but my body is heavy like there are invisible weights pressing me into the mattress. I try to pull my hand away, but I wince as a band of pain locks around my bicep.

"The more you struggle, the more you'll hurt."

I finally turn to look at him. His beard is longer than I've ever seen it, like he hasn't slept in days. His silver eyes are fire-bright, burning as he studies me. There's an intensity there that can only be hate.

But when I move my lips around his name to explain myself, to beg him for my life, my mouth is too dry. Nothing comes out.

"You're thirsty." He grabs a glass from the nightstand and then cups a large hand behind my head. Slowly, like he thinks I'll snap in half, he lifts me towards the glass that he presses against my lips. "Small sips."

It's ice-cold water. I drink until there's nothing left.

With the same care, Samuil lowers me back to the bed. "I had to call a doctor. You were—" He clears his throat, a muscle in his jaw jumping as he does. "He treated your ankle and reset your arm. He also cleaned your cuts and put you on an IV with painkillers and antibiotics. You'll be okay."

For now.

I wait for him to finish that sentence. To explain that he's only healing me so I can be properly interrogated and then disposed of.

Instead, Sam pulls the blanket higher on my chest, cocooning me in warmth that makes me feel drugged.

Maybe I am. Maybe the IV is full of some poison that'll knock me out.

Ilya didn't find poison enjoyable, but maybe Sam doesn't care about the thrill of the execution. Maybe he just wants me gone.

Maybe I'll go to sleep and never wake up.

"You need to rest," Samuil says, his voice a faint rumble in the distance. It's the last thing I hear before my eyes close, and I drift away.

~

There's laughter in the trees. And crackling snarls following me as I run and run.

Every time I look over my shoulder, it's another face—another monster. Ilya and a Labradoodle named Berry and my father.

And Sam. Always Sam.

He's calling my name, his voice hauntingly familiar.

I'm so tired. So sore. I want to stop. I want to see him.

When he calls my name, I call back to him.

"Samuil."

I wake up with his name on my lips. The last few days flicker through my mind in a lowlight reel I want to turn off.

The dog attack, my father threatening Grams, Ilya kidnapping me, running for my life through the woods not once, but twice. My heart kicks into an unsteady rhythm, and each ragged breath hurts.

Then a leg brushes mine.

I still, slowly looking over my shoulder again, and it's Samuil. But his eyes are closed, his expression smooth and calm.

And I'm not afraid.

Maybe I should be, after everything. Part of me tries to be. *Run. Scream. Fight.* But I don't have the energy for anything other than relief that he's keeping me warm, a shield between me and the unfinished wood wall against his back.

As I'm tracing the square of his jaw, the thick, dark tangle of his beard, his eyes flicker open.

Immediately, his face sharpens and shifts. His eyes flare with heat and scan my face like he's already looking for the answers I don't know how to give.

I want to look away—I'm not strong enough to see how much he despises me. But I'm also too weak to look anywhere else.

I've missed him. And no matter what happens next, I'll never be able to bring myself to hate him back.

"I'm going to kill whoever did this to you."

But only because they beat you to it, right? Because someone else broke the toy that was yours to shatter?

Then he leans in slowly.

My breath catches in my throat as he closes the distance between us and brushes my hair away from my face so he can press a kiss to my forehead.

His warm breath washes over my skin, sending a shiver down my spine. "I'm going to take you somewhere safe," he whispers. "Somewhere I can protect you."

He's lying.

He has to be.

My brain churns sluggishly, trying to make sense of how we ended up here.

"Sam…" My voice breaks.

He shakes his head. His hand curls around my cheek. "You need to rest."

His lips brush against my forehead a second time. I close my eyes, letting myself believe for a few seconds that all he wants is to keep me safe. Buying into the fantasy that my betrayal and the gun I saw sitting in Samuil's lap when I walked into the cabin mean nothing.

Maybe we can stay here forever—away from the darkness of his world and the uncertainty of mine. Maybe the Andropovs and Katerina and Ilya and my father will fade away, meaningless outside of how it feels to be with Samuil like this.

But they matter. They'll come for me. They'll kill me.

If Samuil doesn't do it first.

A sob skitters through my chest despite my efforts to choke it down. "Samuil, I didn't— I wasn't—"

He shushes me again, his thumb stroking along my cheekbone in time with his breathing. "You're going to be okay. I'll take care of you."

I want to believe him.

But hope is a dangerous thing.

"Sleep, *krasavitsa.*"

With no other option in front of me, I obey.

4

SAMUIL

"Samuil!"

Myles's voice crackles and cuts out.

I tilt my phone towards the sky like that might make a difference in the shit reception. Unsurprisingly, it changes nothing.

"I was starting to think you'd gone full homesteader on me," he says. "Long time, no chat."

It's only been a little over twenty-four hours since I texted him an update, which is approximately twenty-three hours and fifty-nine minutes longer than he can handle without having a meltdown.

"I've been occupied." The word choice is deliberate. Clinical. A wall between what I've actually been doing—which is holding Nova through fever-dreams and wiping tears from her cheeks and pretending I don't notice how she trembles when I change her bandages.

He snorts. "That usually means one of two things, and since you haven't asked me to come clean up a crime scene, I'm guessing the two of you have been *very* busy."

The suggestion in his voice is obvious, but I'm in no mood to tell him that Nova and I have shared a twin-sized bed for the last three days without me touching her.

I'm also in no mood to admit that the feeling of her curled into my body every night, safe and protected, has been more than enough.

The thought makes me grind my teeth. Since when has anything ever been "enough" for me?

"We can't stay here," I announce, getting straight to the point. "The doctor was back this morning and, according to him, Nova should be fit to be moved in a day or two."

"We have safehouses all over the country. Name your coast of choice, and I can organize—"

"No safehouses. Ilya knows about too many of them. I want —" I scan the rolling meadow in front of the cabin, the dense ring of trees. It's on the tip of my tongue to say I want to stay here. "Forever" would be preferable. "... I want something more secure where Nova can recover."

If Myles is curious why I'm worried about Nova's recovery right now and not her plot with the Andropovs, he doesn't mention it.

I'm glad. Because I don't have an answer.

I've asked myself the same question a million times over the last three days and come up empty every single time. But it's easy to ignore—because there's a voice in my chest purring in contended delight.

She's here. In my arms. She's safe. She's whole, more or less.

And as long as all that is true, everything else is fucking secondary.

"It would help if I knew where the fuck Ilya was." Myles's frustration bleeds through the phone.

"What about Leonid?"

"Sitting pretty in Chicago," Myles informs me. "My intel suggests that he's livid about Nova's disappearance. This is one thing he can't blame on you, since you were out of the country at the time."

"Doesn't mean he won't try." And if history is any indication, he will. Several times. "If anything comes up—"

"Yeah, yeah, I'll let you know immediately. I know the drill. But until then, you need somewhere to shack up." Myles whistles as he thinks.

Suddenly, the line goes quiet.

I check to make sure we're still connected. "Myles?"

"Still here. Just thinking."

"Think out loud."

"I was thinking about Castle Moorbeath."

It's been a long time since I've spared a thought for the crumbling Scottish castle I forgot I own. I bought it on a drunken whim the year after my divorce from Katerina. "The place isn't even inhabitable. It needs millions in renovations."

"Which makes it the perfect cover. Parts of it are livable. That old caretaker you hired still lives up there, right? There must be some running water and lights."

"Running water and lights," I mutter sarcastically. "All you need to run an empire."

"People have done it with less," he replies, unbothered. "And no one but me knows about the place. It could work."

"Except I have a shit ton of work to do. I need to be close in case Ilya, the Andropovs, or anyone else decides to make a move. I'd also like for Nova to have access to healthcare and to be in a position where I can see my enemies coming for miles and miles."

"That's what I like about working for you, Sam—your expectations are so reasonable." He lets loose a long-suffering sigh. "Lucky for you, I'm exceptional at my job. What about *The Sofia*?"

"Now, there's a fucking idea."

Thanks to a deal I brokered for a fellow *pakhan,* Oleg Pavlov, last spring, I was handed a spare set of keys to his superyacht with an open invitation to use her whenever I needed. A floating fortress where I can keep Nova safe while maintaining my grip on my empire.

The thought of having her trapped on a boat with me for weeks makes something dark and hungry twist in my chest.

"I'm full of 'em," Myles brags. "I also know Oleg is in the Maldives for the next three weeks. The yacht is available and outfitted with enough bells and whistles to avoid detection from any radar or satellite. You'll basically be sailing a luxury high rise with an invisibility cloak. It just comes down to whether you're ready to be at sea for weeks. Maybe months."

"Weeks," I counter. "Just until I find somewhere more permanent to settle."

"'Permanent?'"

I ignore the question because, again, I don't have an answer.

For most of my life, there's been a firm five-, ten-, fifty-year plan. I woke up every day knowing where I wanted to be when I was old and gray and even more obscenely wealthy than I already am.

Now, for the first time in as long as I can remember, my future is blurred. It's rippling around a Nova-sized blip, and I'm flying fucking blind.

The strange part is how it doesn't feel strange at all.

"Nova will be ready to move in a couple days, but she has a ways to go before she's recovered. I'm going to keep an eye on her until she's healed, and then..."

I hoped the right answer would tumble out of my mouth, but the rest of the sentence disappears into the void like the rest of my plans.

"And then...?" Myles pushes.

And then... And then what? And then we get married? Then I knock her up as many times as she'll let me, and we fill Castle Moorbeath with a dozen dark-haired little hellions scampering around barefoot? Children with my eyes and her smile?

Then I give up my Bratva and my empire and content myself with spending nights in the Scottish wild with my bride and our family?

Does that really sound so fucking bad?

I clear my throat. "Get the yacht ready. We'll set sail in two days."

Before he can point out my non-answer, I hang up and step back into the cool dark of the cabin.

As soon as I do, I realize I'm making plans to run away with a woman who hasn't even spoken to me in days. Not unless you count whimpering nightmares and groans of pain as I change her bandages.

We need to talk—but I don't know how to start.

No matter how many ways I turn things over and shift them around, I can't make any goddamn sense of the fact that I watched Nova betray me on video, and yet… I'm here tending to her wounds. I'm stroking her sweat-soaked back through nightmares and combing tangles out of her hair and force-feeding her broth I made by hand.

I'm taking care of her, when, if she was anyone else, she'd already be dead.

A fact I'm sure she's aware of, which is why she flinches when I open the bedroom door.

She's sitting on the edge of the bed in nothing but a t-shirt, gray sweatpants pooled on the floor around her ankles. She drops her gaze the moment she sees me and tucks her long locks behind her ears.

"I made broth." My voice comes out rough, hungry in a way that has nothing to do with food.

"I'm not hungry." Her forehead pinches at the center, mouth turned down at the corners.

"Eat anyway."

She turns her head to the side, chin set. "No, thank you."

I sigh and bend to grab the sweatpants to help her pull them on.

"No! Don't—" She wheezes out a breath. "Leave them there. I'll get them."

"A week from now, when you can bend at the waist without crying, you mean? You're going to want pants before then."

"I'm not helpless. You don't have to do—" She gestures with her good arm to me and the broth and the sweats. "—this. Any of it."

I know I don't. By all accounts, I shouldn't be.

In another world, Nova would be wrapped in a trash bag in the back of a freezer somewhere until the police stopped looking for her.

Instead, I'm reasoning with her to eat soup and let me help her get dressed.

I fucking dare someone to make that make sense.

"Well, I don't see anyone else lining up for the job, so I'm what you've got."

"I never asked you to follow me here and play nurse."

"No, you didn't. I came to the middle of nowhere for the simple joy of your company," I fire back.

Her brown eyes are on mine, stormy and stubborn. Then her chin wobbles and the fight drains out of her.

She drops her head, hiding her face behind a curtain of hair. "I'm sorry. I'm— I wanted to take a bath. I thought I could make it, but I can't— I couldn't—"

"No, you can't," I agree, already turning towards the bathroom. "But I can."

Her lips twist together nervously. I'm sure she's thinking what I'm thinking. Well, not exactly what I'm thinking—my thoughts have taken on a hot, gauzy quality all of a sudden.

But our minds are in the same general location: I'm going to see her naked.

I gave her a sponge bath when she was unconscious, cleaning her wounds through her clothes. But this is different. This is skin and vulnerability and trust she probably shouldn't give me.

Her shoulders slump with resignation, and she nods. "Okay."

"Great. While I run a bath, you can eat." I slide the end table in front of her and place the broth there.

She stares at it and then at me until it becomes clear I'm not moving another step until she takes a bite. She rolls her eyes, but I don't miss the way her lashes flutter closed as she spoons the broth into her mouth.

She swallows and a soft moan slips out.

I turn and leave before she can see exactly what that little sound does to me.

Not that it matters much. Five minutes later, I carefully help her limp into the bathroom and pull the threadbare t-shirt she's wearing over her head.

Fresh scrapes and bruises mark her skin, goosebumps rippling down her chest and arms.

But she's still the most beautiful thing I've ever seen.

I swallow down the burning desire rising in me—now is absolutely not the time—and begin to peel away her bandages.

Her lacerations are already beginning to close, but the sight of the mottled skin blending into the silvery scars on her wrists bothers me more than it should.

I've seen men gutted and bleeding out at my feet. I've done the gutting more times than I can count.

But it can't be Nova. I won't let it be. Ever again.

Nova eyes the high sides of the tub and then glances back nervously at me. "I don't think I can— It's high."

Without a word, I bend and lift her naked body into my arms. She's too thin and shivering, but as I lower her into the warm water, she groans.

A dreamy smile slips across her face, and I'm in danger of crawling into the tub with her.

"Better?" I growl through clenched teeth.

She draws her fingers over the surface of the water. "Much."

I try not to stare at the curve of her breasts as I ladle water over her back and shoulders. Nor when I lather my hands with bar soap and begin cleaning her in slow, gentle circles.

She lolls her head back against the lip of the tub. "God, that feels good."

I say nothing, because fuck knows nothing I have to say will be appropriate for where she is, where we are, for what's happened between us and what might still happen in the future.

Instead, I take my time washing her. Because I want to be careful. Because I don't want to hurt her.

It has nothing to do with the ache pressing against the seam of my pants or the way she sighs as I soap and rinse her chest and her stomach.

When my hand slips deeper into the water, her legs part in what can only be an invitation.

I'm nowhere near strong enough to refuse.

Nova's eyes stay closed as my hand curls over the center of her once and then again. When I circle a finger over her, her lips part on a sigh.

It's the first time she's looked relaxed in days, and I want to give her more. Everything.

I keep my gaze fixed on her face as I touch and stroke her beneath the water. Her hips begin rising to meet me. Her brows pinch together and small whimpers slip between her lips. All of it gives me some sick kind of pleasure I can't name. It satisfies some deep part of me that I never knew existed.

It's not the kind of gratification I find in work or sex—it's a selfless kind of joy I never would've thought a soulless fucker like me could be capable of.

But when Nova stiffens and cries out, her body pulsing around the press of my fingers, I don't have to keep a grip on the beast in my chest at all.

It's already content watching her get off.

Somehow, taking care of her is enough.

5

SAMUIL

For two days, I've watched Nova pretend she isn't afraid of me. It would be easier if she was—fear is something I understand.

It's this trust she keeps showing that's driving me fucking insane.

The rage is, too. It hasn't left my blood since I found her in that ravine, broken and terrified. Every time I close my eyes, I see her there—mud-streaked and trembling, injuries that I should have prevented marring her skin.

I've spent these last two days watching her fight through pain, knowing I'm partly responsible. If I'd been in Chicago instead of Moscow, none of this would have happened. She wouldn't have ended up at her father's mercy or in Ilya's crosshairs.

The doctor who treated her injuries left an hour ago with strict instructions about rest and recovery. But Nova's been restless since sunset, tossing and turning in the bed we're sharing out of necessity rather than choice. The cabin only has one bedroom, and I'm not leaving her alone—not when Ilya could still be hunting her.

When I finally slip into bed beside her, it's late. The world is dark beyond the skylight, and I can only see the silvery highlights of Nova's cheekbones and her full lips.

But it's enough to notice the way her lashes stir as my hand finds her hip. To register the hitch in her breathing. To register what that hitch does to mine.

Even beaten and wary, she's the most dangerous thing in this cabin.

"You're not asleep," I whisper into the dark. "But I'll let you pretend if you want to."

We haven't spoken about what happened in the tub earlier. As far as I'm concerned, we don't need to.

Nova was hurt, and I wasn't there to stop it. Now, I am. If there's anything I can do to ease her pain, I will.

Even if it means I have to excuse myself to relieve mine immediately afterward.

She turns slightly, looking over her shoulder. In the darkness, her eyes are liquid gold. "I can't sleep."

"Nightmares?"

A wince crosses her face as she pulls back the cover to adjust her leg. "Pain."

A dozen filthy ways I could help ease her discomfort flash through my mind—each one more depraved than the last—before I reach over her for the painkillers. The motion brings my chest flush against her back, and fuck if I don't want to stay there, pressed against her soft curves.

Instead, I deposit two pills into her waiting palm. She swallows them dry before falling back against the pillow to stare through the skylight.

"So many stars," she breathes. "It's so open out here."

"It looks that way from this vantage point, but then you step outside. There are too many trees and shadows and hidden ravines."

Like everything else in my world, the view is a beautiful lie. Things are rarely what they seem.

The woman beside me should be the prime example of that, but she feels like one of the exceptions. One of the few pure things left in my blood-soaked life.

"Where would you rather be?"

"A place with room to breathe." I could leave it there—probably fucking should—but the truth sneaks out of me before I can stop it. "My father's worst punishments always happened in the dark corners of his woods."

"Men like that want you to feel like you're alone." She gives me a sad smile that rips something open in my chest. "It's why my father locked me in the basement."

The same father who took care of her after her dog attack. The one who drove her to the penthouse so she could steal a server from me.

He never should've been close enough to touch her.

My hand curls into a fist, and I have to tear it away from her hip before I leave bruises.

"He's never going to put you in that basement again. No one will lock you up, Nova."

She blinks hard, gaze darting around the small room like a trapped animal. But this isn't that. This cabin isn't a dank basement. And I'm not her father.

I'm something far more dangerous.

I gingerly place my hand back on her hip, letting my thumb trace the jut of bone there. "Are you still in pain?"

"It's better. The pills are helping."

"Try to sleep, then."

"I can't."

"Are you cold?" It's a pathetic excuse to seal my body to hers, but it's late and I stopped pretending I could resist touching her weeks ago.

She's seen exactly how much I want her. Felt it. Tasted it.

Which is why the next words out of her mouth make no sense at all.

"Why are you here, Samuil?" She turns her head to face me fully, the gold flecks in her eyes catching the moonlight. "You didn't come here with a gun just to nurse me back to health. Why are you *really* here?"

She's right—I came here to kill anyone responsible for her pain. That was my first goal.

But the second?

"I knew you were injured and alone and scared. I knew my brother was hunting you. How could I not come?"

She studies my face with an intensity that makes my skin prickle, searching for lies in the shadows. But I've already given her the truth, as ugly and inconvenient as it is.

Despite everything I saw about her moves against me, I was tearing across Wisconsin backroads to reach her. My empire was under siege in Chicago, but I was moving in the opposite direction to help a woman who'd betrayed me. All because the thought of her being in danger made something primitive rear up in my chest.

Her throat bobs with a swallow. "I know Ilya sent you that video of me. I know what you've seen, Sam… and I know what it looks like. B-but—" She squeezes her eyes closed like she's concentrating. "I didn't do what it looks like. Or, I did, but not in the way they wanted."

I know. Of course I fucking know.

As soon as I clicked "play" on that video, my question was how Nova got into this mess and why she didn't ask for my help.

I never had to wonder if she wanted to move against me. I knew she didn't.

But again, she stops, nervously scanning my face like she's waiting for me to snap.

She chews on her bottom lip. "They wanted your server, so I gave them the one I knew you weren't using."

The second Myles told me which server was missing, I knew what she'd done—how she'd managed to both comply and protect me. My clever, dangerous girl.

"Why take it at all?"

"Because my father gave me no choice." She wraps her arms around her middle, holding herself the way I wish I could. "I woke up after the attack in his house, and he threatened to hurt my grandmother. He said he'd throw her out on the street if I didn't do what he asked."

It's exactly what I expected, but it's so much worse to hear than I thought it would be.

After everything, Nova didn't trust me to take care of her. She walked past my guards and stole from me and put herself within arm's reach of the Andropovs without ever stopping to wonder if she should just pick up the phone and call me.

I could've protected her grandmother and dismantled the Andropovs piece by bloody piece. I could've handled all of it from Moscow and then come home to her safe in our bed.

Instead, we're here.

"Did you really think I would let that happen?" I grit out angrily. "Did you really think I wouldn't step in and protect her? Protect you?"

"I didn't know what to think, Sam." Her voice is hoarse and hollow, matching the emptiness in her eyes. "You weren't there."

There's the truth of it.

The last few days—caring for her, being here with her—doesn't change the fact that I wasn't there when it mattered. My failure is etched into every new mark on her body.

"I want to go back to Chicago, Samuil," she whispers softly. "I need to check on Grams and Hope. I need to make sure they're okay."

She doesn't seem to understand that *she's* not okay.

Or that I'm going to take care of all of it.

I clear my throat. "We can't go back to Chicago yet. It might be a while before we can."

Her eyes shimmer with tears. "Why?"

"Ilya's out there somewhere plotting with my father or the Andropovs or fucking Katerina," I spit. "He's willing to work with anyone and everyone to take me down, and I don't know who else he might be working with. Until I know, I can't let you go back."

"How long will that take?"

The real question is tucked just under the surface. *How long do I have to stay here with you?*

"It'll take as long as it takes."

She flinches like I've struck her. "Will we be— Where will you put me?"

She says it as if she's some doll I'll put away on a shelf. Or a little girl I'll stash in a basement.

She says it like she's afraid.

"I'm going to take you somewhere safe and watch over you."

How many times am I going to have to explain myself? And how many times will it take before she believes it?

Her lips part, and I brace for pushback or pleading. In the end, she snaps her mouth shut and rolls onto her side.

The silence stretches, rippling with tension and all the things I should say to her but don't. All the promises I want to make but can't trust myself to keep.

When her breathing evens out, I let myself touch her again. I lay a soft hand on her waist, her warm skin soaking into my fingertips.

I need to be patient. Let her see that I'm trying to protect her. That keeping her away from Chicago and our families is the only thing that makes sense.

But patience was never one of my virtues.

And at this point, all I've got left are sins.

Nova shifts in her sleep, mumbling something that sounds like my name. It hits me then—what I've been avoiding since I found her in that ravine.

I didn't come to Wisconsin to save her.

I came because I can't live without her.

And if I have it my way, starting tomorrow, I'll never live without her again.

6

NOVA

The worst part about waking up beside a killer is wanting to stay there.

Sam's arm is draped over my waist, his chest rising and falling against my back in a steady rhythm that makes me ache. He runs hot—a furnace of muscle and danger that should send me running. Instead, I find myself counting his breaths, memorizing the weight of him against me.

Stupid. So fucking stupid.

Last night, we talked about monsters in the dark. About fathers who break their children. About basements and woods and all the ways powerful men teach you not to trust. Sam actually listened. Actually shared. Actually made me feel… safe.

That's how I know this is all a lie.

Because Samuil Litvinov doesn't do safe. He does calculated. Strategic. He takes what he wants and eliminates what stands in his way. And right now, I'm just a liability—the girl who stole his server and ran straight to his enemies.

Because how could he believe me? How can I believe him? How can either of us believe anything ever again?

The fact that he hasn't put a bullet in my head yet just means he still thinks I'm useful.

Or maybe he's waiting to see if I'll lead him to something bigger. To someone bigger. To all the secrets I don't actually have.

His fingers twitch against my hip, and my traitor body responds. Heat pools low in my belly as I remember those same fingers bringing me to pieces in the bath yesterday. Remember the way he touched me after he thought I was asleep, like he couldn't help himself.

Like he wanted me as much as I want him.

But want isn't trust. And trust isn't something either of us can afford right now.

I inhale slowly, trying to steady my racing pulse. Outside the cabin windows, dawn is breaking over the trees. Soon, he'll wake up. Soon, we'll have to face whatever comes next.

Soon, I'll have to decide if I'm going to fight or surrender when he inevitably shows his true colors.

For now, though, I let myself have this moment. Let myself pretend that the warmth at my back is comfort rather than threat. That the man holding me is salvation rather than damnation.

Let myself imagine, just for a heartbeat, that we could be something other than what we are:

A mafia prince and his latest victim.

A captor and his prey.

A man who kills traitors and the woman who betrayed him.

Behind me, Sam stirs.

Time's up.

"Nova…" His voice is raspy with sleep as his hand brushes along my shoulder.

I shiver, caught between fear and desire.

This is how it starts.

I force my eyes open. He looms over me, all six-foot-four of lethal grace. His usually pristine appearance has gone feral —beard untamed, dark hair falling in waves over his forehead.

The wildness suits him.

"Good. You're awake." Without warning, he scoops me into his arms like I weigh nothing.

If I thought it would make any difference, I'd fight. Since I know it won't, I don't bother.

"Where are we going?"

He doesn't answer me. He doesn't have to. I can barely walk without his help.

As we pass through the cabin's living room, I notice my duffel bag is gone and the furniture has all been pushed back into place.

"Where are we going?" I ask again. "And 'somewhere safe' isn't an answer."

He says he came to this cabin to keep me safe and take care of me, but all he's done is muddle my head even more than it already was.

I thought I understood who he was. I thought he'd press a gun to my temple the first time he laid eyes on me again.

Instead, he's making me bite back his name in the bathtub and carrying me off to unknown second locations.

I thought I knew Sam, but I'm not sure I know anything anymore.

"Somewhere dangerous then," he deadpans.

If I didn't think it would only hurt me more than it would him, I'd slap his chest. As it is, I hang uselessly in his arms as he carries me down the front steps and across the lawn.

He ducks through a break in the foliage, shielding me from the twigs and branches. When we come out on the other side, a hulking gray jeep with tires up to my waist is waiting for us.

He cradles me with one arm and opens the passenger door with the other, then tucks me inside.

"You're not going to tell me anything, are you?"

He reaches across me to buckle my seatbelt, his hand brushing across my chest. "Correct. Because telling you would actually make this dangerous."

When he opens the door to get behind the wheel, I keep firing questions. "Is it dangerous because you can't trust me? Or because I can't trust you?"

He turns the key in the ignition and takes off down a dirt road. "Trust is apparently a rare commodity these days."

If there was any doubt about whether he bought my story last night or not, it's gone now.

He was probably on the fence, waiting for an explanation from me. Then the half-assed one I gave last night convinced him of my guilt.

I'm a spy. This is my last ride.

"Can I at least call Hope and Grams?"

"No." His eyes stay fixed on the road. "You can't call anyone."

The walls of the Jeep press in, suffocating. "You said you were doing this to keep me safe, not to keep me prisoner. This isn't a hostage situation."

"It'll become one if you can't cooperate. You got yourself into this mess, and now—"

"You think I asked for this?"

Samuil's jaw tightens before he answers evenly. "I think you're uniquely good at attracting the wrong kind of people. I do what needs to be done to protect you. Abduction included."

"I'm not surprised," I grumble. "It runs in the family."

When he finally looks away from the road, his icy eyes locked on mine, I know I crossed a line. He sucks his cheeks in like he's tasting something sour, and as much as I want to take it back, I don't.

Samuil isn't Ilya, but I've bartered away too much of my pride already. If I hand over any more, there will be nothing left of me. And I won't do that. Not even for Samuil.

His grip tightens on the wheel until I swear I hear the leather creak. We spend the next half hour marinating in thick silence, the only sound the crunch of gravel under tires. When he finally turns off the single-lane road, a warehouse looms in the distance like a metal coffin.

"*This* is where we're going to lay low? A warehouse in the middle of nowhere?"

It looks like a remote building where no one would hear me scream.

I begin rehearsing a better explanation—one that might spare me. I don't want to die.

Sam raps his knuckle against the glass, pointing out the open field next to the warehouse. "We're not staying here. It's just for takeoff."

"For taking off what?"

Sam slows to a stop in the gravel parking lot and puts the Jeep into park. "We need to get to an airport with international clearance. We're going to Europe, and we have to get there quickly."

"No." I watch his face, searching for some sign that this is a sick joke, but he's as steely and surly as ever. I shake my head. "Nope. No way. Not gonna happen."

For all I know, Grams is living on the streets. Hope could be dead in a ditch somewhere. As much as I hate admitting Sam's right about anything, he nailed it—I got everyone into this mess. I can't abandon them now.

He gets out of the car, slamming his door behind him hard enough to make the whole vehicle shake. I dig my nails into the sides of my seat as if that could stop him from simply picking me up and carrying me wherever he wants. Like onto a plane, apparently, and off to Europe and wherever the hell else he wants to cart me.

I want to trust Sam—since the very beginning, my instinct has been to trust him—but I have a feeling that if I get on that plane, there's a chance I'll never make it back home.

When the door wrenches open, his eyes burn with molten heat. "Do I need to get a leash and harness to drag you into that helicopter? Because I will, if that's what it takes to keep you alive."

Is that what he wants? To save my life?

The weight in my chest is rising, rising… right into my throat. "It seems the best way for me to stay alive is to stay far away from you," I spit at him.

I'm hoping it'll piss him off enough that he'll change his mind and walk away, leave me here to fend for myself.

Then again, the thought of watching him walk away threatens to unleash another wave of tears.

I have no idea what he wants to do to me or with me, yet I can't bear the idea of letting him go. What kind of masochistic madness is this?

Finally, Sam gets actually angry. I see it as red creeps up his neck, as the vein in his forehead pulses. His mouth presses into a flat line. "You may be right about that, but it's too late now. If you want to stay alive, you have to come with me."

"Sure," I snort. "Sounds like exactly what a kidnapper would say. I'm supposed to give up my freedom and trust you."

"I gave you fucking freedom, and look how you repaid me for it!"

"I told you what happened—"

"Just like I'm telling you what's happening now," he snarls, voice dropping to a register that makes my bones vibrate. "You don't believe that I'm trying to protect you, so why should I believe you?"

He shouldn't—that's the problem. I betrayed him, and he doesn't believe me, so I can't believe him. It's a nasty cycle of distrust that I can't seem to break.

Before I can explain this, he hoists me out of the car and into his arms yet again.

"Are you going to carry me like this all the way to Europe?"

"No, I'm going to carry you to Myles," he snaps. "Because I know you won't fucking believe me. Maybe he'll have a better shot."

"Myles is here?"

Samuil doesn't respond, just scoops one of the duffle bags off the ground and slings it over his other shoulder without slowing. Dust plumes behind his every step as we cross the parking lot towards the warehouse where Myles is waiting in the doorway, a cautious smile on his face.

"Hey there, Nova."

Samuil deposits me on a wooden crate next to the door and then stomps off back towards the car, both hands raking through his hair in frustration.

I watch him go. "I don't care what he says—I'm not getting on that plane. I need to stay here."

I'm expecting him to give me the same *"you don't have a choice"* line as Samuil, but Myles just sighs and drops down on the crate beside me. "As long as you're in the country, Ilya can track you."

"I'd like to point out that I escaped him. All on my own. No help from anyone. And he still hasn't tracked me down."

"He very nearly did," Myles says, voice heavy. "His team is tearing the cabin apart as we speak."

A chill races down my spine. "That's why we left so quickly?"

"You missed him by fifteen minutes. If that. Samuil saved your life."

Maybe it's a good thing I wasn't strong enough to fight Samuil. It could've gotten us both killed.

"Why does Ilya want me so badly?"

"Because he knows the best way to get to Samuil is through you. You're his weak spot."

I laugh out loud.

Myles does not. He isn't even smiling anymore. "Sam is my best friend. He can be a dick and he's colder than an ice rink in Siberia in February, but I love him anyway. Because he's a good man. He's a million times the man his brother could ever hope to be. If you think this escape is some ploy to kidnap you and make your life miserable, you couldn't be more wrong."

It wouldn't be the first time. My track record lately is absolute shit.

"So what is it?" I ask, fearing I already know the answer.

"It's the only way he knows to keep you alive."

My head sags between my shoulder blades, and Myles reaches over to squeeze my knee. "You've survived a lot in the last few days—the last few months, really. You can survive this, too."

I'm not sure anyone is strong enough to survive Samuil Litvinov. Not when he looks at you like you're everything he wants and everything he can't trust. Not when his touch sets your skin on fire even as his eyes freeze your blood. Not when he carries you like you're precious cargo one minute and eyes you like a potential threat the next.

Least of all me, the girl who can't decide if she wants to kiss him or knee him in the balls.

The girl who betrayed him and still can't stop wanting him.

The girl who no longer has a choice.

7

SAMUIL

The last yacht party I attended in Sardinia ended with two dead bodies and a forty-million dollar deal to import black market firearms.

Tonight, *The Sofia* carves relentlessly through the Mediterranean, her hull as black as the secrets she carries. No champagne. No caviar. No elite parasites comparing the sizes of their offshore accounts.

Just the whisper of waves against steel, the echo of the crew's boots on teak, and Nova—my broken bird, who looks seconds away from throwing herself into the endless dark below.

"The security system rivals most government facilities." Captain Andreas drones on about surveillance and defensive capabilities while Nova drifts closer to the railing. Her fingers trail along the polished metal, testing. Searching. "Would you like to see the command center?"

"Later." I dismiss him with a sharp nod.

Nova's shoulders tense at my approach, but she doesn't move away when I join her at the rail. The moon paints silver paths across black water that stretches to infinity. Different from the Wisconsin woods that cradled us, sheltered us. Out here, we're exposed. Vulnerable.

But also untouchable. Let them try to reach us now.

"Are you hungry?" The question slips out before I can stop it. Feeding her, keeping her strong—these are problems I know how to solve. Not like the shadows haunting her eyes or the bruises marking her skin.

"No." Her voice is barely audible.

"Nova—"

"I need to lie down." She turns away, won't even look at me as she asks, "Where is the room?"

"Below deck. First door on the left."

She limps away, every step a reminder of what my brother did to her. Of what I failed to prevent. The Nova who challenged me at every turn, who squared her shoulders and spat defiance in my face—that woman is buried beneath layers of fear and betrayal.

I pace the deck like a caged animal, muscles coiled tight with the need to hunt. To destroy. Ilya is still breathing somewhere on this earth, and that fact alone makes my trigger finger itch. But Nova needs protection more than she needs vengeance.

Even if she hates me for it.

The night wind carries the bite of salt and diesel, but I keep stalking the perimeter, scanning the horizon. She's just below my feet, yet the distance between us stretches wider than this fucking ocean.

I'm doing what needs to be done. That should be enough.

It isn't.

For the first time in my life, I need someone to understand my choices. To trust them. To trust me.

When the cold starts to sink into my bones, I abandon my post and head below.

Nova stands at the porthole in wrinkled sweats and a thin tank top that does nothing to hide the goosebumps on her arms. Her dark hair falls in tangles down her back, wild and unkempt. She looks like a stray who's wandered into a palace —all this gleaming mahogany and brass surrounding her only emphasizes how far we are from her world.

She doesn't acknowledge me until the door clicks shut. Then she whirls, stumbling, one hand flying out to catch herself against the wall. The movement draws a hiss of pain from her lips.

"It's just me." I drag a hand over my neck, fighting the urge to go to her. To steady her. To wrap her in my arms until that haunted look leaves her eyes.

Instead, I keep my distance.

"I've never..." Her voice catches. "I've never been outside Chicago before. Not really. Just...Wisconsin once, for a school trip. And then again, for... other reasons." A bitter laugh escapes her. "And now here I am, in the middle of the ocean, running from the Russian mafia."

The confession hits me in the chest. While I've been thinking of this yacht as a fortress, a sanctuary, she sees only the vast unknown stretching in every direction. No familiar streets. No safe spaces. No home to return to.

She presses her forehead against the cool glass. "I don't even know where we are. What country we're near. Nothing seems real anymore."

"We're off the coast of Sardinia." I take one step closer, then another when she doesn't flinch away. "In the Mediterranean Sea."

"Sardinia," she repeats softly, like she's tasting the word. Testing its reality. "I used to walk dogs in Lincoln Park and dream about traveling someday. Not like this, though. Never like this."

The yacht pitches gently, and Nova's hand flies out to steady herself again. Without thinking, I close the distance between us, my body moving on pure instinct to catch her if she falls.

"The rocking gets easier," I tell her softly. "Your body adjusts to the motion after a day or two."

She nods but doesn't relax. Her fingers grip the window frame so tight her knuckles turn white. "Everything I own, everything I am, fits in that little duffel bag." She gestures to the corner where her hastily packed bag sits. "My whole life in Chicago… it's just gone."

The words carry the weight of everything she's lost. Her business. Her independence. The simple life she'd built for herself, far from her father's corruption. Everything taken from her because she got tangled in my war.

"Your grandmother is safe," I remind her. "Hope, too. And the dogs. I have men watching them all around the clock."

"I know." She closes her eyes, a tear sliding down her cheek. "But I can't even call them. Can't let them know I'm okay. They probably think…" Her voice breaks.

I step closer, close enough to feel the heat from her body, to catch the faint scent of her skin beneath the antiseptic smell of bandages. "What do they think, Nova?"

"That I'm dead." The words come out as a whisper. "Or worse."

My hands find her shoulders, gentle, giving her every chance to pull away. When she doesn't, I turn her to face me. More tears track down her cheeks, and something in my chest constricts at the sight.

"Look at me." I wait until those amber eyes meet mine. "You're alive. You're whole. And I swear to you, on everything I am, that I will keep you that way."

Nova sways forward, her forehead coming to rest against my chest. Her hands stay wrapped around herself, but she lets me take her weight, lets me shelter her from the vast darkness beyond the window.

"I used to rescue animals," she whispers into my shirt. "Strays. Abandoned pets. The ones nobody wanted. And now, I'm the one who needs rescuing."

My arms slide around her, one hand cradling the back of her head. Her hair is silk against my palm. "You rescued yourself. I just provided the getaway vehicle."

A sound catches in her throat—not quite a laugh, not quite a sob. "Some getaway vehicle you picked."

"Only the best for you." The words come out rougher than

intended, weighted with everything I'm not saying. Everything I can't say.

The yacht rolls with a larger wave, and Nova's fingers finally uncurl from around herself to grip my shirt instead. I hold her steadier, stronger, becoming her anchor in the shifting dark.

"I dream about it," she confesses, so quietly I almost miss it. "The warehouse. The cell. Ilya's voice. Sometimes, I wake up and can't remember where I am."

My arms tighten involuntarily. The need to hunt my brother rises like bile in my throat. "You're with me. You're safe."

"Am I?" She doesn't pull away, doesn't look up. Just breathes the question into the space between us like a prayer.

Instead of answering, I press my lips to her temple and whisper against her skin in Russian, "*Ya ne pozvolyu nikomu tebya obizhet'.*"

I will never let anyone hurt you again.

Nova melts further into me, her body softening degree by degree. Her hands stay fisted in my shirt, but the desperate grip loosens slightly. Each breath she takes grows steadier, deeper.

I should move us to the bed. Let her rest. Her body is still healing, still weak from days of captivity and fear. But I'm frozen in place, afraid any movement will shatter this moment of trust.

"Tell me what that means," she murmurs against my chest. "What you said."

My thumb traces circles against the nape of her neck. "A promise."

She shifts, pressing closer, seeking more warmth. More contact. More comfort. "The good kind or the scary kind?"

"Both." I rest my chin on top of her head. "The kind that will keep you alive."

The yacht rocks again, but this time, Nova moves with it, letting me take more of her weight. Her eyes drift closed, exhaustion finally winning over fear.

"I should let you sleep." The words come out, but I make no move to release her.

"Not yet." Her fingers twist deeper into my shirt. "Just... just stay like this. For a minute."

So I hold her in the dark, my broken bird who's slowly learning to trust again. Outside our window, the Mediterranean stretches endless and black. Somewhere beyond that darkness, my enemies plot. My brother hunts. The world spins on with all its violence and betrayal.

But here, in this moment, Nova breathes steady against my chest.

And for the first time since I found her in that cabin in Wisconsin, I feel like I'm doing something right.

8

SAMUIL

She trembles against me in the dark, and for the first time in my life, I'm fucking terrified of breaking something precious.

Nova's pulse flutters beneath my fingers where they rest against her throat. Her skin is silk and heat, so delicate I could snap her in two. But she's not made of glass—she proved that by surviving Ilya, by escaping, by finding her way back to me even when she had every reason to run.

"*Ya ne mogu tebya poteryat,*" I whisper into her hair.

I can't lose you.

The confession slips out in Russian because I'm a goddamn coward. Because saying it in English would make it real. Would make her real. Would make this ache in my chest something I can't ignore.

She shifts closer, seeking warmth, comfort, protection. All the things I want to give her. All the things I'm not sure I know how to provide without turning them into chains.

"More Russian secrets?" Her voice is drowsy, colored with exhaustion and trust she probably shouldn't feel.

My thumb traces the curve of her jaw. "Just truth."

"Mm." She tilts her head, pressing into my touch. "Sounds dangerous."

It is. Christ, it is. Every soft sound she makes, every unconscious display of trust, every moment she lets me hold her like this—they're all fucking landmines in my chest, waiting to detonate.

I should put her to bed. Should give her space to rest and heal. Should maintain some kind of distance before I forget every lesson I've learned about letting people get close.

Instead, I hold her tighter and whisper more dangerous truths into the dark.

"Ya budu zashchishchat tebya vechno."

I will protect you forever.

Her breath catches, though she can't understand the words. Maybe she hears the weight behind them anyway.

She turns in my arms to stare out the porthole, watching the dark waves that carry us further from everything she's known.

"Tell me about Chicago." Her request comes soft and unexpected, like the first drops of rain before a storm. "Tell me what you see when you look at my city."

I could tell her about the corrupt web of power binding the streets together. About the deals made in penthouses while servants scrub blood from marble floors. About the men who rule from corner offices, their hands clean while their souls drip red.

But that's my Chicago. Not hers.

"I see your park," I say instead. "The paths you walked with your dogs. The shelter where you volunteered. The small ways you carved out space for yourself in a place that tried to swallow you whole."

She stiffens against me. "My father…"

"Owns half the cops on the North Side. I know." My fingers find a knot of tension in her shoulder, work it loose. "But you built something real there anyway. Something that had nothing to do with his power or his control."

"And now, it's gone." The words crack like ice. "Everything I built. Every bit of freedom I clawed out for myself. He wins again."

"No." The denial comes fierce and fast. "He loses. Every breath you take away from his influence, every moment you spend healing and growing stronger—those are victories he can't touch."

Her laugh holds no humor. "Is that what this is? Healing? Running away on a yacht that probably has more surveillance than a prison?"

"This isn't a prison, Nova." But the guilt twists in my gut anyway. Because she's not entirely wrong. "This is a fortress. And the difference is that every door opens for you. Every security measure exists to keep threats out, not to keep you in."

She's quiet for a long moment, processing. When she speaks

again, her voice carries the weight of years spent under her father's thumb.

"I used to dream about escaping him. About building a life so far removed from his influence that he couldn't touch me." Her fingers trace patterns on my chest. "I never imagined escape would look like this. Would feel like this."

The raw honesty in her voice cracks something open inside me. Makes me want to show her that not every man with power uses it as a weapon.

For years, I've built walls of wealth and violence, collecting power like ammunition. Every decision calculated to expand my control, to ensure no one could ever make me weak.

Now, I find myself dismantling those walls, brick by brick, to let this woman breathe.

The yacht's engines thrum beneath our feet, a steady pulse of raw power. But for the first time, that power feels hollow. Empty. What good is an empire of fear if it can't give Nova the peace she deserves?

"I made a call today," I tell her, watching her face in the dim light. "Transferred control of Hope's Helpers to a shell corporation. Your friend can keep running it, but my name will shield it from your father's influence. From anyone's influence."

Nova goes very still against me. "You didn't have to—"

"I wanted to." The truth of it surprises me. "My resources should do more than just destroy things. They should protect what matters."

She lifts her head, studies me with those amber eyes that see too much. "And what matters to you, Sam?"

Everything I am screams at me to deflect. To maintain distance. To keep my priorities locked behind steel doors where they can't be used against me.

Instead, I brush my thumb across her cheek and whisper, "You're changing all my answers to that question."

The waves slap harder against the hull, making the cabin creak. Nova lifts her head and whispers, "I'm not going back to Chicago, am I?"

I tense, but keep my arms loose around her. The darkness beyond the porthole makes it easier to face this truth. Makes it easier to be the man she needs right now, not the vengeful bastard I've trained myself to be.

"Not until I know you'll be safe there." My voice comes out rough. Foreign. As if all my carefully maintained control has rusted away in the salt air.

"My father..." She swallows the rest, but I hear it anyway. The weight of his betrayal. The echo of his threats.

I could tell her it doesn't matter. That distance changes things. But her father's influence runs deeper than Chicago's streets. His corruption has seeped into her bones, into the way she flinches at sudden movements and second-guesses her own worth.

"Tell me." I brush my lips against her temple. Not a kiss—a shield.

The story spills out of her in broken pieces. How he'd force her to sit silently at family dinners while his cop buddies talked about "cleaning up" the streets, one broken femur at a time. How he made examples of people who crossed him. The way he'd hold her grandmother's care over her head whenever she tried to break free.

"I thought I'd escaped." Nova's fingers twist deeper into my shirt. "But I was just pretending. Playing at having a real life while he watched and waited."

That hits too close to home. My own father's games. His tests and manipulations. The constant balance of power and punishment.

But this isn't about my damage. This is about Nova.

I slide my palm along her spine, counting vertebrae, measuring the tremors that race beneath her skin. "Your father cannot touch you here."

She exhales against my throat. "Because you're more powerful than him?"

The question hangs between us, heavy with implications. Once, I would have answered with a smirk and a demonstration of exactly how much influence I wield. But Nova deserves better than another man's power games.

"Because I'll never use that power against you."

Her head snaps up, amber eyes searching mine in the dim cabin light. "Those are pretty words, Sam. But you've already made decisions about my life without consulting me. Taking me from Chicago. Bringing me here."

She has a point. Every protective instinct in me wants to argue, to explain how those choices kept her alive. Instead, I force myself to really hear her.

"You're right." The admission costs me nothing but pride, and her startled expression makes it worth it. "I'm used to giving orders and expecting them to be followed. It's how I've survived. How I've kept others alive."

"And now?"

"Now, I need to learn a different way." I brush a strand of hair from her face, letting my fingers linger against her cheek. "With you."

Nova doesn't pull away from my touch, but she doesn't lean into it, either. "What does that mean, exactly?"

"It means we make decisions together." The words feel strange on my tongue. Not wrong, just new. "It means I tell you what I know, and you tell me what you need. We find solutions that work for both of us."

"Even if I disagree with you?"

"Especially then." I trail my hand down her arm, feeling goosebumps rise in my wake. "Your perspective... it challenges me. Makes me think beyond force and fear."

She shivers, but her voice stays steady. "And what if I need space? Time to process things on my own?"

The question stabs at my deepest fears—of abandonment, of betrayal, of loss. But I make myself nod. "Then we find a way."

Nova's shoulders relax slightly, as if she's testing the truth of my words. Testing me. "You're asking me to put my life in your hands," she says quietly. "I need the same from you."

The old me would have laughed at the idea of giving anyone that kind of power. The old me would have kissed her silent and changed the subject. But her steady gaze holds more strength than all my father's threats ever did.

"Tell me what that looks like." I keep my voice neutral, open. This is her moment to define terms.

"No more unilateral decisions about my safety. No more hiding information to 'protect' me." She straightens in my arms, chin lifting. "And no more assumptions about what I can or can't handle."

My jaw clenches. "Some things in my world—"

"Are brutal. Ugly. Dangerous." She presses her palm against my chest, right over my heart. "I know what you are, Samuil. I've seen it. But I'm not asking you to change that. I'm asking you to trust me enough to let me choose how I deal with it."

The request burrows under my skin. In my world, trust is a weapon. A weakness to exploit. But Nova isn't asking for my secrets or my power. She's asking for partnership.

"Okay." I cover her hand with mine, pressing it harder against my chest. "But I need something from you, too."

She tenses slightly. "What?"

"When things get dark—when you're scared or overwhelmed—don't shut me out." I thread our fingers together. "Let me be your strength until you find your own again."

Nova's breath catches. For a moment, I think I've pushed too far. Then she rises on her toes and brushes her lips against mine. "Deal."

The kiss deepens, soft and slow, nothing like our desperate couplings in Chicago. Nova's hands slide up my chest to my shoulders, and I lift her easily, compensating for her injured ankle. Her legs wrap around my waist as I carry her to the bed.

"Your ribs," I murmur against her throat. "We should wait—"

"I'm tired of waiting." She tugs at my shirt. "Tired of being careful. Of being afraid."

Still, I lower her to the silk sheets with deliberate gentleness. Her tank top has ridden up, exposing the purple-black bruises scattered across her sides. My brother's handiwork. I trace the unmarked skin between them, watching her shiver.

"Sam." Her voice holds a warning. "Don't treat me like I'll break."

"Never." I press my lips to her collarbone. "I'll take you to the edge. But I'll never, ever hurt you, Nova Pierce."

She arches beneath me as I map her body with careful touches, learning which movements make her gasp and which make her wince. When I finally slide into her, we both freeze, adjusting to this new intimacy.

"Look at me," she whispers, and I do.

In her eyes, I see everything we've been dancing around. Trust. Fear. Need. Power. All the complicated threads binding us together, stronger than duty or revenge or protection.

We move together in the darkness, finding a rhythm that belongs only to us. Each touch is a promise. Each kiss, a confession. When she comes apart beneath me, crying out my name, I follow her over the edge.

After, she curls against my side, her breathing steady and deep. For the first time since Chicago, her body is truly relaxed.

I know this peace is temporary. Tomorrow will bring new challenges, new negotiations of power and trust.

But for now, I hold her close and let myself believe in something bigger than survival.

9

NOVA

I'm living a nightmare.

I'm sitting on the deck of a private superyacht with a still-warm snickerdoodle muffin and an iced matcha latte in front of me, and I can't even bring myself to look at either one.

Louisa steps back, smiling proudly at the tray she just slid in front of me. "You said these were your favorite, ma'am."

I did say that, didn't I?

One of the crewmembers played cards with me yesterday and used the opportunity to dig for more information on how to take this superyacht to the next level. Apparently, it's not enough to have two exercise rooms, multiple sun decks, and a theater room with every movie I've ever wanted to watch. No, it also needs a chef who can whip up whatever my heart desires with zero notice.

"You and the entire crew are a wonder, Louisa." I beam up at her, hoping she isn't noticing the way I'm sliding the napkin with the muffin on it to the edge of the table. The breeze off the water is sending the smell of cinnamon straight into my nose.

I think I'm going to be sick.

Louisa shifts around the table, blocking my view. That's just as well for me. Watching the waves toss is probably why I'm feeling so queasy this morning. "At least try a bite so I can tell Chef what you think."

I could refuse her. Samuil has made it clear over the last two weeks that I'm free to do whatever I want on this yacht.

Sleep in until noon? Go ahead.

Tan topless on the private deck? Sure, albeit only if he can watch.

Cut dinner short so he can spread me on the table and eat me instead? The crew has now added it to the daily schedule and learned to keep their distance.

But I don't *want* to refuse. I want to thank Louisa for all of her work. I want the chef to know I'm grateful.

So, even as my stomach roils, I pinch off the smallest possible crumb of the muffin and drop it into my mouth.

Some part of me recognizes the burst of flavor. It's buttery and sweet with a punch of spices and cinnamon. I should be crying tears of joy that someone made my favorite treat in the middle of the ocean.

Instead, my insides are churning with the desire to expel the small morsel of muffin along with everything else I've managed to choke down today.

"Delicious!" I chirp, swallowing a gag.

Thankfully, Louisa seems satisfied. She promises to pass the praise along to Chef and then retreats below deck to the kitchen.

As soon as she's out of view, I launch myself out of the sunchair and sprint down the stairs to my suite.

I blow through the door, grateful Samuil isn't inside, and use the bedpost to swing myself into the bathroom like Tarzan. I just barely manage to drop to my knees and lift the lid before everything in my stomach comes back up with a vengeance.

Several unpleasant minutes and several flushes later, I close the lid and press my cheek to the cool porcelain surface. I'm hot and sweaty and so miserable that I don't care that I'm using a toilet lid as an ice pack. I happen to know the maid scrubs this thing twice per day. I could eat off of it without getting sick.

Which means there's no reason at all for me to *be* this sick.

Like the universe is trying to remind me where I am, the yacht lurches ever-so-slightly. But no, we've been here for days. Why would I only get seasick now?

I close my eyes, trying to regain my equilibrium. Nerves and anxiety and fear typically go after my heart, my lungs, my mind. My stomach has always been something I could count on.

But it's been days of on-and-off nausea. Last night, I refused the pre-dinner cheese board, which caught Samuil's eye. Turning down cheese is definitely a distress call in the world of Nova Pierce, and Sam is nothing if not observant. But I played it off well enough.

"I want to save room for dinner," I explained.

Thankfully, by the time the seafood fettuccine arrived, my stomach was settled. I scarfed down my entire plate and then doubled back to the cheese board for good measure.

But I'm paying for it in spades right now.

"Why?" I moan into the crook of my arm. "Why me?"

I peel myself off the bathroom floor and trudge over to the sink.

I slept for nine hours last night, but my eyes burn with exhaustion. Every part of me feels achy and bloated.

I cross my arms over my body and wince when I accidentally graze my boob.

Because of course my boobs hurt, too. The one part of me that wasn't used as a doggy chew toy or scraped up in my tumble down the ravine is now aching of its own accord. Can't a girl catch a break?

I'm bending towards the sink to rinse out my mouth when, like the tumblers in a lock, the facts shift into place.

The nausea.

The soreness.

The fatigue.

For days, I've been attributing all of it to my escape from Ilya, the fall down the forest ravine, the antibiotics, my recovery. I'm certainly not short on things to blame.

But I shouldn't be getting *worse* as time passes, right?

I freeze, my hands gripping either side of the sink as I count back through the days and weeks and months in search of my last cycle. But it's all hazy.

Since meeting Samuil, I've had more sex than I've ever had before. But life has also been more chaotic than it's ever been, and I occasionally forget to take my birth control.

I lunge for my makeup bag, upending the moisturizer and accidentally turning the hot water faucet on high as I rifle through the contents. I pull out my pills and flip open the lid.

"Oh, God," I groan. I press my forehead to the mirror in hopes I'll fall through into an alternate reality where I'm not the dumbest woman alive.

The pill container is like a half-finished tic-tac-toe game. I thought I'd maybe missed one or two doses here or there, but it's more like I'm forgetting as often as I remember. Add to that the kidnapping stress and the antibiotics for my injuries, and there's no way this medicine is doing what it's supposed to.

I press a hand to my stomach, jostling it like it's a Magic 8 Ball.

Am I pregnant?

There's a gurgle. *Reply hazy, try again.*

I try to think through my options. The yacht has a fully stocked medical unit. There could be a pregnancy test in there, but I'd have to ask for it. And it's not as if I could lie and say it was for a friend.

Louisa might keep my secret if I asked her to, but I don't want to put her in that position.

Plus, it doesn't matter. As I breathe through another wave of nausea, the haze of uncertainty clears fast. I can feel the truth in my bones.

I'm carrying a child.

I press my hand to my stomach again, waiting for panic or another bout of heaving. But there's nothing. No dizziness. No feeling of the walls closing in.

Instead, as I circle my thumb over my stomach, I picture a rosy-cheeked baby with Samuil's silver eyes and my dark brown hair. I picture a little human who is part Samuil and part me. I close my eyes and imagine the three of us at the park, a giggling toddler chasing after Rufus and Ruby in the grass. Chubby little hands would reach for Samuil, and he'd scoop our child up and spin in circles until he tumbled dizzily to the soft grass, laughing in that rare, carefree way I love so much.

This isn't happening the way I would have planned it. But then again, nothing in my life so far has gone to plan. Why start now?

"Nova?" My heartrate kicks up, and I snap my eyes open as Samuil's voice slips under the crack in the door.

"In here!" I'm going for an "easy, breezy, beautiful, *CoverGirl*" kind of tone, but my voice comes out shaky and unconvincing.

He tries the knob, but finds it locked. "Louisa said you ran off the deck."

So much for Louisa keeping my secrets. She ratted me out the first chance she got.

"I'm fine," I insist.

"Then let me in."

"I can't. I'm… sick." The best kind of lie has a little bit of truth in it, right?

"Then let me in," he repeats, trying the knob again. "Let me help you."

"You've done enough." I snort with laughter, still processing what I'm accepting, more and more by the second, to be true.

Sam slams a hand against the thin wooden door. "Open the damn door and tell me what's going on, Nova."

I'm not ready, but I don't think I'll ever be. So I pull open the door to reveal Samuil glowering on the other side.

His eyes scrape over me instantly, assessing me for injuries. Finding nothing, he frowns. "What's wrong?"

"I don't know for sure, but… I kind of know for sure."

He frowns. "I don't like guessing games. Tell me what's happening."

My mouth opens, and…

Between abductions, espionage, and all the unprotected sex we've been having, I forgot to take my birth control. Congratulations, Daddy.

"Nova…" Samuil growls, taking a step closer. He fills the small bathroom, making it hard to breathe.

Maybe that's why the truth tumbles out of me with no build-up.

"I'm pregnant."

10

NOVA

My world narrows to Samuil's face as the word hangs in the air between us.

Pregnant.

His silence says everything. I back up, but I only have a foot or two to retreat until I hit the bathroom counter. My eyes dart to the window, to the endless expanse of blue beyond the glass. I've never felt more trapped on this floating palace than I do right now.

"I could be wrong," I whisper, but the words scatter in the air between us. Samuil hasn't moved, hasn't blinked. His face is a mask I can't read, those ice-gray eyes fixed on some point beyond my shoulder.

My heart pounds so hard I'm sure he must hear it echoing. Every bitter comment he's ever made about his mother floods my mind. Every cutting remark about his ex-wife's betrayal plays on repeat. I watch his jaw clench, see the muscle jump beneath his skin, and wait for him to say something. Anything.

For God's sake, give me anything but this silence.

"It's probably just stress," I continue, the words tumbling out faster and faster now, messier and messier, more and more desperate. "Or seasickness. The waves have been rougher today, and—"

Samuil finally moves.

One step forward. His massive frame fills the doorway, blocking any escape route. Not that I have anywhere to go—we're in the middle of the Mediterranean, for God's sake.

The sudden movement makes me flinch, and I hate myself for it. I want to believe I know the man in front of me. This is Samuil. *Samuil.*

But the face he's wearing belongs to a stranger.

Then a harsh sound tears from his throat—something between a laugh and a growl—and everything changes.

That sound reverberates off the marble walls as Samuil's hand finds the doorframe, gripping it until his knuckles turn white. For a man who practically radiates power, he suddenly looks like he needs the support to stay standing.

I've never seen him so stripped bare, so unguarded. His face cycles through emotions faster than I can track them—fear bleeding into something darker, then transforming into what might be wonder. Might be joy. Might be terror. I've learned to read the microscopic shifts in his expression over our months together—or at least, I thought I did.

But right now? I'm lost.

When our eyes finally meet, the intensity in his gaze pins me in place. His irises are molten silver, fever-bright in a way that makes my breath catch. He takes another step forward as Russian spills from his lips, low and guttural. I catch my name among the flow of foreign syllables, but the rest is lost to me.

Still, I don't need to understand the words to hear the storm behind them. To recognize that whatever he's saying comes from somewhere deep and raw inside him.

My arms wrap around my middle without conscious thought. It's instinct—protective—though I'm not sure if I'm trying to shield myself or this possibility growing inside me. Or maybe I'm trying to shield him from what this means. From how it could change everything.

I want to reach for him, but something in his expression keeps me frozen. The air between us feels electric, charged with potential energy. I realize I'm holding my breath, waiting for words I'll understand, waiting to know if this news will break what we have or make it stronger.

His eyes drop to where my arms cross over my stomach, and suddenly, he's moving with purpose toward my cosmetics bag on the counter.

He snaps into focus with predatory intensity as he spots the pink packet of pills among my toiletries. The transformation is instant—from raw vulnerability to pure, driven purpose. In three long strides, he's beside me, his cologne wrapping around me as he reaches past to snatch up the birth control.

My breath catches as I realize what he's about to do. "Samuil, wait—"

But he's already at the porthole, muscles bunching under his white dress shirt as he cranks it open.

Then he cocks back his arm and throws my birth control out of the window.

The pills catch the Mediterranean sunlight as they arc through the air, a flash of pink against endless blue before disappearing into the waves below.

The gesture is so absurdly dramatic—so perfectly, ridiculously Samuil—that a bubble of hysteria rises in my throat. Of course this is how he'd handle it. Not with words or discussion, but with an act of possession so over-the-top it borders on caveman.

When he turns back to me, his face has transformed once again. The earlier turmoil is gone, replaced by something fierce and proud that makes heat pool low in my belly. His eyes burn into mine as he stalks closer.

"There," he says, voice rough and deep. "One less thing to stress about. You don't have to worry about getting pregnant anymore." His hand reaches for my stomach but stops just shy of touching. "Because if you're not already, you soon will be."

Jaw, meet floor.

I should be outraged. Should be furious at his high-handedness, his assumption of control over my body. Instead, I find myself fighting back a smile at the barely concealed hunger in his expression. At the way his fingers tremble slightly in the space between us, betraying that this display of dominance masks something much more vulnerable.

My lips part to challenge him, because someone needs to point out how ridiculous this all is.

"Are you seriously telling me," I say, finding my voice, "that you just chucked my birth control into the ocean, then promised to knock me up?"

His lips curve into something that's not quite his usual smirk. It's softer somehow. Teasing. *Dangerous.* "Would you rather I left it to chance?" His voice drops lower, intimate. "Left us wondering, waiting?"

He moves closer, backing me against the counter again.

"Tell me you don't want this, too." His hand hovers near my belly, not quite touching. "Tell me you don't want it every fucking bit as bad as I do."

My hand finds his where it hovers over my stomach, and I press his palm flat against me. His fingers spread wide, possessive and protective all at once. A small sound escapes him—something so raw and honest it makes my throat tight.

His other hand slides into my hair, tilting my face up to his. "Nova..." he breathes, and I can hear everything he's not saying in those two syllables.

I watch his control crack just a little more as his gaze drops to my lips.

His fingers curl in the hem of my shirt, drawing it up with aching slowness. I shiver as his palms slide over my skin, mapping every inch as if searching for changes that couldn't possibly show yet. His touch sets off sparks everywhere he makes contact, but it's different from his usual intensity. There's reverence in the way his thumbs trace my hipbones, my ribs.

It's worship.

"Obviously," he murmurs against my neck, "I want my baby in here." His hands span my waist, thumbs meeting just below my navel. The possessiveness in his touch makes me tremble, but it's the gentleness that brings tears to my eyes.

"Samuil..." I whisper back, and something in my voice makes him lean away to study my face.

His pupils are blown wide, turning his eyes almost black as they track over my features. When his thumbs brush away tears I didn't realize had fallen, the tenderness in the gesture undoes me completely.

"Are we really doing this?"

I need to hear him say it. Need something solid to hold onto in this moment that feels like standing on the edge of a cliff. Like everything is about to change.

His forehead presses against mine. I feel his breath shudder out. "We're doing this." His voice is rough, like the words are being dragged from somewhere deep inside him. "You and me. Our child." His hand slides back to my stomach, protective and possessive. "Mine to protect. Both of you."

My fingers find the buttons of his shirt as his mouth descends toward mine.

His kiss crashes into me with an urgency I've never felt from him before. It's desperate and tender all at once, like he's trying to pour every emotion he can't voice into the connection between us. My legs wrap around his waist as he lifts me onto the counter, pulling him closer, needing to feel his heart thundering against mine.

His hands roam my body with new purpose, learning me all over again with this fresh knowledge between us. He breaks the kiss to trail his lips down my neck, then comes back up to capture my mouth again, like he can't decide which part of me he wants to taste most.

"Together," I promise, cupping his face between my palms.

He presses closer, deepening the kiss until I'm dizzy with it. One of his hands splays across my lower back while the other tangles in my hair, cradling my head as he moves against me. Every touch feels heightened, charged with new meaning.

Every kiss feels like a vow.

When he finally pulls back to look at me, I see our future written in his eyes. Whatever comes next —whatever challenges we face—we'll face them together. As a family.

His hands slide under my thighs, lifting me off the counter. "Bedroom," he growls against my lips. "Now."

He carries me like I weigh nothing. My legs tighten around his waist, my fingers digging into the hard muscles of his back. The world tilts and spins, a blur of polished wood and shimmering crystal, but my focus narrows to the man holding me.

To the heat radiating off his skin.

To the way his heart hammers against my chest.

He kicks open the bedroom door, not bothering to set me down before he crashes into me with a kiss that steals my breath. His mouth is hot and demanding, his tongue tangling with mine as he backs me against the wall. His hands are everywhere at once, pulling at my clothes, his touch leaving a trail of fire in its wake.

"Mine," he growls against my lips, his voice thick with possessiveness. "All mine. To fill. To breed."

His words are dirty, raw, and they send a shiver down my spine. I've never heard him like this—so unrestrained, so primal. It's terrifying and exhilarating all at once.

He rips open my shirt, his fingers tracing the curve of my breast before his mouth closes over my nipple. A moan escapes me, a sound I've never made before, and it seems to fuel his hunger. He sucks hard, drawing a gasp from my lips, and I arch into him, desperate for more.

"So fucking fertile," he murmurs, his breath hot against my skin. "Ready to take my seed. Ready to carry my child."

He pulls back, his eyes burning into mine as he reaches for the button of my jeans. His fingers work quickly, impatiently, and then he's pushing my jeans down my legs, his gaze fixed on the exposed skin of my hips.

"Tell me you want it, *krasavitsa*," he demands, his voice a low growl. "Tell me you want me to ruin you. To make you a mother."

His words are a challenge, a dare.

I can't resist.

"Ruin me," I whisper back, my voice trembling. "Fill me with your child."

A guttural sound escapes him, a mix of triumph and desire, and then he's spreading my thighs and devouring me until I come hard in a matter of seconds.

As I'm still lying there, quivering and moaning, he steps back and strips off his own clothes. His body is a masterpiece of muscle and sinew, sculpted by years of hockey and hard work.

I've seen him naked before, but tonight, he looks different. Wilder. Hungrier.

He climbs onto the bed, settling between my legs, his eyes

blazing with intent. He reaches for me, his touch sending a jolt of electricity through my body.

"Let's make a baby, Nova," he murmurs, his voice rough against my ear. And then he's inside me, moving with a primal urgency that makes me cry out his name.

It's a quick fucking. After all the build-up, I don't think either of us could ever have lasted more than a few seconds. But one moment, he's splitting me open with his cock, reaching places in me no one has ever reached.

Then he's coming. I am, too, and it's impossible to say where he stops and I begin. We're fused at the hip, at the source of the life between us.

I float back to awareness slowly, my body humming with aftershocks. Samuil's weight pins me to the mattress, his breath hot against my neck. Neither of us seems able to move yet, caught in this perfect moment where we're still joined, still one.

His hand slides between us to rest on my belly, and the tenderness in that touch brings fresh tears to my eyes. I've never felt so cherished, so completely claimed.

"I swear I can feel it," he murmurs against my skin. "Life. Growing inside you."

I laugh softly, threading my fingers through his sweat-dampened hair. "Already? That was fast work, even for you."

He pushes up on his elbows to look at me, and the intensity in his gaze steals my breath. There's something raw and vulnerable in his expression that makes my heart clench.

"If not now, then soon." His thumb traces my lower lip. "I won't stop until you're round with my child."

The possessiveness in his voice should frighten me. Should make me want to run. Instead, it settles something restless inside me. For the first time since this whole mess began, I feel... safe. Protected.

Wanted.

His fingers trace patterns on my skin as we lie tangled together, neither willing to break this bubble of peace we've found. The gentle rock of the yacht beneath us feels like a lullaby, and I find myself drifting, warm and sated in his arms.

I fall asleep with his hand still pressed protectively over my womb, dreaming of a future I never dared hope for. I let myself have this dream, this fantasy, for as long as it lasts.

In the morning, everything will change.

11

SAMUIL

I probably didn't need the best doctor in Sardinia to administer a simple pregnancy test.

But if there's a single fucking person on the planet who thought I *wouldn't* get said doctor, they're out of their goddamn mind.

This is Nova.

This is my child.

I'm not cutting any fucking corners.

That's why we're on this yacht in the first place. That's why, the second my eyes opened this morning, I called Myles and told him to start working on Plan B.

And C.

And D through Z, for good measure.

It's also why, right this second, I'm staring holes through Dr. Floris, ready if necessary to drill straight into his skull to get the information I want to know. The information I need.

If Nova is pregnant, I need to start making plans fucking *yesterday*. Everything has to be accounted for. Every precaution, every defense.

Not one man on this earth will hurt my family.

My phone rings for the third time in five minutes, and I move to silence it. But Nova's hand slips into mine. "The doctor said it'll be a bit before the test is ready." She pushes me gently towards the door. "Take the call."

"It's just Myles."

Probably with an important update about my twenty-five ongoing backup plans. But all of that feels distant for the time being. All I want is the answer to the question that's been burning inside of me since I found Nova in the bathroom yesterday. Since I threw her birth control overboard and fucked her like I'd never get the chance to do it again.

I need to know if she's pregnant with my baby.

And if she is, I need to turn the world upside down to keep her safe.

Her hand slips into mine and she squeezes my fingers. "I'll wait for you. Just take it."

I bring her knuckles to my lips, pressing a kiss there before I reluctantly slip into the hallway.

"What?" I bark into the phone.

"Who is this?" Myles sounds confused. "This can't be Samuil. I know that because my best friend, Sam, woke me in the middle of a damn good dream involving several bikini-clad supermodels to start making calls around Europe for him and his on-the-run mistress. And *that* Samuil would be nothing but grateful to me for all of my hard, thankless work."

"Go annoy someone else if you want a gold star. I'm busy."

"So was I when you called last night," he grumbles. "Some of us are seven hours behind. Some of us are tracking sniveling little brothers around the city instead of living it up on a bougie-ass yacht in the Mediterranean. Some of us—"

"—are wasting my time," I finish. "If you have something useful to tell me, Myles, spit it out."

"I thought beach vacations were supposed to be relaxing. You shouldn't be in such a bad mood."

I have to bite my tongue to keep the news from spilling out.

The truth is, I couldn't be in a better mood. For the last twenty-four hours, my head has been swimming with images of what my future could look like. And for the first time since I took over the Litvinov Group, it isn't spreadsheets and blood feuds filling my head.

It's images of brown-haired, silver-eyed kids clustered around a breakfast table. It's the sight of Nova carrying my children, sundresses draping over her growing belly. It's thoughts of our lives becoming inextricably linked in a way that a signature on divorce proceedings could never undo.

I wasn't kidding with her earlier. If Nova isn't pregnant already, then she will be before we step foot off of this yacht.

No matter how many tries it takes.

"Is Nova okay?" Myles prods.

"She's great."

She's perfect. She's mine.

Having children was always on my to-do list, but only in an abstract sort of way, floating somewhere between diversifying my investment portfolio and cleaning out the freezer. It was an organizational must—to secure my legacy, if nothing else—but I didn't long for it. I wasn't striving towards it with any kind of meaningful effort.

Now, the possessive beast in me roars with approval at the image of Nova growing large with my child, marked forever by her connection to me.

"No need to elaborate." Myles whistles. "I'm suddenly understanding why you're so 'busy,' so I'll make it quick."

"Finally."

"John and May Morris got back to me, and everything will be ready for your arrival. They're thrilled, actually. They didn't think you'd ever actually make good on your investment."

That makes two of us.

"Great. If that's all—"

"Yeah, yeah. Go take care of your woman," he grumbles. "I'll just keep slaving away for next to no gratitude. Don't mind me."

"I won't."

I hang up with the sound of Myles's curse in my ears and a smile on my face.

My woman. It has a nice ring to it.

My wife would be even better.

When I burst back into the suite, my attention stalls on Nova. She's lying on our bed, a blanket pulled over her lap. She looks like a different woman from the one who limped into that cabin a few short weeks ago. Her face is fuller and glowing, the bruises along her jaw are healed, and the bite marks along her arm are fading to soft, pink scars that I'll learn to love just like I love the rest of her.

The thought stops me in place, ringing through me like a frying pan to the top of the head.

I love her.

Fucking hell, I love her.

My face splits into a wide smile, and Nova matches it. She's radiant as she blinks back tears. "I'm sorry—I couldn't wait. I had to know. Did he already tell you, too?"

"Tell me what?"

"You're smiling, so I thought—" She shakes her head, still grinning. "It doesn't matter. I'm pregnant, Sam. For real."

The air leaves my lungs in one heavy exhale. "Pregnant."

She bites nervously at the corner of her mouth, her fingers twisting in the comforter. "Are you happy?"

I turn to the bushy set of eyebrows in the white lab coat. Dr. Floris is marking something on a chart and humming under his breath. "Are you sure?"

"Most definitely," he assures me in a crisp Sardinian accent. "Early, but absolutely pregnant. I've prescribed some folic acid, but that's standard. At this point, everything is healthy and stable."

There's relief, but somewhere deep down, there's something else. Some part of me that snags on his words.

At this point.

As in, at some point in the future, things could turn to shit. At some unknown time, maybe not too far off, everything could turn sideways.

Because that's what love is, isn't it? Giving someone else the opportunity to rip your world to shreds. It's breaking off a piece of your heart and offering it up to the universe or fate or whatever fucked-up force makes decisions about who lives and who dies and who gets happily-ever-afters.

It's not usually men with blood on their hands.

It's not usually men like me.

"Sam?"

Nova's voice cuts through the jarring, unpleasant turn my thoughts have taken. I give her a tight smile and then usher the doctor to the upper deck and onto the transport boat.

I watch the boat glide through the water, reaching the shore, and I wonder if maybe Nova and I should stay here on this ship forever. Maybe I should tell Oleg Pavlov to fuck off when he comes to reclaim *The Sofia*. This little bubble is mine now. It's where I'll keep Nova and our child safe—away from the world, my past.

But when I close my eyes, even the bright, clear sun and open skies can't shake the troubling images from my head.

Images of the dank kennels and damp forests where my father taught me lasting, lingering lessons.

That's my picture of childhood. *That* is what I know about what it means to be a father.

Nova being pregnant is good news. I want this.

So why the fuck can't I envision a world where this doesn't all end in disaster?

Gritting my teeth, I head back downstairs to Nova. I find her standing in front of the porthole, looking out at the ocean with her arms wrapped around her body.

She turns when the door clicks closed. "Are you okay?"

I clear my throat. "The doctor is returning to the mainland, but I'll bring him back if you need anything. Just say the word, and he'll be on this boat for good."

Her eyes are fixed on me, searching. "Are *you* okay?"

I thought so. I was.

Now? I don't know.

That wholesome image of children thronging underfoot, of sundresses and soft smiles and bedsheets fluttering in sunlit breeze… I can't find it anymore.

All I see is darkness in the back of a cage.

All I hear is barking.

Loud, angry, endless barking.

"Of course I am." Or at least, I should be. I want this. I want this so fucking much. "But I have to make some calls."

"What calls?"

"I need to get things organized in Chicago. Make preparations." The energy zipping through my veins suddenly has purpose, and I cling to it. "Now that it's certain we have a baby on the way, I need to make sure I can keep you both safe no matter where we're at."

Nova's mouth slants down in a frown. "And you have to do that right now?"

"I should've had it done already."

"It's not like we knew this was going to happen," she says cautiously.

"But I should've had a plan," I grit out. "We knew it was a possibility. I need to be ready."

"I don't think anyone is ever ready to be a parent." She lets out a soft laugh like this is funny.

"Other people don't have enemies like I do, Nova. I can't afford to take any of this lightly."

She gestures to the wood-paneled walls surrounding us. "We're floating around on forty million dollars of security. I know you aren't taking this lightly. But we have time to celebrate. This is good news, Sam. I'm happy. Aren't you happy?"

I want to reach out and hold her so much, but the longer I look at her, the more I feel that missing piece of my heart. I feel how weak I am—how vulnerable.

"We can't stay on this yacht forever."

I start to turn away from her, but she catches my arm. Her hand slides to my face. "I know this is overwhelming. I know it's scary—"

"I'm not scared."

"Well, I am," she insists, her voice shaky. "Things feel so much realer now. There's no going back. We're going to be parents, Sam. A family. And it's not like either of us have a working blueprint of what a happy, healthy family looks like."

"This is a great pep talk," I drawl sarcastically. "I feel much better."

She drops her hand, brows knit together. "I'm trying to have a serious conversation with you."

"By pointing out that neither of us knows what the fuck we're doing?" She opens her mouth to say something, but I pull away from her. "You must be tired. Go lie down."

"Sam!" she cries, but I don't stop.

Because if I stop, I might just say more shit I'll regret later.

Shit like, *Why the fuck did I think I could do this?*

Why the fuck did I think I could be someone's father?

Why the fuck did I think my past was finished with me?

~

Nova doesn't follow me above deck, and she stays out of sight for most of the evening.

Fucking fantastic. Not only have I psyched myself out of what should be the happy delirium of impending fatherhood, I've also scared away the mother of my child.

Because I can't just accept something good.

I can't just be fucking happy without calculating the thousands of ways it could all be snatched away from me.

I prop my elbows on my knees and drag my hands through my hair. I don't know the first thing about what it takes to be a father. Short of wrapping my child in a plastic bubble and locking them in a steel bunker, I have no idea what it takes.

What the fuck was I thinking?

"Can I join you?"

I glance over my shoulder to find Nova standing behind me. She's barefoot, dressed in a sheer blue cover-up that doesn't cover up much of anything.

"Knock yourself out."

She slides onto the lounge chair beside mine and rakes her hair over one shoulder. "Have you finished making all your arrangements? Is the penthouse decked out with a shark-infested moat and a death ray?"

"Not yet, but I'll add those to the list."

She smiles, but there's an edge to her smile, a sadness in the tilt of her eyes. "Can we talk now?"

I sigh. "You talk; I'll listen."

She fidgets for a moment, like maybe she regrets coming out here to start this conversation. I wonder if she'll turn back. But then she draws in a big breath, straightens her posture, and blurts out, "I'm scared, too."

She lets those words hang in the salty air between us for a long few seconds. "I'm so happy about this baby, Sam—but I'm terrified, too. I mean, my mother left me. Will I wake up one day and regret this? Will I change my mind and abandon my child the way my mother abandoned me?"

"No." I know I'm supposed to be listening, but I can't bite my tongue. "No, you won't. I know you, Nova Pierce. You're protective and loyal. You're devoted to a bunch of flea-bitten dogs you barely know. Our child is going to have your entire heart and soul."

"And I know *you*, Samuil Litvinov." She reaches across the

gap between our chairs to touch my wrist. "You're not your father. You would never do to a child what he did to you."

Her hand grazes up and down my arm, giving me comfort I don't deserve.

Like she can still sense the wall between us, Nova crashes through it. She stands up and settles herself on my lap, her legs wrapped around me, her hands hooked behind my neck. "We can't allow our pasts to get in the way of our future, Sam. This is our chance to do better—to *be* better—than our parents were."

Her words settle deep in my chest, taking root there.

We have a chance to learn from our traumas. We have a chance to turn our pasts into something beautiful for the children and family we're going to build together.

And just like that, I can see the picture again: Nova and I, surrounded by our children and a mess of dogs.

Happy.

Whole.

Together.

She laughs, shifting her hips against the erection growing between us. "Looks like you're feeling better."

I pull the transparent fabric over her shoulder to admire the scraps of the bikini she's wearing beneath it. "It's hard not to feel better when you're wearing this."

"It's my last chance before I'm too big to pull off the outfit."

I shake my head. "You'll always be able to pull this off, Nova. Watching you grow my child is only going to make me want you even more."

I slide my hands down her back and squeeze her waist. Her body rocks against me, and we both groan.

Surely nothing that feels this good could be wrong.

I've made mistakes before. I married the wrong person, trusted the wrong people.

But Nova is the *right* woman.

A woman I know will go to any lengths to protect our children and love our family. And if she believes I can do this, then damn me to hell if I don't do my best to prove her right.

12

NOVA

After weeks on the ocean, with nothing but the gentle wash of the waves against the sides of the yacht and the hum of the engine, I'm used to quiet. Serenity.

Helicopter blades don't fall into that category.

The roar of the chopper wrenches me out of bed. I'm on my feet before I know what's happening, a hand flying to my belly. That reaction already feels natural. Ever since the test, I touch it again and again, all day and all night, like this baby might disappear if I don't check on them often enough.

Samuil's side of the bed is empty. Cold. The sheets still hold the ghost of his warmth, but he's been gone long enough for anxiety to spider through my veins.

The noise grows louder. Metal against metal. Men's voices. Heavy boots on deck.

I force myself to breathe. To think. But memories of Ilya flood back—the warehouse, the blindfold cutting into my skin, his voice promising my death. The nausea isn't just morning sickness anymore.

"Eat your crackers first," I mutter in a poor imitation of Samuil's command voice. But my hands shake too hard to reach for the ginger cookies he insists will settle my stomach.

Instead, I press my forehead against the cold porthole glass, watching black helicopter blades cut through the purple dawn sky.

The door opens behind me. I whirl, smacking my head against the metal frame hard enough to see stars.

"I'm so sorry!" Louisa struggles to keep her tray of tea and cookies steady. "I thought you'd still be asleep."

I can barely hear her over the sound of the helicopter. "Who is here? What's going on?"

She sets the tray beside the bed with practiced care. "Men are coming aboard. Mr. Litvinov is greeting them above deck. He said he'd check on you soon."

Nothing about that sentence puts me at ease. Not one single word of it. Theoretically, it should—if Ilya or the Andropovs were here, Samuil wouldn't be "greeting" anyone. He'd be putting bullets in skulls.

But my throat closes anyway. The walls of our suite—previously a sanctuary of silk and sunlight—press in. Even the gentle rock of waves feels threatening now.

I sink onto the bed's edge, mechanically lifting a cookie to my mouth. If death is coming, at least I'll face it with something in my stomach. The thought forces a hysterical giggle from my throat.

The sight and sound of the chopper has awakened something in me. A fear that I didn't even realize I've suppressed. It's similar to the feeling I had in the woods just before I fell down that ravine.

It's the helplessness of being hunted.

Except this time, the stakes are so much higher.

The door crashes open. Samuil fills the frame, all six-foot-four of lethal grace wrapped in a tailored suit. His jaw is granite, eyes winter-sharp. This isn't my Samuil—the man who kisses my belly each morning and fights me about eating before standing.

This is the *pakhan*, the man who makes other men tremble.

"What's going on?" I whisper.

He eyes the plate in my hand. "Good. You're eating."

"Samuil," I breathe, "what's happening?"

"It's nothing."

Maybe to him. But to me, a helicopter just landed on the superyacht we've been living on. That feels distinctly like *something*.

"'Nothing'?" I throw the cookie across the room. It shatters against the wall, sending crumbs raining onto the plush carpet. "A helicopter just landed on our yacht. That's not *nothing*, Sam."

A muscle jumps in his jaw. "A couple of my men came aboard to escort us to the next port."

"What's wrong with this port?"

"Nothing." But the way he passes his hand over his nape is the equivalent of him screaming like Chicken Little. "It's just time for a change in scenery."

I have no right to be disappointed. Samuil told me this was someone else's yacht. I knew it was temporary. But watching him dismiss me—treat me like some docile pet to be moved at his convenience, the way he *used* to treat me, the way we agreed he never would again… It ignites something primal in my chest.

"Where are we going?" I stand, refusing to let him tower over me.

"You'll find out when we get there." He turns to leave like that's the end of it.

I scramble after him, pregnancy-clumsy but determined. "Are you serious? You're not going to tell me?"

"The men here to escort us don't even know where we're going, Nova."

"The men here to escort us aren't your—" A title for exactly what I am to him slips between my fingers, so I fumble for something else. "—aren't having your baby. I think I should have a higher clearance."

His eyes drop to my stomach, that familiar possessive heat flooding his gaze. For a moment, I think he'll crack. Tell me something. Anything. But as he turns and strides out of the door, he leaves behind only a single word.

"Later."

"Later" turns into hours. Hours of pacing outside of his office like a circus tiger while he conducts his "meeting." Hours of being dismissed by stone-faced Bratva men with guns when I try to get answers.

I'm left to keep pacing and weighing the pros and cons of saying *fuck it* and barging through the door.

Pro: My righteous indignation would love nothing more than a grand entrance.

Con: The guns in that room likely outnumber humans three to one. If I value my own life and my child's, I probably shouldn't surprise anyone armed.

When I finally cave to the insult that is knocking, I raise my fist—only for the door to open and a surly-faced Russian man in a gray suit to block my path.

"Apologies, ma'am," he says, straddling the line between cold and polite. "We're in the middle of an important meeting."

"But Samuil—"

"Mr. Litvinov told me to inform you that we'll be another hour at least."

Then he shuts the door in my face. Not even a proper slam—just a quiet, dismissive click.

I stomp back to our suite, already drafting the long, angry rant I plan to deliver the moment Sam comes to find me.

He said he missed my fighting spirit. Well, I'm about to let him have it. I'll tell him exactly what I think about being treated like property. About being kept in the dark while carrying his child. About how if he wants this relationship to work, he needs to see me as a partner, not a possession. About how we fucking *talked* about this, all of it, ad fucking nauseam, and yet the second that pregnancy test showed up with two pink lines, it all went out the damn porthole window along with my birth control.

But all that will have to come later. In the meantime, I can only go down to the suite and wait for him on our bed.

And wait.

And wait.

The next thing I know, I'm blinking my eyes open to a dark room and the groggy realization that everything is gone.

My luggage, the clothes I had piled on the chair, Samuil's shoes—gone, gone, gone. All of it.

I sit up, the world spinning for a second before I can focus on the broad shape of Samuil standing at the end of the bed, zipping a suitcase.

He glances up at me. "There's a snack by the bed. You should eat."

Sure enough, a plate of ginger cookies sits on my nightstand—the one piece of furniture he hasn't cleared. The gesture should be sweet. Instead, it feels patronizing.

"We're leaving now?" I had a whole speech planned. There were accompanying hand gestures and thoughtful pauses and several brutal, sizzling turns of phrase.

Samuil nods. "I'm glad you woke up on your own. I didn't want to interrupt your sleep."

I snort. "As if that would've stopped you."

Apparently, he doesn't have time for snark, because he heaves the suitcase off the end of the bed and wheels it towards the doors. "I've left some comfortable travel clothes out for you. We leave in ten."

By the time I glance to my sweats and my favorite sweatshirt covered in embroidered dog paws, Sam is gone.

Grudgingly, I throw on the clothes—annoyed that he knows me well enough to pack an unlined sports bra and fuzzy socks—and then haul my ass upstairs, where the transport boat is already being loaded and readied to launch.

Samuil tosses a duffel bag down into the craft as I stop behind him.

"You gonna fling me down there, too?" I hold my arms out as if I'm ready. "I'm luggage, after all. Something you pack up and move around as you seem fit."

He turns to me, mouth quirked in an amused smile.

That throws me for a loop, which I don't appreciate. He's supposed to match my anger. He's supposed to snap back, if only so I can justify slapping him.

"You think this is funny?" I demand.

"Well—" He lays a hand over my belly. "—you are carrying precious cargo. The suitcase analogy isn't so far off."

My eyes go wide. "If you think I'm just some vessel for you and—"

He grabs my hand and presses a kiss to my knuckles. "I think I might need to handcuff you to my wrist like a briefcase full of cash, like the highly valuable package you are."

"I dare you to handcuff me," I snarl. "I fucking dare you."

His eyes dance with amusement and moonlight. "Don't tempt me, *krasavitsa*."

I put my fists on my hips. "I am this close to pushing you overboard."

He turns his face up to the sky and laughs. "You have no idea how good it is to see your fight come back."

Things can't be so dire if he's in this good of a mood, right?

"Where are we going?" I ask for the billionth time.

He doesn't answer. Just gives the men below some unspoken command before he turns back to me. "Say goodbye to *The Sofia*. It's time to leave."

"Translation: sit down, shut up, and don't ask any questions."

I take one look back at the yacht. I really will miss it. For a few weeks, at least, it felt something like home.

He shakes his head and sidles closer to me. I fight him for only a second before his arms wrap around my shoulders. He brushes a kiss against the top of my head. "Translation: take a deep breath and trust me. I'm trying to keep you and our baby safe."

As the transport boat carries us away from the yacht, I feel every dip and ripple on the water. I pull my knees to my chest and think about Grams and Hope. I think about Rufus and Ruby.

Most of all, I wonder if and when I'll ever be able to stop running.

13

SAMUIL

We've been driving on the same bumpy, one-lane road for half an hour with nothing more than Highland cows and Nova's simmering rage to keep us company.

She hasn't spoken directly to me since we left the yacht. Smart girl—talking would mean acknowledging that I exist, and right now, she's determined to prove I don't.

Even when Myles swerves into the passing lane without warning, sending her tumbling toward my lap, she rights herself without a glance in my direction.

A camper van blasts past us, nearly taking off our side mirror.

"Fucking tourists," I mutter.

"We're tourists, too." Nova's voice drips with disdain. "Wherever the hell we are, I know it's not Chicago."

Again, Myles catches my eyes in the rearview mirror.

Again, I ignore him.

I planned to tell Nova where we were headed once we were on the plane, but she spent the entire flight either throwing up in the toilet or trying to steal a burner phone from Vlad. He caught her elbow-deep in his suitcase and discreetly sent her back to her seat, but I got a text less than a minute later informing me of the "incident."

Nothing happens with her that I don't know about.

Except, of course, in that stubborn head of hers.

Who was she going to call? I told her to trust me. I told her I was taking care of her. That should've been enough.

Clearly, it wasn't, and mistrust breeds mistrust, or some shit like that, which is why I chose to keep her in the dark about our final destination. That and she really fucking pissed me off.

Myles is enjoying the tension a little too much. I continue to ignore him even as he starts to whistle "All Star" by Smash Mouth for the third time in as many minutes. Let him enjoy the tension. I'm too busy wondering how Nova will react when she sees where we're headed.

I may have bought the castle during a low point, with visions of living happily off the grid and as far as humanly possible from Katerina, but those dreams are nothing but ash now. They crumbled to dust on the yacht and burnt to a crisp on the plane.

I need to be connected to the world because, whether Nova wants to acknowledge it or not, the world is coming for me. I need to be prepared.

That's tough to do in the middle of fucking nowhere.

"Enough with the goddamn whistling!" I bark.

Nova flinches and curls closer to the door. "I don't mind the whistling, Myles. It's better to hear something than nothing at all."

The dig lands exactly where she intended. I flex my fingers against the leather seat between us, fighting the urge to drag her into my space. I wanted to see her fire return—just not while we're trapped in a car with my head of security playing shepherd.

I grit my teeth. "Maybe you would've heard something if you hadn't decided to pull that little stunt on the—"

"Are we almost there?" She leans forward, making it clear she's speaking to Myles and not to me.

I haven't seen her this alive in days. It's beautiful. It's infuriating. It's exactly what I need and exactly what I can't handle right now.

"It's just up ahead. The next right." Myles shrugs at me in the rearview mirror, and it doesn't matter, anyway. I kept her in the dark as long as possible. We're one turn away from me explaining why we're gonna have to spend the next God-only-knows-how-many months in a decrepit Scottish castle. In terms of being away from Chicago, this is about as far as we could ever get.

She thinks she's mad now.

Wait 'til she sees our destination.

The dense canopy of Scots pines breaks just as Myles takes the final turn, revealing Castle Moorbeath in all its imposing glory. Something flickers across Nova's face—surprise, wonder, maybe a hint of the same madness that possessed me to buy this monstrosity in the first place.

She gasps, and for the first time today, she forgets to pretend I don't exist. "We're staying in a castle? This isn't 'laying low.' There are turrets!"

"The turrets were his favorite selling point," Myles chimes in, clearly enjoying himself. "He was going to live up there and snipe anyone who came too close."

"Shut up, Myles," I grumble.

My best friend is getting too close to revealing exactly how bleak things were when I bought this place. And being here after years of letting it sit empty is a sign that things are beginning to take a bleak turn again. I'd rather Nova not know all the hairy details.

Luckily, she's caught on to another detail.

"You own a castle? Like, the whole thing?"

"They don't sell them in halves," I mutter.

"That's exactly why he bought it," Myles says cheerfully. "Because he could have the whole thing to himself. He was tired of dealing in halves after settling with Katerina."

I punch my fist into the back of Myles's seat. "Watch the road. It's narrowing up ahead."

I turn back to Nova, ready to face whatever wrath is coming my way for bringing her to three hundred acres of wet, overcast solitude. But she's gaping wide-eyed and slack-jawed through the window. She fumbles with the switch for a second before rolling her window down so she can take a deep breath.

As much as I want to believe my eyes are deceiving me, I think she actually might be smiling.

Myles pulls the car through an ancient stone gate crawling with moss and stops in front of the castle. No sooner than the engine is off, two fluffy shapes bound around the far side of the castle, bounding towards the car.

Nova squeals and flies out of the car to meet them.

I watch through the open door as she drops to her knees and greets two floppy-eared border collies. They look like they're fresh from a dog food commercial.

"Look at the two of you!" she coos, accepting their face licks and cuddles with more excitement than she's shown for anything in days.

Myles loops his arm over the passenger seat and turns to look back at me.

"Don't fucking say a word," I growl.

He snorts. "I wasn't going to."

He doesn't need to. The truth is written all over Nova's radiant face as she scratches behind the dogs' ears and asks their names.

Nova loves it here.

~

Two weeks pass with relative ease. It's a quiet existence. With Myles back in Chicago to shore up our operations there, I begin work before the sun is up and I don't stop until long after it's set beyond the pines.

Nova stays quiet, too, which would be troubling if I didn't have the luxury of crawling into bed next to her each night.

That's the only thing holding us together—the fact that, when we're skin on skin, everything else seems to fade away.

Now, it's the middle of the night, and Nova is asleep on my chest. The peaceful in-and-out of her breathing is the only reason I haven't snuck out of bed and gone back to work. There's so much to do, but I've convinced myself it can wait.

Until I see my phone flashing on the bedside table.

With a sigh, I shift her body off of mine and slide to the edge of the bed to answer.

It's Myles.

It's early in Chicago, and I try to think of a single good reason why he'd be awake and calling me before dawn, but I come up empty.

I'm tense before I even accept the call. "Myles?"

"Are you alone?"

I get up, pad into the bathroom, and pull the door closed. "What is it?"

"Have you heard?" he asks.

No, and I don't want to. I want to go back to bed with Nova. I want to kiss her awake and bury myself in her. I want to forget for five goddamn seconds that hell is constantly raining down on our heads.

"What is it?" I growl.

"It's— Is Nova nearby? I don't want her to overhear." He sighs. "It's bad, Sam. It's really bad."

14

NOVA

Two weeks.

Two weeks of radio silence from Chicago. Two weeks of nothing but cryptic texts from Myles showing Rufus and Ruby playing in Sam's penthouse garden. Two weeks of Sam's increasingly creative attempts to "distract" me from asking questions about home.

I trace my fingers over the old stone walls of the castle kitchen, watching Mrs. Morris stir something that smells divine. The kitchen is my favorite room here—all worn flagstones and copper pots hanging from iron hooks, steam rising from bubbling pots into wooden rafters that have absorbed centuries of secrets. It feels real in a way the rest of my gilded cage doesn't.

"More salt?" Mrs. Morris asks, offering me a spoon.

I shake my head. "I think the boys will love it exactly as it is."

And they'd better. I've spent all afternoon here, mostly staying out of Mrs. Morris's way while she works her magic.

But when Myles arrives from Chicago for dinner, I want him to think I slaved over this meal myself. Want him to feel indebted enough to finally tell me what the hell is happening back home.

The dull roar of an approaching helicopter makes the windows rattle. Right on schedule.

I dry my hands and head for the hallway that leads to Sam's office. My bare feet are silent on the stone floor—a skill I've perfected living in this museum of a house. It's pathetic that I have to resort to eavesdropping, but Sam's left me no choice. If he won't tell me what's happening with my family, with Hope, with the life I left behind, I'll find out myself.

The heavy oak door to his office is closed. I can hear the low rumble of male voices inside—Sam and Myles, already deep in conversation. I press closer, holding my breath.

"Have you told her yet?" Myles's voice is clearer now.

"Not yet." The resignation in those two little words has me catching my breath. I barely stop myself from knocking in time.

"Jesus, Sam."

"I've been trying to—" Sam sighs. "I've been waiting for the right time."

"I don't think there is a right time to tell someone their entire family is dead."

My ears fill with a high-pitched whine that drowns out everything else. The castle stones pulse around me, the portraits on the walls blurring into smears of oil paint and judgment as my world contracts to this single, horrible moment.

I see Grams sprawled on her kitchen floor, blood pooling under her silver hair.

Hope, her bright smile frozen forever, throat torn open.

Rufus and Ruby, their precious little bodies riddled with bullets.

My knees quake, and I want nothing more than to sink into the floor. No—beyond the floor. I want to melt into nothing.

They're dead. They're all dead.

That's what Myles said.

And Samuil knew. He fucking *knew.*

Has it been days? Weeks? How long did he keep this secret from me? I want to collapse, but if I do, I'll never get back up again.

And I need answers.

With trembling hands, I shove Sam's office door open. The hinges shriek in protest, making both men whip around to face me. Their expressions are identical masks of concern, which only makes the rage burn hotter in my chest.

Sam rises from behind his massive desk. "Nova—"

"Is it true?" I choke out. "They're all… Everyone is…?"

Samuil's face is drawn tight as he rises and takes a step towards me. "*Krasav—*"

"Don't!" I throw out a hand, my vision too blurred with tears to know if he listens or not. "Just tell me the truth. Are they g-gone?"

Yesterday—just yesterday—I asked Sam if Grams was okay. The day before, I begged him to have Myles check on Hope.

He looked me in the eyes and lied.

Again and again and again, he lied.

"Nova, sit down." Myles stands and tries to usher me into his chair. "We can explain—"

"That you're liars?" I hiss. "Goddamn both of you! You told me Grams and Hope were safe, but—"

"They are." Sam moves like lightning, gripping my shoulders and pulling me against his chest. His heart thunders under my ear. "God, Nova. I didn't think— They're okay. Grams and Hope are safe."

My world is on a bungee cord. I was plummeting to the ground, and now, suddenly, Sam sends me soaring in the other direction.

"Wh...what?" I rasp. I stare at him, trying to suss out a lie in the beautiful words I want to curl up inside of.

They're okay. They aren't dead. They're all okay.

"They are safe." He kisses the top of my head. "I made sure of that."

Myles nods. "I checked on them both right before I flew out. Hope is great—a handful, but safe. And Serena is as scrumptious as ever." He offers me a wink, but it's a thin cover for the anxiety creasing his face.

"Okay, but— You said—" I pull away from Samuil and shake my head. "You said my family was dead."

Samuil's hands fist at his sides like he wants to reach for me, but I feel fragile right now. The next words out of his mouth will change everything, and I want to see his face as he says them.

"There was a shootout," Sam explains haltingly. "The official story is some kind of blow-up between rival gangs. Civilians died... but so did the officers who tried to break up the fight."

I feel cold.

Before, thinking about Grams and Hope, there was white-hot panic.

Now, I'm ice.

"Your brothers," Myles picks up. "They were killed on the scene."

I try to picture Tommy and Mike's faces, but they're blurred around the edges, like old photographs left too long in the sun. When was the last time I even spoke to them? Called them? The silence stretches back years.

My throat closes up. "My father...?"

Sam finally reaches for my hand, and I let him. "He didn't make it."

"But... how?"

It's not possible. My father was always the one wielding the gun. He can't have been taken out like this.

"They're reporting he was shot in the line of duty, but it's a cover-up," Sam grits out. "The Chicago PD doesn't want to reveal how many of their officers were on the take from the Andropovs."

"So, they were... executed?" A tear slips down my cheek, and Sam presses a strong hand to my back, holding me up.

"As far as we can tell, yes."

I shake my head, tears blurring my vision. *Why in the hell am I crying for them?* "But they were working for the Andropovs? Why would they—"

The reality slams into me and Sam's hand on my lower back is the only thing that keeps me from toppling over.

"Me," I whisper. "It was my fault."

The server I delivered was a dud. My father took the Andropovs' lone shot to get inside Samuil's penthouse, and he wasted it on a useless server and a mole who skipped town immediately afterward.

He pinned all his hope on me.

And they killed him for it.

Sam is already pulling me back into his chest, his strong arms squeezing me tight. He smells like oak and frost, and I breathe him in deeply to keep my lungs from clenching tight.

"This isn't your fault, Nova. Your father and brothers knew the kind of people they were getting involved with."

People like the Andropovs and Ilya… and Samuil.

I squeeze my eyes closed.

No, Samuil isn't like them. But maybe my father and brothers would be alive if I wasn't with Samuil. If I'd kept my head down and continued walking dogs, maybe none of this never would've happened.

What makes me feel even worse is that I wouldn't change a thing. I should be devastated. I should be screaming, raging, drowning in grief for my family. Instead, all I feel is sick relief washing through me. They can't hurt me anymore.

They can't threaten Grams or try to control my life or drag me back into their web of corruption.

They're gone, and I'm free.

Maybe I'm as much of a monster as they were.

"I need some air," I croak, pushing away from Sam.

"Nova—"

"A minute," I beg, turning for the door, hoping he can't see the awful person I am all over my face. "I just need a minute."

I make it as far as the front lawn before my legs give out. The grass is damp with evening dew as I sink to my knees, running my trembling fingers through the thick green blades.

My father is dead.

My brothers are dead.

They're all gone.

I repeat it to myself again and again, but it doesn't feel real.

Is this shock? Is that why I'm not horrified or grieving for the men who shaped half my life? Is that why my mind keeps circling back to one terrifying thought:

If the Andropovs executed my father and brothers for failing them... what would they do to me?

My hands curl protectively around my stomach. There it is—real fear finally cracking through the numbness, sending violent shivers up my spine. The evening air feels arctic against my clammy skin.

I picture the people I actually love: Hope's bright laugh, Grams's gentle hands, Myles's steady loyalty, Samuil's fierce devotion. I press my palms more firmly against my belly, where our child grows beneath my heart. Tears blur my vision of the sprawling Scottish grounds, turning the castle into a dark smear against the purple twilight sky.

The Andropovs didn't just kill my father and brothers—they made examples of them. Left their bodies in the street like warnings. My father, who terrorized our neighborhood for decades, died cowering in the gutter.

What horrors would they dream up for the woman who betrayed them? For Samuil Litvinov's pregnant lover?

The grass beneath my fingers suddenly feels like a funeral shroud. I could run. Take the Range Rover and disappear into the Highlands. Keep my child safe from all of this.

But even as the thought forms, I know it's pointless. There's no running from this life anymore. No hiding from who and what Samuil is. No protecting our baby from the legacy of violence it will inherit.

The only way out is through—and the only way through is with Samuil beside me.

I push myself to my feet, one hand still pressed to my stomach. The castle looms before me. Ancient. Dark. Unmoving.

Either this place will be my prison, or it will be my fortress.

It's time to decide which.

15

SAMUIL

I find her by the loch hours later.

She's a silhouette cut against the dark horizon, a shape that would make better men than me fall to their knees and pray. But I stopped believing in divine intervention the day my mother took twenty grand and walked away from her son forever.

Her face is turned up to the sky. Moonlight paints her cheeks silver. But when she turns her eyes on me, they're hard and cold.

I hoped leaving her alone would help her process the news about her family, but Nova has never been one to waste time on grief when anger is an option.

"It's cold. You should come inside."

She tugs her sweater more tightly around her shoulders. "I'm fine right here."

"Nova—"

"Why can't I speak to Hope or Grams?" she demands. "They're not involved in any of this."

I slide my hands into my pockets to keep from reaching for her. "And we want to keep it that way. I have men watching them around the clock. If there's a target on their backs, we'll know about it." The wind bites through my jacket, reminding me that Scottish autumn nights are brutal. "But I've underestimated the Andropovs before. I won't make that mistake again. If they're monitoring Hope or your grandmother, we can't risk giving them more reasons to act."

I don't mention how Ilya or Katerina would love nothing more than to gut Hope or Serena just to watch Nova break. Just to watch me shatter as I hold the pieces of her.

This woman isn't just my weakness. She's a collar around my throat, a target on my chest, and the only thing that makes my black heart beat. My enemies know it.

And now she's paying for it.

"My grandmother lost her son and two grandsons in one day." Her voice breaks. "She's going to be terrified of losing her only granddaughter, too."

"I've sent word as securely as I can to both Hope and Serena. They know you're safe."

The look she gives me could freeze hell twice over. "I suppose you want me to thank you?"

What I want is for her to let me hold her while she falls apart. What I want is to piece her back together with my hands, my mouth, my soul—what's left of it.

But she's planted her feet in the rocky Scottish earth like

she's ready for war, so I stay where I am and meet that frozen gaze head-on.

"You don't need to thank me, but you have to understand. If we're going to make it, Nova... If this thing is going to—" I blow out a harsh breath as I drag a hand through my hair. "I'm not keeping you from them to be cruel. I have to tread carefully. We have to lie low, and—"

"You're still talking to your father, aren't you?"

It's an accusation. For me, it's an unfortunate reality.

"I have to speak with him."

"And you can do that safely, but I can't speak to my family?"

I want to shake her and hold her and toss her in the loch and kiss her. I settle for shoving my hands deep in my pockets. "This is a chess match, *krasavitsa*. There's one board and many players. I have to lay my traps carefully. In order to do that, I have to be patient. *We* have to be patient."

"How many people are going to die while I'm busy being 'patient'?" She stands up, her hair rippling in the wind like the water across the loch.

"I get why you're angry," I say softly. "It's hard not getting the closure you crave from the people who've hurt you the most."

She whirls on me, lips parted for battle. But several heartbeats pass before she finds her voice. "I don't need closure from any of them."

Bullshit.

"I mean it," she doubles down, like she can sense my doubt. "I was never going to get closure from my father or my brothers. They were all assholes and they weren't ever gonna change. The only thing they ever gave me was permission not to mourn their deaths."

"And yet here you are, raging at me because of it."

"I'm not raging at you because they're dead!" The words echo across the water. "I'm raging at you because I can't go home or call my grandmother to ask how she's doing! I'm angry because I'm helpless out here and there's not a damn thing I can do about it. I'm frustrated because this is my life and you're treating it like it's a game."

"Nova—"

"Don't you get it?" she interrupts. "This is not what I signed up for—chess and players and midnight shootouts. Who's the king and who's the pawn? Who comes out on top and who ends up the loser? You think I don't know what that means? It means that sooner or later, every player in your stupid game will end up dead, Samuil! And all the time and money in the world won't mean shit!"

If her words were blades, I'd be bleeding from a thousand different cuts.

"You wanted to know the plan, Nova. That's why I told you. I thought you could handle it."

"I *can* handle it," she snaps defensively. "That doesn't mean I have to like it."

Before I can respond, she strips off her sweater, casts it at her feet, and strides straight into the loch like she's got a death wish. The water reaches her waist, her thin shirt going translucent in the moonlight, and still she doesn't stop.

It's too fucking cold—the kind of cold that can kill. Every instinct screams at me to drag her back to shore, but I know my Nova. The more I try to save her, the deeper she'll go just to prove she doesn't need saving.

Which is why I bite my tongue and follow her to the edge of the loch.

After a few silent seconds of standing with the dark, frigid water lapping at her hips, she picks up a rock and flings it across the surface.

She tries to make it skip, but it just sinks to the bottom with a sad little *plink.* I grab a stone myself and flick it casually across the lake's surface. It skips half a dozen times before it's swallowed up.

With a little growl, Nova picks up another stone and tries again.

Another sad little thump.

Another sinking stone.

I skip another. This one goes nearly twice as far as the first.

She glares at me. "You suck, you know that?"

A laugh escapes before I can stop it. I wade in after her, biting back a curse as the freezing water climbs up my legs. My balls try to crawl back inside my body, but Nova's standing there vibrating with enough rage to keep herself warm.

"Want me to show you how it's done?"

"No," she says. "I'm not interested in more games."

Sighing, I step a little closer and place my hand on her stomach. She freezes, her eyes darting to mine.

"Yes, I play games—but only because I have to. That doesn't mean I take them lightly. Just because I strategize doesn't mean I don't understand the stakes."

She takes a deep breath that I feel against my palm, then looks across the loch to a derelict rowboat that's been rotting in the weeds since before I bought this place.

She nods toward it. "Mr. Morris said that boat's been floating there for a decade. No one's paid it the slightest bit of attention."

"I'll buy a new one, if you want."

"I don't want a new one. I want *that* one." Her jaw sets. "I want to fix it up. Especially if..." She swallows. "If we'll be here for a while."

I nod, wishing I could give her a timeline. Wishing, more than anything, that I could give her absolutely everything she wants.

But all I can do for now is keep her here and keep her safe.

A shiver wracks her body. "I suppose I might as well find a project, then."

It doesn't sound like we're talking about the boat anymore.

"You can try," I tell her. "I know it's in your nature to want to heal what's broken. But not everything can be fixed."

Her eyes meet mine for half a heartbeat before skittering away. "I have to try."

The need to protect her wars with pride in her stubborn strength. I understand why she has to do this—why she needs to believe she can salvage something from this mess I've dragged her into.

But I'm as worried about her succeeding as I am about her failing.

Because the truth is, I am who I am. Son of a monster, brother to a snake, heir to an empire built on blood and bone.

And as fierce and determined as Nova is, trying to fix me might be the thing that finally breaks her.

The moon watches from above as we stand in the freezing loch, her body trembling against my palm, both of us knowing this isn't just about a broken boat anymore.

Some things are meant to stay fractured. Some men are meant to stay damned.

And sometimes, love isn't enough to save us.

16

NOVA

The rain falls like God decided Scotland needed a new loch.

For days, I've watched it through the window. Droplets captured against the glass scurry down like prisoners trying to break free. Can't get in, can't get away, can't go anywhere but down.

Very fucking relatable.

My thoughts are doing the same. It's not grief I'm feeling, not truly. Or at least, not solely. Maybe there's something called grief tangled up in the knot of emotions taking up residence inside my chest. I lost my family, after all. The man who birthed me. The brothers who were supposed to love me.

But there's more than that, too. There's anger, and confusion, and despair, and fuck knows what else. I'd need more dictionaries than this castle's library can handle to puzzle it all out.

I press my head to the windowpane. Outside, another day bleeds into the constant gray. Endless sheets of water steal away the last of the evening's light. The world goes from watercolor green, to slate, to darkness.

It's been seven days of this. Seven days of meandering down endless halls, of pretending I don't hear the hushed Russian phone calls behind closed doors, of ignoring the armed men who patrol our grounds with dead eyes and deadly purpose. Seven days of touching my growing belly and wondering if our child will inherit their father's talent for keeping secrets. Seven days of hoping our baby never learns how family can wound you deepest, the way my father taught me. Sometimes, I catch myself rubbing the scar on my hand and wonder if my father ever loved me at all, or if I was just another thing to control.

During daylight hours, Samuil might as well be a ghost. The only proof he still exists comes from the occasional glimpse of his broad shoulders disappearing around corners, the lingering scent of his cologne in empty rooms, the way his security detail subtly shifts formation when he moves through the castle.

At night, he finds me.

That's when he materializes like smoke, his heat wrapping around me, his breath carrying promises in Russian against my skin. Every evening, I swear I'll resist, demand answers, force him to see me as more than a delicate thing to be protected.

And every evening, I fail.

Sex is our only common language now, the sole bridge between his world of violence and my world of waiting. I'm terrified that if we lose this connection, this raw physical need that draws him to my bed no matter how many bodies he had to step over that day, we'll drift so far apart we'll never find our way back to each other.

"Don't fret, m'dear," Mrs. Morris says, her Scottish lilt cutting through my brooding. "The rain will clear eventually. It always does."

I turn from the window, forcing a smile. "You said that seven days ago. I stopped believing you five days ago."

She sets an armful of fresh linens on the bed—crisp, white sheets that probably hide bloodstains better than darker colors. Everything in this castle serves dual purposes. Everyone except me.

"These are the Highlands, lass. The weather can be as wild as the lochs themselves."

I trace a raindrop's path down the glass with my fingertip. Wild would be better than this suffocating sameness. At least wild would mean feeling something real.

"Mrs. Morris," I say, sitting up straighter as an idea claws its way through my melancholy. "The rest of the castle, the unopened wings. Are they condemned?"

She wrinkles her nose, weathered hands smoothing already-perfect linens. "Nothing's condemned exactly, but—" She hesitates. "Those sections haven't been touched in centuries. The fireplaces are dead, the rooms are full of God knows what."

Her warning ignites something in me that's been dormant since Samuil dragged me to this fortress. A spark of defiance, of purpose. Of power.

"Nothing a little cleaning couldn't fix," I say, already mapping out possibilities in my mind. If Samuil wants to keep me locked away in his castle, I might as well claim some territory of my own. "I could help. I want to help."

She studies me with a frown. "Are you not pleased with the estate as it is now?"

"No! No," I hurry to tell her with a smile. "Everything has been lovely. You and Mr. Morris have made everything so perfect. I just... want to feel useful. I'd like a project. And I think this could be fun. What do you say?"

I make one more wish—one teeny, tiny wish in hopes that the universe will give me this one thing.

Please let her say yes.

Because if she doesn't, there isn't anyone else on the entire grounds who will help.

Her eyes soften. After what feels like years of scrutiny, she says, "You're the lady of the house, Ms. Nova. Whatever you have in mind, I can't stop you."

It's been way too long since I've heard anything like that.

It's music to my ears.

"Nova!"

Samuil's voice echoes up the stone staircase and bounces around the high ceilings of the abandoned turret. Or, to be more precise, the *previously* abandoned turret.

As of late this afternoon, it's mine and Samuil's new bedroom.

"Nova!" he barks again, sending me tunneling deeper beneath the two heavy quilts on the bed.

It's cold up here, but only because the man Mrs. Morris hired to clean out the fireplace can't get here until the morning. Knowing that, I probably should've opted to wear something other than a silk nightie to bed, but I wanted to mark the occasion. It's not every day you move your bedroom into the highest point of a Scottish castle.

Samuil illustrates exactly how high it is when he bursts through the door, panting like an enraged bull. His broad chest expands with every breath, but he stills when his eyes land on me beneath the blankets of our four-poster bed.

The bed that, again, only a few hours ago, was tucked away in our ground-level bedroom on the opposite side of the house.

"What is this?"

I hold up the book I'm hiding behind. "*Native Birds of Scotland.* It's very informative."

"Nova." The way he growls my name sends electricity dancing across my skin.

"I moved our bedroom," I explain as cheerfully as I can with him scowling at me. "What do you think?"

I know what he thinks. Part of the reason I moved the bedroom up here is because I knew exactly what he'd think.

But this is what he gets for giving me so much time to myself.

His jaw tightens as he takes in my handiwork. The candles cast shadows that dance across his sharp features, turning him from man to demon and back again.

"We agreed I should find a project," I remind him.

"I was talking about that damn rowboat. Something small. Something that I'd probably never let you—" He stops himself with another growl, but I know what he was going to say.

"Something that you could watch me fix up to kill some time and then never let me actually use?" I swallow down the new wave of anger that brings up in me and slap on a smile instead. "You like it when I stay close to the house, so, for the last few days, that's what I did."

He's tense and fuming, and he's still the most handsome thing I've ever seen. Despite it all, I just wish I saw more of him.

I throw back the quilts, revealing the pale pink silk that clings to my curves. His anger fractures, desire bleeding through the cracks.

I pat the mattress. "Come to bed."

His jaw works back and forth as his eyes do the same, raking over me again and again. "It took me fucking forever to hike up here," he grumbles, striding across the room towards me.

But as he does, he catches his foot on the gargantuan wooden trunk at the end of the bed. A string of Russian words I'm familiar with only because he often uses them to describe his brother flies out of his mouth.

"Sorry," I wince. "Our clothes are in there since this room doesn't have a closet."

"This room doesn't have fucking anything." His gaze catches on the flickering candles. Understanding dawns. "Is there even electricity?"

I wince again, which must be answer enough because he curses.

No electricity was actually a selling point for me. No Wi-Fi, no devices—when we're in our room, we'll be completely cut off from the rest of the world.

"Is this payback?" he demands. "Are you doing this to prove something to me? Because I'd rather just have it out with you than climb a mountain to get to bed every night."

I roll my eyes and slide out of bed, not missing the way Samuil tracks my every movement. Part of me would rather just "have it out" with him, too.

But he needs to hear this.

"It might've started that way," I concede. "I was bored and lonely and it just kept raining and raining—"

"I think it's still raining." His hand darts out, pinching the soft silk between his fingers like he can't help himself.

"I just wanted to feel useful. But now that I'm up here—now that I see how it could be..." I turn to admire the thick, velvet curtains, the layered rugs over the stone floor, the candles dripping wax on each nightstand. "I like it up here, Sam."

He steps behind me, his warm body molding to my back. I arch against him and drop my head to his shoulder. "There's not even a bathroom up here, Nova," he murmurs in my ear.

The trek down to the bathroom is grim, I'll give him that. As this baby gets bigger, I'm going to have to get used to pitch black, late night walks to the bathroom or go full medieval and get myself a chamber pot.

But I'll deal with that later. Right now—

"Come with me." I take his hand and pull him towards the secret door in the corner.

"Where the hell are you taking me?"

I don't answer. It's nice to lead Samuil around blindly for a change. God knows he's done it to me enough over the last few months.

We take another set of stairs out of the room, which Samuil mounts with more grumbled complaints. But then we step through another door and out onto the top of the turret.

For the first time in days, the rain has stopped. Like it knew we were coming. Like it knew how bad I needed this.

Instead of a hazy mist, the skies are clear. The loch is bright, mirroring the dense smattering of stars in the sky.

I take a deep breath of the damp air and sigh. "It's beautiful, isn't it?"

His mouth is warm on my cheek. "It's a long way down. I don't want you out here by yourself."

"Sam—" I turn to him, pressing my hands to his chest. "I'm not afraid to be up here. Actually, this castle is one of the few places I've ever felt completely safe."

"For a woman who claims she's never left Chicago, you sure have a penchant for feeling at home in exotic places."

I can't help but grin. "Maybe I'm more adventurous than I gave myself credit for. You taught me that. And, I suppose... knowing my brothers and father are gone now makes it easier to embrace the parts of myself I was afraid of."

He moves closer, his hand finding my waist. "You don't have

to be afraid at all, *krasavitsa*. I'm right here. I'll take care of you."

"I know that, Sam. I do. But—" I blow out a breath, trying to decide how to say this. "I don't just want you to take care of me. I don't want to be another responsibility on your long to-do list. I want to feel like I'm included in your life. I want to make decisions."

He looks around, something between a grimace and a smile dancing on his lips. "And your first decision is to make me hike up ten flights of stairs every time I want to take you to bed?"

"It'll be good for your heart."

"*You're* good for my heart," he fires back. He grips my chin and brings my mouth to his in a kiss hot enough I can almost forget I'm wearing lingerie on a windy castle top. He pulls back. "You're sure about this? You want to sleep up here?"

I step closer, bending my body into the hard lines of his. "Right now, I don't want to sleep. Not even a little bit."

His hand fists in my nightie. "Then what do you want?"

I stretch onto my toes, my lips brushing against his in a whisper. "I want to fix up that boat."

"What else?" He holds me closer, almost crushing me against him. What I really want is narrowing down to where he's hard and hot against my stomach.

"I want you to go on a walk with me," I add, pressing my luck. "Every day."

"Nova..." Warning and want tangle in my name.

"And you," I pant. "I want you."

"That's better." All at once, he scoops me into his arms and carries me down the stairs. He tosses me onto our bed, crawling over me with heat in his eyes.

It really does feel like another world up here in this turret. I almost can't believe it's real.

"Are you mine?" I whisper, more to myself than Sam.

He kisses his way up my body. "I'm yours, Nova Pierce. It's all yours. Anything you want."

17

SAMUIL

Rain hammers the windows of my London office like artillery fire. Each drop is another fucking reminder that I'm trapped in this concrete hellhole while Nova's alone at the castle.

My jaw clenches hard enough to crack teeth. I yank the curtains mostly closed and London disappears from sight—I can't even look at this godforsaken city without wanting to set it on fire just to be back with her.

My mind is a mess. I should be strategizing how to destroy my traitorous brother, figuring out my next move now that Ilya's slithered off to fucking Siberia of all places.

Instead, I'm remembering the way Nova hurled that antique vase at my head last night. The way her eyes blazed with rage when I told her she couldn't come with me. The sharp sting as broken porcelain sliced my cheek.

Pregnant women aren't supposed to have that good of an arm.

My phone buzzes with another update from my team in Russia. Nothing concrete, just more speculation about Ilya's location, his next moves, whether Katerina's joined him yet. I rake a hand through my hair, resisting the urge to hurl the device through the window.

A month ago, I had them exactly where I wanted them—Ilya exposed as a traitor, Katerina's schemes unraveling. Then Nova got caught in their crossfire and I had to shift focus to keeping her safe.

Now, here I am, trying to project strength by returning to London to handle Litvinov Group business, while my heavily pregnant girlfriend is hidden away in Scotland.

Mess. It's all just a big fucking mess.

The office door opens and Myles strides in, shaking rain from his coat. His expression tells me he has news before he even opens his mouth.

"Just heard from Artem," he says without preamble.

I straighten, shoving thoughts of Nova aside. "The Siberia lead?"

"Still trying to pin down specifics, but it's definitely Ilya. No sign of Katerina yet."

"Fuck." I turn back to the window. Through the curtain gap, I see umbrellas bob through the streets below like black beetles. "What the hell is he doing out there?"

"Maybe the same thing you were doing in Scotland," Myles suggests. "Hiding."

I shoot him a glare. Myles just raises an eyebrow, completely unfazed after fifteen years of friendship. His gaze flicks to the cut on my cheek. "How's that healing up?"

"I regret telling you about that."

"You deserved it."

I pivot to face him. "Excuse me?"

"You heard me." He meets my stare evenly. "Nova was right. You could have brought her."

"She's pregnant," I growl. The words come out harsher than intended, as if saying them could erase the image of Nova's tear-streaked face from my mind.

"Exactly." Myles drops into one of my visitor chairs, propping his feet on my pristine desk because he knows it pisses me off. "Soon, she'll be stuck at home with your kid. You should let her live a little before that happens."

"If I thought it was safe—"

"It *is* safe. I put enough security measures in place myself." He cuts me off with a dismissive wave. "Don't blame my team for you being overprotective."

My fist clenches at my side. I'm not above punching him. "Am I the only one who sees the danger?"

"You're the only one who sees it where it isn't." That infuriating smugness remains plastered across his face. "In almost everything else, I defer to your judgment. But when it comes to Nova…" He shrugs like the answer's obvious. Maybe it fucking is. "Love makes people do crazy things. Like lock up the person they care about and throw away the key."

"I've never used that word."

"Doesn't mean you don't feel it."

The unease crawling under my skin has nothing to do with Myles making sense. I happen to know another man who kept his woman locked away. She turned to drugs and alcohol to control the demons inside because she couldn't control the one outside. First chance she got, she ran.

I tell myself I'm nothing like my father. But maybe we're just different shades of the same toxic fucking color.

"Do you think I'm like him?" The question slips out before I can stop it.

Myles's head snaps toward me, surprised but not confused. He turns back to the rain-drenched windows with a weary sigh. "Come on, brother. Leonid is a brute all the time. You're only a brute when you have to be."

"He kept her locked away, too," I mutter. The rain intensifies, drowning out the city noise below.

"He didn't love your mother the way you love Nova," Myles says quietly. "He isn't capable of it."

That word again. *Love.* It settles like a steel trap on my shoulders. Am I capable of it? Is that what this burning in my chest means? Is that truly in the cards for someone like me?

"I don't think Nova would call this 'love.'"

"Maybe you should tell her then. Might make her go easier on you."

"I've already given her more than I thought possible," I snap. "I've compromised more than I ever planned to. I've bent until I nearly broke. I'm not sure I have anything left to give."

He eyes me sideways. "What if that's not enough for her?"

The question I've been avoiding. Because I already know the answer.

It's not enough. Nova wants all of me—even the parts I keep locked away in this office. The parts that attend meetings where men die and dirty deals are struck. She deserves the whole truth.

But that truth would destroy her.

With Katerina, everything had been simpler. Her demands were easier to meet: designer clothes, diamond tennis bracelets, luxury vacations where my presence was optional at best. Dangle something shiny and off she went, satisfied long enough for me to be both CEO and Bratva *pakhan* without giving her a second thought.

Of course, she was also fucking my brother behind my back.

So maybe things weren't as simple as I remember.

Either way, everything's become infinitely more complicated. I have so much more to lose.

"I need to end this soon," I rasp, pulling out my phone to check for updates. "For my family's sake."

"Show your father the evidence against Ilya and be done with it," Myles suggests, not for the first time. He's been pushing me to pull that trigger for months.

I shake my head. "Leonid won't believe it. Not now that he has footage of Nova walking into Andropov headquarters with that server—"

"That proved to be fake!" Myles interjects.

"Doesn't matter." I press my palm against the cold glass, letting it ground me. "Leonid's convinced himself that Nova didn't know the server was false. He believes what she did was calculated, premeditated. He'll never accept Ilya had anything to do with it."

"So you've already spoken to him."

"Multiple times." The admission tastes bitter. "He wants her head on a spike."

"I take it he doesn't know she's with you."

"I don't know what he thinks," I say, watching a black car pull up to the curb below. "But he doesn't have proof of her location. I intend to keep it that way until I have a solid plan."

Myles exhales heavily. "That's why you wouldn't bring her to London."

I nod. "The entire Bratva thinks she's an Andropov spy thanks to Leonid and Ilya. The number of men still loyal to me shrinks by the day. Who can blame them? I already have one black mark courtesy of my cheating ex-wife. I can't be seen with another woman whose loyalties are questioned."

"Christ." Myles runs both hands through his hair. "What about telling Leonid about the baby?"

A bitter laugh is my only response.

"Surely he wouldn't order the death of a woman carrying his grandchild?"

The horror in Myles's voice would be touching if it weren't so naive.

"You severely underestimate my father's capacity for cruelty." I turn from the window, needing to move. "I won't risk it. I have no idea how he'd react, and I refuse to gamble with her life."

Myles nods, his jaw squaring. "Then I have one more suggestion. After that, I'll shut my mouth."

"I doubt that. But go ahead."

"Tell Nova," he says simply. "Tell her everything. Let her in."

The vein in my forehead throbs at the mere idea. "This isn't her burden to bear, Myles. She's already got enough on her plate, with worrying about her grandmother and Hope and our baby. I won't add to it." I drop into my chair, spreading my hands on the mahogany desk. "I can be her punching bag. I can take her anger if it means keeping her safe from how high the stakes really are."

"You're a good man, Samuil." Myles claps me on the back. His resignation is proof that I answered exactly the way he expected. "And I'm proud to be your second, your brother-in-arms." He pauses at the door. "I just hope this decision doesn't come back to bite you in the ass."

"Yeah," I whisper to myself long after he's retreated out of my office and left me to resume my pastime of staring at the raindrops racing down the window glass. "That makes two of us."

My phone lights up with another message. This time from Nova.

I'm sorry about the vase. And your face. Come home soon.

Three simple lines that make my chest constrict. This woman who throws pottery at my head one day and misses me the next. Who fights me tooth and nail about staying safe, then apologizes for caring too much. Who's carrying my child and still doesn't realize she already owns every piece of me worth having.

I type back: ***Nothing to apologize for,*** **zaychik.** ***I'll be home soon. Just a few more days.***

18

NOVA

The turret room feels smaller every day Samuil's gone. I've taken to pacing its circular confines like some tragic heroine in a gothic novel, scanning the winding road below for any sign of his return.

Three weeks. Three fucking weeks of "just a few more days, *zaychik*."

Today, I'm changing venues. I'll pace in the library instead of the turret. But I'm barely halfway around the room before I lose all desire to keep moving and collapse into a self-loathing heap on the window seat.

I press my forehead against the cold stone, letting out a breath that fogs the glass pane. The castle that felt like a fairytale now feels like a prison, no matter how lovely the grounds or how kind the staff. Even the Scottish rain seems to mock me, drumming an endless rhythm that sounds suspiciously like "alone, alone, alone."

Not *fully* alone, though. My hand drifts to my growing belly. At least someone's keeping me company.

"Miss Nova?" Mrs. Morris's voice echoes from the entrance. "There's something in the barn you might want to see."

I consider ignoring her. The library's perfectly good for moping, and I've gotten rather skilled at it lately. But Mrs. Morris has become more than just the housekeeper—she's the closest thing to a mother figure I've ever had. If she thinks something's worth dragging my pregnant ass out into the rain for, it probably is.

"Coming," I call back, wrapping my sweater tighter around my growing belly.

The walk to the barn takes longer these days. Not just because I'm getting bigger, but because every path holds memories.

The garden where Samuil first kissed me in the rain. The loch where we went midnight swimming. The meadow where he promised me forever, right before rushing off to London and leaving me here alone.

I'm so lost in memories that I almost miss the sounds coming from the barn—high-pitched yips and excited barks that definitely aren't the usual farm noises. My steps quicken despite myself.

I push open the heavy wooden door—and freeze.

Four black and white puppies tumble over each other in a makeshift pen, their stubby tails wagging furiously as they spot me. A weathered farmer I recognize as Duncan from the neighboring property stands nearby with an adult border collie at his heel.

"Thought ye might want to meet the new additions," Duncan says with a knowing smile. "Their mam passed last week, poor things. They'll need someone with a gentle touch to help raise them up proper."

The smallest pup breaks away from the pack and waddles toward me, front paw slightly turned in, making him trip over his own feet. My heart melts instantly.

"Hello there, little one," I whisper, kneeling carefully to let him sniff my hand. His wet nose tickles my palm before he gives it a tentative lick.

His siblings, noticing his bravery, scramble over to join in the investigation. Soon, I'm surrounded by wiggling bodies and puppy breath.

Duncan chuckles. "They seem to know a good soul when they meet one."

The adult collie—sleek and gorgeous with intelligent eyes—sits primly beside him, watching the proceedings with what looks like maternal concern.

"And who's this beauty?" I ask.

"This here's my Fiona. Best herding dog in the county." He pats her head proudly. "Was thinking, if you're interested, there's a herding clinic next week in the village. Could teach you proper handling techniques. These wee ones'll need structure once they're bigger."

My heart leaps at the thought of having a project, something beyond waiting for Samuil's return and watching my belly grow.

But then reality crashes back. "I should check with—"

"Already cleared it with the boss," Duncan interrupts with a wink. "Mr. Litvinov arranged everything before he left."

Of course he did. Part of me wants to be irritated at his high-handedness, at how he's trying to manage me even from hundreds of miles away.

But as the runt of the litter crawls into my lap and promptly falls asleep, I can't summon the anger.

Damn him for knowing exactly what I need.

"When do we start?" I ask, already mentally planning how to puppy-proof our bedroom. The turret might make an excellent training space…

"Tomorrow morning, if you're up for it." Duncan whistles and Fiona immediately comes to attention. "We'll start with the basics: voice commands, positioning, that sort of thing. These little ones are too young yet, but they'll be watching and learning."

The puppy in my lap lets out a tiny snore. His siblings have collapsed in a heap nearby, worn out from their excitement. I stroke his soft fur, feeling more at peace than I have in weeks.

"Thank you," I tell Duncan. "Both for this and for…" I gesture vaguely, encompassing the whole setup that has Samuil's fingerprints all over it.

He tips his cap. "Pleasure's mine, lass. Though I should warn you: handling border collies isn't for the faint of heart. They're clever as the devil and twice as stubborn."

My mind goes immediately to Samuil, and I snort. "I have some experience with that type."

The puppies are great. I mean, what's not to love about puppies? But entering into week four with still no sign of Samuil is… less great.

It's maddening, actually.

If the puppies were Samuil's attempt to come home to a forgiving Nova Pierce, he's going to need an ark full of them. Puppies of Biblical proportion are the only way I would ever be able to not be livid at him for leaving me for three, going on four, entire weeks.

I'm sitting in the soft grass next to the loch—far enough away that the puppies can't beeline into the water—when I hear footsteps crunching on the dirt behind me.

I turn, and my traitorous heart gallops at the sight of…

Myles, with his hands shoved deep in his pockets.

"You're not the asshole I was expecting."

Where is Samuil? I want to add. *Is he inside? Can I see him? Does he want to see me?*

Before all my pathetic questions can pour out, Myles drops down on the blanket next to me. "That particular asshole got held up in London. I'm afraid he'll be another week or two."

The puppies charge at the newcomer. Myles can't help but smile as they clamber over him.

Meanwhile, disappointment is turning my stomach over. I bring my knees to my chest and wrap my arms around them. "He might as well stay in London. I've gotten used to the quiet around here," I lie.

"He wants to be here, Nova, but things are complicated."

I roll my eyes. "Aren't they always?"

"Cut him some slack. It hasn't been easy for him."

"He could've told me all about it when he called me every night—except, oh, wait, he *didn't* call me every night. We haven't even spoken." My throat tightens with tears I refuse to shed. Because once I start, we might all need that ark full of puppies to escape the flood. "He doesn't tell me anything, Myles. Do you think being kept in the dark is easy for me?"

"He doesn't want to worry you." Myles looks genuinely sorry, but it's hard to see him as anything but Samuil's accomplice right now. Everything going on is partially his fault, too.

"Too late."

I'm worried about Samuil and what he's up to in London.

I'm worried about what will happen with us when he comes back.

Most of all, I'm terrified he won't come back at all. Maybe this whole setup was just a convenient way to stash his pregnant mistake somewhere remote while he handles his real priorities.

Myles watches the puppies wrestle in silence. One tugs at his pant leg until he shoos it away. "They get annoying fast, don't they?"

"Hey, at least they're here."

There's a beat before he can't help himself. Defending Samuil is in the job description. "They're only here because Samuil didn't want you feeling so alone."

I huff out a bitter laugh. "Is that why you're here? He sent you to plead his case for him?"

"No, I'm here because I wanted to come."

"That makes you the only one."

Again, he ignores me. And I'm glad.

Because if he pushed, I'd have to admit that the truth is much more complicated.

I love it here. I'd stay at Castle Moorbeath forever.

But only if Samuil was with me.

The four puppies are romping in four different directions until Myles scoops them all up and deposits them in a squirming pile in the middle of the blanket. "Wanna tell me their names?"

Not really. I want to pin Myles to the grass by his annoyingly thick skull and force him to tell me what Samuil has been doing every single day for the last three weeks.

But seeing as how that's not physically possible, and he wouldn't give me any information even under threat of torture anyway, I allow the subject change.

"Meg is the one biting your toenail. The other three are boys —Finbarr has the brown tail and Rory and Kill are rolling around on the grass."

"Kill? Pretty brutal name for such a fuzzy little thing."

"It's short for Killian," I explain. "Mr. Morris picked it. He had a dog that looked just like that chubby little monster when he was a kid."

Myles chuckles as Kill rolls over Rory and lands on his back, all four little paws pedaling up in the air.

"I heard you and Mr. Morris went fishing yesterday."

I'm not surprised he heard about that. I'm sure he and Sam know exactly what I've been up to the last three weeks.

Even with that bitter thought, though, I can't help but smile. "I've never been fishing before, but it was actually pretty fun. I'm looking forward to taking my boat out on the lake one of these days."

I nod towards the boat floating along the edge of the loch, and Myles's jaw drops. "That thing can't possibly be water-worthy."

"It will be when I'm through with it." I lift my chin proudly. "I'm working on fixing it up. As soon as I learn which end of the hammer to hold, it's gonna be game over. Both for that boat and for Samuil."

Myles laughs, but when I don't join, his chuckle quickly fades away. He clears his throat. "Listen, Nova, I know you feel isolated up here—"

"You don't even know the half of it," I snap before he can even get started. "I lost my father and my brothers in a single day. I've barely begun to process that. Mostly because the only people I might be able to process it with are the people I'm not allowed to talk to."

He runs a hand through his hair and curses under his breath again. But he doesn't interrupt me. Which is good, because I have a lot more to say.

"Grams, Hope… they're the only ones who understood my relationship with my family. I don't even know how my grandmother is doing since she found out she lost her son and grandsons. Do you know how horrible I feel that I can't even check on her?"

"I know it's not easy—"

"Don't tell me you understand, because you don't. Grams is the only family I have left and Hope is my best friend. Unless you're going to tell me that you'll find a way for me to talk to them, I don't want to hear it," I snarl fiercely. "You and Samuil get to do what you want, and I'm the one left to deal with all of the rules."

"Have mercy!" Myles throws up his hands. "Stop beating me over the head with reason and logic. I get it."

"Do you?" I ask, sensing weakness for the first time.

He stares at the puppies, who have gone back to romping in the grass. "Samuil would never approve of this..."

I inch a little closer, determined not to look too eager. "What Samuil doesn't know won't hurt him. And I'll never tell."

Myles gives me a nervous scowl. "Is one phone call to Chicago worth it for you? You're asking me to go behind my friend's back and keep a secret from him."

"As secrets go, it's a small one. And he's keeping plenty of secrets from me."

"That's different."

I shouldn't push my luck—not when Myles is my only shot at contact with the outside world. But still, I roll my eyes. "Because he's the big, bad *pahkan*? Give me a break."

Myles chuckles. "You really are something, Nova Pierce. Samuil met his match the day he met you."

I nudge him in the arm. "Is that a yes? Will you let me talk to them?"

"Fuck me," Myles mutters.

That's a yes.

19

NOVA

My victory becomes less satisfying the longer Myles's list of conditions goes on.

"… less than five minutes. Don't tell them where we are. Don't tell them where you've been. Don't tell them where Samuil is. Don't—"

"This would go faster if you told me what I *can* talk about," I grumble.

I've been bouncing from foot to foot like an impatient child while he prattles on, waiting for him to wrap it up. I'm a few button pushes away from talking to Grams, and my chill disappeared right around the same time he agreed to this plan in the first place.

"Feelings and shit," he concludes. "That's what's allowed. Isn't that what women like to talk about anyway?"

"Don't forget our periods. We love talking about our monthly cycles." I roll my eyes and hold my hand out. "Give me the phone."

He pulls it out of his pocket, but doesn't hand it over. His eyes remain suspiciously narrowed. "There will be hell to pay if Samuil finds out about this, Nova."

My heart kicks against my ribs at the mention of his name. Even now, after everything, the mere thought of him sends electricity dancing across my skin. I force myself to focus.

"You're a good friend, Myles." I soften my voice, letting a hint of suggestion creep in. "I'll mention just how nice you are when I talk to Hope."

With that, his eyebrows zoom upwards in the purest expression of giddy joy I've ever seen. I have to bite my lip to keep from laughing at him. Joke's on me, really—I'd probably already be talking to Grams if I'd led with that. Let that be a lesson for next time.

"Tell her the only thing nicer than my personality is how nice I look without a shirt on," Myles adds with a cheeky grin.

"I'll work that in between the feelings and period talk. It'll go: sadness, your rippling abs, Hope's period cramps, and then we'll wrap up with a lengthy discussion of your stamina in bed."

Finally—finally—he extends the phone. "Work in that I can bench two-fifty, and I'll give you fifteen extra minutes."

I snatch the phone before he can change his mind and blow him a kiss. "You're a doll."

"And a sucker," he mutters as he gets up and wanders away into the nearby meadow.

The moment I have it, my hands start shaking. I know he's listening—he'd be stupid not to—but I don't care. All that matters is the number I'm punching in with trembling fingers, each digit bringing me closer to home.

The ring echoes in my ear like a funeral bell.

Then she answers, and I almost collapse to my knees in relief.

"Hello?"

"Grams!" I choke out, the single word a wobbly, shaky mess.

"Oh my God—Nova?"

"Shhh," I whisper, glancing at Myles's turned back. My pulse thunders in my ears as I lower my voice. "I'm not calling you. This never happened, okay?"

A beat of silence stretches between us before she catches on. "What never happened?"

That puts a smile on my face, though the tears remain stubbornly where they are. "You have no idea how good it is to hear your voice, Grams. I've missed you."

"And I've been worried sick." The strain in her voice makes me fist the blanket harder. "Samuil has been giving me regular updates. He insists you're safe, you're doing well, but I don't think I really believed him until just now when I heard your voice."

Despite how angry I am with him right now, I can't help but agree. "I *am* safe, and I *am* doing well."

"Well, thank God for that."

I stare out over the water as afternoon clouds roll in, trying to decide where to start. So much has happened—not that I can talk about most of it. So I settle on the thing I can talk about. The last thing I want to bring up.

"How are you, Grams? After everything… Are you okay?"

I've been wanting to talk to her about my dad and brothers since the second it happened, but I never actually planned what to say. I don't even know how I feel about it, let alone how she might feel.

Her silence takes on a heavy edge. When I hear her sniffle, my arms ache to pull her into a hug. "I never thought I'd outlive my son. Certainly not Tommy and Mike."

Funny, neither did I. Mostly because they each took their turns threatening me within an inch of a life. If anything, my reigning thought has always been that *one of these days, they'll kill me.*

"It's hard to make sense of any of it. I keep thinking I should feel... different about it. More something." I watch raindrops dapple the flat mirror of the lake. "They were not good people. But it's okay to be sad."

They were worse than that. But the less Grams knows about what her son and grandsons did, the better off she is. Enough of us are tangled up in my father's dirty dealings as it is. She's too innocent to get dragged into the mud.

Let her think of them as angels. She deserves that much.

But that doesn't keep me from being angry. I'm angry at them for existing at all and then for abandoning us in such a cruel fashion. I'm angry that it's all such a fucking mess. That we can't just mourn the loss of our family like normal people. That even this most basic human experience has to be uniquely complicated.

"Are you telling me or yourself, honey?" she asks softly.

I swipe at the tears leaking down my cheeks. "I don't know. Both, I guess. I just… Ever since I found out, I haven't known what to think. I don't miss them. I won't. I'll never, for a single second, wish they were alive and I could call them up and tell them about my life."

My throat closes around the words as memories flash through my mind—bruises hidden under long sleeves, nights spent crying into my pillow, the constant edge of fear. "But part of me wishes that I would. I think I'm mourning the fact that I can't mourn them, if that even makes sense."

She releases a shaky breath. "I wish you could've gone to the funeral with me. I think it would've helped you."

"You went to their funerals?" I don't know why, but I didn't even think about a funeral. The mayor was probably there. I'm sure flags were draped over their coffins. Bullshit honors were probably bestowed on them for serving the city, and stone-faced men probably said too-kind things about them that they didn't come close to earning.

I would've hated every second of that funeral.

"I did," she admits. "Myles escorted me."

That's another surprising blow. "What? He didn't— No one told me."

That's a trend around here, it seems. No one tells me anything.

"Myles said you were safe, but the way he talked about you, it almost sounded like you were sick. Are you… Nova, are *you* okay? Where are you?"

I think back through the rules Myles laid out, repeating them to myself twice before I decide this next topic isn't off-limits.

"I wanted to tell you in person, but at this point, I don't know when that will—" The words lodge in my throat, and I shove the thought away before I devolve into tears and ruin what is already a botched announcement. "I'm not sick, Grams. I'm pregnant."

There's one beat of silence for me to worry about what her response will be before she's happy-shouting through the phone. "Are you serious? Sweetheart! How far along? Oh, honey, I'm so happy for you. I'm so— Are you nauseous? Have you been taking vitamins?"

I laugh and start answering as many of her questions as I can manage. "I'm almost two months, but everything is going well. The baby is healthy and happy, and I'm happy. I'm really happy."

"Oh, my darling, I'm—" She hiccups again. "This is the best news you ever could have given me."

"I wanted to tell you in person," I whisper. "I had this whole plan. We were going to have breakfast at Moody's, with apple pancakes…"

"Oh, honey." Her voice wobbles. "We'll do that. When all this is over, we'll celebrate properly. Have you been craving anything yet?"

I laugh softly. "Everything and nothing. Yesterday, I cried because we didn't have pickles. Then, when Louisa brought some, I couldn't stand the smell."

"That's exactly how I was with your father." She catches herself, the words hanging heavy between us. "I'm sorry, I shouldn't have—"

"No, it's okay." I swallow hard. "I want to hear about it. About the good memories, too. Even if they're about him."

"You're going to be such a wonderful mother, Nova." She sighs. "So much better than… well. My point is, you know what real love looks like. What it feels like to want to protect someone."

Something in her tone shifts then, takes on an edge I've never heard before.

"But I need you to do something for me, sweetheart."

"Okay?"

"Listen to Samuil," she insists. "Listen to him and trust that he's going to keep you safe."

My jaw actually drops. Of all the things I thought Grams would say, that wasn't it.

And she's not done yet, either.

"Your father and brothers were in a mess with the wrong people and they were killed for it. Those people could come after you next. I need to know you are going to be safe, and Samuil can do that. He's a good man."

"Grams—" I jump up and start pacing along the water's edge. "How can you be so sure about him? You barely know him."

"I know enough." Her voice hardens with conviction. "I know he checks on me every day. Makes sure I have everything I need. I know he cares."

I stop in my tracks. "He does?"

"And when he talks about you…" She pauses, and I hold my breath. "Well, a mother knows these things. Even if I'm just a grandmother." So promise me," she continues with surprising intensity. "I want to hear you swear that you'll do what's best for yourself and my great-grandchild. Swear it."

I close my eyes and picture him. It's only the wind tousling my hair, but I could swear it's Samuil's fingers combing through. I know it's only the storm booming, but I could swear it's his voice. I know it's only a drop of rain kissing my cheek, but I could swear it's him.

He's here. He's not actually, but he is in all the ways that matter.

But is that enough? Is the ghost of Samuil as good as the real thing? Or, maybe even worse—is his presence worse than his ghost? Because even when it really is Samuil touching me, kissing me, whispering to me, he comes with so much more. Shadows trailing him, guns tucked in desk drawers, that cold steel of his voice when he switches languages and has conversations I can't understand.

Can I trust that? Trust him?

Do I really have a choice?

In the end, I do all I can do. I sit down in the damp, dark sand and sigh. "Okay, Grams. I promise."

20

SAMUIL

The meeting drags into its ninetieth fucking minute, and all I can focus on is the piece of lettuce wedged between Jonathan Beckett's front teeth. He's flicked his tongue across them four times now, missing the green intruder with each pass. I'm counting. It's become a game—the only entertainment in this suffocating private dining room where old men come to stroke their egos and pretend the glory days of the Soviet Union aren't long dead.

I drain another finger of vodka, grateful for the burn. Maybe if I get drunk enough, this will become bearable.

"I'm throwing a party next week," Mr. Beckett says, his tongue once again missing the bit of lettuce. "Very exclusive. I would've invited you sooner, but you've been a hard man to track down."

There's an unspoken question there that I have no intention of answering.

"I'll be out of town," I reply shortly.

His wine glass wobbles as he blinks at me, nearly slipping from his grasp before a waiter materializes to refill it. "You're not coming?"

I used to be better at this—the smiling, the drinking, the endless fucking small talk. I could endure it all while keeping my eyes on the prize: money, security, power. The holy trinity I've pursued my entire life.

Now, I look at this man across from me, and all I can think is, *Nova. Nova. Nova.*

If I'm going to spend another week away from her, it's not going to be wasted stroking the ego of Jonathan Beckett and his friends at a fucking cocktail party.

"You *have* to be there," he blathers on before I can say anything. "I'm flying in a chef from Amsterdam, and the entertainment…" He lets out a heinous moan that sets my teeth on edge. "The models I'm bringing in will be very entertaining. You'll have first choice."

The offer of sex with random women Beckett has paid to be there wouldn't have tempted me even before Nova. But now, it's as repulsive as the food lodged between his teeth.

"Tempting," I say. "But no."

The man frowns like nothing has ever been more confusing than someone refusing his company. I would've thought it would be a normal enough occurrence for him by now, but it's remarkable what money can convince people to put up with. I'm sure sex isn't the only companionship he's paying for, whether he knows it or not.

Suddenly, his eyes cast over my shoulder. "Ah, well, if you can't make it, perhaps the elder Litvinov can. Let's ask him."

My fist tightens around my tumbler of vodka. “My father doesn’t go out much.”

“He’s out today,” Beckett croons, looking far too pleased with himself. “And he’s coming this way.”

Fuck.

I keep my spine straight, refusing to turn until Jonathan has already extended his hand to my father, the two of them shaking over my shoulder. Only then do I look, meeting my father’s cold blue eyes as they lock onto mine with predatory interest.

I keep my spine straight, refusing to turn until Jonathan has already extended his hand to my father, the two of them shaking over my shoulder. Only then do I look, meeting my father’s cold blue eyes as they lock onto mine with predatory interest.

We both know that’s bullshit.

“Please, take my seat, Leonid.” Beckett rises and steps away from the table, pulling his chair out for my father. “I lost track of time with your son and have another meeting to attend. I’m afraid I’m already late.”

My father nods and lowers himself into the offered chair like a king taking up his throne. “Don’t let us keep you, then.”

Beckett shakes his hand again. “You’re working the boy too hard, Leonid. He has no time for parties and beautiful women, apparently.”

Leonid’s gaze veers lazily to me. “That’s news to me.”

Once Beckett is whisked away by his security team, Leonid’s smile withers and dies on his face. “Odious man. Did you see the food in his teeth?”

I keep my own face utterly impassive. I don't want to give my father any edge to use against me. "He brings in enough money for us that I endure the occasional meal to keep him happy."

"I stopped doing that kind of grunt work a long time ago."

"Only because I picked up the slack."

Leonid inclines his head in acknowledgement and orders himself a bourbon that costs more than the entire meal Beckett and I just indulged in.

"How long have you been in London?" he asks.

"Not long. A few weeks."

"And you didn't think to inform me?"

"No more than you thought to inform me of your presence here."

"The head does not inform the hands of its location; it gives orders and they follow." He sniffles and raises his chin high in the air.

I snort. "Where is your other hand, then? Are you aware of his whereabouts?"

His jaw clenches. Half his bourbon disappears before he speaks again. "This feud with your brother has gone on long enough, don't you think? How did this nonsense even start?"

"Thirty-something years, by the last count," I say, still silently urging myself not to crush the tumbler in my fist. "And I believe it started around the time you decided to make me and Ilya fight over everything we got. Everything we were. Your idea of fatherhood was turning your sons into gladiators for your entertainment."

"Is that your charge against me?" Leonid drawls. "Because I believe I made up for taking away your toys by giving you my empire. And look how you've thanked me for that."

That, at last, gets a rise out of me. I abandon my vodka, leaning forward until I can see every line carved into his face by cruelty. "I will not dignify that with an answer."

"If you didn't want to talk, son, you should've stayed in your backwater hideout in Scotland."

It takes all my willpower not to betray my surprise.

He knows. He fucking knows.

"I just needed a change of pace."

One of Leonid's eyebrows rises skeptically. "You did? Or was it your low-rent girlfriend who wanted the vacation?"

I slide my hands beneath the table before he can see them curl into fists. Before they betray how badly I want to wrap them around his throat.

"You've always been led around by your cock," he spits. "At least Katerina had pedigree. Class. A sense of propriety."

"No wonder she and Ilya got along perfectly."

"Don't make such a fuss, boy. He knows better than to continue any association with that backstabbing bitch. You, on the other hand—"

"Nova Pierce did not betray anyone," I interrupt. "She was a pawn. I've taken responsibility for her, and she is not your concern."

He scowls. "Whoever my sons choose to fuck is very much my concern. Haven't you learned anything from me? A woman is nothing more than a warm hole to stick your cock. Apart from that, they serve no purpose."

"I didn't know you were such a romantic, Father. Your wife is a lucky woman."

"My wife knows her place," he growls. "Can you say the same for that traitorous little cunt you're seeing? She may be able to suck your cock like a cheap American whore, but she will never be worthy of the Litvinov name. She will never—"

"Enough!" The roar rips from my chest before I can contain it.

My heart hammers against my ribs. Red bleeds into the edges of my vision. It's taking everything I have not to flip this table and show him exactly what kind of monster he created.

He arches one eyebrow, daring me to say another word.

Unfortunately for him, I fucking dare.

The blood is pounding in my temples, but my voice remains as frigid as ever. I learned that from the best: *him.*

"I've endured your abuse patiently for thirty-three years to make sure I didn't damage your fragile ego, but I will not sit for another second and hear any of it hurled at Nova."

I know I'm showing my hand here, but I can't stop myself. This needs to be said.

I won't stand idly by while he aims his fangs for her throat.

"Do you know how easily I could take it all away from you, *boy*?" Leonid hisses. He snaps his fingers. "Like that. One word from me and your title, your position, everything you wrongly think is *yours*—gone."

"Ah, we've come to my favorite portion of the night: the inevitable dance where you put me in my place." I lean forward. "You know what, Father? I'm tired of all these games. Go ahead and fucking do it already."

Leonid's eyes go wide.

I bare my teeth in a smile. "You want to kick me off the cliff and hand the reins over to Ilya? Fine. Go right ahead. See how that works out for you. I'll just retire to my 'backwater hideout' and enjoy the implosion from the sidelines."

He freezes in his chair, all color draining from his face. For the first time in my life, I've left him speechless. Because I finally called his bluff.

"This meeting is over." His voice comes out rough, unsteady. "Get out of my sight and get to work proving to me that you're worthy of my legacy."

As I push away from the table, his eyes track me—a predator suddenly realizing his teeth aren't as sharp as he thought. The sight should fill me with victory, but I'm not naive enough to think I've won.

A cornered man is a desperate one.

And Leonid has walls closing in on all sides.

I stride out into London's perpetual gloom, already pulling out my phone to change my travel arrangements. I'd planned to stay another five days, work through the mountain of meetings Myles arranged.

Fuck that.

All I can think about is Nova. The gentle curve of her belly. The way her eyes light up when she sees me. The quiet strength that makes her so different from the women in my father's world.

I need to breathe her in, hold her close, make sure she and my child are safe. Everything else—the empire, the rivals, my father's games—can wait.

It's time to go back to Scotland.

It's time to go back to the only thing that matters anymore.

It's time to go back to my family.

21

NOVA

There are things I won't do for love. I make a list of them while pulling weeds from between the castle's stones:

I won't forgive him for disappearing.

I won't let him touch me.

I won't think about the new scar I glimpsed in the grainy photos Myles reluctantly showed me last week.

I won't wonder who gave it to him.

I won't imagine him bleeding.

The problem is, my body's a traitor. It's been another three weeks of solitude, and my hormones are staging a coup. Every night I wake up aching, sheets twisted around my legs, his name hot on my lips.

"Nova." Myles's shadow falls across the garden bed. "He's here."

I focus on the pea vine tangled in my fingers. If I look up, he'll see the hope warring with fury in my eyes. "Good for him."

"Aren't you coming inside?"

"I'm busy." The lie sits between us like the growing curve of my belly—obvious and impossible to ignore. "I'll be in when I'm done."

Myles sighs. In the weeks since Samuil disappeared, he's watched me cycle through rage and despair with the patience of someone who defuses bombs for a living. Which, come to think of it, he probably does.

I wait until his footsteps fade before slumping into the grass. Meg, one of the border collie pups, nudges my thigh with her wet nose. Unlike most of the castle's inhabitants, she doesn't judge me for talking to dogs more than people.

"Your new master's an asshole," I inform her, scratching behind her ears. "A gorgeous, terrifying asshole who thinks he can vanish for weeks without a word and then just—"

"Just what?"

The voice slides down my spine like steel against stone. I don't need to look up to know he's there—my body recognizes Samuil Litvinov's presence like it recognizes its own heartbeat.

Vital. Necessary. Completely beyond my control.

When I finally lift my head, the sight of him steals my breath. His hair is longer than usual, curling at his nape. A fresh scar traces his right cheekbone like a signature. He's traded his usual designer armor for dark jeans and a black henley that clings to his shoulders, but he still radiates lethal grace. Power wrapped in casual menace.

"Just waltz back in like nothing happened?" I turn back to my plants. "Actually, that's exactly what I expected."

He moves closer, and the dogs swarm him like he's got bacon in his pockets. Traitors, every one of them. "I see you've replaced me."

I follow his gaze to the scarecrow Mr. Morris helped me build last week. "He's better company. Doesn't disappear without warning. Doesn't come back looking like he's been in a knife fight. Doesn't lie about where he's been."

"Jealousy doesn't suit me, *zaychik*." His shadow falls across my hands. "Stand up."

"That's not how this works anymore. You don't get to order me around just because—"

His fingers curl around my chin, tilting my face up. "Please."

That single word—soft and rough and nothing like the commands he usually issues—undoes me. I let him pull me to my feet, but I keep my hands fisted at my sides. I won't touch him. I won't.

I won't look at him, either. I keep my eyes on the garden, on the life I've managed to create in this gilded cage.

Seeds I've planted have sprouted.

Flowers I've tended have bloomed.

Proof that some things can grow even in the shadows of monsters.

"Are you ever going to look at me properly?"

I want to stomp my foot and scream no. But again, that rough, tender hand of his cups my face and guides it up toward his.

His eyes crinkle as he smiles. The puppies are a mosh pit of cuteness at his feet, but he steps over them and brushes the back of his hand along my cheek. "You look beautiful."

"Absence really must make the heart fonder," I mumble under my breath. "I'm covered in sweat and dirt and dog hair."

"I've always liked you dirty."

I cringe away from his hand. It's too tempting to nuzzle into his touch. "You think you can just waltz back here and pick up where we left off?"

He exhales a plume of warm, minty fragrance. "I know you well enough to know you'd never make it that easy on me."

"Good. Then you must also know you'll be sleeping in your own bedroom tonight."

I try to twist around, to let that be the parting kill shot, but I should've known it would never be that easy. Before I can get far, he grabs my elbow and spins me back to face him. His grip is vise-like, but his smile is still soft and amused.

"You can be mad at me, *krasavitsa*. You can hit and scratch and even throw another vase—give me a scar to match the first. But at the end of the day, make no mistake—" He drops his chin and his voice, sending a bolt of awareness lancing directly between my legs. "—you'll be in bed next to me."

Then he sighs and his grasp loosens. Something like melancholy leaches into his voice, though I don't really think he's capable of emotions like that. "I need your warmth and your touch, Nova. I've been away from it for too long."

I plant my fists on my hips. "Whose fault is that?"

Something sad flickers in his silver eyes. "That's a complicated answer. But I wouldn't have left if it wasn't necessary."

That's the thing, though: No matter what, there will always be something that takes him away. There will always be some big, important cause that I'm forced to share Samuil with. He'll leave me again and again and there will always be reasons; there will always be complicated answers to my questions.

I just don't think I'll ever like them.

"Did the dogs keep you company?" He bends down to scratch Finbarr behind the ears as the pup nibbles on his shoelace.

Yes. I love them. I love you. Never leave us again.

"The dogs—" I meet his gaze. "—were a manipulation."

He grins. "But did it work?"

~

"Scotland looks good on you, *krasavitsa*."

I watch his reflection in the patinated mirror as he unbuttons his shirt slowly. Each revealed inch of skin tells a story—scars from battles I'll never know about, victories carved in flesh and bone. Watching him undress is like watching a transformation. The beast shedding the businessman's skin, finally showing his teeth.

"Gardening, shepherding puppies." His voice drops to that dangerous octave that makes my toes curl and my common sense go haywire. "You're going native. Next thing I know, you'll be out birthing sheep with Morris and speaking Gaelic."

"He's better company than my other options." I reach for my sexiest negligee—a scrap of black silk that cost more than I used to make in three months of walking rich bitches' dogs. If he's going to walk around flaunting his washboard abs, I'm certainly not going to drown in my flannel pajama set.

"At least the sheep don't disappear for weeks without a word."

His eyes track my movements as I slip the silk over my skin, and something fierce and feral unfurls in my chest at his sharp intake of breath.

I love seeing that reaction in him, that confirmation that he's actually fucking human after all. That I can still reach him.

Even kings can bleed if you know where to cut.

"The sheep also can't make you scream my name in three languages."

... Well, fuck.

Fuck, because that voice—that dark promise of pleasure twined with pain, of passion tangled with possession—is what started this whole beautiful disaster. It's the voice that whispered filthy promises in my ear that first night in my apartment, when we were both covered in lake water and dog slobber and couldn't keep our hands off each other. The same voice that murmured Russian lullabies against my stomach last month when he thought I was sleeping.

That voice is my undoing.

"Bold of you to assume I'll give you permission to come anywhere close enough to do that," I snap back. I try to inject venom into the words, but they come out breathier than intended. Because he's moving now. Closer. Closer.

I feel like one of Mr. Morris's lambs, locking eyes with a wolf on the other side of the fence.

"'Permission' has nothing to do with it." He's behind me in an instant, one hand splayed possessively over the slight swell of my stomach where his heir grows, the other tracing the edge of my negligee like he's mapping territory he already owns. "This is about truth. About how your body responds to mine. About how you've been wet since the moment you heard my voice in the garden."

His fingers drift lower, and I hate that he's right. Hate that three weeks of silence and anger dissolve like sugar on my tongue the moment he touches me. Hate that my body arches into his hand whether I like it or not.

"I'm still mad at you," I gasp as his teeth graze my neck, his fingers finding exactly where I'm aching for him.

"Good." He spins me around, and the look in his eyes makes my knees weak. Hunger and possession and something deeper, something that looks dangerously like devotion. "Be mad. Be fucking furious. But be mine."

He kisses me like a man starving, like he's been dying in the desert and I'm the first drop of rain. His tongue slides against mine, and I taste his desperation, his need, his silent apology for leaving. For always leaving.

"I hate you," I breathe against his mouth, even as my fingers dig into his shoulders, marking him like he's marked me.

"No, you don't." He lifts me like I weigh nothing, pressing me against the cold stone wall. The contrast of temperatures—his burning skin, the frigid stone—sends shivers down my spine. "You hate that you love me. There's a difference."

And damn him straight to hell, because he's right about that, too.

His hand slides up my thigh, pushing silk aside like it's tissue paper. "Tell me to stop," he murmurs, but his fingers are already moving higher and higher. "Tell me you don't want this—don't want me—and I'll walk away."

That's the biggest lie he's ever told me. We both know he'd sooner burn down all of Scotland than let me go.

Just like we both know I'd never let him.

"Fuck you, Samuil," I moan as his fingers curl inside me, my nails leaving crescents in his shoulders that I hope scar.

His laugh rumbles against my throat, dark and satisfied. "That's the plan, *krasavitsa*. That's always been the plan."

22

NOVA

He's everywhere. My personal demon, marking his territory and chasing away the shadows that have haunted me these past three weeks. Every touch reignites nerve endings I thought had gone dormant in his absence. His hands trace my curves with excruciating tenderness.

Hours pass in a haze of pleasure. Outside our turret room's soaring windows, the Scottish night unfolds like black velvet studded with pinwheeling stars.

Inside, we're cocooned in the aftermath of what we've done to each other. My muscles are liquid, my skin sheened with sweat, and the only coherent thought in my head is *finally*.

Finally, he's back.

Finally, he's mine again.

"You're thinking too loud," Sam murmurs against my hair.

I trace the scar on his chest, memorizing its shape, its texture. "I'm thinking about how much I hate missing you."

"Then stop missing me." His thumb draws lazy circles on my stomach. "I'm right here."

"For how long, though?"

Instead of answering, he pulls me closer, tucking me into the hollow of his throat where I can breathe in the familiar scent of his cologne.

"Long enough to make up for lost time." His voice vibrates against my lips. "Long enough to remind you why you fell for me in the first place."

"Bold of you to assume I've fallen for you at all."

He chuckles. "Your body just spent the last hour proving otherwise, *zaychik*."

I bite his collarbone in retaliation, but we both know he's right. No matter how much I fight it, no matter how many times he leaves, I'll always want him back.

That's the problem with loving monsters: Once you let them in, they nest in your heart and refuse to leave.

His scar glints in the moonlight as I trace it once again, gathering courage like breadcrumbs. "Can I ask you a question?"

He pauses, then exhales. "You can ask."

"What scares you more—Ilya finding us, or becoming a father?"

Sam's hand stills on my belly. For a heartbeat, I think I've pushed too far, crossed one of his invisible lines. But then he shifts, propping himself on an elbow to study my face.

"Both keep me awake at night." His jaw works, and I recognize his struggle to find words that aren't wrapped in thorns. "I never wanted children before. Never saw the point of bringing innocents into this life."

"And now?"

"Now, I dream about our child. About protecting you both." He splays his fingers wider across my stomach. "About being nothing like my father."

"You won't be."

"You can't know that."

"I can. I do." I cover his hand with mine. "You show it every time you touch me. Every time you look at me like I matter more than revenge."

His eyes darken. "You do matter more. That's what terrifies me." He presses his lips to my temple, breath warm against my skin. "My father taught me that love makes you weak. Makes you vulnerable. But when I think about our baby—about you carrying my child—I've never felt stronger."

Something breaks loose in my chest, a shard of ice I didn't know I was carrying. "So you're not disappointed? That it happened so fast?"

"*Krasavitsa.*" He cups my face, thumb brushing my lower lip. "You've given me something I never dared to want. How could I be disappointed?"

I lean into his touch, memorizing this rare moment of total honesty between us. Tomorrow, he might rebuild his walls, but tonight—tonight, he's mine.

Or at least, he was. Then his phone vibrates on the nightstand and a few of those bricks go right back in place between us.

"Your father?" I ask, already knowing the answer from the way his jaw tightens.

"He's requesting my presence in London. Again." Sam reaches for the phone but doesn't check the message. Instead, he rubs the screen's edge with his thumb, lost in thought.

"Are you going to listen?"

"Fuck no. I saw enough of him last week."

I study the harsh lines of his profile in the moonlight. "You said he seemed… different."

"Weaker," he agrees. "He's never backed down before. Not from anything."

"Maybe he's finally realizing what he could lose."

Sam's laugh is nearly lifeless. "He isn't capable of that. If he's showing weakness, it's because he wants me to lower my guard."

"Or maybe he's sick." The thought springs unbidden to my lips. "You said he looked frail."

"The great Leonid? Mortal?" Sam's fingers find my hair, twisting a strand around his knuckle. "That would require him to be human first."

"Everyone's human, Sam. Even mob bosses."

His eyes meet mine, and for a moment, I glimpse the little boy who grew up desperately seeking his father's approval. "Not him. Trust me, *zaychik*. If death comes for my father, he'll negotiate his way out of that, too."

"You make him seem like a god."

"I used to think he was," Sam admits. "You should have seen him back then." A ghost of a smile plays at the corner of his mouth. "Six and a half feet of tyranny. He'd stride into a room and everyone would stop breathing."

"Like father, like son?"

"In some ways, perhaps." His jaw tightens. "Leonid was... magnetic. He'd take Ilya and me hunting in Siberia, tracking bears through snow so deep it swallowed our legs. Or we'd spend weekends on Lake Michigan, learning to sail his racing yacht. He made everything look effortless."

The pride in Sam's voice carries an edge of old pain. "You wanted to be just like him," I guess.

He nods somberly. "Every boy does. Even when their father pits them against their brother in endless competitions." His fingers find my belly again, protective. "I lived for the moments he'd look at me with approval. The times he'd say, '*Molodets*' after I scored a goal or landed a marlin. For years, I thought if I could just be stronger, faster, smarter than Ilya, he'd—"

Sam cuts himself off, throat working.

I press my palm to his chest, feeling his heart thunder beneath my touch. "Our child will never have to compete for your love," I whisper fiercely.

His eyes meet mine, dark with promise. "Never."

Sam's fingertips ghost across my stomach in feather-light patterns, as if he's trying to communicate with our child through touch alone. The tenderness in his caress makes my throat tight.

"I used to think it was normal." His voice drops low, intimate. "What he did to us. How he raised us."

"And now?"

"Now, I look at you carrying our child and I want..." He shifts, pressing his forehead to my belly. "I want lazy Sunday mornings teaching them to make blini. I want to watch them draw terrible pictures that we'll hang on the fridge. I want to read them stories about brave little rabbits who outsmart wolves."

My heart cracks open at the image. This fierce, dangerous man imagining such gentle moments.

"The day I found out about you being pregnant, I realized something." His lips brush my skin. "A good father would have taught us that winning isn't everything. That sometimes, the best victories come from working together, not tearing each other apart."

I cup his jaw, tilting his face up to mine. "You already know more about being a good father than Leonid ever did."

His eyes darken with emotion. "Because of you. You make me want to be worthy of this." His palm spreads wide over our growing child. "Of both of you."

My fingers pass over the stark lines of Sam's tattoos—Cyrillic letters that mark his skin like prayers or curses. "The thing about being born into a family like yours or mine?" I press my lips to each letter. "It's like being assigned a role in a play we never auditioned for."

Sam's chest rises beneath my touch. "Some roles are impossible to escape."

"But we can rewrite the script." I lift my head, meeting his gaze in the moonlight. "You're not Leonid's puppet anymore. You're not his soldier or his heir or his weapon against Ilya." My palm finds his heartbeat. "You're going to be a father. And you get to decide what kind of father you'll be."

His arm curls around my neck, drawing me closer until our breaths mingle. "What if this child grows up hating me the way I hate him?"

"They won't." I pour every ounce of conviction into my voice. "Because you know exactly how it feels to be unloved. To be a disappointment." My fingers find his jaw. "You can give our baby what you always wanted: unconditional love. Real pride. The freedom to be imperfect."

Sam's entire body goes still beneath me. For a moment, he's utterly silent. Then his arms lock around me, crushing me to his chest as if he could absorb my certainty through skin alone.

"*Zaychik*." His voice breaks on the endearment. "How do you see straight through my armor?"

"Because I recognize the cracks." I press my lips to his throat. "They match mine."

23

NOVA

"This secure line won't last forever," Hope's voice crackles through my phone. "Give me something juicy before Myles cuts us off again."

I trace a finger through the condensation on the glass. "Fifteen extra minutes today."

"What did that cost you?"

"My soul. Or yours. I didn't read the fine print."

Hope's laugh comes through staticky but genuine. "You pimping me out to your jailkeeper?"

"More like listening to an hour-long speech about his many dateable attributes." I push away from the window, bare feet silent on thick Persian carpets as I wander through the library stacks. "Did you know Myles can crack walnuts with his—"

"Don't finish that sentence." Another laugh, but it fades quickly. "How are you really doing, Nova?"

Good question. Last night's intimacy feels like a dream now. Sam spent hours whispering promises against my skin, sharing fears about fatherhood and his determination to be better than Leonid.

But morning brought reality crashing back—more meetings, more secrets, more walls between us. The tenderness in his eyes when he touched my growing belly has been replaced by that familiar arctic steel.

Sometimes, I think the only version of him I get to keep is the one that exists in darkness, when his guard drops and his masks slip away. Daylight steals him from me, no matter how hard I try to cling on.

"I'm fine."

"Bullshit."

"I am, really," I insist. "I have Samuil back." I leave out that having him here but unreachable might be worse than when he was gone. At least then I could blame the distance.

"Do you wanna talk about it, babe?"

The lump in my throat feels like I swallowed one of Finbarr's tennis balls. "No. I want to talk about you. Let me live vicariously through whatever is going on in your life."

"Would you like to experience misery and woe?" she offers with false chipperness. Paper crinkles—probably her stress-eating another candy bar. "'Cause that's all I've got."

I've spent so many weeks missing Hope that I almost forgot she's dealing with her own drama back home. Matter of fact, I almost forgot there is a "home" outside of this property. The thought of Chicago—Lakefront Trail, honking cabs, the L rumbling overhead and the smell of deep-dish pizza wafting from every other storefront—seems like another lifetime.

I wince as I tuck my cold toes up under me. "Are the trolls still harassing you?"

"Like it's their fucking job." The defeat in her voice makes my hands clench. "Every time I make a new post or a client leaves a good review, it's immediately bitch-slapped with a dozen nasty comments."

"Has Jerry been able to do anything?" I ask as I once again go back to pacing. Nothing lasts these days—I pace, I sit, I sleep, I don't sleep.

Nothing feels comfortable. Nothing feels right.

"Jerry's a freelance IT guy, not a miracle worker," says Hope. "The most he's been able to do is shut down the comments and review section of our website."

If I had regular access to the internet, I'd take up my sword as keyboard warrior and defend her. It would feel good to be useful. Here, I'm raising puppies and looking after sheep from time to time, watching the seasons change through leaded glass windows—but no one truly needs me. If I suddenly vanished, someone else would fill my role without blinking.

But no one else can be Hope's best friend.

"Is it Katerina?" I guess.

"Who else? But her house is dark. Word is she left Chicago, but her vindictive ass clearly found WiFi wherever she landed."

A gust of wind rattles the windowpanes, making me jump.

Outside, dark clouds gather over the loch, promising another storm.

I shoot to my feet, struck by sudden inspiration. "WiFi!"

Hope chuckles. "I see you're familiar with the concept."

"No, I'm saying *WiFi,* Hope. WiFi! What if that's exactly what we need?"

"Your crazy idea voice makes me nervous, NoNo."

I stride over the cold stone floor from the door to the window and back again, adrenaline thrumming through my veins. Lightning flashes like the world wants to match my energy. "Remember that client you had… What was it, like, a year ago? The one who was starting a cosmetics company?"

"Sure," says Hope, "I remember her. I also remember the rash all of her sample products gave me. My skin looked like I'd tried to exfoliate with poison ivy."

"You never should've accepted tips in the form of untested products," I tease. "But she was looking for women to endorse her brand, right? Models, actresses, popular influencers?"

"Count me out. My skin is traumatized."

"I'm not talking about you, dummy."

I wait, letting it sink in. Hope sucks in her breath. "I see where you're going with this, Nova, but—"

"Improv rules," I interrupt, spinning away from the window. The motion makes my thick sweater—one of Samuil's I'd stolen from his closet—swirl around my thighs. "I want to hear '*Yes, Nova. Good idea, Nova. And…*'"

"*And* how are we gonna use that to get to Katerina?"

"We create a fake beauty brand and say we're looking for ambassadors. Stroke her ego. Get her to respond." My reflection grins back at me from the fireplace mirror, feral and bright-eyed. "She knows how to hide from Samuil's men. But she won't be able to resist being told how gorgeous and influential she is."

Hope sighs, the sound coming out somewhere between a groan and laugh. "Your plan is to lure her in with… makeup? That is the most basic bitch bait I've ever heard of."

"Picture it—she gets a letter from an up-and-coming cosmetics agency." I put on a fake and incredibly cringy French accent. "'*Dear Miss Alekseeva, we would be delighted and greatly honored if you would consider being the spokesperson and face of our cosmetics brand. Your natural beauty, charisma, and charm are exactly what we need to push our company into the world of beauty.*'"

Hope guffaws, her laugh echoing through the phone's speaker. "No one would say that after spending a single minute with her."

"That's exactly the point." I shiver in a sudden draft as cold wind batters the castle. "We'll hit her where it counts: her ego."

Hope still sounds skeptical as she taps her nails against her desk. "Do you really think a woman who left Chicago in order to protect herself from the men hunting her is going to be interested in being the face of a cosmetics brand?"

"No, probably not," I confess. "But I'm hoping her ego will compel her to, at the very least, reply to our email. Maybe then we can track the IP address."

Hope whistles. "I have to admit, you're a little scary, Nova. Like a creepy mastermind."

"Is that a yes?"

"Even better: it's a *yes, and*," she says. "As in, *yes*, I'll do it, *and* you have to create the fake email account. I get enough spam in my normal inbox as it is."

Smiling widely, I turn back to the room just as the sun breaks through the clouds, sending rays of light dancing across the polished floor. The timing feels like an omen. The rain softens to a gentle patter, and somewhere in the distance, a rainbow arches over the hills.

"A little spam will be worth it to catch the bitch."

~

An hour later, Myles is still a no-show, which means I'm still on the phone with Hope. We've spent the last forty minutes cackling about our email to Katerina.

"I hope she reads this again one day—if they allow email in hell, that is—and realizes how many times you actually insulted her," Hope snorts. "Like, this line: '*You're as brilliant as you are beautiful, which makes you the perfect candidate for our campaign.*' God, it's truly inspired."

"Why, thank you. You're too kind." I bow despite the fact that Hope can't actually see me. "Do you think she'll reply?"

"Honestly, I don't even care. It was a fun afternoon. I miss doing stupid shit with you."

"But what if it's not just stupid shit? What if this works?" I sit on the couch, hugging a pillow to my chest. "What if she actually responds?"

"Then Jerry traces the IP address and we hand it over to your baby daddy's team of super-spies." Hope pauses. "Speaking of which, how are we going to explain this if it does work?"

My stomach clenches. "We're not. Samuil can't know."

"Nova..."

"He'd lock me in this tower and throw away the key if he knew I was trying to track down Katerina."

"Maybe he should." Hope's voice turns serious. "This isn't some mean girl from high school we're dealing with. She's actually dangerous."

"So am I." The words come out fiercer than I intended. "I'm tired of being helpless. Of watching the people I love get hurt while I sit here playing princess in a castle."

"You're pregnant."

"I'm not made of glass."

Hope sighs. "No, you're made of pure stubborn spite. Just... promise me you'll be careful? I need my best friend in one piece."

I'm about to respond when, suddenly, a message notification pops up on my laptop screen. My heart stops.

"Holy shit," I breathe.

"What? What is it?"

"She replied."

24

SAMUIL

My rage points me to her like a compass with its needle fixed on hell.

I storm into the barn, that fury burning through my veins. Nova sits on a hay bale by the doors, surrounded by puppies, her hair glowing in the afternoon light. The sight of her—pregnant, peaceful, perfect—threatens to douse my anger.

But the report in my pocket feels like it's on fire, reminding me why I'm here.

This betrayal changes everything.

"Nova."

She turns, and that fucking smile stays on her face despite the murder in mine. "I didn't think I'd get to see you until this evening. Want to take the puppies for a walk around the loch with me?"

Yes. God yes. I want nothing more than to pretend everything's fine, to walk with her and watch her laugh at the puppies' antics. To feel our child move under my palm when I touch her belly. To forget for one moment that my entire world is a house of cards built on shifting sand.

But that's not who I am. Not what I was raised to be.

I shake my head, keeping my voice glacier-cold. "No. Where's Myles?"

Her smile falters. She rises slowly to her feet, ignoring the puppies yapping at her heels. "I don't know. Is everything alright?"

"Not even close."

"Sam...?" Her voice is soft, questioning. It takes everything I have to look away from the concern in her eyes. "What's going on?"

"You'll find out later. After we talk to Myles."

She doesn't question me again as she follows me out of the barn. The puppies try to come with us, but she pushes them into the pen that Mr. Morris made for them and then rushes out after me. She's out of breath as she tries to keep up.

But I don't stop. Or slow down. I can't. I take long strides like I might be able to outrun this. Like, if I move quickly enough, I won't have to deal with it.

We round the corner of the castle, the turrets and gargoyles looming over us like silent judges. And there's Myles, kneeling in the vegetable garden like he doesn't have blood on his hands. Like he hasn't betrayed everything we built together.

The smile on his face dies just like Nova's did.

"What's going on?"

"Follow me," I command. "Both of you."

They fall in behind me as I lead us through the castle's winding corridors to the library. No one speaks, but I can feel them exchanging glances, communicating silently like they've been doing for weeks now. Planning. Plotting. Betraying.

The library doors slam behind us with a boom that echoes off the shelves. Dust motes dance in the sunbeams streaming through the high windows, shining almost like spotlights.

Exactly like spotlights, actually. Too fucking fitting.

I gesture for them to sit.

Nova does. Myles doesn't.

That's fine. It just means that, if I do decide to punch him in the end, he'll have farther to fall.

I pull out the report that has been burning a hole in my pocket since a few minutes before I set out in search of them. The pages make a satisfying crack as they connect with Myles's chest before fluttering to the floor at his feet.

He bends to retrieve them, and I watch his face as he reads. Watch the color drain from his cheeks as reality sinks in.

Nova shifts in her chair, anxiety rolling off her in waves. "What the hell is going on?" Her eyes dart between us like a trapped animal. "Samuil, why are you treating us like we've done something wrong?"

My eyes land on hers. "Haven't you?"

"No, I haven't." Her chin lifts with that stubborn defiance I usually find endearing. Today it just feeds my rage. She turns to Myles, her expression softening. “Myles? What does it say? What’s the letter about?”

Myles’s hand drops, but he’s still gripping the papers tightly, his knuckles white. He answers Nova, but he’s looking at me.

“It’s not a letter,” he says hoarsely. “It’s a report.”

“A report on what?”

“A surveillance report.” His skin is turning a pale shade I’ve never seen before. “One that details new targets in Chicago.”

Nova’s forehead wrinkles with confused lines.

Any other day, I’d smooth them out myself. Kill whoever put them there.

But not today. Today, they just remind me how naive she still is about my world.

I give Myles a curt nod. “Go on, then. Tell her exactly what it means. Tell her what the two of you have done.”

He swallows, his Adam’s apple bobbing up and down. “There have been eighty alerts for Hope Levy in the last twelve hours. And four intersections between one of Hope’s employees, Jeremiah ‘Jerry’ Cuthbert, and a known Andropov enforcer.” He takes a labored pause. “The report also shows several calls made to Chicago that originate from… this castle.”

I watch Nova carefully. I know her face as well as my own, and I see the exact instance she understands what it means.

I also see the exact instance when she decides she doesn’t care.

“You left me no choice, Sam.”

If I wasn't rigid with anger, my jaw would drop. Instead, I watch as she shifts in front of Myles, like she's trying to shield him from me.

"I was drowning in loneliness in this castle, Samuil. I needed someone to talk to, and Myles took pity on me. He let me speak to—"

"'Pity'?" I growl, causing her lips to snap shut. "Is that what you think Myles did? Do you think he offered you a gift?"

Myles steps out from behind Nova. "Brother—"

"Explain to her what this means!" My roar echoes off the vaulted ceiling, sending centuries of dust scattering.

Myles's jaw clenches as Nova turns to face him.

"I know what it means," she insists, that stubborn light still burning in her eyes. "Because of what Hope and I did, it means that you can track down Katerina Alekseeva now. You're welcome."

I shake my head, but it's Myles who speaks first. Every word drips with a shame he deserves.

"Nova… you don't understand. Because I allowed you contact with Hope, it exposed you to the Andropovs. But it's not just you. It also—" He drags his free hand along the nape of his neck, tugging on the hair hard enough to yank it out. "Hope and her employee are in danger now, too. The Andropovs will be tracking them. I put their lives at risk."

All at once, the defiance drains out of her. Her shoulders droop, and her eyes go wide with new fear.

"Wait. Hold on. So you're saying… Wh-what does this mean?"

This time, I don't afford Myles the opportunity to speak. "It means that Jeremiah Cuthbert will have to leave Chicago or forfeit his life. He'll have to change his name and live in hiding for as long as it takes the Andropovs to forget about his existence. And Hope..."

Nova flinches as though I'm throwing daggers, not words. I don't stop. Because this shit never stops. Because it keeps coming, and I need her to realize that.

"Hope," I continue, "will have to do the same. All your meddling and detective work has made your best friend a target. Not just to Katerina, but to one of the most dangerous Bratvas in the world."

The last vestiges of color have completely vanished from Nova's face. She looks like she might collapse, one hand pressed against her belly as if to shield our child from the harsh reality of my world.

"No..." she whispers. "I... I thought that if we just found her, then—" She breaks off, her eyes lifting towards me without ever quite meeting mine. "I didn't think..."

"That's right," I snap. "You didn't think."

Then I turn to Myles. The weight of a decade of friendship hangs between us. Every mission, every close call, every victory we've shared—it all comes down to this moment.

I'm not sure if I'm grateful that he's silent and expectant, waiting for me to land the final blow. Or if I'd rather him put up a fight.

He stands there silently, waiting for judgment. Part of me wishes he'd fight back. Make this easier by giving me a reason to hate him.

My voice comes out low and deadly. "Myles Hagerty."

He risked the Bratva. Innocent civilians. And Nova...

He put Nova in danger.

That is a mistake I cannot overlook.

That is a mistake I cannot forgive.

"Pack your shit and get the fuck out."

25

NOVA

What kind of colossal ass—

What kind of power-hungry maniac—

What kind of supposed *friend* would do something like this?

My hands tremble as I pace the tower bedroom for the hundredth time, my footsteps echoing off stone walls that have witnessed centuries of drama but surely never anything this absurd. The portraits of stern-faced Scottish lords seem to judge my life choices as I stomp past them. Even Finbarr has taken shelter under the massive four-poster, only his judgmental green eyes visible as he watches me wear a path in the floor.

"This is insane," I tell him. She blinks slowly, unimpressed.

Myles is packing his bags right now, and it's all my fault. Myles, who snuck me phone calls to Hope and Grams when I was crying myself to sleep. Myles, who remembers my weird pregnancy cravings for haggis and strawberry jam. Myles, who's been Samuil's right hand through god knows how many riots and wars and business dealings that definitely aren't in any company prospectus.

Gone. Exiled. Never to darken Castle Moorbeath's door again.

Because he was kind to me.

"Goddammit!" I cry at the empty room. The syllables echo back, mocking me.

I wonder if Samuil can hear me. I wonder if, down in whatever dark, cobwebby corner he's found to hole up in, he's hard at work convincing himself he's done the right thing.

It would be fitting. I'm up here hating myself—he's down deep, so utterly certain in his own convictions.

I can't help but remember the look on Myles's face as he left the library. I remember the awful things Samuil said. And I remember that all of it was because of me.

My fault.

My fault.

My fault.

As I make the hundred and fiftieth circuit around my room, my jaw sets with determination.

I have to find Myles. I have to speak to him before he leaves.

I'm halfway out the door when I come to an abrupt stop, my hand gripping the centuries-old brass handle. The corridor stretches before me. More dark portraits of stern-faced Scots watch my indecision.

On second thought, it's not Myles I should be looking for.

It's the stubborn brute who is making him leave in the first place.

New target in mind, I charge through the castle, my nervous energy suddenly chomping at the bit now that it has a purpose and a nemesis. I need to track Samuil down before it's too late.

I'm so set on my mission that I almost bowl poor Mrs. Morris over on my way to the ground floor.

My hands shoot out to steady her frail shoulders as guilt floods me at the thought of adding yet another soul to my hit list today. The wool of her cardigan is rough against my palms. "Mrs. Morris, where's Samuil?"

She squints at me over the tops of her bifocals, nostrils flaring in alarm. "Are you alright, sweetness?"

"I'm fine. I just really need to speak to Samuil."

She pushes me in the direction of the kitchen like she'd love me to be someone else's problem. "You'll find him in there, lass. I just put a plate out for him."

I mutter a hurried thanks at her and follow the trail of savory scents through stone corridors, each step fueled by righteous, pregnancy-powered fury. The massive kitchen hearth blazes, and there he is: the lord of the castle himself, hunched over his dinner like a gargoyle made flesh.

The fire throws his shadow against the far wall, twenty feet high and monstrous. I have half a mind to shove his face in his shepherd's pie.

He straightens up when he sees me, broad shoulders squaring beneath his black sweater, eyebrows furrowing like he already knows what I'm here to say.

"Not now, Nova."

"Actually, I think now is the only time to have this conversation. If we don't, it'll be too late." I stride around the table to face him. "How can you sit here and eat while Myles is packing his bags?"

He doesn't look at me, focusing instead on mutilating his dinner with surgical precision. "I have the appetite of someone whose conscience is clear."

"What is that supposed to mean?" I wait for him to answer, but he just spears another piece of meat. "You think I should feel guilty?"

Guilt might be what drove me from my tower, but I'll be damned if I'm admitting that now. Not when I need every scrap of moral high ground I can get.

"Before you," he remarks, "Myles was never so easily persuaded."

"Glad to know that some men are capable of evolving."

He sighs tiredly. "It's been a long fucking day, *krasavitsa,* and I haven't eaten for most of it. Can you save the dramatics for the morning?"

Without thinking, I lunge forward and grab the fork right out of his hand.

He looks merely bored as he gazes back at me. "Planning on stabbing me with it?"

"I haven't ruled it out yet." The fork does feel good in my hand. Getting a reaction out of him other than apathy—say, by stabbing the tines into his giant shoulder—might feel even better.

Samuil gestures for me to continue. "Well, get on with it then. I'd like to get back to my dinner once you're done commandeering my cutlery."

He cares, insists a voice in my head. *Somewhere under this rock-hard veneer, the cold-hearted bastard actually fucking* cares.

"He's your best friend," I whisper, my voice breaking. My throat feels tight, like all the unsaid things are choking me. "Your right-hand man."

His jaw hardens, muscle ticking beneath his skin. "Which is exactly why he should have known better."

"He didn't think he was doing anything wrong."

"He knew exactly what the fuck he was doing. He knew he was crossing a line." He sets his plate on the stones of the hearth and rises to his feet. His silver eyes simmer dangerously. "That's why he kept it from me."

"I made him do it. If you have to punish someone, punish me."

He takes a step forward until the points of the fork I'm holding touch his chest like a trio of metal fingertips. "This is not a negotiation, Nova. You don't have a say in this."

I jab the fork upwards, in front of his face. "Look at this fork, Samuil. Look at the tines."

His face screws up into a frown. Clearly, he has no idea where I'm going with this.

That makes two of us.

"There are three tines." I touch them one by one. "You. Me. Myles." Samuil's frown recedes back into simple impatience, but I'll take it; it's better than the rage back in the library. Or the forced indifference. I might be able to work with this. "We're like these three tines. They're separated, but always connected at the root. Always moving in the same direction. Always."

He arches a dark eyebrow. "And which direction do you think the three of us are headed?"

"Towards cornering Katerina once and for all."

He sighs, like there are entire universes of darkness in his head that I can't begin to comprehend.

"You don't understand, Nova. This is so much bigger than just Katerina. She may be manipulative and psychotic, but she's just a cog in a much bigger wheel."

"I get that—"

"No." His words are sharp and curt. "You don't. Because if you understood, you wouldn't have wanted to contact Hope or your grandmother in the first place. If you'd truly grasped what was at stake, you would've known that contacting them meant risking their lives."

My chin starts to wobble.

Samuil steps towards me, his fingers curling over the sharp tips of the fork. If it hurts him, he shows no sign of it. "You see three parts of a whole connected by a solid base? Well, I see three separate, rigid entities—standing in isolation, never meeting."

My mouth is too dry to work well. I have to wet my lips before I can speak again. "You can't be that pessimistic."

"I'm not. I'm realistic. You should try it some time."

I relinquish the fork, abandoning it on the stone island with a sad, muted clatter. "This is stupid, Samuil. We should be working together. We should be in this together."

"We were," Samuil intones. "Then Myles betrayed me by going behind my back. He understands why he was exiled. So should you."

I shake my head. I know I'm pushing against a mountain, expecting it to bend. And still, I try. Because the guilt is eating me alive.

I have to fix things.

"Please don't do this, Samuil." Pride is a small price to pay if it means Myles can stay. "You can go to him, rehire him, ask him to stay... Please."

A log shifts in the fire, sending up a shower of crimson sparks. The kitchen suddenly feels too small, too confined, like the stone walls are closing in with the weight of Samuil's words. Outside, a gust of Highland wind howls against the castle walls. The world itself is warning me.

"Since you seem to enjoy cutlery metaphors so much, here's one for you." Samuil takes a step back and plucks the knife off his plate. "The Andropovs are a knife, Nova. Made of ruthless, relentless steel. Their only job is to sever and divide. If they set their sights on you, they will cut until they draw blood." It feels like he's looking right through me. "My orders were clear. Myles chose to ignore them, and by ignoring them, he put you directly in harm's way. If he can do that once, he can do it again—"

"He won't if you just—"

"I'm not taking that risk." He drops the knife back onto his plate. His chin is raised, his posture defiant, but his eyes are seeing things that I can't. "Myles knew the rules."

A bitter laugh rips from my throat. "'Rules?' Do you even hear yourself? Fuck rules! There are things that don't need 'rules,' and relationships are one of those things."

He simply shakes his head. Sad. Solemn. Unyielding. A mountain cloaked in rain. "Not in my world," he says. "This is how things are."

"But they don't have to stay that way." My voice is shaky, but I force the words out—my last chance to make things right. "Those are the rules your father wrote, but you can change them, Sam. You can be better than the men who came before you. You swore you would. Don't you remember?"

Something flickers in his expression—pain or rage or regret, I'll never know. Because he stands, adjusts his sweater, and walks out.

Leaving me alone in the massive kitchen with nothing but dying embers, cooling shepherd's pie, and the weight of everything we've lost.

I press my hand to my belly. "Your father," I whisper, "thinks he has to choose between love and survival." My voice breaks. "I just pray he figures out they're the same thing before it's too late."

The Highland wind howls its answer.

It sounds an awful lot like grief.

26

SAMUIL

Whoever said misery loves company doesn't know a fucking thing.

I've always preferred getting shitfaced on my own. There's no need for anyone to see me miserable and self-destructive. No need for anyone to judge as I sit in the library and pour myself another glass of scotch, all alone in this empty, godforsaken castle.

Every time I blink, I see Myles's face floating in front of me. Or Nova's.

I can't decide which one makes me feel worse.

Rather than blotting out the unwelcome thoughts, the first few drinks only made their faces clearer. It stabbed a hole in my cold façade and exposed the regret curdling just beneath the surface.

The next drink is supposed to drown it out altogether. My hands shake as I pour. Surely this'll do it. This'll be the one that fixes me.

But when I drain the last drops and still feel every bit as shitty as when I started, I abandon my glass and grip the crystal decanter by the throat.

If Leonid could see me now, he'd laugh in my face. He'd call me a sorry excuse for a *pakhan*. A real leader doesn't hesitate between duty and friendship. A real leader doesn't lie awake wondering if protecting his empire is worth losing the only two people who've ever truly been loyal to him. How could I let something as insignificant as my conscience derail the justified sentence I passed down on Myles?

This is why you don't make business personal, Leonid would say. *This is why shit like "best friends" and "girlfriends" isn't meant for men like us. They don't fit.*

"Fuck off," I mutter back.

So much for being alone. Even my demons won't allow me a moment of drunken peace.

But if I'm hearing voices, I might as well talk back.

The creak of the door has me gripping the crystal decanter a little tighter. I twist around in my seat as the silhouette approaching grows clearer.

"I thought I told you to leave," I slur.

"Jesus, Sam." Myles's voice is pitched with concern. Ironic, considering it ought to be laced with anger. "How much have you had to drink?"

I take an extra-long chug. "S'not your fuckin' business anymore."

Myles steps into the dappled moonlight and all the phantoms haunting me race for cover. "We need to talk."

I scoff and turn away. "You were supposed to say that before you went behind my back." I attempt a careless laugh but, despite all that scotch I've downed, my throat is dry. It comes out like a hyena's cough instead.

"You're drunk."

"And you're a traitor," I growl. "Since we're stating the obvious, let's start there."

In his reflection in the dark window, Myles's chin drops. "I know. I did betray you, and… Fuck, Sam, you have no idea how sorry I am."

A crack of thunder peals across the sky beyond the window. The room is darker than it was a few minutes ago, the silver moonlight devoured by the clustering storm clouds. These damn things keep coming in, every evening without fail. Like nature intends to match my mood.

All this bullshit would be so much easier if Myles was defiant. His repentance makes everything more difficult.

I turn to face him. "It's too late."

Myles lifts his eyes to me. "It's not. Not if you don't want it to be. I've been with you from the very beginning, brother—"

"Stop calling me that." My grasp on the decanter tightens. I can practically sense the glass screaming beneath my fingertips.

"I *am* your brother, whether you like it or not," he insists. "A truer brother than Ilya ever was—and you know what that means in our world. Blood might be blood, but loyalty…" He lets the words hang unfinished. "You know that as much as I do. I would take a bullet for you, Samuil."

The scotch wants me to deny it. So do my demons. So does my father's voice in my head—the same voice that taught me betrayal and family were synonymous. The same voice that showed me videos of my mother choosing drugs over her son.

But goddammit, Myles is right.

I give him the smallest of nods. "I know."

"Then you know that I would do just as much for Nova and your baby. I would sacrifice myself for them in a heartbeat."

My jaw tightens. I have to look away from him. Leonid would curse me for being weak—but then, he's never had a friend he trusted. One who would jump in front of a bullet for him.

"You say that," I snarl, "but you're the one who put her in a situation that might make your sacrifice necessary. Every call she made, every connection reopened—it's like painting a target on her back. On my child's back. Ilya's watching. He's always fucking watching."

"I did, and I know," Myles says. "But it wasn't intentional, Sam. I was stupid and shortsighted and careless—but I wasn't malicious."

"This doesn't change anything. You have to go."

"I made a mistake—"

"A mistake that has put my family in danger!" The word "family" catches in my throat—so foreign until Nova, until our child.

Now, it's everything.

Family. My bellow echoes against the stone walls. Even the thunder seems to go quiet at the sound of it, as if the storm itself recognizes the weight of what I could lose.

Neither of us says anything. The storm churns outside, the sky blacker than black.

"I thought I was part of your family," Myles says softly, just as the rain starts to fall.

"You are— You were," I correct. The alcohol is making me sluggish, slow, stupid.

"Doesn't that entitle me to a second chance?" Myles takes a tentative step forward. "I'll beg you if that's what it takes, brother. This is the only life I've ever known. My place is with you, by your side. I didn't want to plead my case earlier in front of Nova. I didn't want to question your decision in front of her. But now… I can't leave without—"

"If you don't leave willingly," I interrupt, "I will drag you out myself."

His fist tightens by his side. "You're a stubborn ass, Samuil Litvinov."

"No, I'm your *pakhan*."

"Not anymore." There's steel in Myles's tone that matches mine now. "That's your father talking—the same man who taught you power matters more than people. The same lesson you swore you'd never pass on to your own child." He pauses for breath, chest rising and falling in steady rhythm. "Do you want to know why I did it?"

Getting to my feet, I wave the decanter in his face like it's a weapon. "I don't fucking care why you did it."

"Well, you're going to listen anyway, you drunk son of a bitch. It's because you left Nova here like she was a damn dog locked in a crate. You gave her nothing to rely on, no one to turn to. She was lonely. She fucking missed you. I tried to help, believe me." He shakes his head in bitter frustration. "Hell, that fucking boat sitting on the lake right now is floating because *I* fucking repaired it. But she didn't want me. She wanted *you*."

I hoped the scotch would make seeing reason a little more difficult. Apparently not, because every one of Myles's words is another cold bucket of water in my face.

More unwanted images flash through my mind: Nova alone in our bed, Nova walking the grounds with no one to talk to, Nova staring at her phone like it's a lifeline I've cut.

The scotch burns in my gut. It no longer numbs—it nauseates.

"Get out of my sight, man." I shudder at the sight of the library shelves looming over me. They feel like prison bars.

I need out of this fucking place.

I shove to my feet and stride for the door. But Myles refuses to move out of the way. Instead, he blocks my path, raising his voice over the crash of rain lashing against the window in violent sheets.

"You want me to go?" Myles asks. "I will. But first, you'll listen. Nova doesn't need a *pakhan*—she needs a fucking partner. She needs someone she can talk to. And since I couldn't make you do the decent thing, yeah, I let her have some contact with her grandmother and her best friend. It was the right choice. It was the humane choice."

I slam the decanter down. The crystal doesn't shatter, but something inside me does. The careful walls I've built, the control I've maintained—it splinters like the sound I wanted to hear.

"Enough."

"No, not enough!" Myles raises his voice for the first time in as long as I can remember. "Not even fucking close to enough! You say you want to be better than your father. You say you want to be different from him. But instead of learning from his mistakes, you're intent on repeating them."

My mouth hangs open, slack and stupid. I see myself at twelve, watching another security video of my mother's betrayal, my father's voice behind me. *This is why we can't trust anyone, son.*

"You fucking dare—"

"Why not?" Myles shrugs carelessly despite the fire blazing in his hooded eyes. "What have I got left to lose?"

"Your tongue, for one," I warn. "Because I'm about to cut it out myself."

He just shrugs again. "Won't stop anything I've said from being true. You know why I'm telling you all this? Because I'm your best friend. Because I know you well enough, and I care enough, to tell you the truth. No one else does. No one else will. And if you keep pushing away everyone who actually gives a damn about you, you'll end up exactly where your father did—powerful, feared, and completely fucking alone."

Damn him. Damn him to hell.

I knock Myles aside with a brutal shoulder check, but instead of charging toward the door that opens into the guts of the castle, I opt for the French doors that lead outside. When I throw them open, the wind takes over and sends them clattering against the wall. Some of the glass panes shatter. I don't stop to deal with the mess.

I just keep moving. I have to move. If I stay still, the demons catch me—and if the demons catch me, the demons win.

So fuck it. One step after the next. Out of the office and out into the night, the brutal night, the raging, furious night, with wind like whips and rain like knives and lightning like God's disappointment.

But my demons keep coming. Funny how they take the shape of my best friend.

"Sam!" I hear Myles call out after me. "Samuil!"

I ignore him. I keep striding away from the light and deeper into the wild dark until Myles's voice and my father's voice and the thoughts swirling around in my head all fade away in the howling of the wind.

I don't want to think anymore.

I don't want to fucking *think* anymore.

I draw in a sharp breath as ice swallows my right leg. I look down to see my ankle disappearing into murky water that thrashes and moans like it wants to claim me.

I've walked myself right into the loch.

The surface of the water churns and sloshes, splashing farther and farther up toward my waist. I take one more step. Then another. The water is up to my hips. If I keep wading in, the currents will drag me under.

Then something stirs in the water up ahead.

I squint into the rain as a shape moves back and forth, a great, hulking beast, groaning softly, wailing louder and louder. Lightning cracks, bursting through the darkness, and I see it for what it is.

The boat.

Nova's boat.

The one that Myles repaired, because I wasn't around to help.

Without a second thought, I push onward into the lake until I reach it. I throw myself over the side and grab the only oar that I can find. The wind must have pitched the other one into the water.

It doesn't matter. I'm going nowhere in particular.

I have no destination, no goal in mind as I paddle. I just want to get away from here—from the taint of regret that's clawing deeper and deeper into the gaping void in my chest. Away from the reminders of my own failings. Away from all the disappointment I know is waiting for me back at the castle.

The wind continues to keen. Rain slashes against my back. Thunder and lightning rip across the sky, illuminating the loch with eerie, silver light.

Through it all, I keep paddling.

I make it to the middle of the loch before wind like a freight train pitches the boat sideways and tosses me off-balance.

The oar slips through my fingers, cracks in half, and disappears into the black water.

Just like that, I'm trapped. Stuck hundreds of yards from shore with no way out of this loch or this storm.

Nova would tell me to fight. Our child would beg me to fight. But the black water calls like absolution—an easy way to ensure I never become my father, never hurt them the way he hurt everyone who loved him.

I could dive in if I chose. That would fix it. That would save me.

But I don't deserve such a simple, painless ending.

Maybe *this* is what I deserve.

The cold. The rain. The loneliness.

So I close my eyes and take it.

27

NOVA

The storm wakes me up.

I should be used to it by now—it's been storming every day here for weeks. It's like clockwork: night falls and storms break. I ought to be snoozing right through them.

It's not like I was sleeping very deeply, anyway.

Finbarr and the rest of the puppies are huddled together in the nest of blankets I made for them in the corner, yapping with terror at every rumble of thunder. Samuil's side of the bed is still empty.

I fell asleep waiting for him to show up. I was sure he'd find his way to bed when it suited him. Very few things have kept him from it so far. Even when we fight, he doesn't stay away.

But it's late and there's no sign Samuil ever made it up.

Surely, he's not still in his office. What kind of work could he be getting done when it sounds like the castle is being ripped apart stone by stone? The only reason I'm not shaking in a heap with the puppies is because I keep telling myself this castle has stood here for hundreds of years—it'll last one more night.

Or maybe he gave up work and found some unfinished part of the castle to sit by himself and feel like an ass for how he treated Myles.

I'm hoping for the latter, but a part of me is still not sure he's capable of anything as human as regret.

Sighing, I slide out of bed and walk over to the window.

Rain falls against the window in pitch-black sheets. I'm not sure I'd be able to see my hand in front of my face.

Then lightning strikes overhead. A jagged flash of white heat searing over the loch. And for a single second, I see my boat, bobbing in the middle of the loch.

Then full dark descends again.

Frowning, I squint, trying and failing to make out its shape in the night. My boat should be anchored to the shore. It's not supposed to be in the middle of the lake. Maybe the wind untied my knot, but I doubt it. What I lack in gardening skills, I make up for with my knots. Mr. Morris said I was a quick study.

Another flash of lightning. Whiter. Hotter. I press my face to the window, flattening my nose against the glass. There's the boat—and, even more bizarre…

… Someone is in it.

Who would be stupid enough to go out on the water in this storm?

In answer, another bolt of lightning zags across the sky, illuminating things long enough for me to see the broad, stubborn shoulders and dark hair I know so well.

"Samuil!" I scream out, like there's any chance at all he can hear me.

Then, without a second thought, I sprint out of my room and down the staircase.

Even in the heart of the castle, it feels like the walls are quaking. Does Samuil have a death wish? Is that why he took my boat out in this storm? Is he a fucking madman?

Each peal of thunder sends my heart crashing in response against my chest, desperate to get out. To be with the man it loves, despite it all. The man who thinks he can fight Mother Nature herself and win.

I have just enough presence of mind to throw on some rain boots and a coat before dashing out onto into the rain.

Although "rain" feels like a woefully inadequate word for what I walk into. Even with my jacket, I'm soaked through in seconds. The cold bites at my fingers and my face. Every drop of rain is another tiny dagger slicing into my exposed skin.

I really must love that stupid brute. Nothing short of love would induce me to brave this kind of weather in my condition.

The wind tries to knock me off-course, hurtling this way and that over the mossy hills. I stumble through the thick grass and brambles. Thunder booms, shaking the ground beneath my feet, and I drop to my knees.

"This is insane," I mutter furiously as I push myself up and keep moving towards the lake. "The moment we're both dry, I'm going to kill him. With my bare hands."

If this storm doesn't kill us both first, that is.

I cling to my anger and frustration. I cling to the hope that we are both going to get out of this and that there is a future where I can rail against Samuil for scaring me this much, for putting me through this.

Because the alternative is unthinkable.

I finally make it to the loch's edge. My boots squelch in the boggy grass, heather whipping against my bare knees. The familiar scent of peat and pine mingles with the metallic tang of lightning in the air. Through it all, I'm close enough now to confirm what I already know: Samuil is sitting in my boat.

"SAMUIL!" I scream.

He twists around, scanning back and forth until his gaze falls on me. It's dark and he's far and the rain is heavier than ever, but I still see the panic that crosses his face.

He roars something I can't decipher and waves back toward the castle. It doesn't take a genius to interpret, though.

This idiot is in the middle of a lake in a freaking lightning storm, and he wants *me* to go inside?

"I'll go inside when you do!" I scream back. But my voice is lost to another crack of thunder.

Samuil stands up, waving his arms at me until the boat starts to wobble. "Samuil! Stop it! You're gonna make the stupid boat top—"

Before I can finish my warning, the boat spills over.

And Samuil disappears into the water.

I run forward far enough for my feet to dunk into the frigid water. Even if I wanted to go after him, I can't. Not with our baby. God only knows what the loch would do to life that fragile.

It doesn't care about who lives or dies. It just churns and waits for people stupid enough to wander into its maw.

People like me.

People like Sam.

I cry his name again and again. "Samuil! Samuil!"

He'll come back up. He'll be fine. He'll swim to the shore. He can swim, can't he? I saw him swim laps around our yacht when we were out to sea. He's strong. He's capable.

So why the hell hasn't he come up for air yet?

I squint through the choppy waves as panic threatens to pull me down.

What if the boat struck Samuil in the head when he fell? What if he's unconscious, sinking to the bottom of the lake right this second?

What if I don't do something and I lose him forever?

I shuck my coat off, ready to risk absolutely everything to get him back—what is all of it without him, anyway?—when a hand grips my arm. One hand on each arm, actually.

Myles pulls me back out of the way as Mr. Morris appears over the other shoulder, a spool of rope looped on his forearm.

I don't even know what Myles is still doing here. He should've left hours ago. But I'm too terrified to question it.

"Myles, it's Samuil," I gasp. "He fell out of the boat and he hasn't come up for—"

"I know. I saw it happen." Myles takes the rope from Mr. Morris and ties it around his waist. "Don't worry—I'll get him."

Without another word or look back, Myles begins to wade into the lake, aiming in the rough direction of the rocking boat. But it's like the storm is working against us. The rain comes down harder and seeing farther than the water's edge is near impossible. Myles is reduced to a blur, a shadow on shadows.

"B-be c-c-careful!" I stammer, my teeth chattering from the cold.

How much worse must it be for Samuil?

"Dinna fash, lass," Mr. Morris croons, feeding Myles more of the rope's slack. "He'll be alright. He's a brawny man, yer Samuil."

Normally, I'd say the same thing. Except we're in the throes of the most violent Highlands storm I've seen yet and I'm finding it hard to cling to hope.

Especially because Samuil still hasn't come up for air.

"Bring him back to me, Myles," I croak just as Myles dives into the depths of the lake.

I can only stand frozen, eyes fixed on the spot where I think Myles disappeared. Where I think Samuil disappeared.

This can't be the end. Samuil Litvinov is too stubborn to die.

Still, my heart aches with the possibility that we might not have another conversation. That he might never wrap his arms around me and surround me with his solid warmth.

That he might never meet his child.

I think I'm crying, but I can't tell because of the rain. My entire world is submerged in water, and there's nothing I can do but let it rinse me clean.

Then there's a disruption. A wave that moves in the wrong direction. Ripples. More sharp, angular shadows breaking the surface, ducking below. Rising up. Falling down.

The only reason I don't dive in is because Mr. Morris grabs my arm.

"Whoa there, lass. Myles may be able to drag in one body, but let's not give him another one."

Body. The word is an ice pick to my heart. Samuil is more than a body. He's alive. He has to be.

"Myles!" I scream. "Do you have him?"

The rope pings, taut and moaning. Mr. Morris starts to heave, but he's huffing from the effort. Desperate for something to do, I grip the rough-hewn rope and pull with all my might.

Then: more motion. Myles's white face bobs just above the surface of the water. I can't make out much more than that. I just close my eyes and tug as hard as I possibly can.

It isn't until he's closer that I realize Samuil is draped lifelessly across Myles's back.

"No!" I cry, tearing forward.

But Myles holds up his hand. "He's alive," he pants. "I feel him breathing."

He drags Samuil onto the sloshy grass and rolls him onto his side. Immediately, water bursts out of Sam's mouth as he coughs and retches.

It's the most beautiful thing I've ever seen.

He's alive.

I drop to my knees in front of him. "Samuil."

He rolls to one side, breathing hard.

But Myles doesn't give him any time to recover.

"'Alright?'" he roars. "I hope he's not alright! It would serve him right for— What the fuck were you thinking, you jackass?! Drunk boating? In a storm? At fucking pitch black midnight? Who the hell do you think you are, fucking Poseidon? You could have died!"

Samuil raises his head an inch. His eyes meet mine. He's drunk. I see it in the red of his eyes. I can also see that nearly dying is sobering him up fast.

He groans, clutching his side. I lean in and place my palm over his. "Are you hurt?"

"Tired." He coughs up more water. "Sore."

"Good." I pinch his hand hard enough that he yanks it away.

"*Blyat',* woman. Have some mercy."

"You're lucky I don't leave you here after what you just did!"

Around us, the rain has begun to slow. The wind sighs and eases, too. Sam forces himself up to a seat. His wet shirt clings to every muscle on his body. What does it say about me that, even under the circumstances, I'm not above noticing?

"You didn't have to come in after me," Samuil remarks to his best friend stiffly. "I had the situation under control."

Myles scowls. "You did, did you? What were you planning on doing? Soaking up the lake like you did that bottle of scotch?"

"I didn't need your help with either task."

Myles's eyes gleam like the last of the lightning rattling over our heads. Not that anyone seems to be paying attention to the storm anymore. We might as well be standing in front of a roaring fireplace for all the concern the men give our current surroundings.

"Maybe I'll push you back in then," Myles snaps.

"And waste all your effort? You worked hard to get me out."

"I didn't do it for you, you self-important bastard," Myles spits. "I did it for Nova and the child she's carrying. Because, despite what you might believe, I care about them."

"I know that."

"You have a funny fucking way of showing it."

My gaze bounces between the two men as I try to decide if I should jump between them or let them brawl it out.

Samuil rises, then sways on his feet, tottering a step closer to Myles. His hand darts out for balance on Myles's shoulder, but it's not in anger. Then he sighs and squeezes. "Don't leave."

Raindrops pelt Myles's face, but he doesn't so much as blink. His jaw is working overtime, but whether to hold back emotion or anger, I can't say.

Then Myles clasps a matching hand on Samuil's shoulder. "As if you could get rid of me that fucking easily."

All at once, the tension dissolves.

Samuil pulls Myles into a hug, and Myles slaps him hard on the back. I'm glad it's still raining gently, because it hides the tears running down my cheeks.

I shake my head at the both of them. "Boys. The most incomprehensible species on this planet."

Samuil smirks, offering me his hand. The moment I slip my fingers through his, he pulls me into the hug, too.

We're all soaking wet and chilled to the bone, but I feel warm all the same.

We stand there in a tangled embrace, the three of us, while the storm whimpers and recedes. Through my palm pressed against his chest, I feel Samuil's heart beating—strong and steady now, like it never stopped. Like it never could stop, not while he has people to come back to. People who won't let him drift away.

"Next time you feel like testing the loch's patience," I murmur against his wet shirt, "remember this moment. Remember what you almost lost."

Samuil's arm tightens around me. "I remember," he says roughly. Then, so quietly I almost miss it: "I'm sorry."

Above us, Myles snorts. "You can prove it by giving me a raise."

"Technically, I haven't rehired you yet."

"Technically, you still owe me a new suit. This one's ruined."

I feel Samuil's laugh rumble through his chest—rusty, like he's forgotten how to do it, but real.

28

SAMUIL

I wake up feeling like I've gone ten rounds with the Loch Ness Monster.

And the monster fucking won.

"*Blyat*'," I groan as I try to sit up. My ribs are extremely pissed off at me and they have no issues letting me know about it. It's like every single one of those fuckers is trying to stab me in the lungs.

"Hurts, doesn't it?"

Nova's voice catches me off-guard. I turn too quickly and regret it immediately. My brain is liquid. It sloshes against the inside of my skull. But the headache isn't so intense that I miss the upward curl of Nova's lips, the telltale dimple in her cheek.

She's enjoying my pain. At least a little.

Given what I put her through last night, I probably deserve it.

"I need a more compassionate nurse," I mutter.

"What you need," Nova retorts, rising from the worn leather armchair where she must have spent the night watching over me, "is a swift kick in the ass. Maybe several."

She marches barefooted to my bedside, then takes a loose pillow and shoves it behind my spine to help me sit more upright. I've never seen someone wield a cushion aggressively before, but she's found a way. If I wasn't busy trying not to vomit, I'd be impressed.

"I nearly died last night," I say as I rub the sleep out of my eyes. "Shouldn't you be happier to see me?"

Her scowl remains unchanged. "We all saw more than enough of you last night." She straightens up after arranging the pillow, one hand automatically moving to support her lower back—a new habit since her belly started showing. The sight sends another wave of guilt through me, sharper than any hangover.

"What do you mean by that?" The way she's looking at me—part exasperation, part lingering fear—makes my stomach clench with something worse than nausea.

"Well, let's see." She purses her lips and taps a finger against them. "After Myles pulled you out of the lake, and he and Mr. Morris helped drag your immobile, blue-lipped carcass up to the castle—"

"I remember all of this."

She arches a brow. "Then you definitely remember when you dropped trou in front of Mrs. Morris and scandalized her for life."

Actually... I don't. At all. The gap in my memory sends a chill down my spine that has nothing to do with being naked under these quilts.

Speaking of which…

I lift the heavy tartan fabric, confirming my state of undress. "Fucking hell. I thought you were the one who undressed me."

The idea of Nova taking care of me like that feels right. Safe.

The reality appears to be far more mortifying.

"Oh, no." A ghost of amusement flickers across her tired face. "You did the honors all by yourself. Right in the foyer. Nearly gave poor Mrs. Morris a heart attack—though I notice her gaze lingered longer than strictly necessary."

"Wonderful," I mumble darkly. "Anything else I should know?"

"Nothing too major." That dangerous sparkle returns to her eyes. "You let Myles help you up to bed and then you vowed, just before passing out, that you would let me make all decisions from this point. I'm the *pakhan* now."

I cock an eyebrow at her. "That doesn't sound like me at all."

She only shrugs. "Your near-death experience must've made you more reasonable. I'd say it's long overdue."

"Sounds like you think it made me gullible, too."

She turns away to hide a smile, though I still catch a glimpse of it. Then, schooling her face back into steely disdain, she pokes a finger into my ribs. "Let me check your bruising."

I bite down a grunt of pain and snag her hand before she can shiv me with that fingernail again. "You're heartless."

"Actually, 'heartless' is risking your life when you have a child on the way," Nova snaps. "'Heartless' is scaring me half to death by throwing yourself into a lake in the middle of a freaking thunderstorm. 'Heartless' is making your baby's mother and your best friend wade into cold, dark waters to drag your ungrateful ass back to shore."

I press her warm knuckles to my lips. "Did I not apologize for that last night?"

"Not anywhere close to my satisfaction."

I turn her hand over and press another kiss into the center of her palm. "I guess I'll have to think of a way to make it up to you."

"It might take a long time."

"I can be patient."

She snorts. "That would be a first."

"For you, I can be."

There's a beat of silence then. Not an angry silence, not a hateful silence. But just the tiniest pocket of space to let me know that not all is lost. That I didn't abandon hope for a less-than-happy ending at the bottom of that godforsaken fucking loch.

That we might still make it after all.

"Good to know," she says suddenly, pulling her hand from mine. The loss of contact aches more than my bruised ribs as she pushes herself to her feet, one hand automatically steadying her changed center of gravity.

"Where are you going?" I ask as she retreats.

I can't help drinking in the sight of her. The pale pink slip she's wearing catches the morning light, clinging to the new curves of her changing body. Her breasts are fuller now, her hips softer, her belly a gentle swell beneath the fabric—every change a reminder of what we've created together.

My body may be battered, but my hunger for her is working exactly as designed, and then some.

Nova pretends to be busy with a cart of medical supplies stationed against the far wall, her back to me. "I promised Mrs. Morris I'd help her with harvesting today," she says as she rearranges bottles needlessly. "I figured I should throw the poor woman a bone after you nearly gave her a heart attack with the peep show of yours. Though she did mention at breakfast that you've been holding out on her all these months."

I lunge for her when she passes closely by the bed, but I don't even get halfway there before the pain forces me to lie back down. Every motion is sending lightning bolts of pain up and down my side and Nova into a fit of giggles.

"Nuh-uh. Stay in bed and rest," she scolds, wagging a finger in my face. "That's an order."

"I'm the one who gives orders around here."

"For the next few days at the very least, the only thing you're doing is lying down in that bed. Understood?" Then, with a sparkle in her eye that says trouble is coming, she sashays over to the bureau and strips that slip of hers right off.

It lands in a pink puddle at her feet, not that I'm paying much attention to the garment. My eyes are fixed on her body, tracing every curve, every line, every inch of skin I want to taste and touch and press my lips into again and again.

I never thought I'd see something this beautiful again. Last night, with dark water surging everywhere, even the thought of warmth and softness felt too good to be true. Now, it's there—just out of reach, but closer than I deserve.

She's tempting me with it. Teasing me with it. And that's fine —I deserve that, too.

But I'm going to fucking make it up to her. I'm going to take the punishment I've earned and then give her the apologies and the happy endings that *she* has earned.

Because Nova Pierce is my woman, goddammit. She is my family and my future and I'm never going to leave her alone again.

Not.

Fucking.

Once.

She twists just enough to look at me over her bare shoulder as she steps into a clean dress and shimmies it up over her hips.

"Someone doesn't know how to give a lady her privacy," she remarks lightly.

I hold out a hand. My dick is aching.

"Come over here," I growl.

She just shakes her head and smiles that devil's smile. "Can't, I'm afraid. I told you—I'm going downstairs to help Mrs. Morris."

I groan in agony. "Help *me*. I've got a raging hard-on and the world's worst hangover. You're not really going to leave me like this, are you?"

She finishes tying up the bow of the dress and walks over to me, leaning in seductively as her breath tickles my face. "After what you put me through last night," she says in a low, raspy voice, "you deserve to suffer with both."

I try to grab her, but she dances away from me, laughing wickedly.

"Nova…!" But she's already blown me a kiss and disappeared through the door. "Goddammit."

I could rub one out, but it wouldn't do a damn thing.

So I haul my ass gingerly into the shower, cursing at the water pressure but reveling in the heat. It soothes all the tortured knots in my back, and by the time I'm heading downstairs for some coffee, I feel somewhat human again.

As I approach the kitchen, I can hear the insistent yapping of the puppies. Apparently, Nova left them in the kitchen to make sure I really feel my headache.

But before I can even cross the threshold, the lead of my private IT team walks through the arched passageway that leads to the library.

"Morning, boss!" Adam's voice bounces off the vaulted ceiling with demonic enthusiasm.

I resist the urge to sink my fist into his open-mouthed smile. It's not his fault that I chose to drown my control issues in an entire bottle of Macallan last night. Though his volume control could use some work.

"Adam," I acknowledge, far less brightly.

"I've got good news for you." His grin stretches wider, if possible.

Must be why he's fucking shouting about it. Christ, did Nova brief everyone on optimal torture techniques?

"What is it?"

He hands me a crisp sheet of paper with the Litvinov crest pressed on top as letterhead. "See for yourself."

I scan through the intel report, then read it again, my hangover momentarily forgotten. The words swim into focus: location coordinates, bank transactions, communication logs.

All pointing to one person.

I lift my eyes to Adam, keeping my voice carefully neutral despite the adrenaline suddenly coursing through my veins. "Is this information legit?"

"I've triple-checked everything." He winks. "We finally have solid intel on Ms. Alekseeva. And here's the kicker: that little social media scheme Ms. Nova and her friend put together? It created exactly the digital breadcrumb trail we needed. Your wife-to-be has better instincts for this than half our security team."

You have got to be fucking kidding me.

"Are you saying that it actually worked?" The words come out rough—part disbelief, part something dangerously close to admiration.

While I've been playing chess, Nova's been changing the entire game.

The realization hits me like another wave of cold loch water: I've been so focused on protecting Nova that I never stopped to consider she might be capable of protecting herself—protecting us both—in ways I never imagined.

Maybe it's time to rethink more than just my drinking habits.

He nods, barely containing his excitement. "I was able to track Katerina's IP address from the email address she responded with. Amateur mistake—it wasn't even encrypted."

"Fuck me," I murmur, scanning the intelligence report again. The coordinates mock me from the page. All this time, all these resources, all my careful planning... The best IT team in the world at my disposal, surveillance networks spanning continents, decades of Bratva connections...

And who's responsible for tracking down Katerina?

A pint-sized dog walker and her busy-bodied best friend.

I dismiss Adam with a grateful nod, and he makes a beeline back to his office. Then I turn into the kitchen and hunt down some coffee.

As I pour myself a cup, watching the steam curl up like Scottish mist, I contemplate how to tell Nova that her scheme actually worked. That, while I was busy being an overprotective ass, she was quietly orchestrating Katerina's downfall using nothing but Instagram and her understanding of human nature.

Letting her think she was right to take matters into her own hands seems like a dangerous precedent to set. The last thing I need is Nova thinking she can wade into Bratva business whenever she pleases.

Then again, I do have to make amends somehow. And maybe... maybe it's time to admit that my way isn't always the best way. That, sometimes, the biggest victories come from the most unexpected directions.

Admitting I was wrong is a start.

The day passes in a blur of business calls and strategy sessions. But as the sun arcs through the sky, my thoughts keep circling back again and again to Nova and that intelligence report. By evening, the castle has settled into its usual twilight rhythm: the clip of sheep hooves in the distance, the whisper of wind through stone archways, the soft glow of lamps against darkening horizons.

I find her in our bedroom, curled up in the window seat where she spends most evenings now. The door frames her like a Renaissance painting, all soft curves and tangerine light. A book lies forgotten in her lap, but her gaze is fixed on the misty hills beyond the glass, one hand absently stroking her swollen belly.

I've seen that look on her face before—the tight pull of her eyebrows, the press of her full lips, the slight furrow between her brows that appeared the day I dragged her to Scotland.

She's overthinking. Worrying. Probably about me, about us, about the future we're building in this moss-covered fortress so far from everything she's ever known.

I don't want that for her—that weight on her heart. That burden.

But I'm man enough to recognize that it's my fault it's there in the first place.

I clear my throat to let her know I'm here, watching as she blinks away from whatever vision held her captive. The sight of me doesn't exactly light up her face—though there's something softer in her eyes than there was this morning—so it's safe to assume I'm still the cause of those worry lines.

"I didn't see you today," I say.

She closes her book. "I was out in the woods, trying to recreate your naked rain dance for posterity. The villagers have already added it to the list of local legends. *The Mad Russian Man and His Midnight Swim.*"

I scowl. "There was no rain dance."

"How would you know? You were drunk."

"Not that drunk."

She snorts. "You were drunk enough that you decided to take a casual stroll in the torrential rain. Drunk enough that you thought it was a good idea to take my boat out while the sky opened fire. Drunk enough that you nearly drowned in that ice-cold lake. Need I go on?"

I purse my lips. "Are you going to bring this up forever?"

"As long as I draw breath."

I join her by the window. She's still in the blue dress from this morning. The neckline dips low to reveal generous acres of cleavage.

Just like that, I'm hard again.

You'd think after my midnight swim with death, she'd want to revel in how alive I am, let me worship her body until we both forget yesterday's terror. Or maybe that's just how I would like to celebrate continued survival—by drowning myself in her instead of scotch.

My woman clearly prefers holding grudges. Though the way she's looking at me now, lips parted and eyes dark in the fading light, suggests she might be fighting the same battle I am.

"Nova..."

Her eyes flicker to mine, amber catching fire in the sunset. She's holding her breath—I can see the tension in her shoulders, the slight tremor in her hands where they rest protectively over our child.

But as our eyes meet, her lower lip trembles with something more complicated than anger. I cross the room to her.

Unlike this morning, when I reach for her now, she doesn't dance away. The castle's shadows lengthen around us as I lift her out of the chair and pull her into my lap.

"I'm sorry," I whisper into her hair.

She sniffles. "For what?"

"I was a beast yesterday. Myles didn't deserve to be treated like that. Neither did you." She bites down on her bottom lip, trying to maintain her severity even as she melts against me. She's failing miserably. "It just drives me mad to think of you exposed to the Andropovs. Anything that puts you in danger makes me—"

"Crazy? Reckless? Completely unreasonable?"

"Reasonably unreasonable," I counter. "This is your life we're talking about here, Nova. Yours. Our baby's." I spread my hand across her stomach, stroking the swell with my thumb. "Nothing matters more to me. I'll do whatever it takes to keep you safe."

She sighs. "I know you were just being protective, but I don't want to spend the rest of our lives worrying about how you'll respond every time I'm in danger. I can't live like that, Samuil. Our child can't grow up like that."

Then never be in danger.

It seems like an easy enough solution to me. I keep her locked away here, safe and sound in this castle, and we all live happily ever after.

"I'll work on it," I relent. "I can't promise to change overnight, but I'll do my best. For you. For us."

Her fingers twist into the hair at the back of my neck. "I suppose that's enough for now."

My hands slide down her back until they reach her ass. I give her a good squeeze, pulling her flush against my erection. But she holds herself back from me.

She sits back, and in the gathering darkness, I can see tears gleaming in her eyes. "You really scared me last night, Samuil." Her voice cracks on my name.

"I know."

She shakes her head. "No, you don't. I—I saw you disappear underneath that water and… I couldn't breathe. I thought my heart had actually stopped beating."

"I know the feeling." I place my hand over her chest. "Before you, I wasn't even sure I had a heart. Now, you're the reason it beats at all."

She presses her forehead to mine. "I love you, Samuil."

Emotion clogs my throat, making it impossible to say the words back. But she has to know how I feel about her. This fierce, stubborn woman who walked into my life with an unruly Great Dane and proceeded to turn my whole world upside down. There's no other person in heaven or earth who could've coaxed an apology out of me, who could make me want to be better, softer, more worthy of the family we're building.

"I have something for you, *krasavitsa*."

She tilts her head to the side. "What is it?"

I hand her the intel report. "Information on Katerina. A lead on her location… all thanks to you."

Her eyes widen as she scans the page. "You're kidding. It actually worked?"

"It worked."

She claps her hands against my chest, her body gyrating against mine as she celebrates. "I can't believe it. I didn't really think she would— This is great! I have to tell—" She breaks off, realizing suddenly that telling Hope would put her in danger again and bring us back to square one.

I breeze over the tense moment. There will be time for that later. "You're quite something, Nova Pierce, you know that?"

"See?" She puffs out her chest. "You shouldn't underestimate me."

I press a kiss to the side of her neck. "Never again. I've learned my lesson."

29

NOVA

"What fresh hell is this?"

I eye the pink monstrosity Samuil's packing like it's about to sprout fangs and bite me. If anyone is going to put their mouth on me, though, I'd rather it be him. I'm not sure if it's the pregnancy hormones or if he just looks extra good today, but Sam's eyes are burning like a winter storm as he looks up from his task to drink me in.

"It's packing," he replies. "What does it look like?"

"It looks like you're about to leave me again. Although—" I squint at the last item he just stuffed into the case. "—we might need to discuss why you're packing my panties for a business trip."

His gaze bounces between me and the eyesore at his feet. "Princess, if you believe I'd choose *that* as my getaway gear, we need to have words."

I can't help but grin. "Pink brings out your eyes, though."

In a heartbeat, he eats up the space between us. One hand connects with my ass while the other hauls me against his granite chest. "The Versace limited edition is yours."

I sigh and melt against him. He's so warm and solid and so *Sam* that it hurts. "Seriously, though. Why are you packing? Last time you packed without warning, we ended up as fugitives in Scotland."

"You make it sound so dramatic." He straightens to his full height and looks down at me, six-foot-four of pure muscle and danger. "I seem to recall you falling in love with this castle."

"Stockholm Syndrome. Don't get it twisted."

Speaking of "twisting," though, his fingers are doing interesting things with the hem of my nightgown. Pushing it up, teasing it higher and higher. And with every inch of skin he exposes, I get a little bit weaker in the knees.

I force myself to push him away and keep him at arms' length. "Answers, please."

He chuckles. "I thought for sure the Gianni would put you in a more compliant mood."

"Designer labels don't make me wet, Sam. Intel does." I press my palm against his pecs, secretly counting his heartbeats. "Who's trying to kill us this time?"

"What happened to my ray of sunshine who couldn't stop smiling? You're turning cynical on me." He tucks my hair back behind my ear, and damn him, even that whisper of a touch has me craving more. "Can't a man surprise his woman?"

"She got kidnapped by the Russian mob and knocked up by their boss." I arch an eyebrow. "Ring any bells?"

His laugh rumbles through his chest and into mine. "Best mistake I ever made."

"The kidnapping or the knocking up?"

"Both." Like the touch-starved fool I am, I lean into his palm with my cheek. "There's nothing to fear, Nova. I just thought we could use a trip."

I scan our bedroom, our sanctuary, and sigh. As beautiful as this place is, as Pinterest-perfect, as secluded and safe, it would be nice to change the scenery for a little while.

"Fine. But tell me we're coming back."

He engulfs me in his arms, tucking me under his chin. "This isn't another escape plan, Nova. Just a shopping spree."

I frown in suspicion. "Keep talking."

His mercury eyes dance with mischief. "Time to upgrade our wardrobe. Lord and lady have certain standards to maintain."

If this is manipulation, it's fucking masterful. I've been MacGyvering my pre-pregnancy clothes with rubber bands and living in Sam's sweats for weeks now. I'd sacrifice my firstborn for some proper maternity wear.

I'm about to demand we leave immediately when suspicion creeps back in. "We do have internet access, do we not? Could order everything online."

He exhales. "Still doubting me?"

"Can you blame me?"

He grazes my forehead with a kiss. "Different story this time, angel. No one's hunting us down. No hidden agenda. Cross my heart."

"Prove it then. Where are we going?"

"London."

Electric anticipation zips through me. "London... didn't you just come from there?"

"Yeah, but you weren't with me. Plus, I was keeping my head down. Barely counts." His arms snake around my waist. "This time will be different. We're living the high life at the Ritz Carlton. Trafalgar Suite."

I nearly choke. "Holy shit— Hope's gonna lose her mind! That's the *Notting Hill* suite! Julia fucking Roberts stayed there, Sam! I'll be breathing her air!"

"Pretty sure that air's long gone by now."

But I'm already halfway to cloud nine. Finally breaking free from this stone prison. *With* him.

I surge up, claiming his mouth. "That movie's my absolute favorite! Did you plan this?"

His mysterious shrug comes with another kiss to my crown. "A magician never tells. Now, make moves—we're wheels up in fifty-seven minutes."

"Oddly specific."

"So are your spa appointments."

My jaw unhinges. "You're shitting me."

"Three hours of pure queen treatment. Nothing less for my woman."

My mind short-circuits. The closest I've gotten to spa-level luxury was face-masking with Hope and playing amateur pedicurist. Maybe that's why my brain starts throwing up roadblocks.

"The puppies, though…" I chew on a nail. "And my garden… Mr. Morris needs help with—"

"Don't tell me you're choosing potatoes over paradise."

I try to protest—God knows why—but then Sam captures my face between his palms and shuts me up with a kiss that makes my toes curl.

When he breaks away, my head's spinning like a carousel on acid. "Come on, baby," he purrs, voice pure sin. "Run away with me."

Bastard's playing dirty.

What's a girl to do but surrender?

~

The trip from Moorbeath to London feels like someone hit fast-forward on reality.

After weeks of isolation, seeing the world still turning is a mindfuck. Every building is a symphony. Every passing stranger looks like the Mona fucking Lisa.

Then we hit the suite, and I'm counting thread counts like a psychopath. Can't miss a single detail.

I'm on our balcony, getting high on rose perfume when Sam materializes behind me.

His arms cage me in. "Worth it?"

"That's rhetorical, right? Only a crazy person would hate this. It's fucking insane."

"Good. Because we're calling it home for the next week."

I shake my head. "I've only ever been in one hotel room before this. It was on the ground floor of the Red Roof Inn in Illinois for my cousin's wedding."

Samuil's mouth twists to the side. "Sounds… quaint."

I snort. "You don't have to be polite. It was about as good as it sounds."

"Did you enjoy yourself?" he asks, still making an effort to be a gentleman.

"Well, I was fifteen and forced to share a room with my brothers. So no, not really." I break off. It's the first time I've casually mentioned Tommy and Mike since they died.

It's bizarre, knowing they're dead. A part of me still has trouble believing it.

Samuil pulls me from my thoughts with a gentle caress against my cheek. "That's behind you now, Nova. Time to enjoy this moment."

"You're right." I give him a huge, fake smile and point to my face. "This is me, enjoying the moment."

He thumbs my bottom lip. "Cute. Now, come inside with me."

"But right now, I'm enjoying the view."

"You can admire the view later. After I've given you your gift."

"'Gift'?" I tug my hand out from beneath his. "I thought *this*—" I gesture to our surroundings. "—was the gift."

"It's one part of your gift," he admits, tugging me towards our suite. "The other part is waiting for you on the other side of this door."

I'm not sure my nerves can take any more surprises. One or two more whelms, and I'll be firmly in overwhelmed territory.

But Samuil looks so handsome smiling at me, and I don't want to disappoint him after everything he's done. So I throw the door open, prepared to *ooh* and *ahh* over whatever brand name gown, world-class meal, or chest of gold he's got waiting for me.

But absolutely nothing prepares me for what's waiting on the other side.

"Hey, babe."

Hope is dressed in a tartan skirt and a fuzzy white sweater, leaning against the doorframe with her arms crossed casually over her chest. So calm, cool, and la-di-freaking-da that I want to scream just looking at her.

I promptly hurl myself forward and we collide in a tangle of hair and limbs. "Don't 'hey, babe' me, all cool! What in the hell are you doing here?!"

She laughs and squeezes me back just as hard. "What, you think I'd let you live your best Julia Roberts life without me? Please."

"I can't believe you're here!" My voice breaks embarrassingly, but I don't care. I just keep squeezing her until she wheezes, but it still isn't enough.

Is she real? Am I? Is this really happening?

"I flew in a few hours ago. First class, no less. It's almost enough to make me forgive your man for keeping us apart all this time. When I give him the knee to the balls he deserves, I'll be a touch gentler."

Yeah, it's Hope, alright.

I twist to look at Sam, finding him leaning against the wall with that infuriating half-smile that makes my knees weak.

The bastard planned this perfectly.

"You're welcome," he drawls.

All I can do is laugh.

30

NOVA

I peek around the corner like a creeper.

I'm pretending to rifle through my half-dozen bags' worth of Harrods haul—courtesy of Samuil's AmEx black card, which is still sizzling hot from how many times I swiped it today. What I'm really doing, though, is playing voyeur to the scene unfolding in the doorway.

With the boss man tied up in meetings, Myles got stuck playing tour guide and watchdog to *Hope and Nova's Great London Adventure,* coming soon to a theater near you.

What that means for yours truly, however, is that I was instantly demoted to "third wheel," and my best friend and bodyguard each promptly forgot all about my existence.

Not that I'm complaining. Watching Hope and Myles slink around each other all day like cats in heat has been almost as fun as the shopping.

Since we got back to the suite ten minutes ago, they've both been loitering in the doorway, neither willing to say goodbye just yet.

"Those bags look heavy," Myles remarks for the millionth time. "Sure I can't help?"

Hope's cherry-red lips curl into a wicked smile. "My bedroom's a fortress, soldier. Not that easy to breach."

He peers down the hall to the room in question. "There an application process I should know about?"

"Big time. Long. Grueling. Only the elite make it through."

"Good thing I've got a perfect track record." His massive shoulders rise in a casual shrug that's anything but casual. "And I always finish what I start."

Pink floods Hope's cheeks—a rare sight on my usually unflappable friend. She busies herself with her shopping bags, but I catch her sneaking glances up at him through her lashes. "Cocky, much?"

"I prefer 'determined.' I usually get what I want."

"I'm sure you've been 'determined' to get a lot of women."

Myles presses a hand to his chest. "You wound me. I'm like a penguin. A one-woman kind of man. It's quality over quantity for me."

"Which am I?"

"Quality." His voice drops to a rumble that makes even my toes curl. "Crème de la crème."

She giggles shyly, a sound I've literally never heard from her before. "Paris is on the other side of the Channel, lover boy."

But Myles is completely undeterred. "Close enough." His palm connects with the wall by her head. And holy mother of foreplay, this is it.

Then Hope's eyes find mine. I cringe, stifle a scream, and try to duck back around the corner.

But no dice. Busted.

The door clicks shut moments later. Hope floats in while I fold my new clothes with fake concentration.

"He's a charmer, that one," she remarks, aiming for casual and missing by a mile.

"The Bratva boys do bring the heat."

She face-plants onto the mattress with a dramatic sigh. "He's nothing but trouble, though."

I park myself next to her. "I might be slightly biased here, but it must be said: Myles is a good egg, Hope. You could do a whole lot worse."

"You're supposed to tell me to be careful and not get emotionally involved. I was counting on you to be the voice of reason here." She pokes me in the thigh and laughs, though it fades quickly.

I don't give her the easy out of the joke. "You like him, don't you?"

She rolls her eyes toward the crown molding. "Duh. He's walking, talking book boyfriend material. Ink, muscle, danger—the unholy trinity. My lady bits are doing the mambo."

"Ew, Hope, spare me the details."

"Is this how Samuil got you? The whole dangerous-and-delicious combo?"

I wrinkle my nose. "Let's leave my lady bits out of this."

She flops onto her stomach with a dramatic groan. "Dating Myles would be like… like juggling. Juggling chainsaws, maybe. While walking a tightrope. And the tightrope is on fire."

"Can't argue with that."

"Is that you being the rational angel on my shoulder? Are you telling me to run for the hills? Will you and your Russian sugar daddy fund my new identity and help me start fresh somewhere tropical?" Before I can answer her jumbled nonsense, she sighs. "But his *smile*, NoNo. Have you seen his smile? Every time he smiles at me—"

"When you're gushing about his smile," I warn, "you're already drowning. My rational advice won't save you now."

"Then give me the crazy version." Hope sits up, crossing her legs and fixing me with her *I promise I'm being serious* look. "You've tamed your Russian beast. Share your secrets."

I snort. "'Tamed' is doing a lot of work in that sentence, babe."

"Oh, please. I've been watching you two. You're head over heels—"

"I wouldn't say *head* over—"

"—and trust me, baby girl, it's mutual."

My traitorous heart skips. I roll the thought around before curiosity wins. "You think?"

"Nova, seriously?" Hope's eyes bug out of her head. "The man moves mountains for you. His methods are questionable as fuck, but his devotion isn't. I'm here living large literally just because he wanted to see you smile." She points at her feet, then taps her temple. "Head. Heels. I know it."

I let out an exhale as my chin droops to my chest and the dress I was folding goes fluttering out of my hands.

"Things have been good lately," I admit softly.

"Exactly. So when's he gonna make you his queen?"

That unleashes a rain cloud right over my parade. Things have been good, yes. But "good" doesn't mean "forever-after" good.

I shouldn't indulge these fantasies of Samuil on one knee, or waiting at the altar in a tailored tux. What we have is enough.

It has to be.

"You're on the spot and I'm not letting you out of it," Hope says with another gentle poke in my belly. "It's a valid question. You're carrying his spawn."

"That's different. We'll be family, but... marriage isn't Samuil's style."

"Bullshit," she retorts. "He married that psycho Katerina. You're an upgrade in every way."

"And look how that ended!" I plop back down on the mattress next to her. "He's not exactly rushing back to the altar."

"That's like…" Hope's face scrunches as she thinks. "Getting mauled by a tiger, then saying you don't like puppies. You're nothing like her."

"That's the issue," I mumble. "She belonged in his world."

"And that matters because...?"

Restlessly, I get to my feet. "Because it means she knew what she was getting into. She knew how to be a Bratva wife. She understood his world, his life, what was expected of her."

"And yet, she's his *ex*-wife and you're his pregnant girlfriend. So maybe this whole *I'm-not-the-right-woman-for-him* bit is just a way of sabotaging yourself and this relationship so you can avoid getting hurt."

Oof.

I start pacing, if only to put a little distance between myself and Hope's blunt brand of truth-telling. "I'm not trying to sabotage anything. I'm just…" I huff out a breath. "I'm trying to be realistic, Hope. When it's just the two of us, that's one thing. But I don't know how to be in Samuil's world."

"I got news for you, honey. That baby in your belly means you're going to be a part of his world permanently, whether you like it or not."

I turn my gaze towards the London skyline. The clouds overhead are gray, dense, cottony. A light drizzle is misting over the roses out on the balcony.

"You make a good point."

She rises and joins me at the window, looping her arm through mine and resting her head on my shoulder. A gesture so familiar it makes my throat tight. "You know what I see when I look at you two?"

I shake my head slightly, not trusting my voice.

"I see the way he watches you when you're not looking. Like you're this rare, beautiful thing he can't quite believe is real. And I see the way you soften around him. How your walls come down brick by brick." She squeezes my arm. "That's not about being a perfect Bratva wife or fitting some mold. That's about two people choosing each other despite everything."

I place my hand over my belly. The baby is still a bit too young to kick, but I talk myself sometimes into believing he or she is already moving, breathing, thriving, loving. It's enough to remind me I'm never truly alone anymore.

There's a part of me that desperately wants to believe in Hope's version of love conquering all. The part that melts when Samuil wraps his arms around me at night. The part that thrills at how his presence fills every room. The part that wants to believe I'm enough—more than enough—to be his equal partner in this life we're creating.

But there's another part of me that can't forget what I've seen. What he's done. What he might still do in the future.

The imagined flutter comes again, gentle but insistent, like a reminder that some choices have already been made. Some bridges already crossed.

Hope presses her cheek to my shoulder. "Stop thinking so hard. You're going to give yourself wrinkles."

"I can't help it." I rest my forehead against the cool glass, watching London blur through the fog. "Everything's changing so fast."

"Yeah," she agrees softly. "But maybe that's not such a bad thing."

I close my eyes and let out a long breath, thinking of Samuil's arms around me, his voice in my ear, his hand protective over our growing child.

Maybe she's right.

Maybe change is exactly what we all need.

31

SAMUIL

Blood and sweat stain the tape wrapped around my knuckles as I step back up to the punching bag. We're in a private gym and the air in here reeks of luxury—premium leather, polished hardwood, and the particular kind of silence that only serious money can buy.

"Your form's getting sloppy," Myles taunts as I execute another combination on the heavy bag. "Too much time lounging on that yacht with your baby mama?"

I shoot him a look that would make most men piss themselves. Myles just grins wider.

"Speaking of Nova…" He lets the words hang there like bait.

"Don't."

"What? I was just going to say—"

"You were going to stick your nose where it doesn't belong. Again." I increase the intensity of my strikes, letting the satisfying impact drown out whatever bullshit he's about to spew.

"Fine. But Hope mentioned—"

"Hope needs to mind her own fucking business." The bag swings wildly as I unleash a particularly vicious combination. "And so do you."

"Alright, alright." Myles holds up his hands in mock surrender. "No talk about the beautiful, pregnant woman you're in love with but won't commit to. Got it. Message received."

I stop mid-strike, fixing him with a cold stare. "You're fired."

"Again?" He laughs. "That's, what, the third time this month?"

"Keep pushing and I'll make it permanent."

We both know I won't. Myles has been by my side since college—through the disaster with Katerina, through Ilya's betrayal, through enough bloodshed to fill the Thames. Add the Scotland debacle to that, and he's earned the right to push my buttons.

Doesn't mean I have to like it.

"Come on," he says, nodding toward the door. "Let's grab some air. I know a good route for a little jog."

I recognize the glint in his eye. The same look he gets before doing something stupid that will probably end with someone bleeding.

But the workout has barely taken the edge off the constant tension thrumming through my veins. The kind that comes from having a pregnant woman you'd kill for, a brother you need to kill, and an empire that demands blood to keep running.

"Fine," I concede. "But I'm not looking to set any records."

Myles's grin widens. "When do I ever push you too hard?"

The memory of him fishing my drunk ass out of a Scottish loch flashes through my mind.

"Do you want the list chronologically or alphabetically?"

We hit the London streets at an easy pace. The late morning fog has burned away, leaving behind the kind of crisp autumn day that makes the city almost bearable. Almost.

I notice immediately when Myles veers us off the direct route back to the hotel. The same way I notice the three men who've been tailing us since we left the gym. They're good—professionals keeping a careful distance.

But I'm better.

"Our fan club's still with us," I murmur, keeping my stride casual.

Myles nods almost imperceptibly. "Andropovs?"

"No. These are government types. Probably MI6 keeping tabs while I'm in their jurisdiction."

"Should we lose them?"

I consider it. It would be easy enough—I know every rat hole and bolt spot in Mayfair from years of doing business here. But sometimes, being watched is useful. Let them think they know where I am, what I'm doing.

Let them think I'm just a businessman out for a morning run.

"Let them live," I decide. "For now."

Myles leads us down increasingly posh streets, past boutiques with eye-bleed-inducing price tags. The kind of places Katerina used to frequent, draining my accounts dry while fucking my brother behind my back.

When he slows to a stop in front of Graff, my jaw tightens.

"Really?"

"What?" He bends to adjust his already-perfect laces. "Just thought we could browse. Maybe pick up something sparkly for that gorgeous woman carrying your child."

"You're about as subtle as a bullet to the head, man."

"Hey, I'm just saying, if you're going to mark your territory, might as well do it with diamonds."

I scan the street, cataloging exits and angles of fire. Old habits. "This isn't about marking territory."

"No?" Myles straightens, his expression turning serious. "Then what's it about? Because from where I'm standing, you've got a queen-level woman who somehow puts up with your shit. And instead of locking that down, you're acting like a scared little bitch."

The muscle in my jaw jumps. Anyone else who spoke to me like that would be gargling their own teeth.

But Myles isn't anyone else. And he's not entirely wrong.

"You want to have this conversation? Fine." I claim a bench, positioning myself to watch both the street and the MI6 team trying to look inconspicuous across the way. "But you're not going to like what you hear."

"Try me." Myles settles beside me, his casual posture belying his alertness. Like me, he's tracking every movement around us.

"Marriage in our world isn't about love. It's about alliances. Power. Creating weaknesses that can be exploited." My phone buzzes—a message from Nova. I ignore it, even though every cell in my body screams to check it. "I won't make her a target."

"She's already a target." Myles's voice hardens. "Or did you forget about Ilya taking her? The warehouse? The fact that she's carrying the next generation of Litvinov?"

A growl builds in my chest. As if I could forget. As if I don't see her terrified face in my dreams, hear her screams when I close my eyes.

"That's different."

"How?"

"Because..." The words stick in my throat. Around us, London flows by in its endless parade of tourists and businessmen. None of them know that two killers sit discussing marriage like it's a tactical decision. "Because making her my wife tells everyone exactly how to hurt me."

"And you think they don't already know?" Myles snorts. "You really think Ilya doesn't see how you look at her? How you'd burn the world down to keep her safe?"

"I'd burn it down anyway."

"Exactly. So what's the real reason?"

I clench my fists, fighting the urge to check my phone again. To see what Nova sent. To make sure she's safe.

"You know what happened to my mother."

"Nova isn't your mother."

"No. She's stronger. Better." My laugh comes out bitter. "Which makes it worse."

"Then why are you treating her like she's made of glass?" asks Myles.

"Because the stronger they are, the harder they break." I lean forward, remembering the videos my father made me watch. The way my mother's hands shook as she signed away her rights. "Nova thinks she can handle this life. But one day, she'll wake up and realize what being a Litvinov really means."

"And what's that?"

"Blood." My voice drops low enough that only Myles can hear. "Always blood. There's no escape."

"So you'd rather keep her in limbo? Not quite yours, not quite free?"

A sleek black Mercedes crawls past. I catalog the plate, the driver, the tinted windows.

"I'd rather keep her alive."

"Bullshit." Myles's hand clamps on my shoulder. "You're not protecting her. You're protecting yourself."

"Careful."

"No, you need to hear this. You're so fucking scared of her leaving that you won't give her a real reason to stay."

My phone buzzes again. This time, I check it.

NOVA: ***The baby just kicked. Wish you were here to feel it.***

Something in my chest cracks. I thumb the ring box in my

pocket—platinum and diamonds, custom-made weeks ago. I've told no one.

"She deserves better than me," I mutter.

"Probably." Myles stands, stretching. "But she chose you anyway. The question is, are you man enough to choose her back?"

I rise, my decision already made. It was made the moment I saw her in that park, covered in dog slobber and sass.

"Race you back?" I ask, already moving.

"You're changing the subject."

I am. Because I can't tell him about the ring. Can't admit that I've been carrying it for weeks, waiting for the right moment.

Waiting to be worthy of her.

"Come on, old man." I pick up the pace as Myles scrambles to catch up. "Unless you're scared?"

His curse follows me down the street as I run. Not *from* the truth this time.

Toward it.

32

NOVA

Some people would say playing *Scrabble* with the elderly caretakers of a Scottish castle is a far cry from living it up in a luxurious suite in the center of London with your boyfriend and best friend.

Those people would be right.

"That's a double word score, lass." Mrs. Morris crunches the numbers on her yellow legal pad. "You're in the lead now."

"Am I?" I give her my best smile, but it doesn't go well.

Smiles have been in short supply since we got back to the castle late last night.

They've been in even shorter supply since I woke up this morning and found my bed empty.

I'm not sure what I was expecting, but our week in London was so magical that I guess I was hoping that it would continue once we were back home.

Or, in Scotland, anyway. Maybe this is home now. I'm not sure.

If Samuil ever comes out of the library, maybe I'll ask.

"She *was* in the lead," Mr. Morris crows, placing his tiles with a gnarled hand. "Until now."

His wife leans over the board to read his answer, then immediately swats her husband on the shoulder. "John! You can't talk like that in front of a lady."

"I didn't say a word." He grins proudly at his placement, turning "head" into "fuckhead" on a triple word score.

I can't help but grin back.

"You are a child," Mrs. Morris scolds. "You're just being naughty to make Nova smile."

"And what of it? Worked, didn't it?"

It did.

But not for long.

By the time I drag myself up to my tower post-game—and isn't that just perfect? I'm literally Rapunzel, minus the useful hair—the temporary amusement has evaporated. What's left is a bitter taste in my mouth and a gnawing emptiness in my chest.

Maybe London spoiled me, but days spent with sheep and the Morrises and curled in bed by myself with a book aren't enough anymore. No matter how great the sex is, I don't want to be Samuil's bed-warmer. I don't want to loiter around, waiting for him to have enough time for me.

I don't want to be his crown jewel, locked away in a tower, or his clandestine baby mama, or his dirty little secret.

I want *more.*

And tonight, I'm going to demand it.

So I climb into bed, intent on avoiding sleep. The plan is to wait for Samuil to come join me, exhausted from a day of whatever the hell he does all day, so I can corner him and lay out my demands while I stand a chance of actually winning an argument for a change.

Things are going to change around here, dammit.

~

Except, the next time I blink, I'm staring groggily up at the ceiling.

I fell asleep. *Masterful execution of your plan, Nova,* croons a snide voice in my head. The sky outside my window is dark, so I'm unclear on what time it actually is or how long I fell asleep for. I'm fumbling for a clock or watch or phone when—

"Ahh!"

A sound at the end of the bed sends me snapping upright, yelping as a tall shadow stalks across the room towards me.

"When I say I like to make you scream," the shadow rumbles, "that's not exactly what I had in mind."

I frown and rub my eyes. "What time is it?"

"Midnight." His voice is whiskey-rough as he lifts a candelabra, its seven flames painting gold streaks across the darkness.

The light slashes across his face, shoving darkness below the cliff of his jaw and into the hollows of his cheeks.

My resolution crumbles like a sandcastle. Every cell in my body screams to drag him into these sheets and ruin us both.

Christ, one look and I'm already drunk on him.

I'm a lightweight.

But Samuil doesn't look inclined to join me. He holds out a hand. "Come with me, *krasavitsa*."

"Now?"

His smile gleams in the candlelight. He looks otherworldly. "Put on your coat and follow me."

He doesn't offer any more of an explanation. Why should he explain anything to me?

I'd follow him to the ends of the earth wearing nothing but a smile. But I'm so, so sick of doing it blindly.

"Why?"

"Because it's cold outside."

"No," I grumble impatiently, "I mean, why should I follow you?"

"Because I'm asking nicely." His voice drops an octave. "And because you're too curious not to."

I grit my teeth. Damn him.

I throw off the covers and storm over to my robe, snatching it off the hook like it personally offended me. "This better be worth interrupting my beauty sleep."

Though who am I kidding? Sleep isn't what I'd been planning for tonight anyway. But he doesn't need to know that.

I make my way toward the heavy oak door connecting the bedroom to the castle halls, but Samuil lingers instead by the cramped entrance to the rooftop. He still says nothing. Just holds the candelabra high and waits for me.

With exaggerated annoyance masking my burning curiosity, I stomp up the narrow spiral staircase, making sure each step lets him know I'm displeased.

The moment I step out into the night, the wind slices through me. He was right: I should've brought my coat. But I pull my robe more tightly around me.

Then I look up, and all of my annoyance drains away.

The sky is perfectly clear. The moon hangs above us, full and bright. I've never seen so many stars. I literally did not *know* there were this many stars.

"Holy shit," I breathe before I can stop myself. My words are visible as silver plumes in the air. "It's gorgeous out here."

Samuil places the candelabra on the stone ledge and gazes out over the vista like he owns it. Which, to be fair, he does. I join him reluctantly at his side, though I stay a few defiant inches away from him. The same inches that have felt like miles since we returned.

The world is so still. The waters of the loch are eerily calm, so it becomes like a mirror reflecting infinity above.

But it's all so cold and remote and dark and distant that it lands a little too close to him. *I'm* all those things, too.

Especially cold.

"Why are we up here, Samuil?" I ask, teeth chattering. "It's past midnight and it's freezing."

He doesn't look down at me. "I wanted you to see the view."

"I've seen the view. Many times. Usually by myself while you're holed up in your office working late. Which is most nights."

"You're angry."

"I'm annoyed," I correct, though that's the understatement of the century. "And you should know better."

He turns to face me and I panic. Because this—this is why I needed those few inches of space. He's warm and huge and confident; I'm cold and small and vulnerable. One touch and I'll dissolve into a puddle at his feet.

Which is precisely why I retreat, desperate to keep this fragile distance between us intact.

"Forgive me," he says, his hand falling back to his side. "I've been preoccupied today."

"Clearly."

"I've had a lot on my mind. I had a big decision to make. There was a lot to consider."

My heart stumbles. "And what is it you're considering?"

He's not smiling, but his silver eyes twinkle. "Us."

My heart drops. "'Us?' What do you mean, 'us'?"

"My world is a dangerous one, Nova."

'Nova'? He never uses my actual name anymore. It's always "*zaychik*" or "baby" or—when he's really trying to get his way —*krasavitsa*. Hearing my name in that deep voice sends ice through my veins.

Even worse is the way his hands keep fidgeting—behind his back, at his sides, clenched into fists. Samuil Litvinov doesn't fidget. He calculates. He conquers. He controls.

What the hell is happening?

"Ever since you entered my life," he continues, "you've been in constant danger."

I know that. We've talked about this.

But why is he bringing it up now?

My stomach is in knots. A second ago, I wanted to step away from him. Now, I want to grab him by the front of his shirt and shake the words out of him.

"Your life before you met me was simple and quiet. You separated yourself from your father and your brothers. You'd built a business and a life for yourself that you loved."

My throat is dry, my heartbeat coming in erratic bursts that hurt my rib cage. I can barely breathe. "What are you trying to say, Samuil?"

"I'm trying to say that your life would be simpler without me in it."

My hand falls to my stomach, like I'm trying to remind him of the life we created together. The life I already love. "I… I don't understand."

"We're so different, Nova."

This is the gentlest Samuil has ever spoken to me, but each word is a punch to the chest.

He's breaking up with me.

I sat around most of the day, debating how I could get *more* from him, while he was locked away imagining *less* with me. He wants to leave, and I'm not going to have a say in it.

He wants to leave, and I'll have to watch him go.

"You once asked me if I'd leave everything behind. Surrender the company and the Bratva to my brother and father and disappear. Well, that will never happen. The company and the Bratva, that's who I am. I can't give it up, Nova. Even if I tried, it would follow me. This life isn't something I can quit."

"I know that now," I whisper. "And… I've made my peace with it."

"Have you?" he questions. "Because I'm not quite sure you understand what you've signed up for."

I stumble forward half a step, gripping the stone wall. I need something to keep me steady. My knees are wobbling. My entire world is crumbling around me.

"I understand everything," I croak, my voice surprisingly sharp considering how shaky I feel. Funny how anger can make you stronger even when you're falling apart. "So don't use that as an excuse."

One dark eyebrow rises. "'Excuse'?"

"To break up with me." The words are poison on my tongue. "If you want to leave, do it because it's what you want. But don't pretend it has anything to do with me."

Samuil's eyes snap wide, reflecting the white light of the moon.

Before I can stop him—before I can protect what's left of my heart—his warm hand wraps around mine. I hate that I still lean into his touch. Hate that my body still recognizes him as home even as he's tearing my world apart.

Then the asshole smiles. "I'm not breaking up with you, *krasavitsa*."

I don't let myself feel relieved. I stare at him, cautiously tracing his handsome face. He stares back, taking me in like I'm a miracle he just plucked out of the sky.

"Tell that to your speech. Because you just listed all of the reasons we shouldn't be together."

Samuil nods. "I did."

"Why?"

His smile topples sideways. "To illustrate that, despite our differences, we fit together. Despite everything conspiring to tear us apart, we're still here, Nova—you and me."

A tiny ripple of relief washes through my chest. "Samuil, I…"

Then he drops to one knee in front of me, and I'm overcome in a wave of the stuff.

Oh.

Oh.

He looks up at me from bent knee and pulls something out of his pocket.

"Oh my God…"

Tears stream down my face like the traitors they are. I swipe at them frantically, not wanting to miss a second of this impossible moment.

"Nova Pierce—"

I wave a hand at him, stopping him from opening the box. "Are you sure?"

"I'm supposed to be the one asking you a question."

"But this is— I can't believe this is happening. I want you to be sure."

Sam runs his thumb over my hand, circling my ring finger once and again. He looks up at me. "I don't make decisions I'm not sure about. It's why I left you alone today. It's why I locked the library door and sat there all day, wondering if this life is enough for you."

"It is."

"Questioning if I can make you happy."

"You do," I blubber.

"I sat in silence for hours, trying to decide if I was a good enough man to let you go if I thought it would be best for you. If I thought you'd be safest that way."

The question lodges in my throat, but I force it out. "And? Are you?"

Samuil gives me a sad smile. "No. When it comes to you, Nova, I've always been a selfish, reckless bastard. Which is why—" He opens the small black box in his hand, revealing a glimmering diamond I can barely look at because I'm too busy staring into his eyes. "—I'm going to ask you to marry me, Nova. And I'm going to need you to say yes."

I shiver, but I don't even feel the cold anymore.

Not with the fire raging inside of me.

"Of course I'll marry you," I sob. "Of course I will."

Laughing, Samuil rises to his feet and pulls me into his arms. He kisses me and I forget all about the cold. We could stay here forever. I never want to leave the circle of his arms.

And the ring between us now means I won't ever have to.

My lips are wet and trembling when we finally pull apart. Samuil traces his fingers over my face. "Don't you want to try on your ring?"

I nod and offer him my finger.

He slides it on, and I gasp as the huge rock weighs down my hand. "This is too much."

Not that I'd ever let him take it back. It's mine now.

"It's no less than you deserve." He holds my hand up to the moonlight, letting the diamond refract starfire across my skin. "Do you like it?"

A laugh bubbles up from deep in my chest, half disbelief and half pure joy. Everything I've been holding back—the fear, the loneliness, the desperate hope—comes pouring out in that sound.

"I love it. And I love you."

"Remember that, *krasavitsa.* Remember that whenever I'm being a—what was it you called me—a 'stubborn asshole'?"

"Sounds about right."

He yanks me hard against his chest, one hand splayed possessively across my lower back. "And now, you're stuck with me for life."

"Is that a threat, Mr. Litvinov?" I arch an eyebrow, going for sass even as my heart threatens to explode.

"No. A promise." His voice drops to that dangerous register that makes my knees weak. "One I intend to keep."

I press my lips to the column of his throat, tasting his pulse. "Then let me make a promise of my own." I pull back just enough to meet his eyes. "Your world is chaos and danger and darkness. But I promise to bring you peace whenever I can. To be the calm in your storm."

He studies me for a long moment, this man who could break me in half but treats me like I'm made of glass. This man who's done unspeakable things but touches me like a prayer.

Then he claims my mouth in a kiss that tastes like forever.

Without breaking away, he scoops me into his arms. I wrap myself around him, clinging tight as he carries me down the narrow stairs to our bedroom.

To our bed.

To our future.

~

Back in our bedroom, he lays me on our bed with reverence. The ring on my finger winks in the candlelight, each sparkle a reminder that this is real. This is happening.

Holy shit, I'm engaged.

Samuil hovers above me, his eyes molten with need. Then he bends in half to claim my mouth. His kiss starts gentle but quickly turns savage, matching the desperate rhythm of my heart.

"I love you," I breathe into his lips. "So much." The words feel like loose change when I want to give him gold bars, but they're all I have.

Samuil's growled answer sets me on fucking fire. "Then show me."

And I do.

I show him with fingers that tangle in his hair and hold on for dear life. With a body that curves into his touch and whimpers for more. With his name falling from my lips again and again until pleasure chokes out my voice completely.

I'm trembling, skin glazed with sweat, as Samuil maps my neck with his lips. His hands conquer every curve, every inch of me, as he sheds layers one by one.

When my robe is lying in a heap at the floor beside us, his fingers toy with the band of my panties—the final barrier between us. He pauses, his breath scorching my ear.

"Is this okay?" The question rumbles through me like thunder.

I swallow hard. "Yes." My voice is barely there. "Please."

He grins against my throat before sliding the fabric down my legs with devastating patience. I kick them away, my pulse a war drum. Naked beneath him, I've never felt more exposed —or more wanted.

His gaze devours me whole. "You're so fucking beautiful, Nova. You were made for me. Every piece of you belongs to every piece of me. And I'm just as much yours as you are mine."

His hands cup my breasts, thumbs teasing my nipples until I gasp and arch.

When his mouth replaces his fingers, I lose myself in sensation. He worships first one peak, then the other, until I'm writhing beneath him, desperate for more.

His hand blazes a trail down my body before finding my center. I cry out as he works me open, his fingers stretching and preparing me with expert precision. I'm dripping for him, aching to be filled.

"Samuil," My voice breaks. "I need you. Now."

He nods, eyes locked on mine as he positions himself. The first press of his hardened cock against me has me wrapping my legs around his waist, urging him closer.

He enters me slowly, stretching me perfectly. My nails score his back as I adjust to his size. He stills, forehead pressed to mine.

"Okay?" The word is strained.

I smile softly. "More than okay. You feel amazing."

His answering smile melts into concentration as he begins to move. Slow at first, then building to a punishing rhythm that has me meeting him thrust for thrust. The world narrows to just us. Just this moment of perfect unity.

Joined.

Bound.

Perfect.

His clever fingers find my clit, and pleasure builds to an unbearable peak. I'm teetering on the edge of oblivion.

"Samuil," I gasp. "I'm going to come."

He groans, his pace turning frantic. "Come for me, *krasavitsa*. Let me feel you fall the fuck apart."

He fills me completely, perfectly, and I fracture into stardust. It's different now than it's ever been before. Deeper. More intense. Maybe it's the ring on my finger. Maybe it's because we've walked through fire together. Or maybe it's just him: my anchor in the storm, my safe harbor in the chaos.

"Samuil!" I cry out, marking his shoulders with crescent moons of possession.

He growls my name into my neck as he follows me over the edge, the word vibrating through both our bodies like a shared heartbeat.

Time stutters and stills. We stay tangled together, breathing in sync, while the candles paint shadows on the walls.

Finally, he rolls us to our sides, his fingers tracing patterns on my skin.

"I want to give you everything, Nova," he murmurs roughly. "Everything good in this world."

"You already have." I burrow closer. "You've given me peace. Hope. Family."

He laughs, the sound reverberating through me. "I've given you headaches and heartburn and a lifetime of watching your back."

"Worth it." I kiss his heart. "Every second."

He studies my face. "Are you sure? About all of this?"

I nod, emotion stealing my voice. *I've never been more sure of anything.*

His smile—his real smile, not the calculated one he shows the world—transforms him into something softer. More vulnerable.

More *mine.*

"Then let's get married." He clutches me harder. "Let's build a life together. A real one. Nothing like what our parents had. I want that. I want you."

He pulls me close, his arms wrapping around me like a shield. I close my eyes, breathing in his scent. It used to smell like smoke, like cedar, like sandalwood. Now, it smells like things only I can sense.

Safety. Protection. Love.

For the first time in my life, I feel like I'm exactly where I'm supposed to be.

33

NOVA

I rotate my hand, watching my engagement ring catch the light from the tower window. The stone is massive, throwing rainbow fractals across my face and the weathered wood beneath my fingers.

A week ago, I would've felt like an imposter in front of this ornate mirror with its gilt frame and centuries of tarnish.

Now, it feels right. Like I belong here.

Funny how much can change in a few nights.

The morning after Samuil's proposal, I woke up to find a team of tailors and stylists in the castle's great hall. Apparently, my new fiancé doesn't believe in wasting time—the engagement party is tonight. Half of London's elite and most of Chicago's Bratva will be here in a few hours to "celebrate our union."

More like size me up.

"There now, lass." Mrs. Morris's expert fingers weave tiny braids at my temples, pulling them back to cascade with the rest of my dark waves. Her eyes meet mine in the mirror. "You look like you were born to this."

"Born to what? Play dress-up in a castle?"

"To stand tall." Her gnarled hands settle on my shoulders. "This castle's seen its share of nobility, but it knows the difference between real grace and fancy plumage."

I touch my growing belly, barely visible in the deep green silk of my dress. "I just want to make him proud."

"Oh, love." She squeezes gently. "That's been done since the moment he first saw you."

A knock at the door makes us both jump.

We turn in unison to see my fiancé. *Fiancé*—God, that will take some time to adapt to. Three days of saying it in my head again and again and it still feels like an alien word.

Samuil fills the doorway, his massive frame making both the ancient wood and my heart creak. His eyes lock onto me, and I watch his pupils dilate.

Good to know I clean up okay.

"Mrs. Morris." His voice is quiet thunder. "Could you give us a moment, please?"

The housekeeper pats my shoulder and shuffles out, closing the door behind her without another word. Sam crosses to me in three long strides, his hand sliding beneath my hair to cup my neck.

"You look..." He swallows hard.

"Like I belong in your world?"

"Like you own it." His thumb traces my jaw. "Which is what we need to discuss."

I turn to face him fully. "The great Samuil Litvinov needs to discuss something? Alert the media."

"Actually, that's exactly what we need to talk about. The media. The attention. All of it."

"Sam—"

"Listen to me, *zaychik*." He crouches before me, taking my hands in his. "Tonight isn't just about announcing our engagement. It's about protection. When you're publicly mine, certain rules come into play. My enemies will think twice."

"And your friends?"

"Will kiss your feet or answer to me." His eyes harden. "But they'll test you first. Watch you. Judge how you handle the pressure."

I squeeze his fingers. "No pressure at all then."

"You're carrying my child. Wearing my ring. About to become my wife." He rises, pulling me with him. "You can handle anything."

His certainty wraps around me like armor, and I lift my chin. If he believes in me, what choice do I have but to believe in myself?

~

The party guests flood into our great hall like vultures circling fresh meat. I stand at the top of the stone staircase, gripping the banister, and take a deep breath of cold Scottish air.

You've got this, I tell myself. *You survived a cop father with a God complex. You can handle a few rich assholes.*

My emerald silk dress whispers against the stairs as I descend, each step measured and careful. The weight of my engagement ring anchors me, a constant reminder of why I'm doing this.

For Sam. For our baby. For us.

Below, a cluster of people mill around drinking champagne and downing caviar. Designer suits, couture gowns, and enough diamonds to feed a small country—these are Sam's people now.

Which means they need to become my people.

"Nova." Samuil appears at the bottom of the stairs like a knight in shining Brioni. His hand extends upward, steady and sure. When our fingers touch, warmth floods through me despite the arctic mask he wears for his guests.

Part of me wants to beg him to kick everyone out, bar the doors, and just look at me like *that* for a long time. Why do we need these other people? We have each other, after all. Right? Isn't that enough?

But the look in his eyes from upstairs is still seared into my retinas. That control that hides a deep, primal desperation. The thought of losing me.

I can relate. The merest inkling of ever being alone again makes my heart swan-dive into my stomach acid.

Sam pumps my hand to drag me back to the present moment. "May I present Nela and Josef Dvorak?"

The couple standing at the foot of the stairs oozes old money and older judgment. Nela's scarlet lips curve into something adjacent to a smile while her eyes dissect every inch of me.

"So this is the woman who's captured our Samuilka's heart," she remarks in a posh croon.

Our Samuilka? My spine stiffens. I didn't realize Sam came with communal ownership rights.

Josef's gaze sweeps the tapestries hanging on the walls. "The castle is... quaint. Do you plan to modernize?"

Sam's thumb traces my knuckles—a silent reminder that these people's opinions mean nothing.

"Actually," I say, channeling my inner queen, "we love it exactly as it is."

A few more conversational exchanges that feel more like fencing than chit-chat later, I watch the Dvoraks melt into the crowd, their disapproval trailing behind them like designer perfume.

But they're only the beginning. More guests arrive in waves, one after the next after the next. Sam guides me through introductions that blur together like watercolors.

An hour in, and I've cried mercy, played the pregnant card, and claimed sanctuary on a crimson velvet settee older than America. From here, I can observe the subtle war game playing out in our grand room.

My dangerous man works the crowd with lethal grace, his genuine smile tucked away for safekeeping. This is pure business—calculated charm and measured responses designed to strengthen his position.

Our *position,* I remind myself. *We're in this together now.*

"First time hosting?" A willowy blonde sinks onto the cushion beside me, champagne flute dangling from manicured fingers. "I'm Annika. Viktor's wife." She tilts her head toward a bear of a man currently engaged in intense conversation with Sam. "God, I remember my first dinner party after marrying Viktor. Absolute disaster."

"The soup was cold?" I venture, grateful when she laughs.

But her eyes are sharp, assessing. "The soup was fine. It was me who wasn't ready. These people..." She waves her glass at the room. "They smell weakness like sharks smell blood."

"Good thing our girl here isn't weak." Paige, a statuesque brunette I met earlier, joins us. She stretches her endless legs out, radiating practiced ease. "Honey, you've got nothing to worry about. The way Samuil looks at you? That's worth more than any social graces."

I catch Sam's eye across the room. For a heartbeat, his mask slips and I see *my* Sam—the one who proposed under the stars, who touches me like I'm precious.

Then Josef asks about profit margins, and the ice slides back into place.

"It's strange to see him like this," I murmur, more to myself than to my two new friends. "So… in his element."

"You can't deny that it gets results, though," Annika says, swirling her champagne. "People love him or fear him, no in between. The stories I've heard about what happened to the last person who crossed him..."

"It's just not the Sam I know. That's all I meant. People have a lot of sides to them. We all contain multitudes or something like that, right?"

Paige snorts delicately. "Smart girl. Half the stories these people tell are bullshit anyway. Though I have to ask—is it true about the Great Dane incident? Because if so, that's the best meet-cute I've ever heard."

Heat floods my cheeks. "You know about that?"

"Everyone knows," Annika says. "The fearsome Samuil Litvinov, taken down by an oversized puppy and the tiny woman who couldn't control it? It's practically legend now."

I groan and bury my face in my hands. "Fantastic. Just what I needed to hear before meeting all these people."

"Oh, honey." Paige pats my knee. "That story is the reason half these vultures are actually giving you a chance. You made him human. Do you have any idea how rare that is?"

I peek through my fingers to find both women watching me with something like respect.

"Besides," Annika adds, "any woman who can make Samuil laugh in public is someone worth knowing. Now, about these renovations you're planning—I simply must introduce you to my interior designer. She specializes in historical properties..."

The conversation shifts to safer ground, but I can't shake Paige's words. *You made him human.*

I catch Sam's eye again across the room. This time when he looks at me, a hint of that legendary smile plays at the corners of his mouth.

Maybe we're humanizing each other.

The chime of a triangle draws everyone's attention. Mr. Morris stands a few steps up on the main staircase, dressed in a tuxedo that might predate the castle, complete with a top hat and coattails.

"Ladies and gentlemen," he says in that rolling brogue, "dinner shall be served momentarily. If your lords and lasses would like to join us..." He beckons to the formal dining room and the dozens gathered begin the slow shuffle inward.

I'm one of the last through the archway. On the other side, the endless dining table gleams beneath a sea of candles, their flames dancing in crystal goblets and gilded platters.

I trace the rim of my wine glass—sparkling grape juice, of course—and try not to fidget as forty pairs of eyes study my every move.

A slew of townspeople hired as catering support staff help everyone to their assigned seat. Annika catches my gaze from across the table and winks as a hush falls over the room. Her silent support steadies me, but my heart still thunders when Sam rises to his feet.

I know what he's going to say.

I know why he's going to say it.

That doesn't stop it from scaring the ever-loving fuck out of me.

His voice rebounds around the room, poised and graceful. "Colleagues. Friends. Thank you for joining us tonight."

His palm claims my shoulder, and I lean into his touch, drawing strength from his warmth. From his certainty.

"Many of you have wondered why I've been spending so much time in Scotland." Knowing chuckles ripple through the crowd. These people think they understand everything.

They don't know half of what we've survived to get here. "The answer is sitting right here."

The box he withdraws isn't the one that held my ring. This one is longer, heavier with promise and threat.

"I won't banter or belabor the point. I'm a man of few words, so here is what matters: Nova and I are engaged to be married." His words drop like depth charges into the pristine social waters. "And in about six months, we're expecting our first child."

Reaction explodes around us—gasps, whispers, the scrape of chairs as people lean forward for a better view of my belly. But I'm transfixed by Sam's hands as he opens the box. By the way candlelight ignites the rubies and diamonds within.

"May I?" he murmurs.

I nod, not trusting my voice.

The necklace settles against my throat—heavy, cold, then warming to my skin. Sam's fingers brush my neck as he fastens the clasp, and suddenly, I understand. This isn't just jewelry. This is a statement. A warning. A promise written in precious stones.

I am his now. His to protect. His to cherish.

And God help anyone who tries to come between us.

The rubies at my throat pulse with each breath, like droplets of blood marking my transformation. One accessory, and suddenly I'm worthy of these people's attention.

Amazing how quickly money and power can change people's attitudes. An hour ago, Nela was cutting me with her eyes. Now, as appetizers hit the table, she's cooing over my "perfect" bone structure and how the necklace suits me "as if it were made for you, darling."

I suppose that's the point.

Annika touches my arm as she passes. "Welcome to the family, sister." Her voice drops. "We'll have to get together soon. There's so much to discuss."

I'm not naive enough to think she means wedding colors.

The men treat me differently, too. Now, they include me in their conversations, testing my knowledge of business and world events. I hold my own—thank God for all those nights discussing Sam's work over dinner. When I make a particularly sharp observation about market trends in Eastern Europe, Josef's eyebrows shoot up.

"She has a brain behind that pretty face," he tells Sam, like I'm not sitting right here.

Sam's smile is shark-like. "She has *everything* behind that pretty face."

My hand drifts to my stomach, where our baby grows, blissfully unaware of the political theater playing out around us. These people can dress up their power plays in Chanel and champagne, but underneath, it's all fangs and territory markers.

Through second and third courses, I relax. By dessert, I can breathe. But as coffee begins to make the rounds, Paige passes behind my chair and clears her throat softly.

I turn to see her face—which has been full of laughter since the moment she arrived—looking strangely stricken. I don't know her well at all, but all my alarm bells are going off.

"We need to talk," she mumbles. "As soon as possible."

"That would be lovely," I say, both because it seems like the right response and because she seems like a genuinely kind soul in a room full of hyenas and trained killers.

Her French-manicured nails dig into my arm. "No, you don't understand. We need to *talk*. About Leonid."

My stomach lurches. "Sam's father?"

"He's..." She glances around, then leans closer. The scent of her expensive perfume makes my head spin. "Listen, when he comes—and he will come—don't let him..." She trails off as the door to the dining room creaks open.

"Speaking of the devil," someone mutters.

The room goes silent. Like someone hit pause on a movie. Even the candles seem to stop flickering.

Then Leonid Litvinov fills the doorway like a storm cloud.

His presence swallows all the air in the room, leaving nothing but cold anticipation. His dark eyes sweep the gathered guests before landing on me.

Unlike the last time we crossed paths, I no longer see any trace of Sam in his face. No proof of warmth or humanity at all. Just calculation and hunger as his thin lips curve into what might be a smile.

Or a declaration of war.

"Well," he says, his raspy voice carrying to every corner of the suddenly breathless room, "isn't this a charming family gathering?"

34

SAMUIL

It takes everything in me to stay unmoving.

"You still flinch when doors slam," my father used to tell me. *"Like Mother's departure left permanent echoes."*

Tonight, his entrance silences the dining room like a gunshot.

My first thought is for Nova. I reach for her and find her hand under the table. It's cold and trembling, but you wouldn't know it by looking at her face. From the shoulders up, she's ready for fucking war.

But she won't have to fight those fights. That's why I'm here. That's what I'm for: to go to battle on her behalf.

And if it's my father on the wrong end of my displeasure? So fucking be it.

He's earned his grave many times over.

But even then, she manages to surprise me. I'm halfway out of my seat, already clearing my throat to tell Leonid to fuck back off to whichever rat hole he crawled out of, when another voice cuts me off at the pass.

"Welcome to our home, Mr. Litvinov." Nova's voice carries clear across the room. Every eye turns on her. "I trust your journey from London was pleasant?"

Leonid's cold, gray eyes—the ones I inherited, but with hardly an ounce of the life in them—assess her from head to toe. He waltzes toward us with the measured steps of a predator. His cane tip scrapes over the flagstones. Nails on a chalkboard. Not an accident.

"My dear, I wouldn't have missed this for the world. And please, call me Father."

Nova's fingers curl into fists at her sides. "I reserve that title for those who've earned it."

The other oligarchs at the table shift uncomfortably. My muscles coil, ready to intervene, but Nova continues with perfect poise.

"Your place is set at the far end." She gestures to the opposite end of the table from where we sit. "I'm told you prefer distance from family gatherings."

Fuck. Even I feel the sting of that one.

My father's lips twitch. Amusement? Anger? It's never clear with him. "Far be it from me to wander where I shouldn't," he says. Then he reaches into his jacket and produces a small velvet box. "But before I go, a gift for my future daughter-in-law."

Something in my gut withers and dies. It's my body recognizing the object long before my mind does.

I can't look away as she takes it. As she opens it. As the flickering lights of the candle-lit chandelier overhead catches the familiar grooves and jewels of a ring.

The one my mother used to wear every day of her life.

It's silver and worn. It wouldn't look out of place in a pawn shop. But it sure as fuck looks out of place here—in this place that's supposed to be happy, supposed to be secure. It doesn't belong under this roof.

And it doesn't fucking belong in my fiancée's hands.

Nova, oblivious—because how could she know?—accepts it with a graceful nod. "How thoughtful. I'll add it to the collection of family heirlooms we keep in the east wing. The ones we never use."

The muscle in my father's jaw ticks. He inclines his head and moves to his assigned seat, but I catch the dangerous glint in his eye.

He didn't come here to make peace.

Unfortunately for him…

Neither did I.

The rest of dinner plays out like a game of Russian roulette. Every time my father lifts his fork, every time he opens his mouth to address one of my guests, I brace for the bullet.

But the bullet never comes.

Instead, he plays the gracious guest. Compliments the food. Makes small talk with Petrov about his recent acquisition of a Formula One team. Even manages to keep his snide comments about the castle's "rustic charm" to a minimum.

Nova handles it like she was born to this life. She directs the conversation with subtle grace, never letting silence linger too long, never allowing topics to stray into dangerous territory. More than one of my associates sends appreciative glances her way.

I should be proud. Should be focused on how perfectly she fits this role.

Instead, my mother's ring burns a hole in my brain. I see it every time Nova's hand moves, even though she tucked the box away. Even though she handled the situation perfectly.

She couldn't have known what that ring means. What giving it to her means.

But I do.

And so does he.

When the final course is cleared, my father dabs his napkin against his lips and rises. "Son," he says, "join me in the billiards room? For old times' sake?"

Nova's fingers find my thigh under the table. A gentle squeeze. Reassurance, maybe. Or a warning.

I stand, buttoning my jacket. "After you."

Time to play another round of Russian roulette. Only this time, I know the chamber's loaded.

And I know exactly where I want to aim.

A few of the men follow along, though they stay behind in the library to drink brandy and smoke cigars while my father and I venture deeper, into the rarely-used billiards room.

It stinks in here. Dust, cobwebs, fear. I take one glance back at our dinner guests before the door shuts behind me. They all look back, eyes wide like terrified rats. At least they're wise enough to stay away. There's violence brewing on this side of things.

Leonid positions himself where the shadows eat half his face. He sets his cane down and picks up a pool cue, chalking it with slow, deliberate twists of his wrist. "Shall we play for stakes, son?"

I cross my arms and regard him. "You're looking frail, Father. Sure you're up for it?"

His hands still on the triangle rack. Just for a heartbeat. But it's enough.

"My hands are steady enough to sink the black." He lines up the cue ball. "Unless you'd rather forfeit now. Like your mother did."

The rage builds slow and cold in my chest. He wants me to react. Wants me to give him an excuse.

Not tonight.

I chalk my cue with precise strokes. "Name your stakes."

"Simple enough." He breaks, scattering reds and yellows across the felt. "Your brother comes home. Takes his rightful place. And you—" His eyes glitter in the dark. "You get to keep playing happy families in this sheep-shit castle with your pregnant whore."

I sight down my cue at the perfect shot presenting itself.

Sometimes, the universe hands you exactly what you need.

"Counter offer."

I lean over the table, line up my shot. "You walk out of here tonight. Never contact me, Nova, or our child again. And in exchange, I won't burn everything you've built to the ground."

The solid green ball drops with a satisfying thunk.

"So angry." Leonid's smile slithers across his face. "My boy. My precious firstborn." He circles the table, tapping his cue against the floor with each step. "I came here tonight to congratulate you. On the engagement. On the baby. Such joyous occasions deserve family, do they not?"

He sinks a red without looking. "This is a prosperous time for us, Samuil. The Litvinov name commands more respect than ever. Our influence spans continents." Another shot. Another striped ball disappears. "But there's a shadow over us. A rift that needs mending."

I grip my cue tighter. "Ilya made his choices."

"He did. But he's young. Impetuous. The thing with Katerina —" Leonid waves his hand dismissively. "You were both fools over that woman. But now, you've found happiness. Real happiness. Shouldn't your brother have the same chance?"

"The same chance he tried to take from me?" I bark out a laugh. "The same chance that ended with him plotting to destroy everything I built?"

"The past is past." Leonid misses his next shot. On purpose. "Invite him here. Let him see what you've created. Show him there's a place for him in our future."

I study the table. Study the angles. Just like I study my father's face for signs of the trap I know lurks beneath his words.

"And if I refuse?"

Leonid shrugs. Sets his cue in the rack with careful precision. "Then I suppose we'll never know if your child could have had the family you never did."

The laughter bubbles up from somewhere deep and dark inside me. A place I didn't know existed until Nova crawled in there and made herself at home.

I line up another shot, focusing on the cue ball like it's Ilya's head. "You want me to give him another chance? After what he did to me?"

"Family is—"

The cue strikes true. But it's too much. Too angry.

The ball rockets off the table and explodes against the wall in a shower of composite fragments.

Father's eyes widen a fraction. Good. Let him see what decades of his psychological warfare have created.

"Let me tell you what family is." I stalk toward him, leaving the broken pieces where they fell. "*Family* is the woman out there who carries my child. *Family* is the friend I almost lost because I was too much like you. Family is what I'm building —what I'm protecting—from the poison you and Ilya represent."

"Such dramatics!" But his voice wavers. "I only want—"

"I know exactly what you want." The laughter comes again, soft and deadly. "You want me to take the snake back into my home. Give him another chance to strike. But here's what you don't understand, Father."

I lean in close. Close enough to see the pulse jumping in his throat.

"I'm not that little boy anymore. The one desperate for scraps of your approval. I'm not the man who married Katerina to please you. And I'm sure as fuck not going to risk my child's future on your games."

His eyebrows climb toward his hairline. "This isn't the reaction I expected."

"No." I grin. "I bet it's not."

Turning back, I lean against the rack. "Three months ago, your precious Ilyusha took my pregnant fiancée. Tied her up. Made her think I was coming to execute her." My voice stays conversational. Almost bored. "Before that, he used her as bait to start a war with the Andropovs. A war that's already claimed lives."

Father opens his mouth, but I hold up my hand.

"And that's just what he's done recently. Should we discuss the years of sabotage? The clients he's poached? The deals he's torpedoed?" I straighten my cuffs. "Or maybe we should talk about how he fucked my wife while planning to steal my company?"

"The past—"

"—is exactly where Ilya belongs." I push off from the rack. "If you think I'd let that rabid dog anywhere near Nova or my child, you're even stupider than he is."

I stride toward the door, pausing with my hand on the handle. "One more thing."

He raises an eyebrow.

"That ring you gave Nova? Mother's ring?" I meet his eyes. "I remember the day you made her sign it over. Remember how you played that video of her choosing drugs over me. Over and over."

His face pales.

"Touch my family again," I say softly, "and I'll make sure everyone knows exactly what kind of father you really are."

A beat.

A long beat.

Too long.

My father's face contorts into something monstrous as he swings the cue at my head. *"Svoloch! Ublyudok!"*

I catch the stick mid-arc, wood splintering in my grip. For a moment, we're frozen in this grotesque dance—him snarling, me calculating exactly how much pressure it would take to drive the shattered cue through his throat.

But Nova's upstairs. Carrying my child. My future.

I won't stain our home with his worthless blood.

"I'm going to give you five minutes to leave," I snarl. "If so much as a toe of yours is still on my property by the time those five minutes are up, I will sever it and drain you of every drop of toxic fucking blood left in your body. Do you understand me, Father?" I let the cue clatter to the floor between us. "Five minutes. Not a second more."

He draws himself up, shoulders squared. "You dare—"

"Four minutes, fifty seconds." I check my watch. "Tick tock, old man."

"This isn't over." His voice drops to a whisper. "You think

you can protect them? Your little *krasavitsa?* Your bastard? Ilya will—"

My hand finds his throat. Squeezes. Just enough to remind him how fragile life can be. "Four and a half minutes. Should I start counting body parts instead?"

He claws at my fingers, face purpling. I release him and he stumbles back, gasping.

"Four minutes." I straighten my jacket. "I'd hurry if I were you. The roads are awfully dark this time of night."

He snatches up his cane, backing toward the door, never turning away from me. "You'll regret this."

"Three minutes, forty-five." I smile. "And Father? Next time you raise a hand to me, make sure you finish the job. Because I sure as fuck will."

The door slams behind him. I count his uneven footsteps as he flees.

My phone buzzes. Nova.

Everything okay down there?

I type back: ***Never better, krasavitsa. Never better.***

35

SAMUIL

Red bleeds into my vision as I stalk the castle corridors. My father's words ricochet through my skull.

Your mother was weak. Your woman is weak. You, my son, are weak. And your child will be the weakest parts of each of you.

Each syllable drips with the same venom he used to poison my childhood, his voice still able to find those deep, raw places inside me where the scared little boy lives. The one who watched that video of his mother choosing drugs over him, over and over, until the truth was branded onto his bones.

I want to tear these stone walls down with my bare hands.

Fuck him.

Fuck every cold, calculating lesson he ever taught me about power and control.

Fuck the part of me that still desperately wants to prove him wrong.

Outside, the Scottish night wraps around me like a cold compress. The rage in my blood cools little by little with each breath of Highland air. Stars pierce the darkness overhead, countless pinpricks of light that remind me of winters in Moscow, of everything I've fought to leave behind.

Everything except the duty. The burden.

Protect what's mine. Always.

When Leonid says it, it's with that greedy, vengeful sickness that runs through his veins. Dirty fuel. Black, clotted, rotten fuel. And for the longest, whenever I said it, I meant it in the same way.

Because that's how he raised me. That's how he molded me.

But things have changed now. *Protect what's mine*—not so that no one else can have it, and not so that I can keep adding to my hoard, my empire, my wealth, my reach. It's *protect what's mine*—so that my strength guards the purity of the ones I love. It's *protect what's mine*—use my darkness to safeguard the light.

There's no denying one truth: I'm a beast. From tips to tail, inside and out, I am a monster.

But I can be a monster for the right reasons. I can be the thin black line between the nastiness of this world and the goodness of it. Nova, my child, the dogs—that is my empire now. That is what matters.

That's what I'll protect with my dying fucking breath.

And with that resolution, I can finally unclench. With them, I have purpose. I have clarity. I have calm—

Until movement near the barns snaps me back to high alert. My body knows what to do long before my mind does, muscle memory from years of looking over my shoulder, of expecting Katerina's claws or Ilya's knife in my back.

A lantern bobs through the darkness. Voices drift on the wind. My hand finds the Glock at my hip.

I ghost across the grounds at a silent sprint, keeping to the shadows. The barn looms higher as I approach, a block of black against the indigo night sky. The voices from within grow clearer—one definitely female. Nova? My finger curls around the trigger guard.

The barn door is cracked open, spilling warm light onto the grass. I sneak up to it. Crouch. Peer within.

I'm ready for fucking anything—whether it's Andropovs or my father's men or Leonid himself, I'll slaughter them all if they've dared to lay a hand on—

But no. It's not that. It's not anything like that at all.

The scene inside the barn steals my breath away.

Nova kneels in the straw, still decked out in her finest. Her emerald evening gown pools around her, diamonds glinting at her throat as she gently wipes a squirming newborn pup with a soft cloth. Her movements are precise, tender.

Infinitely caring. Endlessly loving.

"There you go, sweet girl. You're doing so well." Her voice carries that special tone she uses with animals, all warmth and encouragement. The mother collie pants, exhausted but trusting as Nova helps deliver another squirming puppy into Mrs. Morris's waiting blanket.

Something cracks open in my chest. A fissure in the granite walls I've spent decades building. Because this—this raw, pure moment of creation and nurturing—this is what I've been fighting for without even knowing it.

Not the endless power plays. Not the brutal chess matches with my father. Not the blood feuds or territory wars or offshore accounts with so many zeroes that it makes me sick just to look at them.

But *this.*

This woman. This fierce, beautiful soul who refuses to let this world's darkness dim her light. Who faces down crime lords without flinching, then turns around and delivers puppies in a drafty barn.

Mr. Morris, kneeling at the collie's head, spots me in the doorway and opens his mouth, but I shake my head slightly. *Not yet,* I mouth. I want to enjoy this for just one moment longer.

Nova's hands move with surgeon-like precision as she guides the last pup into the world. Even from here, I can see the tiny thing is struggling more than its siblings. Her fingers work quickly but gently, clearing its airways, rubbing life into its body.

"Come on, sweet one." She cradles the newborn close to her chest, uncaring that its wet fur is ruining her designer gown. "Fight for it. That's right."

The pup lets out a weak cry. Then a stronger one. Nova's shoulders sag with relief as she places it near its mother's belly with its littermates. It starts to suckle and only then do I realize that I've been holding my breath, too.

Something fierce and tender unfurls in my chest watching her. The way she gives herself over completely to caring for these creatures. The absolute focus. The boundless compassion.

My father would call it weakness. Would sneer at the very idea of the future Mrs. Litvinov playing midwife to farm dogs, kneeling in shit and hay, dripping jewels.

But I see the steel in her spine. The quiet strength it takes to remain soft in a hard world. To choose kindness over cruelty, time and time again.

She wipes her brow with the back of her hand, leaving a smudge of something I don't want to think about on her forehead. Her smile could light up the whole damn countryside as she counts the puppies one final time.

"Seven healthy babies." She beams at the Morrises. "Mama did beautifully."

I step fully into the barn then, unable to stay hidden any longer. Nova's eyes find mine, and despite everything—my father's poison, the weight of the Bratva, the constant danger —I know with bone-deep certainty that I will spend the rest of my life making sure that smile never dims.

I clear my throat softly. "Mr. and Mrs. Morris. Thank you for helping Nova. I'll take it from here."

They gather their things with knowing smiles, leaving us alone in the lantern-lit sanctuary. The mother collie whines softly in her nest of blankets, her newborns mewling as they find their way to milk.

Nova looks up at me, those gold-flecked eyes wide and questioning. Her cheeks are flushed, wisps of dark hair escaping her elegant updo. There's straw caught in the hem of her dress, and a smear of something on her shoulder that will probably ruin the fabric forever.

She's never been more beautiful.

When I pull her to her feet, she comes willingly. Her body trembles against mine—from the chill or from emotion, I'm not sure. Don't care. I just need to feel her, taste her, remind myself that this is real.

I cup her face in my hands. "My father sees weakness where I see strength. He thinks love makes you vulnerable. Makes you breakable." I press my forehead to hers. "But watching you tonight, *krasavitsa*... I finally understand what true power looks like."

Nova's fingers curl into my shirt. "Sam? Did something happen with your father?"

"That doesn't matter right now." I brush my lips across her temple, breathing in the scent of her skin beneath the barn's earthy musk. "The only thing that matters is you."

She makes a soft sound of protest, but I silence it with a kiss. Gentle at first, then deeper as she melts against me. Her mouth opens under mine, tasting of champagne and promises I'm finally ready to keep.

When we break apart, she studies my face in the lantern light. Those gold-flecked eyes see too much—always have. But for the first time, I don't feel the need to hide from her scrutiny.

"You're freezing," I murmur, shrugging out of my jacket to wrap it around her shoulders. The fabric swallows her small frame, and something primitive stirs in my chest at the sight of her wearing my clothes.

"The puppies—" she starts.

"Will be fine for a few minutes. Right now, I need you more than they do."

She looks at me. Squints. Wonders. But then she nods, and when my mouth finds hers, I wonder if it's possible to live in this moment forever.

Our second kiss starts soft but quickly blazes into something deeper, hungrier. More desperate. Nova's fingers dig into my shoulders as I lift her, pressing her back against a wooden beam. The silk of her dress whispers as it slides up her thighs.

"Sam," she breathes against my mouth. "Please."

That one word shatters my control. I take her there in the barn, surrounded by new life and old stone, my father's poison burning away into the ether with each gasp and moan she makes. When she cries out my name, her voice echoing in the rafters, it feels like forgiveness. Like grace.

It feels like coming home.

36

NOVA

The sheep look like cotton balls scattered across the misty fields below. I turn from the window and look again at the chaos engulfing the castle feast room. Just as she's been doing since the first hint of dawn this morning, Mrs. Morris barks orders at the staff like a four-foot-eleven general commanding troops into battle.

"The linens must be pressed twice, Callum! And for heaven's sake, Malcolm, polish those doorknobs until I see my reflection. If I spy so much as a hint of a fingerprint, so help me God..."

I hide my smile. The castle's already gleaming, but our housekeeper won't rest until every surface sparkles like the diamonds Sam gave me last week.

Speaking of my fiancé...

I descend the spiral staircase and find him at the breakfast table, phone in hand, dark brows furrowed in concentration. Nothing abnormal there. But his jaw twitches when I enter, and he checks his Patek Philippe three times in the thirty seconds I spend standing in the doorway, shamelessly admiring him.

"Important meeting?" I slide into the chair beside him, stealing a piece of bacon from his plate.

"Mm." He doesn't look up from his screen, but his free hand finds my thigh under the table, squeezing gently.

"Must be. Mrs. Morris is treating today like the Queen's coming for tea."

"Mrs. Morris is... enthusiastic." His lips quirk. "She takes initiative."

"'Initiative.'" I snort. "Is that what we're calling this not-so-covert military operation?"

Sam finally meets my eyes, and the tenderness there makes my heart stutter. "You deserve the best, *krasavitsa*."

"I already have it. Though if you'd like to tell me what the hell is going on, I really wouldn't mind that at all." I lean in to kiss him, but before I can Mrs. Morris's voice rings out again.

"—no, no! The flowers must be arranged precisely as I showed you. No, not like that—"

I sigh and pinch Sam's chin between my thumb and forefinger so he has no choice but to look at me. "One more time—and I really am begging this time—please, for all that is good and holy, tell me what is happening."

Sam grins and starts to give me the same answer he's given me for the last week, ever since the dinner party disaster, when he started dropping hints about a great "surprise" that will "blow me away." "You'll—"

I press a finger to Sam's lips. "If you say 'you'll see' one more time, I swear I'll—"

The familiar deep woof echoing across the castle grounds stops my heart mid-threat.

That bark.

I know that bark.

I'm out the door before the bark has even stopped echoing, nearly face-planting on the front gate's steps in my rush. The Scottish morning mist parts like a curtain as I sprint across the drive, my heart thundering against my ribs.

One black Range Rover has already stopped in front of the courtyard fountain. Another crawls through the gates and eases into park behind it.

Suddenly, I'm that seven-year-old girl again, watching life unfold in slow motion. But this time, instead of fear coiling in my gut, it's pure joy exploding within.

And then something actually explodes through the rear door of the first car.

Two somethings, actually. A pair of furry black shadows, each slobbering in their effort to outrace the other. I'm on my knees, ready to greet them, but there's no such thing as "ready" for what happens next.

Rufus and Ruby hit me like the runaway trains that they are. We flop backwards onto the soft sand of the driveway, a tangled mess of limbs and tails and tongues and me laughing again and again as tears I can't stop pour unchecked down my cheeks.

"Ru! Ru!" I keep crying out again and again. They whine, bark, squeal, squeak, and when they can't figure out how else to express their happiness, they run frantic circles before jumping on me to start the process all over again.

Through my happy tears, I spot two more figures emerging from the Range Rover. My heart, already full to bursting, somehow expands even more.

"Nova, darling!" Grams's voice carries across the courtyard.

Then I'm up and running, and I collide with Grams almost as hard as Rufus and Ruby collided with me.

"Be careful with her!" Hope scolds, hovering like a mother hen as I squeeze my grandmother in the hardest hug I can muster.

Grams waves off her helping hand. "Oh, hush. I may be old, but I'm not made of glass." Her eyes sparkle with their familiar mischief as she leans away, though she keeps her hands on my elbows so I can't go too far. She takes in the castle looming behind me. "Though I must say, this place looks like it's made of something even more precious."

I crash back into them both, wrapping my arms around them as Rufus and Ruby dance circles around us, barking their joy to the hills.

"Holy shit, Nova, you really undersold this place." Hope's practically vibrating with excitement. "You literally live in Hogwarts. Are there secret passages? Please tell me there are secret passages. And dungeons. There have to be dungeons."

"Language, young lady," Grams chides, but she's beaming as she cups my face in her weathered hands. "Let me look at you, sweetheart. My goodness, you are more beautiful than ever."

I can barely see through my tears, but when I turn to share their view of Castle Moorbeath, I catch a glimpse of Sam standing on the steps, hands in his pockets, satisfaction written in every line of his body.

He did this. He brought my family to me, gave me back the pieces of my heart I thought I'd have to live without.

The magnitude of what this means—what *he* means to me—sets the waterworks free all over again. Just when I thought I couldn't possibly love him more, he goes and proves me wrong.

Mrs. Morris's voice rings out from somewhere inside, probably having an aneurysm over the dogs tracking mud through her pristine halls, but for once, I couldn't care less about the chaos.

I have my family back.

We start the slow trek up the stairs to meet Samuil at the top.

"Serena," he remarks coolly as he kisses her cheek, "you look well. I hope the travel wasn't too strenuous."

"Oh, it was just awful," interjects Hope, her voice dripping with sarcasm. "Private jets and in-flight caviar service are just pure torture, you know?"

Myles comes trotting up from behind the wheel of one of the Range Rovers, grinning from ear to ear. "If you hated that, wait until I show you the three-thousand-thread-count silk sheets we'll be sleeping—I mean, *you'll* be sleeping on…"

I roll my eyes, laugh, and smack both Hope and Myles on the shoulder simultaneously. "For God's sake, save that for when I'm out of hearing range."

Mr. Morris materializes from nowhere with Rufus and Ruby trotting at his heels like they've known him their whole lives. "Lords and ladies, it would be my pleasure to take you on a brief tour of the grounds as the staff conveys your luggage to your quarters. If you'd be so kind as to follow me..."

He takes us on a circuit through the main parts of the castle, chest puffed with pride. He and Mrs. Morris have really gone above and beyond: custom-made beds for the dogs, a luxurious spread of bath products ready for Hope to use in the clawfoot tub, and at the end of proceedings, a tea service awaiting us in the library, with steam spiraling from the top of the china cups.

Grams and Mrs. Morris hit it off immediately, gossiping like the two old hens that they are. Hope and Myles disappear so he can "assist her with her luggage," which is an absolutely raunchy euphemism if I've ever heard one. And the dogs go gallivanting off to chase sheep under Mr. Morris's supervision. Even through the thick castle walls, their joy-filled barks are audible.

I'm still floating on cloud nine when Sam and I finally retire to our tower bedroom post-dinner. The happiness bubbles through my veins like champagne, making me giddy even hours after everyone's settled in.

Moonlight streams through the arrow-slit windows, painting silver stripes across our bed. I roll to face Sam, overwhelmed by the depth of emotion threatening to spill over.

"Thank you," I whisper, tears pricking my eyes. "Having them all here... it makes everything feel real."

Sam's arm slides around me, his large hand settling protectively over the slight swell of my belly. His touch grounds me, anchors me to this perfect moment.

"The castle needed more life in it," he admits, voice soft in the darkness. "More chaos. More family."

I feel his smile against my hair as Ruby's excited barking echoes up from the grounds. She's probably spotted the foxes that like to hunt near the sheep pen at night. Hope's bright laughter floats up from somewhere below, followed by Myles's deeper chuckle.

"Though perhaps slightly less chaos than Rufus trying to herd the sheep tomorrow," Sam adds dryly.

I laugh, burrowing deeper into his warmth. "He'll figure it out eventually."

"Like owner, like dog?"

I pinch his side in retaliation, but can't help grinning. "I'd say you're the one who needs herding, Mr. Litvinov."

Instead of arguing, he captures my mouth in a kiss that steals my breath and melts my bones. His hand slides lower, and suddenly, I'm very grateful for the thick stone walls between us and our guests.

"Show me how well you can handle an unruly beast," he murmurs against my lips.

"I've got a better idea," I whisper back. "Why don't you run wild for a change?"

37

NOVA

I wake before dawn. My fingers automatically seek Sam's warmth, but his side of the bed is cold.

I'm not worried, though. When I crane my neck to peer through the windows, I catch a glimpse of him running the dogs around the castle perimeter—his new morning ritual since Rufus and Ruby arrived.

It's funny how quickly we've all settled into our rhythm. Two weeks since I cried so many happy tears that Mrs. Morris worried I'd get dehydrated and forced a literal gallon of tea down my throat, life feels like we've always done it this way.

Samuil runs the dogs. Grams and Mrs. Morris stroll the loch. Hope and Myles "sleep in" until second breakfast is served, though there isn't a single soul in the castle who believes they're doing much actual sleeping.

It's easy. It's simple. It's perfect. It's pure.

But today, everything changes.

My stomach flips at the thought. For once, it's not morning sickness. It's because, today, we find out if this tiny spark of life inside me is real. If it has a heartbeat. If it's healthy.

If it's a sign that Sam and I can create something beautiful together.

The thought sends me sprinting to the bathroom, where I promptly dry heave into the toilet. It's the first time I've done that in a while.

"First ultrasound jitters?" Hope leans against the doorframe, already dressed in yoga pants and one of Myles's old Dartmouth hoodies.

"That obvious?" I mumble, wiping my mouth as I rise back to my feet.

"Only to someone who's known you since you tried to rescue that three-legged raccoon in tenth grade." She hands me a cup of ginger tea. "Come on. Mrs. Morris made those little egg things you like."

But the mini quiches—usually my favorite—sit untouched on my plate while everyone else demolishes breakfast. Even Grams, who usually picks at her food like a bird, helps herself to seconds.

Sam's hand finds my knee under the table. "Eat, *zaychik*. The appointment isn't for hours."

I nod. "Yeah. You're right." But I barely manage two bites before my fork clatters to my plate. "What if something's wrong, though? What if—?"

"Then we'll handle it." His voice carries the same steady conviction that made me fall for him in the first place. "Together."

Grams reaches across the table to squeeze my hand. "That's right, dear. And you've got all of us right here with you."

The lump in my throat makes it impossible to respond, but as I look around at my family, I realize they're right.

Whatever happens today, I'm not alone anymore.

"Anyway!" Hope claps to signal a change of subject. "Let's talk about what's really on everyone's mind: wallpaper. The nursery absolutely needs a woodland theme. You know, since you two met because of a certain four-legged menace."

Right on cue, Rufus lifts his head from where he's sprawled at my feet and gives a low *woof*.

"Speaking of menaces," Grams says, her eyes twinkling, "did I ever tell you about the time Nova was born? She came three weeks early, right in the middle of a blizzard. Your father had to—"

I tense at the mention of my dad, but Sam's fingers tighten on my knee, grounding me. The familiar weight of his hand anchors me to this moment, to this room full of people who actually love me.

"More tea, dear?" Mr. Morris swoops in with the pot before I can answer. "And a scone. You'd best finish that, or Mrs. Morris will have your head. The wee bairn needs its strength for its photo shoot today."

I open my mouth to protest, but before I can, I catch Sam watching me from the corner of my eye. The ice in his gray eyes has melted into something molten, something that makes my breath catch.

It's the same look he gave me that first day with Rufus, when the Great Dane knocked us both into Lake Michigan. Like he sees past all my carefully constructed walls straight to the scared girl inside who just wants someone to stay.

"One more cup," I concede, letting Mr. Morris fill my mug. "But only because you're all being so nice about my impending mental breakdown."

"You'll do nothing of the sort, lass," he scolds me playfully. "You've got too many of us here to keep you upright."

~

For a local spot in this quiet Scottish town, the clinic is surprisingly fancy.

The waiting room looks like it was plucked straight from a London magazine spread, all gleaming teak and soft, recessed lighting. But what catches my attention isn't the décor—it's how the receptionist's face lights up when she sees Sam.

"Mr. Litvinov! And this must be Mrs. Nova." She beams at me like we're old friends. "We're so delighted to have you here with us today. Dr. MacPherson's been reviewing your file personally."

Of course he has. My mountain of a man may act like this is just another Tuesday morning, but I know better. The way his hand stays pressed against my lower back, the slight tension in his jaw—he's been planning this appointment down to the smallest detail.

Grams squeezes my fingers as we settle into the plush chairs. "Remember when we used to play doctor with your dolls?" she whispers. "You always insisted on being both the doctor and the worried mama."

I let out a teary laugh. How many times did I drag my toy medical kit to her apartment, seeking refuge from the chaos at home? She never turned me away, not once.

"I still have that little stethoscope," she continues. "Been saving it, just in case."

My eyes burn. Stupid pregnancy hormones. "Grams…"

"None of that now, sweetness." She pats my cheek. "Save the waterworks for when you see your little one."

Before I can respond, a nurse appears. "Ms. Pierce? We're ready for you."

Sam helps me up, and as we follow the nurse down the hallway, I catch his reflection in a glass panel. His face is carved from stone, but his eyes—his eyes tell a different story.

He's just as nervous as I am.

The exam room is warm and dim, like a cocoon. I lie back on the padded table, my hand finding Sam's as the technician bustles around with practiced efficiency. Her Scottish lilt reminds me of Mrs. Morris as she explains each step, each piece of equipment.

"This might be a wee bit cold," she warns, squirting gel onto my stomach.

I flinch at the temperature, and Sam's fingers tighten around mine. His thumb traces circles on my palm—the same soothing pattern he uses when I wake from nightmares.

The technician's wand glides over my belly as she chatters with Grams about the weather, but I barely register their voices over the *whoosh-whoosh* sound filling the room. Is that—?

"Ah, there we are." The technician taps a few keys, freezing the image. "Look at that strong heartbeat."

"Just like her grandmother." Grams leans forward, squinting at the screen. "I had two miscarriages before Nova's father, you know. The doctor said my heart wasn't strong enough to carry, but I showed him."

The technician laughs appreciatively. "We do love to see fighting genes in our mamas-to-be. And it's so nice to have this many generations here for support! Will other grandparents be joining for future visits?"

The technician's innocent question slices through our bubble of calm.

Sam goes completely still beside me. The temperature plummets.

My heart aches at the thought of the empty spaces in this room. Two ghosts hover at the edges of our happiness—a junkie who sold her son for a fix, and a man who recorded the transaction just to torture that same little boy for decades.

The worst part? I can picture exactly how this scene *should've* played out. In a different world, a better world, Leonid would've worn that pinched expression he gets whenever something threatens his control. He'd lean against the wall, pretending indifference, but there'd be a heart beating beneath that mask that would love his grandson like no other.

And Samuil's mother? In that parallel universe where she chose her son over her addiction, she'd be here clutching Sam's other hand, weeping with joy over her first grandchild.

Instead, we have these shadows. These what-ifs. These could-have-beens. These severed, bleeding stumps of the family tree.

"We're keeping things intimate for now," I cut in quickly, forcing brightness into my voice. "Just immediate family."

The technician's professional smile never wavers as she positions the wand. "Right then. Well, let's see what we can see, shall we?"

I hold my breath, grateful when she launches into technical explanations about measurements and markers and this and that. It's all gibberish to me right now. Sam's grip on my hand remains vise-like, but I feel the exact moment some of the tension leaves his shoulders.

This is our family now—the one we're building together. The one we chose. The one that includes my grandmother's gentle wisdom and Hope's infectious laughter, but not the grim shadows of our pasts.

The technician adjusts something on her screen, and suddenly, a new rapid swooshing fills the room. "Ah-ha! There we are," she says softly. "That's your baby's heartbeat."

I can't breathe. My world narrows to the grainy black-and-white image on the screen, to the frenetic flutter that means our baby is alive. Real. Growing inside me.

Sam's fingers crush mine, but I barely notice the pain. I'm too busy memorizing every detail of this moment—the catch in Grams's breath, the way Hope sniffles behind me, the steady *thump-thump-thump* that proves Sam and I made something miraculous together.

"There's your baby." The technician's voice is gentle as she points to a tiny shape on the screen. "Would you like to know the sex?"

Sam and I shake our heads in perfect sync. After everything that's happened, this one surprise feels right. Sacred, almost.

His breath tickles my ear as he leans down. "*Krasavitsa*," he whispers, and for the first time since I've known him, his voice cracks on the word.

It's all he needs to say.

I tear my gaze from the screen to look at him. His gray eyes shine with unshed tears, and the sight undoes me completely. This man who calculates every move, who guards his emotions like nuclear codes, is crying over our baby.

"Everything looks perfect," the technician continues, but her words fade into background noise. I'm lost in Sam's expression, in the way his thumb taps a rhythm on my knuckles, in the realization that this is what unconditional love looks like.

We're going to be parents. We're going to give this child everything we never had—safety, stability, the knowledge that they're cherished beyond measure.

The future stretches before us, bright with possibility.

For once, I'm not afraid.

~

Back at the castle, I'm floating, weightless with joy, as Sam's security detail crowds around him to examine the ultrasound photos.

"Look at that nose—definitely yours, boss." Viktor peers closer at the grainy image. "Poor kid."

"Nah, that's all Nova." Dmitri jabs a thick finger at the picture. "See that stubborn little chin?"

"The head shape," Myles cuts in. "I'd know that ugly melon anywhere. That's your kid, Samuil. Apologies, Nova—your son or daughter will no doubt grow into it eventually, but the Litvinov skull is like a bowling ball on steroids."

"You're all wrong." Sam tucks the photos away carefully, reverently. "This child will be perfect because he or she is ours." His eyes meet mine, molten silver and fierce with pride. "*Krasavitsa,* we made this."

Hope squeezes my hand as fresh tears spill down my cheeks. "Yeah," I whisper. "We did."

Mrs. Morris comes bursting from the kitchen to wrap me in a bone-crushing hug that smells of lavender and fresh-baked scones.

"Come, come!" She practically drags me toward the great hall. "We've been dying to show you."

The hall has been transformed. Tiny white flowers spill from porcelain vases, and the afternoon sun streams through stained glass windows, painting everything in ruby, turquoise, and honey-gold light.

But what stops me in my tracks is the wooden cradle beside the crackling hearth.

Mr. Morris, standing behind it, shifts anxiously from foot to foot. As soon as he sees me, he starts blabbering. "Solid base. Articulating joints to rock the wee 'un. Oak's traditional, see?

For strength. Proper flex in the cold weather, too." His callused hands hover over the perfectly smooth rails. "Been working on it since you arrived. The carvings, they're protection runes—old Highland magic and such. Silly old nonsense, I'm sure, but... well, you never know. Can't hurt. Anyway, enough rambling."

I trace the intricate Celtic knots with trembling fingers. "It's... it's beautiful."

"And this!" Mrs. Morris thrusts an impossibly small package into my arms. "For the wee bairn's first winter."

Inside lies a cream-colored, hand-knitted sweater, so delicate it feels like holding a cloud. Tiny cables twist up the front like vines.

I gather them both in a hug and cry some more.

~

The sun has barely begun to set when Sam guides me up the winding stone steps to our tower room, his palm warm against my lower back. The ultrasound photos are still clutched in my other hand—I haven't been able to let them go.

He pauses at the threshold, then scoops me into his arms. "Let me take care of you tonight, Nova."

My heart stutters at the raw tenderness in his voice. This is a different Samuil than the one who I used to know. His touch is worshipful as he undresses me, each brush of his fingers igniting sparks under my skin.

"So beautiful," he whispers, laying me back on our bed. His

lips trail fire down my neck, across my collarbone. "*Ya lyublyu tebya*."

I arch into his touch, desperate for more, but he takes his time. Gone is the demanding passion that usually drives us both wild. Instead, his hands drift over my body like he's memorizing every inch, paying special attention to my starting-to-swell stomach.

"Our miracle," he murmurs against my skin. "You're giving me everything I never dared want."

The emotions of the day crash over me like a wave, and tears spill down my cheeks. Sam kisses them away, one by one, his gray eyes rippling with love.

"A family," he breathes between kisses. "A future."

I wrap my arms around his broad shoulders, pulling him closer. In this moment, wrapped in his strength and warmth, I've never felt safer or more cherished.

"I love you," I whisper, and his answering kiss tastes like promises kept.

When he moves into me, it doesn't feel like sex. It's too soft and tender and seamless for that. It's just the beautiful friction of his skin on mine, and with the fire chuckling happily in the corner, I'm bathed in warmth from it and him alike.

He kisses me as he fucks me, and he holds me all the while. I come fast and then I just stay there, hovering on the edge between one orgasm and the next.

"Come with me," I beg Sam. As I do, I lock my heels behind the small of his back so he has no choice but to empty himself inside of me. There's only the briefest instance of panic on his face before he's laughing as he explodes.

I feel like we're sharing one breath when he kisses me. When he holds me. When he stays nestled inside me and we fall together onto the pillows, laughing again for no reason at all.

I'm not sure how long we lie there. I'm still floating in that hazy space between dreams and reality when the mattress shifts. Sam's warmth disappears from behind me, and the loss draws me partially awake. Through heavy lids, I watch him pad to the window seat where he left his phone.

The castle's stones glow in the moonlight streaming through the curtain gap, casting strange shadows across Sam's bare chest. His face illuminates in the blue glow of his screen, and for a heartbeat, I glimpse the ruthless Bratva boss beneath my gentle giant.

Ice crystallizes in his eyes. That familiar muscle ticks in his jaw. His shoulders bunch with predatory tension.

Then his gaze finds me in our bed, and the frost melts away. The twinkle in his eye reignites.

He sets the phone aside and rejoins me. The mattress dips as he slides under the covers. His arms cage me against his chest, one broad palm cupped possessively over my stomach where our child grows. His breath fans warm against my neck, and despite that flash of darkness I just witnessed, I've never felt more protected.

"Sleep, Nova," he murmurs, pressing a kiss behind my ear. "All is well."

I should ask what message disturbed his peace. I should worry about what new threat lurks on the horizon.

But right now, wrapped in Sam's strength, feeling our baby flutter beneath his palm, I choose to focus on this moment of perfect contentment.

Tomorrow will bring what it brings. Tonight, I let myself drift away in my fierce protector's embrace, choosing to believe that whatever storms gather, Sam will shelter us from the rain.

38

SAMUIL

The sound of Nova's laughter drifts across the library, every bit as warm as the sunbeams slanting through the stained glass. She's curled up with Hope on the leather sofa, both of them pouring over a pile of books while discussing their plans for some animal sanctuary they plan on building out by the sheep pens.

Their enthusiasm makes the musty old shelves and creaky floorboards feel more like home than any of my penthouses ever did.

Everyone else has caught the same peaceful vibe. Rufus and Ruby are sprawled at Nova's feet like furry throw rugs, with all the puppies scattered between them. Through the window, I spot Serena and Mrs. Morris mapping out the spring gardens, their gestures animated as they debate the merits of various vegetable placements.

My security team's settled in, too. Viktor is sprawled at one door, Mikhail at another. Myles has been in and out all morning, whistling everywhere he goes like one of Snow White's fucking dwarves.

It's a rare sight.

It should probably set off warning bells.

Instead, I find myself memorizing the moment. This implausible snapshot of contentment.

The way Nova's hair catches the light. Her free hand absently stroking her growing belly. How Hope teases her about naming all the future sanctuary animals after romance novel heroes, and the way Nova shamelessly says, "Yes, as a matter of fact, I am."

This is what I've been fighting for without even knowing it. A fortress not built on fear, but filled with life and—

"Samuil."

Myles appears in the doorway. My chest tightens before he even opens his mouth.

I know that look. I despise that look. I hoped to never see that look again.

"I got a report." His voice is low, meant for my ears only. "We need to talk. Now."

I rise. Nova glances up, her smile fading as she reads my expression. "I'll be back in a moment," I tell her. "Keep the fire going."

I follow Myles into my study, leaving warmth and laughter behind. The moment the door closes, his shoulders square.

Bad news incoming. I find myself wishing I'd kissed Nova goodbye.

"Ilya's gone." Myles runs a hand over his buzzcut. "The safe house in Novosibirsk is empty. Clean as a fuckin' whistle, man. Like he was never there."

Ice surges through my veins. "How long?"

"Unknown. Our guy missed two check-ins. When the backup team arrived, they found him with his throat slit. Professional job."

Fuck. My brother's always been a snake, but this is different. This is calculated. Patient.

Not Ilya's style at all.

I cross to the window. From here, I can see the north wing where our bedroom used to be. Where Nova spent those first weeks after I brought her here, scared and unsure. Before she made this drafty pile of stones into something worth protecting.

The muscles in my jaw ache from clenching my teeth. When I turn my head, I have a vantage into the library I just left. Through the window, I watch Nova lean closer to Hope, pointing at something in one of their books.

So innocent. So pure.

So fucking vulnerable.

"Triple the security detail," I rumble to Myles, forcing my voice to stay measured. "I want four men on Nova at all times, rotating in six-hour shifts. Get Dmitri's team down from Edinburgh. And contact our London crew—I need eyes on every property Ilya's touched in the past five years."

"Already started the calls." Myles pulls out his phone, his fingers flying. "But Sam… this isn't like him. Ilya's always been a hothead. Leaving zero trace? Taking out our guy that cleanly? It's—"

"Like someone's coaching him." As always, Myles is thinking exactly what I'm thinking. "Someone patient. Someone who knows how to play the long game."

"Someone like Katerina."

I nod. "She's had years to work on him. To channel all that raw hatred into something calculated. Looks like she did a good job."

"Fuck." Myles scrubs a hand over his face. "Want me to send the team in right now?"

"No. She'll be expecting that." I drum my fingers on the windowsill, mind racing through scenarios. "Focus on the places they wouldn't think we'd look. Storage units. Dead drops. Those old shipping containers by the docks that the Andropovs think we don't know about."

Nova's laugh drifts through the walls, and my chest constricts. Everything I love is right here in this castle.

Which makes it the perfect target.

"And Myles?" I turn from the window. "Not a word to Nova or the others. As far as they're concerned, nothing's changed."

He nods grimly. "What about the FBI operative? Boyko—remember him? Could reach out—"

"No. This stays in the family."

After a moment of hesitation, he inclines his head. "As you wish, *pakhan.*" Then he turns to begin carrying out my orders.

I watch him go, already coordinating teams through his earpiece. The library's warmth beckons, but I can't face Nova right now. Not with murder on my mind.

My phone buzzes. It's Viktor, forwarding the latest surveillance photos from that email trap Hope and Nova set, right on time with his regular daily submission.

I flick through the pictures. Katerina's Aston Martin, parked outside a boutique hotel in Geneva. Her platinum hair gleaming as she kisses some oligarch on both cheeks. Her stilettos clicking across marble floors to the elevator.

I've been sitting on this intel for weeks, telling myself there was time. That I could afford to play the long game while Nova settled into the castle, while we built something real here. Something worth protecting.

But Ilya's new patience changes everything. The brother I knew would have stormed the castle gates by now, guns blazing. This calculated ghost routine? That's pure Katerina. She's finally managed to leash his rage and aim it in the right direction.

And I won't stand to have guns pointed at my family.

I just told Myles not to unleash the wolves, but…

Change of fucking plans.

I pull up the command chat and type out a message to the inner circle: ***Execute Option Red. No witnesses.***

Twelve of my best are already in position around that Geneva hotel. They've been there for days, waiting for my word. Within moments of my text being sent, I watch their body cam feeds flicker to life on my monitors, checking weapons, moving into formation.

In a few short minutes, Katerina will be dead.

I take a seat at my operations center. Through a dozen live camera feeds, I watch my men creep through Katerina's hotel like black-clad ghosts. Their night vision equipment bathes everything in an otherworldly green glow.

Empty bathtub. Abandoned bedframe, no mattress. Dust motes dancing in flashlight beams.

Too empty.

Too clean.

My fingers drum against the mahogany desk as I toggle between views. Something's off. Katerina's precise, methodical—a shark in stilettos—but this level of pristine organization isn't her style. She enjoys leaving a trail of breadcrumbs, little fuck-you souvenirs designed to get under my skin.

"West corridor clear," Anatoly murmurs through my earpiece.

"En-suite bathroom clear," adds Igor.

I lean closer to the monitors, scanning for any hint of movement. The place should be crawling with signs of my ex-wife's presence.

Instead, there's nothing but shadows and silence.

"Sir." Alexei's voice crackles. "You need to see this."

His body cam swings toward a wall. At first glance, it appears blank. But as he moves closer, I spot faint marks in the concrete. Letters carved with painstaking precision:

TICK TOCK

Below the message is today's date. And beneath that, lying forlornly on the carpet…

… is the ring I gave her on the day we were married.

"Pull out," I order, my voice deadly calm even as my heartbeat pounds like fucking thunder in my temples. "Now. Fucking *NOW!*"

My men don't hesitate. They know that tone.

As their feeds show them retreating toward the exit points, my mind races. Katerina's letting me know she's always one step ahead. That ring—it's not meant for me. It's meant for Nova.

My queen.

My weakness.

I reach for my phone to call Myles, but before I can dial, all twelve camera feeds suddenly go black. The audio channel lives one moment longer—long enough to hear an earsplitting *boom,* laced with the sounds of my best men dying.

My phone erupts. Alerts from my teams in Chicago, Moscow, Dubai—all hitting simultaneously.

Not random. Not coincidence.

I scan the incoming reports with numb fingers. Each one is worse than the last. Our Dubai shipping operation—decimated. The Chicago data center—breached. Three warehouses in Moscow's industrial district—burning.

Sixteen dead. Twenty-eight wounded. Millions in assets, gone.

The timestamps tell the story. Every attack executed within the same five-minute window. This wasn't just Katerina being clever with a hotel trap. This was a masterpiece of timing and coordination, planned down to the second.

And I fucking missed it.

I've been too distracted building my fairy tale here in Scotland. Playing lord of the manor while Katerina and Ilya meticulously tied a noose around my throat. They used my own tactics against me—patience, precision, the long game.

All those surveillance photos of Katerina in Geneva? Bait. The IP address she "accidentally" revealed? Bullshit. She wanted me focused there while they positioned their pieces everywhere else.

My phone buzzes again. Myles.

"Three more locations hit in St. Petersburg," he says without preamble. "They're going after everything, Sam. Even the legitimate businesses. They just blew up a fucking laundromat in Queens, for God's sake."

Through the window, I catch a glimpse of Nova still laughing with Hope in the library.

I've tried to keep her separate from this darkness. To give her the peaceful life she deserves.

But now, my enemies have declared total war. And I'll have to become the monster she fears to keep her safe.

Myles bursts into the room, panting. "Sam—"

"Get Artem's team in Chicago to summon all hands on deck," I tell him, my voice dropping to the arctic register I haven't used since coming to Scotland. "And call in every favor we're owed from every fucking family in Chicago. We're going to war."

"Sam, I—"

"War means follow fucking orders, Myles. The only thing I want to hear from you is *yes, pakhan*."

He sighs. I see all the questions in his eyes, the dying hope, the withering belief that maybe the man I used to be was actually gone for good. Fuck, I'd almost believed it, too.

Katerina and Ilya have proved us both wrong.

"Pull in every soldier we have between here and Moscow. I want a strike team ready in four hours."

"Sam," Myles says one last time, "you're talking about a lot of people losing their lives. You're talking about Armageddon."

"They already started it." I check my weapons, the familiar weight of my Glock settling against my ribs like an old friend. "I'm going to finish it."

Through the study door, I hear Nova's laughter fade. Soon, she'll realize her fairytale is over. That her prince is actually the dragon.

"What about Nova?" Myles asks quietly. "She's going to—"

"She knew what I was when she agreed to marry me." The words come out sharp as broken glass. "This is who I am. Who I've always been. I just forgot for a while."

I move toward the door, already plotting trajectories and kill zones. The monster my father created is wide awake now, and he's thirsty for blood.

"Sound general quarters," I order. "We're going hunting."

I stride down the hallway, my footsteps echoing off stone walls that have witnessed centuries of violence. Fitting, since I'm about to add a new, bloody chapter to the history books.

The library's oak door swings open before I reach it. Nova stands in the opening, her gold-flecked eyes wide with concern. "Sam, I—" She sees my face and frowns. "Sam…? What's happening?"

Her voice—so soft, so fucking tender—makes my hands curl into fists. I shoulder past her to the walk-in closet, yanking tactical gear from hangers.

"Go back to your books," I snarl. "This doesn't concern you."

She flinches but plants herself in place. Always so brave, my little queen. So determined to save everyone, even the monsters who don't deserve it.

"Like hell it doesn't. We're in this together."

I whirl to face her, letting her see the ruthless killer I've kept caged these past months. The one who's executed men for far less than the destruction Katerina and Ilya just wreaked.

"No, we're not." I loathe the sound of my own voice. So hateful, so cold I want to shiver. "This is my world, and you need to stay the hell out of it."

Devastation crashes across her face. Her hand flies to her stomach—to our child—and something inside me fractures. But I force myself to keep moving, to stuff weapons into my go-bag while she watches in mute horror.

Better she sees the truth now. Better she understands that the man she fell in love with was just a fantasy. A temporary fiction we both allowed ourselves to believe in.

The real Samuil Litvinov deals in blood and bullets, not happily-ever-afters. And it's time I remembered that.

It's time she did, too.

I zip the bag closed with brutal finality. When I turn, Nova's tears shine in the dim light, but she lifts her chin defiantly.

My beautiful, stubborn woman.

I pray she lives long enough to hate me for this.

39

NOVA

"That's not the man I love."

I keep saying that to myself again and again. I'm still shaking from Sam's transformation. One moment, he was my Samuil —the man who held my hand during our ultrasound, who kissed away my morning sickness, who's learning to let others into his carefully guarded world.

The next? A stranger with glacial eyes barking orders in Russian while his men scattered like roaches. *This is my world, and you need to stay the hell out of it.*

The late afternoon sun casts long shadows across the castle grounds as I trudge down the lane. Rufus and Ruby flank me like bodyguards. My hands rest on my swollen belly, protecting our child from the darkness that's crept back into our lives.

"What do you think, guys?" I scratch behind Rufus's ears. "Think Daddy will—"

My foot catches on something solid and I stumble forward. Ruby's quick reaction is the only thing that saves me from face-planting.

"Thanks, girl." I steady myself on her broad back and peer at the obstacle.

The shape sprawled across the path isn't a fallen branch or wandering sheep.

It's a man.

A badly injured man. Blood mats his hair and stains his torn jacket.

Rufus's hackles rise. A low growl rumbles in his chest.

"Hello?" I squeak. "Sir, are you hurt?"

His eyelids flutter. Chapped lips part. "Need... Litvinov." The words rasp out in an American accent—weird, given that we're deep in the middle of rural Scotland. "Only... him."

My heart thumps against my ribs. This is exactly the kind of situation Sam warned me about—strangers who might be friends or foes. The smart thing to do would be turn and run. But I can't leave an injured man lying here, bleeding into Scottish soil.

I reach for my phone, then remember it's still in the war room where Sam's holding court.

Shit.

I glance back down. His face is a mess of cuts and welts, one eye swollen completely shut. Someone worked him over good. The kind of beating meant to send a message.

I scan the perimeter, looking for signs of how he got here. The castle grounds are surrounded by state-of-the-art security. Guards patrol the gates 24/7. Sam's paranoia means every inch is monitored by cameras.

Yet somehow, this guy slipped through.

My fingers hover over his wrist, checking his pulse. Strong but erratic. "Sir? Can you tell me your name?"

His good eye snaps open—sharp, alert despite his injuries. He grabs my arm with surprising strength.

"Tell Litvinov..." Blood trickles from the corner of his mouth. "They're... they're..."

Ruby barks a warning as the man's grip goes slack. His eye rolls back, consciousness slipping away again like the tides.

My pulse hammers as the stranger's grip tightens on my arm. Even when barely conscious, he's surprisingly strong. Blood smears across my skin where his fingers dig in. The dogs circle us, hackles raised.

A groan rips from the man's throat when I shift him into a more comfortable position. His face contorts, and fresh blood wells from a gash above his eyebrow.

"Rufus." I turn to the dog. "Go get Sam. Find Sam."

Rufus's ears prick. He lingers for another moment, but when I say Sam's name again, he whines and takes off toward the castle, huge paws eating up the ground with every stride.

"Help is coming." I touch the stranger's shoulder, careful to avoid his obvious injuries. "We have a clinic in the village. They're discreet and—"

"No." His fingers clamp down harder. "No village."

"You need medical attention. These wounds—"

"No people." His good eye fixes on my face with laser focus. "Only… only Litvinov."

I try for reason. "Sir, you're hurt. Let me at least call—"

"Samuil." The name comes out as a wet rasp. More fresh blood wells up and stains his teeth pink. "Need… Samuil."

A chill skitters down my spine. Ruby whines and presses against my leg as thunder rumbles in the distance.

"C'mon, Rufus," I mutter under my breath, looking up again and again toward the thin slice of the castle I can see through the trees. "C'mon, Sam."

The storm is getting denser and darker overhead by the time I finally spy motion at the head of the trail. Dark shapes grow, along with the growl of matching engines, until finally, pebbles spray as a pair of ATVs skid to a stop ten feet away.

Samuil vaults off the first one before the engine dies, moving with lethal grace despite his speed. His expression shifts from concern to recognition to rage in the space of a heartbeat. Mr. Morris watches warily from the second.

"Get back, Nova." The command cuts through the evening air.

I stay put. "He needs help."

"Nova." Steel threads through Sam's voice. "Move away from him. Now."

Reluctantly, I scoot a few feet back. The stranger tries to cling to me as Samuil approaches, but his torn jacket falls open, revealing a nasty gash leaking dark blood, and he groans again in a way that sounds worse than any noise he's made yet.

Sam's jaw ticks as he takes in the man's battered face, the blood-soaked clothing. Recognition flares in his eyes, followed by something darker. More dangerous.

"Your wife…" The stranger coughs wetly. "Quite… helpful."

"Fiancée." Sam's correction is automatic, but his focus stays razor-sharp on the injured man. "What happened?"

"Need to… talk." Red-flecked spit bubbles at the corner of his mouth. "Private."

Ruby growls as Sam crouches beside us. His hand replaces mine on the stranger's wrist, checking his pulse. "You appearing here like this—it's a message. From whom?"

The man's eyes roll back once again, eerie déjà vu from just a few minutes ago. He fades back into silence.

"Mr. Morris," Sam orders, "call the doctor. The one who knows how to be discreet." He slides his arms under the unconscious man's armpits and hauls him upright. "And Nova? We need to talk about your habit of helping strays."

The way he says it—like I'm some naive child who needs scolding—makes my blood boil. But the iron in his eyes stops my retort cold.

He and Mr. Morris carefully lift the stranger into the ATV's cargo bed. The unconscious man flops like a rag doll, head lolling against the metal rim.

"He said no clinics." I wrap my arms around my belly, the baby kicking as if sensing the tension. "He was adamant about only talking to you."

"Of course he was."

"You know him?" I step closer, but Sam's sharp look pins me in place.

"Yes." He wipes his muddy, bloody hand on his slacks. "We need to get him to the castle immediately. Mr. Morris—"

"Already messaging the doctor, sir."

"Good." Sam's shoulders bunch with tension as he scans the darkening lane. "I need to check the perimeter, see how he got here. Nova—" He turns to me, expression softening fractionally. "Go back with Mr. Morris. Find Myles. Stay with him until I return."

"But—"

"No arguments." His thumb brushes my cheek, the gesture at odds with his commanding tone. "And don't call the police. Under any circumstances."

Thunder cracks overhead as Sam strides off into the gathering gloom, leaving me with more questions than answers. The stranger moans from the cargo bed, muttering something I can't decipher.

Mr. Morris guns the ATV's engine. "Coming, Mrs. Nova?"

I climb on behind him, my engagement ring catching the last rays of sunlight. The gold band feels heavier than usual, weighted with the mud of the trail, the blood of a stranger, and secrets I'm not sure I want to know.

Mr. Morris guns the engine and we shoot off down the path toward the castle. I take one last look over my shoulder as we go. Samuil is a shadow amongst shadows.

Then the darkness swallows the last of him.

40

SAMUIL

The trail cuts through dense pines, their branches swaying in the wind like dark sentinels. My feet know this path—every rock, every dip, every spot where a sniper could perch. I've mapped these grounds obsessively since bringing Nova here.

And now, there's a new guest joining us.

Angelo fucking Boyko. Of all the poor bastards to stumble onto my land, it had to be the one who's been tracking my family for a decade.

Last time I saw him, he was trying to flip me against the Andropovs in a Chicago steakhouse. *"Your father's methods are outdated,"* he'd said, sliding onto the barstool next to mine at Gibson's. *"The world is changing. The old ways of doing business won't protect you forever. I can offer you a way out."*

Now, he shows up here, beaten half to death, right after Kat and Ilya's latest attack decimated my holdings.

The timing's too perfect. Ilya's recent strike, Katerina's disappearance, and now, a battered FBI operative materializing on my doorstep? The universe doesn't hand out coincidences like party favors.

There's a bloody line connecting these dots.

Boyko was wrong about one thing, though: the old ways are the *only* thing that will protect what matters. Nova, our unborn child, Myles and Hope and Serena and the dogs—all those lives depend on me reverting into what my father raised me to be.

Cold. Fucking. Blooded.

My phone buzzes. Myles confirms they've got Boyko settled in the east wing's secure room. A doctor's en route.

Nova's with them, too, which simultaneously relieves and irritates me. She shouldn't be anywhere near this mess. But trying to keep her away is fucking impossible. It's a miracle she agreed to go back to the castle at all.

I pause at the edge of the tree line, scanning the rocky hills beyond the castle. Someone chased Boyko here. Had to. The question is whether they wanted me to find him—and why.

The Andropovs could be using him as bait, or maybe the feds are finally ready to make their big move against the Russian mob families in Chicago.

Either way, I need to hear what Boyko has to say. But first, I need to secure the perimeter.

It doesn't take me long to pick up the trail. And when I follow it long enough, I come to the source of the broken glass and twisted metal strewn across the forest floor.

The rental car sits half-buried in bracken, its front end crumpled in a ditch. Even from twenty yards away, I can tell it's one of those cheap European compacts tourists love—perfect for blending in on narrow Scottish roads.

Not so perfect for outrunning whoever fucked up Boyko.

I circle the vehicle twice, checking sight lines and possible ambush points. The steep embankment above the crash site would make a decent sniper position, but the thick evening mist provides decent cover. Still, I keep my movements precise and unpredictable as I approach.

The driver's side door hangs open. Dark arterial spray paints the windshield and dashboard in an arc consistent with someone taking a blow to the face. More blood soaks into the upholstery of both front seats. The position and pattern suggest Boyko was driving when he got hit, managed to stay conscious long enough to crash, then dragged himself out and down the hill toward the castle.

A Glock 19—standard FBI issue—lies on the floorboard under the steering wheel. I retrieve it using my handkerchief, check the magazine. Full except for one round. If Boyko fired, he missed.

The rest of the car is clean. Too clean. No phone, no badge, no wallet, no briefcase. Either Boyko ditched everything before he ran, his attacker took it all, or he came here more incognito than he should have.

I pocket the gun and start back toward the castle, taking a different route than before. The fog's getting denser, making it hard to see, but I know these grounds by heart now. Every hollow, every rise, every spot where someone could be waiting.

Boyko may have come alone, but that doesn't mean he wasn't

followed. And I've got too much to protect to take unnecessary risks.

By the time I get back, my clothes are soaked through with mud, dew, and fog. Myles meets me at the side entrance. His usual easy smile is nowhere in sight.

"Doc's twenty minutes out. My guys found tire tracks near the south gate but nothing else suspicious. No chatter about any ops gone sideways, either." He falls into step beside me. "Think he came solo?"

"For now." I scan the security feeds on my phone. "Double the patrols anyway. And get eyes on the village. See if anyone heard or saw anything out of place."

The kitchen's warmth hits me as soon as I push through the door. Nova sits at the worn wooden table with Serena and Mrs. Morris, their hands wrapped around steaming mugs. The air smells like fresh-baked bread and worry.

Mrs. Morris jumps up. "Here now, you must be starving." She slides a plate of shepherd's pie in front of me. "Eat while it's hot."

I force myself to take a bite, but the rich flavors turn bland on my tongue. Nova's eyes track my every movement, reading between the lines of what I'm not saying.

"The perimeter's secure," I tell them, trying to project calm authority. "Our guest came alone, and he'll get the medical attention he needs. My team's investigating how he ended up here."

Serena and Mrs. Morris exchange relieved glances. Nova's jaw tightens—she sees right through my carefully constructed reassurance.

"I should check on him," she announces, pushing back from the table.

"Stay." The word comes out sharper than intended. I soften my tone. "Please. Let the doctor handle it."

She settles back, but her eyes promise this conversation isn't over.

The kitchen door swings open and Myles's expression tells me everything I need to know before he opens his mouth. "Doc's here. Wants a word."

Nova pushes her chair back, but I rest my hand on her shoulder. "Stay. I'll fill you in soon."

Her eyes narrow. She hates being left out, but right now, ignorance might save her life. Serena—bless her heart—asks Nova to help her brew more tea.

Nova's shoulders slump in resignation. "Alright, Grams. Lead the way."

With her occupied—for now—I follow Myles down the stone corridor to where the doctor waits, his lined face grim in the lamplight.

His Scottish brogue is thick as he outlines Boyko's condition: "Concussion. Heavy bruising. No broken bones, but we'll need to monitor for internal injuries." He pauses. "He should be in hospital."

"Thank you, Doctor. Myles will see you out." I slip him an envelope thick with cash. Sometimes, the old ways are still the best ways.

The sitting room is dim when I enter, lit only by a brass lamp that casts long shadows across Boyko's battered face. His eyes flutter open as I approach—sharp and alert despite the beating he's taken.

Good. I need him coherent.

I pour water from a crystal decanter and hold it out. "Drink."

He takes the glass with trembling hands but manages not to spill. His body may be battered, but the steady way he watches me over the rim tells me his mind's clear enough for what comes next.

"Talk." I settle into the leather armchair across from him. "Why are you really here?"

His split lip curves into something between a grimace and a smile. "Because your brother just made a deal with the devil, and I'm the only one who can help you stop him."

I wave a hand. "Say more."

Boyko leans forward, wincing with the motion. "Ilya brokered a formal deal with the Andropovs last week. Not just a friendly chat—we're talking full alliance. Military-grade weapons. Black market tech. The works." He takes another sip of water. "Chicago is imploding in your absence, and your brother's positioning himself to fill the power vacuum."

I keep my face blank, but my mind races. Katerina and Ilya have been flirting with the Andropovs for years. If they finally signed on the dotted line, does that mean my father approved? Does that mean they're coming for the whole Bratva...

... or just for me?

"We've been building a case against the Chicago syndicates for damn near a decade now." Boyko's voice drops lower.

"Your brother just handed us almost everything we need. But you—" He jabs a finger at me. "You've got the final key to bringing it all down. Those surveillance records you keep? The data you've collected on every rival family? That's our smoking gun."

"And in return for my cooperation?"

"Full immunity. Witness protection for you and your family. A clean slate." He leans back, studying me. "Your father's on his way out and you know it. The old alliances are crumbling. You really want to raise your kid in this world, Samuil?"

Nova's face flashes through my mind—the way she looked at our ultrasound, full of hope and fear. The way she touches her growing belly when she thinks I'm not watching.

The way she looked at me when I lashed out at her earlier today.

Which Nova do I want?

Which future can I have?

"Think about it," Boyko continues. "One decision. That's all it takes to give your family a different life. A safe life."

A different life.

A safe life.

If only it were that simple.

But there's no such fucking thing, is there? Every time I delude myself into thinking there might be, my father or my brother or my ex-wife come barreling in to fuck it all up again. And now, here is a federal goddamn agent, bleeding on my sofa and telling me *he's* the one who can fix it for me.

Yeah fucking right.

I didn't believe him the first time he offered me this bullshit deal, either. The Chicago steakhouse's mahogany walls blur in my memory, replaced by sand and surf and an unruly Great Dane. Boyko's words now are a precise echo of the ones he spoke to me that day—right before Rufus knocked me into Lake Michigan.

I'd been so furious then. At the dog, at the situation, at this fed's presumption. But mostly at myself, for feeling that flicker of temptation.

A different life. A safe life. Right there for the taking.

A clean slate had seemed possible back then, before I truly understood what I was protecting.

Now?

Now, I know better.

A laugh escapes me now, harsh in the dim room. "The devil you know beats the devil you don't." I pour myself two fingers of scotch, not offering any to my guest. "Your agency can't protect my family from what would come after. The moment you dismantle the current power structure, every ambitious piece of shit with a gun and a grudge will start a war. And they'd come for mine first."

Boyko's shoulders slump. "We can hide you—"

"Like you hid the Gambinos? The Gottis?" I knock back the scotch. "Don't let your mouth write checks that neither your badge nor your team nor your whole fucking agency has the balls to cash. You can't do a single thing you're promising me, Agent Boyko. So don't waste your breath lying and saying that you can." I set the empty glass down. "Stay here and recover. You'll be treated as a guest, given medical care, good food. But don't mistake my hospitality for weakness. And don't insult me by voicing that offer ever again."

He nods slowly. The fire illuminates his cheeks but casts the pits of his hollow eyes in shadow. "Your father would be proud."

"My father was an idiot who created the mess I'm cleaning up." I head for the door, then pause. "But he was right about one thing: this is the life I was born into. I was a fool for ever thinking there was a way out."

As I stride away, I feel sick and hollow and light-headed all at once.

I need to find Nova. Need to hold her. Need to remind myself why I'm choosing this path.

Need to make her understand that sometimes, the monster is exactly what she needs.

And as I emerge, there she is.

But one look at her face tells me it's not how I wanted this moment to be.

She stands frozen in the hallway, one hand pressed to her mouth, the other curled protectively over her belly. Her tears glisten in the lamplight, and for a moment, all I can think is how fucking beautiful she is, even when she's breaking.

I understand in an instant. What she overheard. What she must have understood. The deal she thinks I turned down.

"You could have gotten out." Her voice wobbles, wavers, shatters like glass. "You… you could have saved us."

I reach for her, but she jerks away, bumping against the stone wall. The tapestry behind her shifts. Dust motes go spiraling in the air between us.

"I *am* saving us." My hands clench at my sides. "By my fucking self. The feds can't protect shit. The moment I flip, every two-bit thug with delusions of grandeur comes gunning for what's mine."

"What's *yours*?" She laughs, bitter and sharp. "What do you mean—your empire? Your reputation?"

"I mean my family." I step closer, crowding her against the wall. "You. Our child. Everyone we love. They'd all be targets."

Her chin lifts. "We already are targets, Sam."

"And I can protect you." I press my forehead to hers, breathing in the vanilla-honey scent of her skin. "I know every player. Every move. Every weakness. But we can only win if I stay in the game."

"That was a ticket out of this game, Samuil." She shudders. "That was our chance to… to… Fuck. Fuck! I told you, Sam: I don't want our baby growing up in this world."

"Then we'll make a better one." I cup her face as tenderly as I know how to do. "But we do it my way. The smart way. Not by throwing ourselves on the FBI's mercy and hoping they can keep their promises."

Nova's eyes search mine, and I see the moment she realizes I won't bend on this. Won't risk everything on Boyko's honeyed words and empty guarantees.

"You really mean it," she whispers. "You really think you're the only one who can win this."

I sigh. I nod. "I know I am."

She tears away from me and swallows hard. "I need some air," she mumbles. "One more breath of outside before you lock us all back in the cages you love so much."

41

SAMUIL

The screens covering my war room's walls show my father's empire dripping in red.

Casualties. Compromised assets. Security breaches.

Each alert represents another crack in the foundation that Leonid Litvinov spent fifty years building. I've been staring at these screens for hours, watching dominoes fall, calculating moves and countermoves until my vision blurs.

I glance out of one window. A black Range Rover is exiting the grounds. I know that in the back of it sits Angelo Boyko, bandaged like a fucking mummy and accompanied only by what little he brought in his pockets, the Glock I found in his car, and my refusal of his deal.

Good fucking riddance.

I check the other window, the one with a view into the library. The room is dark. The fireplace is cold. The couch is empty. No Nova sitting alongside Hope, laughing and oohing and ahhing over bodice ripper romance novels.

The women are in their respective rooms, and I can practically feel the icy chill of Nova's mood rippling throughout the castle air.

She might as well be standing behind me, whispering her last words in my ear again and again.

I need some air. One more breath of outside before you lock us all back in the cages you love so much.

I had a nightmare in the few short hours I slept last night. Nova, on the other side of a veil I couldn't reach through, gasping and choking as the oxygen drained from her lungs.

I couldn't save her, no matter how hard I tried.

I wrench my attention back to the screens. It's a bloodbath in every corner of the Litvinov territory. No matter how hard I try, I can't seem to get an upper hand anywhere. Katerina and Ilya, backed by the might and reach of the Andropovs and with a sizable head start, are too much to overcome.

Myles raps his knuckles on the cracked door. When I nod, he slips in and shuts it behind him. There's a sheaf of papers in his hand.

"Check it out." Myles tosses a photo onto my desk. "Surveillance caught this at Heathrow two hours ago."

My throat tightens. The grainy image shows my father's unmistakable profile, his broad shoulders stooped with age. And next to him—a baseball cap pulled low, but I'd know that arrogant strut anywhere.

Ilya.

"Facial recognition to confirm?" I keep my voice level despite the rage bubbling beneath my skin.

"Ninety-two percent match on both." Myles spreads out three more photos. Different angles. Different timestamps. Same conclusion. "They're traveling under Venezuelan passports. Our contact at MI6 confirms Ilya booked a suite at the Connaught under the same alias."

I lean back, steepling my fingers. "Father never stays anywhere but Claridge's."

"Already have a team watching both hotels, just in case."

The pieces click into place. Ilya choosing London—taunting me by being close enough to strike and yet utterly untouchable. Taking Father there when he should be resting at his dacha. The synchronized attacks across my holdings.

"He's making his move." I stand, energy thrumming through my veins. "Get Vladimir and his crew on the next flight to England. I want our best hunters on this."

"And you?"

"Have a chopper ready in thirty." I check my watch. "But I need ten minutes with Nova first."

Myles nods and heads for the door, then pauses. "Sam. What if this is another trap?"

"Then we spring it." I bare my teeth in what might pass for a smile. "And this time, we make sure my dear brother doesn't walk away."

He doesn't look convinced. "You're sure?"

"He threatened my family, Myles. He threatened *us.*" I clear my throat. "There are no more questions left worth asking."

My best friend shifts his weight from foot to foot, exhaling wearily. His face is drawn long and haggard, bags under his eyes looking bigger and grayer than I've ever seen them before. "This goes without saying, but Nova's already worried sick about—"

"Nova is—" Her name catches in my throat. In my mind's eye, I see her standing in the doorway earlier, belly peeking out from beneath the hem of her shirt, eyes wide with fear when I ordered her out.

The cages you love so much.

I shake my head. "Don't talk to me about Nova. Nova needs me to end this. Now. Before our child is born into a world where Ilya can reach them."

"Copy that." Myles pulls out his phone. "I'll tell Vlad to bring down the—"

My phone vibrates against the mahogany desktop. The screen lights up with an incoming call.

From, of all people…

Ilya.

Myles follows my eyes, sees what I see, and blanches pale white. "Don't answer." He takes a step forward. "Let me trace—"

I hit accept and put it on speaker. "Calling to surrender, brother?"

I expect laughter. I expect taunting.

All I hear is an animalistic sob.

The sound coming through my phone's speaker isn't human. It's the wail of a wounded beast, and even out here in the wilds of Scotland, as violent and untamed a place as exists, it sounds like something that doesn't belong on this earth.

"Father—" Ilya chokes. "Otets, he's—" More Russian expletives follow, each more broken than the last.

I grip the edge of my desk, knuckles white. Waiting. Is he actually saying that Leonid is—

"Dead." The word explodes from him in another wail. "You killed him. You and your fucking stubbornness killed him."

"What happened?" I grit out.

"His heart. Fucking blew up on him." Ilya's voice cracks. "Right the fuck in front of me. One minute, we were talking about—about you—and the next..." A harsh, grating laugh. "The great Leonid Litvinov, taken down by his own fucking body."

My legs won't hold me. I sink into my chair, phone clutched to my ear.

"The doctors say it was quick." Ilya's tone shifts from grief to venom. "But you weren't here. You weren't here to hold his hand or call for help or—"

"Shut up." The words come out barely above a whisper.

"You were too busy playing house with your whore and your bastard to—"

I end the call.

The silence that follows is an anvil on my chest.

Myles hasn't moved. His face is a mask of shock and sympathy I can't bear to look at.

"Get the helicopter." My voice sounds distant, foreign. "And tell Nova..."

What? That the man who terrorized my childhood is dead? That we're free of him?

"Tell her I need her."

Myles runs off.

I slump back in my seat.

Dead.

The word sears through my skull like a bullet searching for an exit. It's suddenly burning hot in here, but when I wrench open the closest window, bitter cold comes pouring in. My breath is a plume in the frigid room.

Dead.

Dead men can't make amends. Dead men can't earn forgiveness. Dead men can't suffer for their sins or beg for mercy as you choke the life from them.

The burn behind my eyes intensifies. I squeeze them shut, willing away memories of hockey games and vodka shots and bruising backslaps that felt like approval until I learned better.

When I open them again, Nova's reflection appears in the glass beside mine. My chest constricts at the sight of her—belly swollen with our child, face drawn with worry. She's wearing one of my sweaters, the sleeves rolled up four times to free her hands.

I brace for her lecture about the FBI's offer. About how we could be free of all this, if I'd just take their deal.

But she doesn't speak. Instead, her small hand slides into mine, fingers threading through my own. Her other palm presses against my back, right between my shoulder blades, and starts moving in slow circles.

The gesture is so tender, so *Nova,* that something inside me cracks. I turn and pull her close, burying my face in her hair. She smells like lavender and safety and home.

"I'm sorry," she whispers against my chest. "About your father. About earlier. About all of it."

I tighten my grip. Probably too hard, but she doesn't complain. Just keeps rubbing my back. Keeps holding on.

Maybe dead men can't give closure. But living women—the right ones—can give something better.

They can give grace.

It's a while before anyone speaks. Nova is the one to break the silence.

"What happens now?"

I stroke her hair. "There will be a funeral in Chicago. Three days from now."

She stiffens. "Chicago? But that's—"

"Neutral ground. Sacred ground, by Bratva law." My jaw clenches. "No blood can be spilled at a patriarch's funeral. Even Ilya will honor that."

Nova pulls back, searching my face with those gold-flecked eyes that see too much. "And after the funeral?"

"What comes after doesn't matter yet," I whisper. "All that matters is paying proper respects. Making the right moves. Showing strength."

"It sounds like another game." Her voice carries an edge of frustration. "More chess pieces for you to position."

"Because it *is* a game." Myles steps into the room, phone pressed to his ear. He covers the mic. "And if we fuck up the opening moves, we lose before we start."

Nova's shoulders slump. I can see the fight drain from her posture, replaced by bone-deep exhaustion.

"You should rest," I murmur, pressing a kiss to her temple. "Doctor's orders."

She nods, but her fingers clutch my shirt. "Promise me something?"

"Anything."

"Promise you won't let this funeral turn into your grave."

I meet her gaze, seeing all the fear she's trying to hide. "I promise."

But when I glance over her shoulder, Myles's expression reflects what we both know—some promises are harder to keep than others.

He clears his throat. "A toast before you go. To the dead old bastard."

Myles crosses to the bar cart, his footsteps echoing in the war room's suffocating silence. The crystal decanter he selects—Russian Imperial, because Father would accept nothing less—catches the light from my screens. A hundred broken beams of blue and red glow dance across Nova's face.

He pours three shots with practiced precision. Water for my pregnant queen, vodka for us.

The familiar scent hits my nostrils—hints of wheat and pepper that take me straight back to Father's study. To lessons learned between sips about power, about weakness, about the price of trust. To mastiffs barking and snarling in dark, cold forests.

"To Leonid." Myles raises his glass. "The worst man I've ever met. Who did one good thing in life, despite all his best efforts to undo it. Cheers, you miserable fuck."

The vodka burns sweet and clean down my throat. Nova sips her water, one hand still locked in mine beneath the desk.

Myles pours again, faster this time, and passes my glass back to me. "And to you, Samuil. The one good thing."

I throw back the second shot. The alcohol works quickly to numb the ache in my chest. When I stand, my legs feel steadier.

Nova wraps her arms around my waist, face pressed to my chest. Her tears soak through my shirt—silent drops of grief for a man who never deserved them.

Then Myles is there, too, pulling us both into a bear hug that smells like vodka and friendship and loyalty. I thump his back, harder than necessary, trying to convey everything I can't say out loud.

Thank you for staying. Thank you for saving me. Thank you for being the brother I should have had.

When we break apart, his eyes are wet but his jaw is set. "The chopper's waiting."

I nod, already reaching for my coat. Time to face whatever comes next.

With my brother-in-arms and my woman at my side.

42

NOVA

The Chicago skyline looms over me like a dark, jagged wound against the November sky. I used to find comfort in these familiar buildings. I knew these shadows, these hot dog vendors, the smell of this air and these cars and these people.

Now, it all feels like strangers wearing masks of my memories.

Samuil's hand rests on my lower back as we exit the private jet and step straight into the car waiting on the tarmac. The trip has made me more aware than ever of his protective instincts—they radiate from him like heat.

"You okay, *zaychik*?"

I nod, but we both know it's a lie. Everything about being back feels wrong. The air smells different. The sounds grate differently. Even the wind whips around us with an edge I don't remember.

Our driver weaves through traffic toward downtown, and I lean my cheek against the bulletproof glass. The city slides past, one block at a time. My fingertips trace circles over my barely-there bump. They haven't stopped since we left Scotland.

It's like my body longs to be back there. Back in the castle that has become home in a way Chicago never was. There, surrounded by rolling hills and bleating sheep, I discovered pieces of myself I never knew existed.

Here, the concrete and steel feel like a cage closing in.

I can tell I'm not the only one wondering if the jet has enough gas to take us back over the Atlantic. During the flight here, I watched Samuil fold his massive frame into the leather seat across from me. From takeoff to touchdown, his jaw stayed locked so tight I could see the muscle spasming. For seven airborne hours, he alternated between staring out the window and reviewing reports on his tablet, barely touching the spread of caviar and champagne the flight attendant kept refreshing.

The death of Leonid has carved new lines into his face. Hard, bitter ones that make him look more like his father than ever.

But unlike Leonid, whose cruelty lived in his eyes, Samuil's gray gaze holds something else entirely when he looks at me. Something that makes my chest ache.

He hasn't cried. Hasn't raged. Just… retreated into himself, speaking only when necessary. Even now, as we drive through Chicago's crowded streets, his fingers drum an agitated rhythm against his thigh—the only outward sign of his inner turmoil.

I want to reach across the space between us and smooth away the tension in his shoulders. Want to pull him close and remind him that he's nothing like Leonid. That our baby will know a different kind of father.

But the weight of what awaits us at the cathedral sits heavy in my throat.

He's told me a bit of what to expect. The whispers will be vicious. The stares calculating. And somewhere in that crowd of mourners will be Ilya, undoubtedly waiting to twist the knife of grief deeper into his brother's heart.

Samuil swears that Bratva law will keep us safe. *No blood shall be spilled at a funeral.* I have my doubts. But I trust him. I trust him to the ends of the earth.

The car slows as we approach our destination, and I slip my hand into Samuil's. His fingers close around mine.

And then we're there. Parking. Emerging. The cathedral's stone facade is huge before us, dark and twisted and impossibly old in a way that looks so wrong in this buzzing, bustling city I once knew.

My stomach lurches as we step from the car, but I swallow hard and squeeze Samuil's hand tighter. He has enough weighing on those broad shoulders without my morning sickness making an unwelcome appearance. I thought I left that back in the first trimester. Apparently, violently inclined mafia funerals can bring it back.

A fine drizzle mists my face as we climb the steps, but sweat still prickles beneath my black dress. My skin feels too tight, like it belongs to someone else.

"Samuil." A silver-haired man in an impeccable suit steps forward, speaking rapid-fire Russian.

Samuil listens patiently without ever letting go of me. He nods when the man is done. Offers a single, clipped word in response. The man bows and departs.

And then another man comes to take the place of the first.

And another.

And another.

I lose count of how many people come to pay respects—each more expensively dressed than the last, each with harder eyes and colder smiles. Their wives drift by like exotic birds in couture plumage, appraising me with sharp glances, but the women know better than to speak, it seems.

I scan the crowd. I don't know if it's Samuil's influence or my own paranoia, but I can't help categorizing faces into potential threats. This man's smile doesn't reach his eyes. That one's hand lingers too long on Samuil's shoulder. That group over there whispers too suspiciously and stares too intently.

This world is still mostly foreign to me, but it's beginning to take on a fuzzy, indistinct shape. I get the gist, if not the details.

And the gist is that we are seated on a precarious throne. Leonid built his empire on broken bones and stolen dreams. Now, all his enemies will be circling Samuil like sharks scenting blood in the water. Wondering if he's fit to take up his father's place.

And that's on top of Ilya and Katerina and the Andropovs still gunning for him. God only knows which pocket of shadow they're lurking in.

My free hand drifts to my stomach. The baby kicks. *It's okay, little one,* I think to it, trying to send telepathic messages of soothing. *Sam is going to take care of us.*

But even as I say it, I can't help but feel that pang of hot anger low in my gut. Listening to him turn down that FBI agent's offer... It felt like a slap in the face. From where I stood, it seemed like he had the key to a happy ending being handed to him on a silver platter. And he said *no.*

I want to understand why. I trust him, I do, I swear I do.

But trust is a hard thing to cling to when everyone around us has murder in their stare.

A flash of familiar blonde hair catches my eye, and my heart stutters. But when I look again, it's gone—swallowed by the sea of black suits and somber dresses filing into the church.

I must have imagined it.

"Could we find somewhere to sit, Samuil?" I whisper to him during a break in the tide of well-wishers. "I'm feeling a little dizzy."

Sam's gaze darts to me in concern. Then he snaps his fingers and the crowd parts. His arm is tight around my waist as he guides me to the pew in the front of the cathedral. I sink onto it gratefully. My hands shake slightly as I smooth my dress over my thighs.

"Water's coming," Samuil murmurs, his thumb brushing my cheek. "And Myles will stay with you during the service."

Myles materializes beside us. "I've got your six, Nova. Not leaving your side until the boss says otherwise."

I manage a weak smile. Grams, Hope, and the dogs are back in Scotland for their own safety, but having Myles here helps

—he's become like a brother to me these past months. A brother who could probably snap a man's neck with his pinky finger, but isn't that what brothers are supposed to be for?

The water arrives a moment later. I take small sips, willing my stomach to settle and my head to stop spinning.

But as more people file into the cathedral, the air grows thick with incense and whispered Russian. My nausea rises again, and this time, it's not just morning sickness. It's the weight of a hundred calculating sneers boring into my skull from every angle.

It's almost funny how trite and standard the service is. Who picked this? Who approved this? Myself and most of the people in here have met Leonid Litvinov, and cliched eulogies about his "generosity" are outright laughable. I'd sooner have expected Satan himself to come conduct proceedings. Not this stooped, graying Russian Orthodox priest with a voice that barely rises above a dull mumble.

A *slow,* dull mumble, at that.

The service drags like a funeral dirge played at quarter-speed. The priest's voice rises and falls in waves of Russian I don't understand. The incense keeps burning. A pot too close to me spews smoke, making my nostrils sting and my eyes water.

Or maybe those are real tears. It's hard to tell anymore.

I shift on the hard, wooden pew for the thousandth time, trying to find a position that doesn't make my lower back scream in protest. The baby is equally uncomfortable. He or she does somersaults, stomping against my bladder with determined little feet.

Beside me, Samuil sits like a statue carved from granite. His shoulders are squared, his chin lifted. Only the muscle thrumming in his jaw betrays any emotion at all.

I want to reach for his hand again, but something in his rigid posture warns me away.

The endless stream of prayers and hymns finally peters out. As the last notes of the choir fade away, a collective exhale seems to ripple through the crowd. No one wanted to be here—not really. This was obligation, not grief.

I struggle to my feet, my pregnant body protesting every movement. The pressure on my bladder has reached critical mass.

"Myles." I catch his eye and make a desperate gesture.

He nods, already moving to escort me. We hustle down the aisle, dodging condolences and curious stares. When we reach the bathroom, Myles does a quick sweep of the inside before positioning himself outside like a sentinel.

"All clear," he says. "I'll keep watch."

I duck inside, grateful for a moment alone. The black-marbled bathroom is freezing cold, but right now, all I care about is blessed relief.

I pee, finish up, and head to the sink. My mind is already wandering to what fresh hell might await us at the reception. The counter is ice-cold under my palms as I lean forward to check my makeup in the mirror.

That's when I hear it—a dull thump outside the door, like a sack of meat hitting tile.

My throat closes. "Myles?"

Silence is the only thing that answers. Not even the shuffle of feet or murmur of voices from the hallway.

I grip the edge of the counter, willing my racing heart to slow. *It's nothing. Just paranoia. Pregnancy hormones making me jumpy.*

But Myles would answer. He always answers.

I edge toward the door, my heels clicking against marble in a staccato rhythm that matches my pulse. Three steps away, I freeze.

Dark red seeps under the door, spreading across the black tile like spilled wine.

Blood.

The metallic scent hits my nose at the same time as the recognition. My stomach heaves. I clamp a hand over my mouth, stumbling backward until I hit the wall. My other hand curves protectively over my belly.

The door handle starts to turn.

Slow.

Deliberate.

Think, Nova. Think. What would Samuil do?

My phone is in my purse—which Myles was holding for me.

I scan the bathroom desperately. No windows. No other exits. Just me, my unborn child, and whatever horror waits on the other side of that door.

The handle keeps turning with excruciating precision, like whoever's out there wants me to feel every microsecond of terror.

I kick off my heels. If I'm about to die, it won't be tripping over four-inch Louboutins.

The door creaks open.

And a familiar head of platinum blonde hair sneaks in.

"Your watchdog is taking a little nap." Katerina's whisper slithers down my spine. She shuts the door behind her, then looks down in distaste when she realizes she's stepped in Myles's blood. Her nose wrinkles.

I try to speak and fail, so I swallow, lick my lips, and try again. "Did you kill him?"

Kat laughs. "I'd worry more about yourself, sweetheart." She saunters toward me. "I must say, you've been a delightful pest. Leading us on such a merry chase across Europe. Or was it me who was leading you? Impossible to tell, really."

My back presses against cold stone. I force myself to meet her ice-blue stare, channeling every ounce of Samuil's steel into my voice. "If you're going to kill me, spare me the fucking lecture and get on with it."

She laughs—a tinkling sound like broken crystal. "Oh, darling. I'm not going to kill you. Not yet." She raises her hand to reveal a snub-nosed pistol. "This is just to ensure your cooperation."

"Cooperation in what?" I ask.

"Excellent question. First, you're going to help me ruin Samuil. If you play nice, maybe I'll let you live long enough to see your bastard born."

"You really are insane."

Her perfectly painted lips twist. "Insane? No. I simply understand something you don't." She steps closer, lifting the gun to level its black eye right between mine. "Men like Samuil don't change. They don't learn to love. They only know how to possess and destroy."

I gulp. "You're wrong about him."

"Sweet, sweet little Nova." She sighs, almost sadly. "Still so naive. Even after everything." She comes close enough to kiss the tip of the gun to the arch of my belly. "Tick tock, though. Time's a-wasting. You're coming with me, and we're going to give Samuil a choice—you or his empire. And trust me, I know exactly which one he'll pick."

43

NOVA

The blood is almost beautiful.

I can't stop staring at it. It's running in perfect channels down the grooves of the tile grouting. A geometric latticework of flowing crimson against gleaming midnight black. Too flawless to be real.

But it *is* real. It's real and it belongs to Myles, the one who's been there for Sam and for me more times than I can count. On the other side of this door, he's dying—fast or slow, I can't be sure, but every second that passes does him no favors.

"Oh, quit with the fucking tears," snaps Katerina. She pokes me in the ribs with the gun. "We're going to get him right now." She points toward the door with one toe. "You're going to open it. Slowly. *So* fucking slowly. And don't even think about screaming."

My fingers tremble as I reach for the handle. The metal is frigid, or maybe that's just my body going into shock.

The knob turns. One groaning gear at a time. When I pull, the door creaks open with glacial slowness. Beyond it, the dim hallway beckons.

Empty. Still.

But not quiet. Organ music drifts from the sanctuary, along with the drone of prayers in Russian. Sam is out there somewhere, probably wondering where I am. The thought of him sends a fresh wave of terror through me—not for myself, but for what this will do to him.

My gaze drops to Myles's crumpled form and my heart seizes. If he finds us like this… If Kat does what I think she might do…

But then I see it—the subtle rise and fall of his chest.

He's alive. Thank God, he's alive.

For now.

The gash on his temple looks nasty but superficial. Head wounds always bleed like crazy. What concerns me more is his complete stillness. In all the months I've known him, Myles has never been still—always alert, always watching, always ready to move at a millisecond's notice. It's not right to see him so frozen stiff.

"Quit stalling," Katerina growls, shoving me forward. My bare feet slip in Myles's blood as I stumble toward him.

A single tear slides down my cheek. Not from fear, but from fury. This bitch really thinks she knows Sam better than I do. Thinks she can predict what he'll choose.

She has no idea what love looks like on Samuil Litvinov. No idea at all.

I'm so close to Myles I can smell the stench of his blood mingling with his aftershave. The combination makes my stomach roll.

I swallow hard, willing myself not to vomit. Not now. Not when one wrong move could mean the difference between life and death for two—no, for *three* of us.

My baby's life is hanging in the balance, too.

"Pull him inside." Katerina gestures with the gun toward Myles. "Careful. Remember who and what you're carrying."

My palm slides instinctively over my rounded belly. Our baby kicks, as if sensing my distress. At four months, it's already strong—like her father. The thought of Sam gives me strength, even as fear claws at my throat.

Keeping my movements slow and deliberate, I grip Myles under his arms. His head lolls against my shoulder as I begin to drag him across the floor. My back screams in protest, but I refuse to let him go. If I can just get him somewhere safe, maybe buy us some time…

"Faster!" Katerina barks, but I hear the tremor in her voice now. She's starting to crack. And cracked things are dangerous—they can either shatter completely or slice you open.

I pray Sam finds us before we discover which way she'll break.

Inch by inch, we retreat back into the bathroom. When we're inside, Katerina shuts the door and throws the lock. She turns to face me. It's then that I can look her in the face for the first time.

She's wild-eyed. Her hair is mussed, unmade, split ends fraying in every direction. It's so alien on her that I have to blink to be sure I'm truly seeing it.

But I am.

It's desperation in Dolce & Gabbana.

"Stop fucking staring at me!" she seethes, surging forward suddenly to crack me across the face with a wicked backhand.

The unexpected blow snaps my head to one side and my neck screams in protest. One of her many rings cuts open my cheek, too, and I feel the wet heat of blood trickle from the wound.

But my mouth stays sealed shut. If she wants me to beg for mercy, she'll have to do a hell of a lot worse.

She spits on the floor next to Myles's unmoving body. "We have a few minutes," she announces with a flourish of the Cartier watch on her wrist. "And he's looking awfully pale, don't you think? Fix him up. He's still worth more to me alive than dead. Barely, but still."

She doesn't have to tell me twice.

I drop to my knees, seize up the hem of my dress in both hands, and rip until a strip of it comes free. I loop that around Myles's head, then go back to work making more.

The ripping sound fills the silence between Katerina's ragged breaths and Myles's shallow ones. I press the wadded silk against Myles's temple, watching crimson soak into the black fabric. His pulse flutters against my fingertips whenever I stop to check his neck, faint but real.

"Such tender care for the help." Katerina's voice drips sardonic acid. "He was always loyal to Samuil. Even when Samuil didn't deserve it."

I arrange Myles's arms by his sides, buying us a few more precious seconds. Every moment he stays unconscious is another moment he's not in danger from her twitchy trigger finger.

"Myles is loyal because Sam earned it," I say, keeping my voice soft and steady. "Through friendship. Through trust."

Her laugh bounces off the bathroom tiles. "Trust? In *our* world?"

But something passes there—a flash of raw hurt in her eyes, gone as quick as it appeared. A word that struck too close to home, I think.

I press another strip of silk over the first, letting my hands shake. I want her to see it. Let her think I'm terrified. Let her think I'm weak. She's not the first person to underestimate me—and if I survive this, she won't be the last.

The bathroom door rattles suddenly, making us both jump. "Is someone in there?" a woman's voice calls. When we don't answer, she tries the door again. "Hello? Nastya, are you in—"

But she never gets to find out if it's Nastya or not.

Because before she finishes her question, the rest of her words dissolve in a scream.

Then comes the sound that made her scream—a sharp crack that echoes off marble and stone. Another follows. And another.

Gunfire.

My brain stutters and buffers. This isn't happening. Can't be happening. But the next burst of gunfire is closer, unmistakable.

And the screams…

Those are real, too.

I've heard animal sounds like this before—when a predator breaches what should have been a safe space. The recognition scorches through me, instinctive and electric: we're all prey now.

Katerina's head snaps toward the chaos. Her body goes rigid. I'm waiting for her to laugh, for her to taunt me, to paint pictures of what must be happening to Samuil marooned out amongst the chaos…

But then I see how pale her cheeks are. How white her knuckles.

She's just as surprised as I am.

And, more surprising: just as terrified.

Male shouts boom throughout the church, a cacophony of Russian and English, accompanied by bursts of gunfire and the crunch of bullets meeting plaster, wood, and flesh. Among the multilingual chaos, a single voice rises above the rest.

At first, it's just another thread in the tapestry of mayhem. But it plucks at my attention the longer it goes on, until I realize why it sounds so familiar.

It's Ilya's.

I know that voice, though I've never heard it like this—loud, commanding, almost exultant. The words are gibberish to me, but the tone isn't.

It's the voice of someone claiming what they believe is rightfully theirs. Someone who's finally letting their mask slip to reveal the monster beneath.

"*Nyet*!" The word tears from Katerina's throat. Her grip on the gun wavers for a fraction of a second. "That lying piece of shit! He swore we'd wait until—"

She catches herself, but it's too late. I see the truth written in the tremble of her perfectly lined lips, in the way her chest heaves beneath her neckline.

Ilya has betrayed her. Whatever plan they had—whatever carefully orchestrated move they were going to make together—he's thrown it all away. And now, Katerina is trapped in here with us, a heavily pregnant hostage she never wanted and an unconscious man bleeding out on the floor.

"He promised," she whispers hoarsely. "We were going to do it together. After the funeral. Just to Sam. Not like… Not like this."

Another burst of gunfire. Closer now. Katerina's head whips toward the sound.

"He's going to kill us all," she says, and for the first time since this nightmare began, I hear real fear in her voice. "That psychotic bastard is going to—"

A massive explosion rocks the building. The mirrors rattle in their frames. Dust sifts down from the ceiling.

And beneath my palm, Myles stirs.

My first thought is that I can't let her see. If she sees him waking, she'll slaughter him just to eliminate a variable.

"Ilya doesn't love you, Kat," I announce. "He isn't capable of it."

She laughs hysterically. "What the fuck would you know about it?"

"I know love," I reply patiently. "Sam—"

"Sam!" she screeches with more unhinged laughter. "You stupid little bitch! You think he loves you? You think you're special?"

I draw in a deep breath to calm my nerves. We're teetering on the edge of death here, and this insane woman's gun is dancing wildly between us. "I think you're in trouble, Katerina. Let me help you before—"

"Don't fucking touch me!"

She whips away from my outstretched hand and the butt of her gun strikes the nearest mirror. I wince as glass rains down, landing in shards amongst Myles's blood.

Outside, more gunfire and chaos and who the fuck knows what else. It's madness inside and out, here and there, every fucking place I look.

And at my feet, Myles is slowly dying.

I inch back toward Kat. She raises the gun, but it doesn't frighten me. She won't use it. Not yet.

"The baby's kicking," I murmur. "Would you like to feel? It might be your last chance to touch something pure."

She opens her mouth to spit something heinous at me, I'm

sure. But before she can, the bathroom door explodes inward in a shower of splinters and marble dust.

Through the chaos, a familiar voice rings out—deep, commanding, and absolutely furious.

"Hello, little mouse."

44

SAMUIL

"My father believed that love was weakness."

My voice rings out across the cathedral. It echoes. Doubles. Triples. Fades. Though some part of me thinks every word is somehow sticking to the beams arcing overhead. That what I say here today will remain here for the rest of eternity.

"My father believed that love was shameful."

My gaze sweeps across the sea of black-clad mourners. Their faces blur together. I don't bother noting who they are, what they've done, whether they are a threat, an ally, or a pawn to be manipulated. I used to do that out of sheer habit. I don't anymore.

Because none of them matter. They might take what's mine or add to it, but they will not change what I have. What I've done. Who I am.

I have Nova.

I have Myles.

I have my child.

What the fuck else could possibly matter?

"My father believed that love was a sin." I work my jaw from side to side. "He taught me that lesson repeatedly. He made damn sure it stuck. Today, I stand before you to tell you he was wrong."

Utter silence has the crowd by its throat.

"Leonid Litvinov built an empire through fear. He wielded power like a scythe, cutting open those closest to him first. But empires built on fear eventually crumble. True strength —true power—comes from having something worth protecting. He didn't know that."

My hands grip the podium's edges. "I used to think I needed my father's approval. His respect. His love. I don't anymore. Because I've learned that real love doesn't demand proof of worthiness. It simply is."

The tension in the cathedral grows thicker with each word.

I turn to the casket. "So I thank you, Father, for your final lesson. In showing me everything a leader shouldn't be, you helped me become the man I am. May you find peace knowing the Litvinov name will endure—not through fear, but through loyalty freely given. Not because of you, but in spite of you. Not with you, but without you—and we are all better for that. So let this be a sign: today, I put you behind me. I put you beneath me. And in whatever hell you end up in, whichever lowest circle of the fucking afterlife will take you… I can only hope that God shows you the mercy that you never showed anyone else."

As my last word dies in the rafters, I step back from the podium. The crowd eyes me strangely—no surprise there.

What's surprising is how little I care.

Let them whisper. Let them wonder.

The frightened Samuil desperate for his father's approval died long ago.

So did the Samuil who gives a fuck about the intricacies of life in this city's underbelly. Once upon a time, I would've been cataloging every whisper, every sideways glance, trying to assess the twisted web of alliances and brewing betrayals. Now, my eyes look for only one person.

But they find empty space where she ought to be.

Where the fuck is Nova?

My chest constricts as I scan the pews again and again. No sign of her golden-brown eyes or Myles's tall frame.

I saw him escorting her toward the bathroom during a break in the service, but that was fifteen minutes ago or more.

They've been gone too long.

Way too long.

Viktor stands rigid by the cathedral's stone wall, hands clasped behind his back. When our eyes meet, I give him the slightest nod. He peels away from his post and floats through the crowd like smoke on the wind.

Ilya's missing, too. My brother hasn't shown his face today, which is fucking bizarre. He didn't come to grieve? To gloat? To threaten me some more, if nothing else?

The hair on the back of my neck rises. Something's wrong. Everything inside me screams to tear through this place looking for Nova, but I force myself to stay put. To keep playing my role.

Mourners approach with hollow condolences. I accept their words with practiced grace while tracking Viktor's progress through my peripheral vision. He reaches the back of the cathedral and disappears through a heavy wooden door.

The seconds crawl by like years.

A muffled sound echoes from somewhere deep in the building. Could be nothing. Could be everything.

My phone vibrates in my pocket. I pull it out to check. One word from Viktor:

Hurry.

I'm moving before I finish reading, shouldering past the crowd without bothering to apologize. If they think I'm grieving or growling or just plain fucking losing it, I don't care. They can believe whatever they like.

All that matters is getting to Nova.

But I don't get close enough.

Before I can even reach the mouth of the hallway, the cathedral doors slam open with enough force to make the hinges scream.

I know who it is. I've been waiting.

Ilya's footsteps echo off marble and stone, each strike a countdown to violence. The crowd parts around him. The murmurs intensify.

I pivot slowly, letting my brother see exactly how little I care about his dramatic entrance. But the sight of his "honor guard" freezes my blood. Those aren't our people flanking him. Those aren't even Andropov thugs.

Those are a motley collection of fifty or more of the city's foulest, nastiest mercenaries. I recognize their dead-eyed stares, the snaking tattoos, the guns with the serial numbers filed off.

What has Ilya done? What deal has he struck, and with what devil? What price did he promise to pay?

"Such a beautiful eulogy, brother." Ilya's lips curl into that familiar sneer. "You always did have a way with words. But actions speak louder, don't they?"

He gestures, and more mercenaries materialize from the shadows. They're carrying assault rifles under their suit jackets. The kind of hardware that says they're ready for war, not a funeral.

My phone vibrates again in my grasp. I don't need to look to know it's Viktor, probably telling me Nova's in trouble. Ilya's timing is too perfect for this to be coincidence.

He's played his hand well. I'm trapped between my pregnant fiancée and an army of killers, with a church full of witnesses as collateral damage.

"What do you want, Ilya?" I call out.

His smile widens. "Everything you have. Starting with that pretty little bitch you knocked up."

Another vibration. A voice memo begins to play automatically. Viktor, panting, panicked in a way I've never heard him before: "Blood by the women's bathroom. Myles down. Signs of struggle."

My brother watches me, savoring my reaction. I keep my face blank, but inside, I'm drowning in memories of Nova this morning—adjusting my tie, touching my chest, whispering, "I love you."

I should have seen this coming. Should have kept her closer.

The mercenaries spread through the church like a virus. They cluster around every exit—thick, clotted, dying to unleash violence.

"You always were slow, Samuil," Ilya mocks. "While you played house, I built an army. The Andropovs were just the start. Every rival you've angered or neglected—they're all mine now. And brother… they want *blood*."

I meet his gaze. "Touch her and I'll tear you apart."

He laughs. "Oh, *I* won't touch her. Katerina will. Fair is fair, after all. Nova stole what was rightfully Katerina's. You stole what was rightfully mine. Surely you both knew the bill would come due eventually, right?"

I just gave a speech about leaving my father as what he is now: ashes. Worm food.

But Ilya is here to prove that Leonid isn't dead. Everything the man tried to make me—selfish, callous, violent, cruel—lives on in the second son.

Ilya is what Leonid wanted.

But me? I'm not.

Not anymore.

Not ever again.

"The Litvinov Bratva needs new leadership," he announces, raising his voice so all of the assembled mob families can hear him. "Stronger leadership."

I sweep my gaze around the cathedral, marking positions, counting heads. My security detail shifts into defensive formations, but we're badly outnumbered. Behind Ilya, amongst the rag-tag hired guns, stand soldiers from the Petrov, Volkov, and Kozlov families—Chicago's most ruthless Bratva clans.

My little brother's been busy.

"You want leadership?" I keep my voice steady, eking out precious seconds to figure out what the fuck to do. "Look around, brother. Look at the kingdom I've built while you played at being Father's good little boy. The Litvinov Group has never been stronger."

"'Strong'?" Ilya barks out a laugh. "You're the farthest thing from it, Samoshka. Love has made you weak." He steps closer. It's just him and me at either end of the aisle that runs between the pews, maybe fifteen yards apart. "But don't worry. I'll take good care of everything—your company, your woman, your child. After all, what kind of uncle would I be if I didn't?"

My hands curl into fists. Every instinct screams at me to rip his throat out. But Nova needs me thinking clearly. Strategic.

I force myself to breathe. To focus.

Because my brother's about to learn exactly what kind of strength love can give a man.

What Ilya doesn't see—what he *can't* see—is that there is no point in burning down an empire just to rule over the ashes. He thinks he can rip this from me and make it his own.

But it's a heart, a beating, pulsing heart—and he doesn't know the first fucking thing about how to nurture life.

The proof is in the pudding. We came here today under a sacred agreement: no blood is to be spilled on the day of a funeral. For generations, that rule has held firm.

And now, Ilya spits on it.

I look around at all the men whom he convinced to spit on it with him. Dmitri Petrov, Aleskandr Volkov, Ivan Kozlov, all battle-tested *pakhans* in their own right… they've all thrown their lot in with this rabid, flea-bitten dog? Why?

I meet Dmitri's eyes. His mouth is a grim, unreadable slash, but there's a glimmer of… something in his eyes. Understanding, maybe.

Or regret.

Because he knows what I'm just now realizing—Ilya didn't *convince* these men to join him. He found a way to force their hands. The question is, how?

"What did you promise them, brother?" I swallow grimly. "What kind of leverage did you need to make the great families bow to a spoiled child throwing a tantrum?"

Ilya's smirk falters for a fraction of a second. "I promised them freedom from the old ways. From dusty traditions that hold us back."

And there it is. The truth, laid bare in my brother's burning eyes. He doesn't want to rule the Bratva—he wants to destroy it. To reduce centuries of culture and connection to rubble, just so he can plant his flag in the wreckage.

I nod, meet Ilya's gaze, and smile. "Then let's give them a show, little brother."

My timing is impeccable.

Not that I intended it as such.

The last syllable of *"little brother"* has scarcely left my lips before the rear wall of the cathedral implodes.

Fountains of dust and debris erupt. Two dozen of Ilya's mercenaries are promptly trampled beneath a herd of FBI agents in SWAT gear. Riot shields, batons held high, all of them dripped head to toe in the government's finest battle armor.

Gunfire drowns out screams. Smoke grenades hiss and pop. The cathedral becomes a war zone of ricocheting bullets and shattering marble.

But I barely register any of it. My world has contracted to two singular points:

The bathroom.

And my brother's face as he stalks toward me through the chaos, lips pulled back in a rictus of rage.

I can't face both. Time slows to a crawl as I weigh my options, each heartbeat an eternity of indecision.

Nova.

Ilya.

Hope.

Heartache.

My future or my past.

Love or vengeance.

In the end, it's simple. If I let my brother walk away now, he'll keep coming. He'll never stop until Nova and our child are dead.

But if I abandon her…

… then there's nothing left worth fighting for.

So I turn and run. I carve through the mayhem, each step precise and measured despite the bullets whizzing past my head. The cathedral's sacred silence has shattered into a hellscape of screams and gunfire.

But all I hear is the steady thump of my own pulse.

I see Viktor standing at the end of the hall. He signals me and I close the gap to him.

I reach the bathroom door just as Katerina's voice rises to a fever pitch inside. "You stupid little bitch! You think he loves you? You think you're special?"

Nova's response is quieter but steady as stone. "I think you're in trouble, Katerina. Let me help you before—"

"Don't fucking touch me!"

Something crashes. Glass shatters. My finger tightens on the trigger as I ease closer to the door.

Nova speaks again, her tone deliberately soothing. "The baby's kicking. Would you like to feel? It might be your last chance to touch something pure."

Clever girl. She's buying time, keeping Katerina distracted. But there's an edge of exhaustion in her voice that sets my teeth on edge.

We need to end this. Now.

I catch Viktor's eye and gesture toward the hinges. He nods once, understanding perfectly. We've done this dance before.

He positions himself to breach while I align my sights with where Katerina's head should be, based on the acoustics of her voice.

One clean shot. That's all I need.

But first, I have to make absolutely certain Nova's clear of the line of fire.

I draw breath to call out to her.

Three.

Two.

One.

Viktor kicks the door.

I charge in.

"Hello, little mouse."

45

NOVA

Three heartbeats. That's how long it takes between Sam appearing in the doorway and Katerina realizing she's lost.

I count them against the pulse of our baby.

One.

Sam fills the frame, his Sig Sauer trained on Katerina's head. The bathroom's fluorescent lights catch the sweat in his beard. Like a net of diamonds.

Two.

Dark-suited men materialize behind him. Shadows given form. They move like they've done this countless times before. In the span of a breath, they've surrounded us.

Three.

Katerina's gun hand trembles against my temple. Her perfume carries notes of desperation now.

"You weren't supposed to be here," she hisses, pressing closer to use me as a shield. My shoulder blades dig into her chest, and I feel her rapid breathing. "Your men were supposed to be—"

"Dead?" Sam interrupts. "Like the ones you and my brother bombed?"

Myles groans from his spot on the floor, trying to push himself up despite the blood seeping through his dress shirt. I want to help him, but Katerina's grip tightens.

"Stay down," I whisper to him.

Sam hasn't moved. That gun stays fixated on Katerina where her face bobs over my shoulder. I see that face reflected in the thousand pieces of broken mirror that litter the floor around us. A murky, indistinct version of it floats in the pool of Myles's blood, too.

She looks terrified in every single one.

"You really thought I wouldn't have a contingency plan for my father's funeral?" continues Sam. "You thought I'd leave this all to chance? To *tradition?*"

More shadows join the first crew. The difference is that, whereas Samuil's men are clad head to toe in black, these men have three letters stamped on the front of their riot gear in bright, undeniable white.

***FBI*.**

And bringing up the rear is a face I recognize—although the last time I saw it, it was beaten into a pulp.

Angelo Boyko.

My throat constricts as it all comes together, so blindingly obvious that I can't believe it took me this long to see it. All those times I pleaded with Sam to work with law enforcement, he was already ten steps ahead. The arguments, his cold dismissals, the way he kicked me from the war room —it was theater. A performance to keep everyone, even me, in the dark.

"Drop it, Ms. Alekseeva," Angelo barks, his own weapon joining the bristling arsenal aimed at Katerina. "You're surrounded by two tactical teams, and there's nowhere left to run."

Katerina's laugh splinters against my ear. "You think I care about running?" The gun digs deeper into my temple. "Your precious FBI can't protect you from what's coming, Samuil. Ilya's already—"

"Being taken into custody as we speak." Angelo's voice booms with the finality of a coffin lid closing. "Along with the Andropov leadership. Simultaneous raids across three continents. Game over."

I meet Sam's gaze through the forest of weapons. His eyes hold mine, steady and sure, like they did the first day we met. When an unruly Great Dane brought chaos to both our lives.

The gun at my temple suddenly feels lighter. Katerina's grip loosens, her breath hitching.

"You planned this," she whispers in horror as she comes to the same realization I just did. "All of it. The funeral. The attacks. You *wanted* us to think we had you cornered."

Sam's lip curls. "I learned from the best, didn't I? You taught me everything about playing the long game when you married me."

Katerina's arm snakes around my throat as she drags me backward until we collide with the rear wall.

"Stay back!" Her scream hits a pitch that makes my ears ring. The gun digs deeper into my temple, cold metal kissing bone.

Through the bathroom door, chaos erupts in the main hall. Ilya's voice carries over the mayhem—no longer the triumphant boom we first heard. He's spewing Russian curses now, each word more venomous than the last. The sound of his world crashing down.

Katerina's breath comes in ragged gasps against my ear. All traces of perfume are gone. There's only the acrid scent of fear-sweat. The arm around my neck trembles.

"You don't understand," she murmurs, though I'm not sure if she's talking to Sam or herself. "*We* were the ones who had it all planned. Every detail. The funeral was supposed to be your ending, not ours."

Sam takes one deliberate step forward. "You still think you know me, Kat?" His voice drops to that dangerous velvet that sets my skin on fire. "After all this time, you still haven't learned?"

The gun at my temple wavers as Katerina processes the truth: she never really knew him at all.

Her desperation rolls off her in waves. The same turbulent terror that clings to abused dogs when they're cornered. Ready to bite because they see no other choice.

I'm not out of the woods just yet.

I meet Sam's eyes over the wall of tactical gear between us. His finger hasn't moved from the trigger, but something in his expression shifts when I give him the tiniest shake of my head.

"You don't have to do this, Katerina," I say quietly. "There are other ways out."

Her laugh is like stones crumbling. "You think I have options? I never had fucking *options.* Ilya made sure of that. The moment I agreed to his plan, he owned me. Every move, every breath—" Her voice quivers. "He used me, just like your precious Samuil did."

"The FBI can protect you," I murmur. "You could start over, build something real—"

"Shut up!" But there's a frantic edge to her command now. "You don't understand what it's like to lose everything."

"Don't I?" I think of my father, my brothers. The family I lost to corruption and greed. "Sometimes, losing everything is how you find what really matters."

The raw anguish in Katerina's face is jarring. For the first time since I've known her, the polished mask slips completely.

"I loved him," she spits out, and her grip on me loosens just enough that I can finally take a full breath.

I frown. "Sam—?"

"No," she snaps. "Not Samuil—never Samuil. Ilya. Since we were young, I loved him."

Through the bathroom door, the agent's voice rings clear as he reads Ilya his rights. The charges roll off his tongue like a grocery list: racketeering, conspiracy to commit murder, money laundering, trafficking. Each one drives Katerina's nails deeper into my shoulder.

"I thought, once we took power, we'd finally be together."

She sniffles and hiccups. "But he lied. Didn't even tell me he was making this move. I was just another pawn."

The gun slips a fraction lower. I scoot a fraction farther.

My eyes find Sam's again. He hasn't moved, hasn't holstered his gun. But there's something in his gaze now—not quite sympathy, but understanding. He knows exactly what it's like to have love turned into a weapon.

"You have a choice," I tell her softly. "Right here, right now. You can be more than what Ilya made you."

For a heartbeat that stretches into eternity, the bathroom fills with the sound of Katerina's ragged breathing and the echo of Ilya's curses from the hall.

And for that heartbeat, I feel like we're all going to make it.

She's going to drop the gun. Going to surrender. Going to make the right decision for once and—

Then she wrenches me closer and jams the gun into my belly. Her finger goes to the trigger.

Men shout.

Things move.

Then the shot rings out before I can scream.

My ears explode with white noise. Time warps and stretches like taffy as two things happen in rapid succession.

The first comes from below. Myles rises from beneath us, unsteady but roaring a wordless battle cry as he knocks Katerina aside. She screams, too, and whirls the gun from my gut toward him. From this close, I don't see how she could miss.

The second thing comes from afar. A blur comes flying in and Samuil dives in front of the gun…

Right as it erupts.

Boom.

Blood sprays across the mirror shards, turning their reflective surfaces into rubies. My throat burns from a scream I can't hear over the ringing in my ears.

Katerina's grip on me goes slack in her shock. I drive my elbow back into her sternum. Her hold breaks completely. The gun clatters to the floor as she stumbles.

FBI agents swarm the space, piling on top of Kat, but I'm already dropping and crawling toward Sam. His blood soaks into the knees of my black dress as I reach him. He's conscious, gray eyes blazing as they find mine.

"The baby…?" His voice sounds far away through the lingering echo of gunfire.

I press my hands over his wound. "We're fine. I'm— We're— Fuck, somebody help me!"

Myles kneels beside us, pressing his balled-up jacket against Sam's shoulder where it's pouring blood. His face is pale from his own blood loss, but his hands are steady. "You really went and took a bullet for me, you melodramatic bastard?"

Sam's laugh turns into a cough, then a grimace. "Consider us even for the boat rescue."

Behind us, Katerina's hysteric sobs mix with the sounds of handcuffs clicking shut. But I can't look away from Sam's face, can't stop counting his breaths, because each one means that he's still here, still with us.

He caught a bullet meant for his friend. Meant for me.

Just when I didn't think I could love him any more.

I can't stop shaking as Sam's blood seeps between my fingers. The shoulder wound gushes with each beat of his heart, dampening his crisp white shirt into a grotesque watercolor.

"Stay with me," I whisper, pressing harder. His muscles tense under my hands, but he doesn't make a sound.

I glance over my shoulder in time to see a glimpse of Kat's face through the tangle of black-clad limbs. She thrashes and screams, mascara turning her tears into black rivers. The blood of the two men she tried to kill paints her cheeks red.

"Target secured," one of the FBI agents barks. "Room clear."

Boyko appears beside us, his previous injuries now just yellowing bruises on weathered skin. He squats next to Sam and pats him on the knee.

"As agreed, Mr. Litvinov. Full immunity in exchange for your brother and the Andropov network."

Sam manages a tight nod, his jaw clenched against the pain. "Make sure… Nova and the baby are protected, too."

"Already done." Boyko stands and retreats as paramedics rush in. "Your family's safety was part of the deal from day one."

The medical team works quickly, their practiced movements a stark contrast to my trembling hands. As they load Sam onto a stretcher, his fingers find mine, squeezing with surprising strength.

"*Krasavitsa*," he murmurs when he sees my shell-shocked face, "didn't I tell you to trust me?"

I laugh through my tears, following as they wheel him out. "Next time, maybe fill me in *before* taking a bullet."

His answering smile is weak but genuine. "Where's the fun in that?"

He catches my hand and brings it to his lips as his smile fades into something more serious. "It had to be done like this. I hope you know that. Your reactions had to be genuine for her and Ilya to believe."

"You orchestrated all of this?" My other hand finds his face, fingers threading through his sweat-damp beard. "The raids, the FBI, everything?"

He manages a shadow of his usual smirk. "I had a hand in things here and there."

The paramedics start to guide Samuil's stretcher down the hall. But as we emerge into the belly of the church, an anguished bellow stops us. We all turn in unison.

Ilya bucks against his zip-ties and cuffs as agents march him toward an armored vehicle. His suit is torn and bloody, his once-perfect hair wild.

But it's his eyes that make my skin crawl. They burn with the kind of hatred that could set the world on fire.

"*Brattan,*" he spits in Russian, zeroing in on Sam. "Always the chess master. Always three moves ahead, eh?"

Sam's fingers interlace with mine. His wound is bleeding through the pressure bandage, but his face remains impassive. Like his brother's venom simply can't touch him anymore.

Behind Ilya, Katerina stumbles as agents drag her toward a rear exit. Her black-and-red-stained face crumples when she catches Ilya's eye. Some strange, almost tangible kind of ripple passes between them—a current of betrayal and broken dreams that makes my chest ache despite everything.

I can't help pitying them. They're violent, yes, and broken, most definitely.

But no dog is unredeemable.

Give them time. Maybe they'll find a way back to the light.

Then Ilya's gaze finds mine. His lips curl into a sneer. "*Shlyukha*," he hisses.

On second thought, maybe not.

I open my mouth to say something, but Sam catches me with one hand looped around the back of my neck. "He's not worth the breath of telling him to go to hell," he rasps to me. "Let him go."

I look at him. Not at Ilya, not at Katerina, but at *him.*

He's right.

The only people left who matter are us.

The paramedics rush Sam through the church doors, but his hand never leaves mine. Even with blood soaking his shirt and pain etching lines around his eyes, he refuses to let go.

Outside, a sea of flashing lights bathes everything in red and blue. FBI agents herd handcuffed mercenaries into armored vehicles. Katerina's sobs fade into the distance. Ilya's curses turn to echoes, then to nothing.

But all I can focus on is the steady beep of Sam's heart monitor as the EMTs hook him up. The way his chest rises and falls. The warmth of his fingers threaded through mine.

"Your blood pressure's dropping, sir," one paramedic warns. "We need to move."

Sam's eyes find mine through the chaos. "Come with me?"

As if he needs to ask. As if I'd be anywhere else.

They help me into the ambulance beside him. The doors slam shut, muffling the circus outside. In this metal cocoon, it's just us and the rhythm of his heart on the monitor.

His hand slides from mine to rest on my belly. Our child kicks against his palm—strong and alive and *real.* Despite everything, a smile tugs at his lips.

"Worth it," he mumbles, fighting to keep his eyes open as the morphine takes hold. "All of it. For this."

I lean down to press my forehead against his. "Rest now. We'll be here when you wake up."

His other hand finds my cheek, thumb brushing away tears I didn't know I'd shed. Even half-conscious, his touch is gentle. Reverent.

The last thing I hear before the sirens start is his whispered *"Ya tebya lyublyu."*

I love you.

And for the first time since this nightmare began, I know we're going to be okay.

EPILOGUE: NOVA

FIVE MONTHS LATER

I feel like an overstuffed crow.

It's Samuil's fault. I'm eight months pregnant, but he swore black would be "slimming." But a slim whale is still a whale, no matter how much silk you drape her in.

Sighing, I look up. The woman in the mirror is both familiar and strange. Gold-brown eyes lined with kohl, dark hair swept up in an intricate twist. Who is this girl, this Cinderella who stumbled and bumbled her way from the dog park to the throne?

But my fairy godmother came packing heat, and my glass slippers left bloody footprints. Love didn't find me in a ballroom—it found me in the crosshairs, when I chose to dance with the devil instead of running from him.

"You're overthinking again, *krasavitsa*." Samuil appears behind me, his gray eyes meeting mine in the mirror. The fresh scar above his collarbone peeks from his crisp white shirt—a badge of survival from that day at his father's funeral.

"I'm not built for this." I gesture at the formal attire, at the weight of expectations pressing down harder than my swollen belly. "Your people want a queen. I still trip over my own feet."

His hands settle on my shoulders, warm and steady. "My people want what I want: someone real. Someone who brings light into dark places." He presses a kiss to my neck. "Someone who tamed the beast."

I lean back against his chest, letting his strength shore up my wobbling confidence. Tonight, dozens of powerful men and women will pledge their loyalty to Samuil Litvinov, the new king of Chicago's underworld. And I'll stand beside him, their unlikely queen, carrying his heir.

He kisses me on the temple once more, then starts to leave. "I'll meet you downstairs. Five minutes," he warns, "or else I'm coming back to fetch you—and if that happens, we might never make it out of this bedroom."

I laugh and pinch his ass as he saunters out of the room.

But when he's gone, the nerves creep back in again. It's one thing to feel confident when Sam is with me. Unfortunately, I can't stay plastered to his side *all* the time.

A soft whine breaks through my anxiety spiral. Ruby and Rufus sit at attention beside me. He's wearing a custom, midnight-black bowtie that matches my dress perfectly, as does the onyx bow tied around Ruby's head.

"Look at us," I say aloud, scratching behind their ears. "The dogs and their walker, living in a fairy tale."

Rufus tilts his head, studying our reflection with an aristocratic air that makes me snort-laugh. It's like he knows he looks good. The sound bounces off the marble floors and crystal chandeliers of our dressing suite. Ruby whines like she's telling him not to be a pompous ass.

"At least we all clean up nice." I smooth my hands over the silk stretched across my belly. "You, too, little one," I add, just so my baby doesn't feel left out.

Rufus bumps his cold nose against my palm, then sits regally beside me again. Always on guard, always watching. Just like his master taught him. On the other side, Ruby is just as alert.

"You're right," I tell them, squaring my shoulders. "Time to own this."

The diamond at my throat catches the light, throwing rainbow prisms across the walls. Not a collar marking ownership, but a crown declaring partnership. Samuil didn't just give me safety or luxury—he gave me purpose. A chance to protect others the way I once needed protection.

Two tails thump against the floor in approval.

The yacht club's grand staircase feels like a stage, and for a heartbeat, I freeze. Hundreds of faces turn toward me—craggy faces that have seen more darkness than light, more death than life.

But then I see *him*.

Samuil commands the front of the room like he was born to it—which, I suppose, he was. His tux fits him like sin, and the way he holds himself—shoulders back, chin lifted—screams of brutal, unchecked power.

But I know better. I see the way his throat works when our eyes meet. The barely-there softening of his expression that tells me exactly where his heart lives.

My Bratva king isn't made of ice anymore. He's flesh and blood and *mine.*

Rufus gives a quiet "woof" of greeting, and I swear Samuil's lips twitch. The gathered men and women—Chicago's elite mixing with Moscow's most dangerous—collectively hold their breath. They're waiting to see how the new boss handles his queen's entrance.

I lift my chin and descend. One hand on the rail, one held gently over my belly. Rufus and Ruby move in perfect sync beside me, more bodyguards than pets.

When I reach Samuil, he takes my hand and brings it to his lips. *"Moya koroleva,"* he murmurs. *My queen.*

The room relaxes fractionally. This is what they needed to see—their leader claiming his woman, his heir, his future. But I know what they don't: that behind closed doors, this man kneels for me. That the most feared boss in Chicago whispers poetry against my skin and melts when he feels our baby kick.

That the most powerful thing you can do is let love change you.

Samuil's fingers tighten around mine as he steps up to the microphone to address the crowd. I expect him to let go—to assume the stance of power these people recognize. Instead, he keeps me anchored to his side.

"Many of you knew my father," he begins, voice carrying to every corner of the yacht club's grand ballroom. "Leonid Litvinov was respected. Feared. Obeyed." His thumb traces circles on my knuckles. "But he forgot the most important lesson about power: it means nothing if you're alone at the top."

The crowd shifts, uncertain where this is going. I am, too, if we're being honest.

"My father taught me that love makes you pathetic." Samuil's jaw tightens. "That trust is for fools, and mercy is for cowards." His eyes find mine. "But I stand before you today because a woman who had every reason to hate me chose to save me instead."

My throat closes up. This isn't the speech anyone expected—least of all me.

"Nova Pierce walked into my life and showed me that real strength comes from having something worth protecting. Worth dying for." He places his free hand on my belly. "Worth living for."

Rufus and Ruby press against my leg as tears threaten.

"So yes, I am your new leader," Samuil continues, addressing the room again. "And I will be stronger, more ruthless, more successful than my father ever was. Because unlike him, I understand where true power comes from." He raises our joined hands. "From this."

Then, lifting a champagne flute to the sky, he adds, "To the future of the Litvinov empire—and to the queen who makes it worth building."

The room erupts in cheers and raised glasses, but I barely notice.

I'm too busy falling in love with Samuil all over again.

One Year Later—Castle Moorbeath

It's been almost two years since the funeral. There are probably still enemies out there, old and new alike, who'd love nothing more than to hurt Samuil, hurt me, hurt our family.

But they aren't in here.

In here, spring sunlight pours through leaded glass windows, turning dust motes to fairy lights as they dance around my man and our daughter.

In here, the air smells like Mrs. Morris's scones.

In here, Samuil cradles eleven-month-old Louisa against his broad chest while Grams—our terrifying wedding planner—rattles off ceremony details at a frankly astonishing pace.

"The flowers from Holland arrive Thursday, the custom vodka Friday, and—"

"Papa!" Louisa's squeal cuts through my grandmother's logistics. Her tiny hand reaches for Samuil's face, and just like that, Chicago's most feared *pakhan* transforms into putty.

"*Moya printsessa,*" he coos, pressing kisses to her dimpled fingers. "Tell this scary lady that weddings can wait, yes?"

I hide my smile behind my teacup. "Sam, Grams will slaughter you in your sleep if you suggest postponing again. We're doing this. Next week. Come hell or high water."

"But you're tired, *zaychik*." His gray eyes find mine, softening in that way that still makes my knees weak. "Between the baby and running the household—"

"And that's precisely why we need this." I cross to them, running my fingers through his hair. "To mark how far we've come. To show our daughter that love wins, even in the darkest places."

Louisa babbles agreement, patting her father's stubbled jaw.

My grandmother clears her throat. "If I may remind you both, postponing now would be… unwise." The steel in her voice could sharpen knives.

Samuil and I share a look. We've faced down rival mobs, corrupt cops, and murderous relatives. But neither of us is brave enough to cross Serena Hogan when she's got that gleam in her eye.

"Wonderful," deadpans Grams when neither of us pipe up to argue any further. "So glad we're all in agreement. Now, come this way. Lots to show you…"

We follow Grams outside and down the worn stone path to the barn, Louisa's tiny hand wrapped around my finger as she toddles between Samuil and me. It's no surprise that she's an early walker—they make the Litvinovs very headstrong, as it turns out.

I don't mind going slow while she gets her feet under her, though. It's beautiful in Scotland during the springtime. The morning sun gilds everything in sight—the towering castle walls, the dewy grass, my daughter's dark curls, my man's strong profile.

My heart skips when I see Hope directing workers near the barn doors. She's wearing her assistant wedding planner face, which means something's about to happen.

The massive oak doors swing wide, and I freeze.

Three baby goats—black, white, and dappled gray—bounce and play in a custom-built pen. Their mother, a gorgeous Nubian with floppy ears, keeps watch from a raised platform nearby, chewing contentedly on fresh hay.

"For me?" The words escape in a whisper, though I already know the answer. I remember a night on the yacht last winter, tipsy on champagne, telling Samuil about my dream of having goats at our wedding.

His arms slide around me from behind, one hand splaying possessively over the curves that motherhood left behind. His breath tickles my ear. "You wanted goats. I got you goats. I deliver what my woman asks for."

I turn in his embrace, fighting back tears. "I didn't really expect—"

His kiss steals my protests. When he pulls back, his gray eyes burn with an intensity that makes me swallow hard. "You've given me everything. A daughter. A future. Let me give you this."

Louisa squeals and points at the baby goats, breaking our moment. But that's okay. Watching him and her, the life we created and the man who helped me do it… That's as beautiful as anything in this world has ever been.

~

The bagpipes start playing, and I burst into tears.

"Don't you dare ruin that makeup." Hope dabs at my eyes with a tissue. "Do you know how long it took to make you look this ethereal?"

But I can't help it. The music carries across the castle grounds like a warrior's cry—fierce and proud and undeniable. Just like the man waiting for me at the end of this flower-strewn aisle.

Rufus prances ahead of me, head held high, the silk pillow with our rings balanced perfectly in his mouth. The sight of him in his little tuxedo vest sets off fresh waterworks.

A commotion from the goat pen draws his attention. The babies are putting on their own show, bouncing and bleating like tiny circus performers. Rufus's ears perk up, and he veers off-course.

"Focus, buddy." I giggle through my tears.

He rights himself with a dignified sniff, but then Louisa starts fussing in Grams's arms. That does it. Ring pillow forgotten, he bounds over to my daughter, pressing his cold nose to her cheek until she giggles.

Ruby, not to be outdone, lets out a series of happy barks from her post next to Hope. The sound echoes off the castle walls, making the crowd chuckle.

And there, at the end of it all, stands Samuil. His gray eyes lock onto mine through my veil, and suddenly, I'm that girl in the park again, tangled in a leash with a handsome stranger. Only now, I know exactly where this path leads.

To him. To us. To forever.

The bagpipes fade into Mendelssohn's Wedding March, and my heart stutters in my chest. Here we go. I can do this.

One step, then another. The late afternoon sun filters through clouds in honey-gold shafts, turning everything magical—the stone walls, the Highland roses that Mr. Morris grew special, my daughter's cherub face as she waves from Grams's arms.

But it's Samuil who steals my breath.

My fierce, damaged, beautiful man stands tall at the altar. His shoulders are straight, chin lifted—but I see the muscle jumping in his jaw. The way his fists clench and unclench at his sides.

I'm not the only one fighting tears.

When I reach him, he takes my hands in his. They're shaking. The great Samuil Litvinov—trembling like a schoolboy.

I never thought I'd see the day.

"Dearly beloved..." the priest begins, but I barely hear the words.

All I can focus on is the storm in Samuil's eyes. The way decades of pain and rage have transformed into something else.

Something pure. Sacred.

When it's his time to speak, his vows pour out in that growly rumble I've come to associate with home. "Nova, I vow to protect you, cherish you, honor you. To give you the freedom to fly and the safety to land. To love our children with everything I am, and to show them that real strength comes from having an open heart."

Louisa babbles, "Papa!" and the gathered crowd laughs once more.

My own vows catch in my throat, but Samuil's grip anchors me. Steadies me. Just like always.

"I vow to be your shelter in the storm," I whisper when it's my turn. "To love your darkness as much as your light. To build a family where trust isn't weakness and love isn't a liability."

A single tear escapes down his cheek. I reach up and brush it away, feeling like my heart might burst from all this joy.

My hands still shake as Samuil slides the ring onto my finger. The platinum band nestles against my engagement ring, catching the golden Scottish sunlight. Two circles of forever.

"By the power vested in me…" the priest continues, but I'm once again lost in the beautiful turbulence of Samuil's eyes. In them, I see our future stretching out before us—more babies, more adventures, more battles fought side by side.

A commotion erupts from the goat pen. The kids have escaped and are making a break for the flower arrangements. Hope's eyes go wide with panic, but before she can move, Rufus and Ruby spring into action. They herd the wayward babies back to their mama with practiced efficiency, tails wagging proudly at a job well done.

Samuil's lips twitch. "Even our dogs know how to protect what matters."

"I now pronounce you husband and wife," the priest declares once the mayhem has been contained. "You may kiss your bride."

My new husband—*husband*—cups my face in his calloused hands. His touch is reverent, like I'm something precious. Something holy.

"*Moya zhena*," he breathes against my lips. *My wife.*

Then he kisses me, and the world falls away. No more mob wars or family betrayals. No more running or hiding or doubting ourselves.

Just this moment, this man, and this love we've fought so hard to keep.

When we break apart, Louisa squeals from Grams's arms, reaching for us with grabby hands. Samuil scoops her up, and suddenly, we're a tangle of limbs and laughter and happy tears.

The crowd erupts in cheers, but I barely notice. I'm too busy memorizing how it feels to finally, *finally* be whole.

~

The string lights shimmer like fallen stars, casting everyone in a dreamy glow. Even the hardened Bratva soldiers look softer somehow, their sharp edges blurred by candlelight and copious consumption of Scottish whisky.

Samuil's hand finds the small of my back, his touch electric even through layers of silk and lace. "Dance with me, Mrs. Litvinov?"

The way he purrs my new name sends shivers down my spine. I let him guide me onto the dance floor laid out in the castle courtyard. Myles and Hope have beat us out there, but they're too busy exploring each other's tonsils to notice us.

"They'll be next," I murmur, nodding at our best friends.

Sam's chest bobs with quiet laughter. "Myles better not fuck it up. I need Hope around to keep you out of trouble."

"Me? Trouble?" I bat my eyes innocently. "Never."

His grip tightens possessively. "You're nothing *but* trouble, *krasavitsa*. And now, you're my trouble forever."

I melt against him, breathing in his familiar scent of spice and leather. Across the courtyard, Grams rocks a sleeping Louisa, her weathered face peaceful in the golden light. Our daughter's curls spill over Grams's shoulder like ink, her tiny fist clutching the pearl necklace Sam gave her this morning.

The sight of my daughter sleeping in my grandmother's arms makes my throat tight. All those months ago, when I first discovered I was pregnant on that yacht, I never imagined we'd end up here—surrounded by love and laughter instead of violence and fear.

"You're thinking too hard yet again." Sam's lips brush my temple as we sway to the music. "I can practically hear the gears turning."

"Just grateful." I trace the scar on his collarbone through his shirt. "For everything that brought us here. Even the bad stuff."

His hand slides lower on my back, possessive and heated. "The bad stuff made the good stuff sweeter."

I shiver. Even after everything we've been through—the betrayals, the battles, the blood—he can reduce me to putty with just his voice.

"Speaking of good stuff…" His fingers thread through my hair, carefully avoiding the crystal pins Hope spent an hour arranging. "Are you ready to escape? I have plans for you that aren't suitable for public consumption."

Heat pools low in my belly. "What about our guests?"

"Let them drink and dance." His lips graze my forehead. "I need my wife alone."

I glance around one last time, taking in this magical moment. Bratva soldiers are teaching our Scottish neighbors traditional Russian dances. Ruby and Rufus lie sprawled at Mr. Morris's feet, worn out from their goat-herding adventures. This unlikely family we've built, against all odds.

"Lead the way, Mr. Litvinov."

The moonlight turns Samuil's shoulders to marble as he leads me up the winding stone steps of our highest tower. My wedding dress whispers against the worn flagstones, each step taking us further from the party below.

"Almost there." His voice is rough velvet in the dark.

The door opens to a nest of silk pillows and furs beneath an open patch of stars. White roses perfume the air, their scattered petals glowing silver in the starlight.

"When did you—"

His mouth captures mine, stealing my question. His hands find the buttons of my dress with practiced ease, and before I know it, I'm drowning in sensation—the scratch of his stubble against my throat, the burn of his palms on my bare skin, the sweet bite of night air on my exposed flesh.

"My queen deserves a proper crown." He pulls back just enough to drink me in. The hunger in his gray eyes makes me shiver. "Made of starlight and diamonds."

I reach for his tie, needing to feel his skin against mine. "Less poetry, more action."

His laugh is wicked and warm. "As my wife commands."

We come together like waves crashing on rocks—inevitable, unstoppable. His hands map my curves like he's discovering them for the first time, drawing gasps and sighs that float up to mingle with the stars.

When he finally slides home, I arch beneath him, caught between the softness of fur and the hard planes of his body. The position opens me deeper, makes everything more intense.

"Look at me," he growls, and I do.

The universe wheels above us, but all I can see is him—my dark angel, my fierce protector, my inked Adonis.

Mine.

Forever.

EXTENDED EPILOGUE: SAMUIL

Download the exclusive Extended Epilogue for a glimpse into the warm, fuzzy future of the growing Litvinov family!
(Plus, you'll get a sneak peek at another one of my bestselling mafia romance novels!)
https://dl.bookfunnel.com/rn7j7b0vo4

ALSO BY NICOLE FOX

Groza Bratva

Cashmere Cruelty

Cashmere Ruin

Kuznetsov Bratva

Emerald Malice

Emerald Vices

Novikov Bratva

Ivory Ashes

Ivory Oath

Egorov Bratva

Tangled Innocence

Tangled Decadence

Zakrevsky Bratva

Requiem of Sin

Sonata of Lies

Rhapsody of Pain

Bugrov Bratva

Midnight Purgatory

Midnight Sanctuary

Oryolov Bratva

Cruel Paradise

Cruel Promise

Pushkin Bratva

Cognac Villain

Cognac Vixen

Viktorov Bratva

Whiskey Poison

Whiskey Pain

Orlov Bratva

Champagne Venom

Champagne Wrath

Uvarov Bratva

Sapphire Scars

Sapphire Tears

Vlasov Bratva

Arrogant Monster

Arrogant Mistake

Zhukova Bratva

Tarnished Tyrant

Tarnished Queen

Stepanov Bratva

Satin Sinner

Satin Princess

Makarova Bratva

Shattered Altar

Shattered Cradle

Solovev Bratva

Ravaged Crown

Ravaged Throne

Vorobev Bratva

Velvet Devil

Velvet Angel

Romanoff Bratva

Immaculate Deception

Immaculate Corruption

Kovalyov Bratva

Gilded Cage

Gilded Tears

Jaded Soul

Jaded Devil

Ripped Veil

Ripped Lace

Mazzeo Mafia Duet

Liar's Lullaby (Book 1)

Sinner's Lullaby (Book 2)

Bratva Crime Syndicate

**Can be read in any order!*

Lies He Told Me

Scars He Gave Me

Sins He Taught Me

Belluci Mafia Trilogy

Corrupted Angel (Book 1)

Corrupted Queen (Book 2)

Corrupted Empire (Book 3)

De Maggio Mafia Duet

Devil in a Suit (Book 1)

Devil at the Altar (Book 2)

Kornilov Bratva Duet

Married to the Don (Book 1)

Til Death Do Us Part (Book 2)

Heirs to the Bratva Empire

**Can be read in any order!*

Kostya

Maksim

Andrei

Princes of Ravenlake Academy (Bully Romance)

**Can be read as standalones!*

Cruel Prep

Cruel Academy

Cruel Elite

Tsezar Bratva

Nightfall (Book 1)

Daybreak (Book 2)

Russian Crime Brotherhood

**Can be read in any order!*

Owned by the Mob Boss

Unprotected with the Mob Boss

Knocked Up by the Mob Boss

Sold to the Mob Boss

Stolen by the Mob Boss

Trapped with the Mob Boss

Volkov Bratva

Broken Vows (Book 1)

Broken Hope (Book 2)

Broken Sins *(standalone)*

Other Standalones

Vin: A Mafia Romance

Box Sets

Bratva Mob Bosses (Russian Crime Brotherhood Books 1-6)

Tsezar Bratva (Tsezar Bratva Duet Books 1-2)

Heirs to the Bratva Empire

The Mafia Dons Collection

The Don's Corruption

Printed in Great Britain
by Amazon

58317059R00238